AFTERMATH

AFTERMATH

L.A. WITT

VINO & VERITAS

HeartEyes Press

This book was inspired by the True North Series written by Sarina Bowen. It is an original work that is published by Heart Eyes Press LLC.

1

BRENT

"Dude, you're turning into a hermit."

I glared across my kitchen at Ethan, my best friend since forever. "I'm not turning into a hermit. I just don't want to—"

"You don't want to go out." He cocked his head. "You don't want to see anyone. You don't want to do anything except stay here all by yourself. You're not even on social media. Honey, that's the literal *definition* of a hermit."

Frowning, I looked away from him and out the window at the lake. That view usually relaxed me even when I was wound tight with frustration, and it usually helped to pull me from the dark pit of tar my mind seemed to like wandering into these days. Going out and peopling only stressed me out and depressed me more. Staying home and gazing out at Lake Champlain was a hell of a lot more appealing. The view was peaceful and calm, and everything here was way less taxing than anyone or anything in town.

Which…damn.

"Okay, maybe I *am* becoming a hermit." I shifted a little, wincing at the relentless ache in my back and my left hip, and I faced him again. "But I'm just not ready to be social again."

The concern in his expression deepened as he came closer. "I get it, hon. I do. It's been a hell of a year, and I'm sure you still have a lot you need to work through."

Now wasn't *that* an understatement.

"Look," Ethan went on, "I'm not suggesting we go clubbing or anything. But there's a wine bar in town that's low key, and maybe the change of scenery would do you some good, you know? Plus it's attached to a bookstore, so if nothing else, you can wander over to that side and find something to read while you hermit."

I had to admit, the bookstore sounded tempting. I'd done a lot of reading the past several months, especially when I couldn't move enough to do much else, and I was itching for some new material. I could always download another ebook or order another paperback, but the idea of actually wandering a bookstore and thumbing through pages did have some appeal.

"Hmm. Maybe."

Ethan reached across the space between us and squeezed my forearm. "I know you've been through hell, and I know you're still recovering. But I'm worried about you. This isn't healthy, and it isn't like you."

"What isn't like me?" I asked with more annoyance than I usually directed at him. "Being in pain all the time?"

He tsked. "You know what I mean, Brent. Holing up. Avoiding everyone. Playing the recluse instead of the life of the party."

Just thinking about being the life of any party made me tired. On the other hand, I remembered being the guy he was describing. And I'd loved it. My friends and I were always getting into mischief when we were kids, finding new and innovative ways to entertain ourselves, and I'd been one of the ring leaders. In college and in my pro career, same thing. One of the best parts about hockey had been the camaraderie with other guys who liked to play pranks, raise hell, and enjoy life.

The person I'd been up until that fateful night last spring? He was a stranger to me now. Could I learn how to be him again, though? Did I even have the energy for it? Because my body was never going to be the same. How could I expect my mind to be?

"Brent?"

I sighed and rubbed my eyes. "I don't know. I just… I don't really feel like me anymore, you know?"

"Because this isn't you. It never has been." He squeezed my arm again. "Just come with me and give the wine bar a chance." He paused. "One hour."

I met his gaze. "What?"

"One hour." Ethan put up his index finger. "If after an hour, you think it sucks and you've had enough and even the bookstore won't keep you there, then we'll bail. No questions asked."

I quirked my lips. An hour didn't sound like too much. It also kind of sounded like way too much—I still had to get dressed, and we had to get into town, and what if we had to walk from the car to the place? I was walking more comfortably than I'd been a few months ago, and I didn't feel like I'd need my cane tonight, but parking five blocks away and hoofing it to the front door wasn't something I could do as easily as I had in my past life. What if the bar was on a hill? Or the ground was uneven? Or there was a thick crowd? A goddamned headwind? Every walk had to be planned for. Strategized. Mentally calculated against whatever physical and psychological reserves I had during a given hour.

Christ, I felt like an old man.

I kind of wished Ethan *had* suggested we go clubbing. It would've been so much easier to shoot down the idea since the club scene meant not only people and noise, it meant dancing (which hurt), hooking up (which wasn't happening), and drinking (which only depressed me more).

But a low-key wine bar and bookstore…

Oh hell. How bad could it be? At least it probably wouldn't have sports on the screens, which meant no hockey to rub salt in my wounds. Plus wine bars were usually fairly quiet, so I wouldn't have to deal with sensory overload on top of pain and body image issues before I told Ethan, *"I was right. This sucks. I'm out."* I could just have a single glass of wine, stay long enough to make it seem like I was giving it the old college try, and then *I told you so* right out the door without feeling like I'd been through the wringer.

With a heavy sigh, I turned to Ethan. "Fine. *Fine*. Let's go check out the wine bar."

His face instantly lit up. "Sweet! Oh honey, you'll love this place."

I smiled weakly. As much as I enjoyed seeing him this excited, his enthusiasm only emphasized my lack thereof. Gesturing down the hall, I said, "Let me go change clothes." I didn't imagine this place expected club attire, but they might look askance at gym shorts and an old ratty T-shirt.

So, while Ethan waited in the kitchen, I changed into some comfortable jeans and a plain black shirt. Just for good measure, since I wasn't sure what the vibe of this place would be, I threw on a blazer I hadn't worn in I didn't know how long.

Then I looked at myself in the full-length mirror, and that was a mistake. A year of surgery, recovery, physical therapy, and muscle atrophy had left me with a body I barely recognized. Some of the muscle tone had started coming back in recent months, and my upper body hadn't lost quite as much as my legs had. The jacket and jeans masked a lot of it, though it was painfully obvious I'd lost the hockey physique I'd been so proud of.

As the weather had slowly shifted from a bitter New England winter to a milder spring, I'd been spending enough time out on my back deck to add a touch of color to my skin. I wasn't pale and emaciated like I'd been after the last surgery, but I still didn't look like me. Not even close. Especially not with the pair of jagged scars on the left side of my face. They weren't as obvious as they'd been a few months ago, having finally faded from angry red to a silvery shade that didn't contrast as much with my skin tone, and I doubted many people noticed them anymore.

I noticed them.

My heart sank. People sometimes recognized me in this town. It took them a minute these days because I was a gaunt shadow of the hockey player featured on their posters. I'd had a high profile. I'd loved that spotlight. I'd *basked* in it.

Now I just wished people would forget they'd ever seen a jersey with WEYLAND across the shoulders. Then they wouldn't get all excited when they realized it was me, only to suddenly look concerned and even a little alarmed at what I'd become. No wonder there was speculation I'd turned to drugs after losing my career.

This is why I don't leave the house, Ethan. Because everyone knows the man I'm trying to forget I ever was.

The thought made a familiar lump rise in my throat. No, Ethan was right. I needed to start getting out again. No matter how much I wanted to just hole up here and turn into the washed-up famous guy the town's kids whispered about and bragged about catching glimpses of, I needed to start living again. I'd never be who I was before, but I had to find my way to something better than this.

Step one—get dressed. Check.
Step two—swallow a couple of anti-inflammatories.
Step three—go to the wine bar with Ethan.
Step four?
Hopefully I'd figure that out.

There must have been something going on at one of the churches or the university or at some business or another. That, or Burlington was just busier than it'd been when I'd lived here years ago. Whatever the case, by the time we got to the Church Street Marketplace, parking was a nightmare. The garages in the area were full. On-street parking wasn't happening. Every nearby lot was jam-packed.

"Ugh." Ethan huffed as he glared at yet another LOT FULL sandwich board beside a parking lot. "You know what? Fuck it." I had about two seconds to enjoy the glimmer of hope that we'd just go back home, but then he said, "I'll drop you off as close as I can get to the wine bar, and I'll go park in New Hampshire or some shit. You can wait out front or grab us a place at the bar."

I wanted—really, *really* wanted—to tell him I could handle the walk from the car. Even if he had to park clear down by the waterfront or Battery Park, I could handle it.

But I couldn't. So I didn't. I just mumbled, "I'll wait. Thanks," and when he pulled up to the bustling row of shops and restaurants, I got out.

Ethan drove away, and I stepped as far out of the path of foot traffic as I could get. Partly so I wasn't in people's way, and partly because I couldn't risk someone crashing into me. I was in enough pain already today.

While I waited for my friend to come back, I leaned against the wall between a couple of storefronts and looked around. Along the sides of the brick road, there were occasional boulders and people sat on them to check their phones or drink their coffee. A couple of little kids were climbing on one while their parents kept an eye on them. As I watched, I was envious. At their age, I'd have been turning my mom's hair gray by scrambling up and balancing on the tip top, probably on one foot or something. I could hear my mom gasping whenever she thought I was about to fall, and my dad bellowing, *"Get down from there before you hurt yourself bad enough you can't play hockey!"* Of course I'd have kept right on doing it too, because I was young, tough, and immortal.

Now, whenever one of the little ones playing on it so much as wobbled, my breath hitched, and I envisioned them falling and getting hurt. Except kids tended to bounce—my nieces and nephews were evidence of that—and while they might scrape a knee, and they might cry because they'd scared themselves, they probably weren't going to wind up with a broken pelvis and a hip replacement. Hell, at twenty-eight, *I* shouldn't have ended up with a broken pelvis and a hip replacement, but here I was. Thanks to some complications and stubborn soft tissue injuries, a year later I was still dealing with more pain and mobility issues than my doctors had predicted. Amazing how much a person's life could change with some squealing tires, shattering glass, the punch of an airbag, and—

I realized one of the rock-climbers' moms had noticed me watching, and she was shooting daggers out her eyes.

I quickly looked away, which probably made me look guilty as sin. She and her friends gathered their kids and moved on, glaring at me as they passed by. Honestly, I didn't blame her. My sister was super protective of her kids out in public too, and even I'd gotten suspicious whenever someone seemed too interested in them. And how long *had* I been staring while my mind had been wandering?

Ugh. Maybe this meant I really wasn't ready to rejoin society.

The jingle of tags turned my head, and my attention went straight to an Irish Setter strolling beside a good-looking guy. The dog's gaze swung around, taking in his surroundings, tail wagging and tongue hanging out.

As they came closer to me, I cleared my throat. "Do you mind if I pet your dog?"

The guy broke into a smile and halted. "Sure! She's friendly, but she'll probably lick you."

"I can live with that." I carefully leaned down and offered my hand. Sure enough, she slurped all over it, and her tail went even wilder as I laughed and petted her.

A moment later, they continued on their walk, and I couldn't help smiling. Maybe I wasn't so sure about getting out of the house and rejoining society, but I got to pet a dog, so it wasn't all bad.

"Oh my God." Ethan appeared beside me, out of breath and faintly flushed. "I swear, if I'd had to drive for one more minute, I'd have offered to blow someone for their parking space."

I laughed, which was a nice break from my usual funk. As we started walking, I asked, "How far away did you park?"

He made an unhappy noise and gestured in the general direction of the water. "Far enough that I will definitely be going to get the car and not making you walk."

That soured me again. I appreciated the consideration, but I hated that I needed it.

Is it too much to ask to feel like me *and not like I body-swapped with an old man?*

But I'd promised Ethan an hour, so I followed him up the street toward the wine bar. The bricks were slightly uneven beneath our feet, so I had to walk slower than I would have liked. God bless him, Ethan adapted to my speed without saying a word. I still had to remind my mom, who habitually walked fast and sometimes forgot that the hip replacement hadn't magically fixed everything like we'd hoped. I always had to struggle with my dad, who didn't get why I couldn't keep up. Ethan never said a word.

Mercifully, we didn't have to walk far before he gestured at a sign. "This is the place."

I looked up. In neon letters, the sign declared we had arrived at Vino and Veritas.

Another sign by the door almost drove a groan out of me: *Live Music Tonight – 8pm!*

So much for low key and quiet.

One hour. That gave me forty minutes before the music started, and I'd only have to grit my teeth through twenty minutes of it before I called time and retreated to my house.

One. Hour. I could do this.

I followed him inside, and we found a table that was far enough back from the stage that we'd theoretically still be able to hear each other once the musician started. Hopefully he wouldn't be the type to crank up his amp to fifty-thousand-seat-arena level and drown out any conversation within a five-block radius.

The chairs were comfortable, which was a godsend. There'd been a time when chairs were a challenge because playing hockey meant my ass and thighs didn't fit into things like pants off the rack or narrow seats. These days, I'd lost that physique, but I still regarded chairs warily because it didn't take much to mess with the various muscles and joints that were still recovering. That was temporary, according to my doctors. A lot of the pain I had these days was muscle atrophy and slow-healing soft tissue, plus old injuries coming back to haunt me now that said muscle atrophy had destabilized everything.

"So how do I know what's atrophy and what I'm stuck with?" I'd asked my physical therapist a month or so ago.

"When we recondition your muscles and see what still hurts."

Great. Because that sounded awesome and promising, especially when I'd been warned time and again that, thanks in part to all the damage and deterioration that had been there *before* the catastrophic injury, that whole reconditioning thing was going to take a while.

So. About that wine…

I followed Ethan's lead and ordered a glass of something that he could pronounce and I couldn't. Despite my pessimistic brain wanting to stubbornly insist that everything was terrible, the wine was good. And the ambiance was nice, too. Plus I couldn't complain about the company. Ethan and I had been tight since kindergarten, and one of the few silver linings of returning home was that we got to see each other more often.

He was also one of the rare people in my life who still treated me the same. My mom handled me with kid gloves, as if a strong wind would undo everything the surgeons had done. Old friends kept me at arm's length, like they weren't sure how to interact with me anymore. My dad… Well, he never wasted an opportunity to remind me that other professional players had come back after worse injuries, and maybe if I just put my head back in the game and started training instead of babying myself, I could play again.

"I don't care what your dad says," one of the surgeons had said to me. *"When someone your age has this much damage already and* then *has a serious injury like this? Whether we replace your hip or not, hockey is out of the question. Period."*

That had been heartbreaking, but also validating. Even if I would never in a million years convince my dad that maybe hockey was a bad idea when my body was so fucked up that I needed a hip replacement before thirty, at least I knew I wasn't just a weakling or a failure. I sometimes forgot that, especially after I'd been at my parents' house, but I knew it.

"Oh, I've heard him play before!" Ethan snapped me out of my thoughts as he gestured at the stage. "He's *good*."

Sure he was. Because musicians in places like this were always top notch.

But I'd promised my friend an hour, and the clock still had twenty minutes on it, so I turned in my chair toward the stage and—

Whoa.

The last time I'd been with a man had been maybe a week before I'd gotten hurt, and I hadn't even considered hooking up since my injury. My libido had vanished the same night my career had ended.

But unlike my hockey career, apparently my libido wasn't dead and gone after all. Just dormant.

And dear Lord, it was waking up now, thanks to the broad-shouldered silver fox onstage tuning an acoustic guitar and wearing jeans, a pair of hiking boots, and a black button-up shirt. He wasn't someone who'd have landed on the cover of a magazine, but holy fuck, he had my attention.

Watching his long fingers move on the guitar strings… Watching his mouth when he took a quick sip from his water bottle… Watching those dark eyes glance around the room and exchange something unspoken with someone I couldn't see…

"Is it just me?" I murmured to Ethan. "Or is he hot?"

"Girl, he is *ridiculously* hot."

"Uh-huh."

As the singer started his set, his faintly gravelly voice did nothing to help me find my breath. He had a bit of a country vibe. Not the stereotypical whiny lyrics and twangy style, but definitely country. I had no idea if these were original songs or covers, mostly because I couldn't concentrate on the lyrics when I was too busy focusing on him. His voice, his face, his eyes…

Yeah, no joke—this guy was ridiculously hot.

He was white with mostly gray hair cut short and neat, and he was starting to get that widow's peak some guys got in their thirties or forties, right around the time they started sweating about losing their hair. I had no way of knowing since I didn't know this guy from Adam, but something about his laidback vibe made me think he'd be the type who would just shave his head if he decided his hairline had receded too far for his taste. And I kind of wanted to see him like that. He was hot like this, he'd be hot with a shaved head, and was it getting hot in here? Why was my wineglass empty?

He finished a song and as the room applauded politely, he smiled and glanced around. And I swear to God, he locked his eyes on me. Only for a couple of seconds, but long enough to make my heart go wild.

Then he broke that eye contact and took a swig of water before continuing into his next song, leaving me wondering how I hadn't evaporated during those few seconds of being on his radar.

Maybe I'd imagined it. Maybe he'd been looking past me or at someone else for a cue about how much time he had or whatever. I didn't know.

I just knew I was absolutely looking at him.

2

JON

If there was one talent I had while performing onstage, it was engaging my audience without being distracted by them. The lighting here at Vino and Veritas didn't mask the crowd in shadows like bigger venues did—no blinding stage lights in my eyes obscuring the people beyond them—which meant I could make out a lot of faces. And there was usually a fair amount of activity, too. People came and went. Waiters brought out drinks and food. Bartenders poured drinks. Quiet conversations went on. Some loud ones, especially as more alcohol flowed.

I was used to it, and I was never distracted by it. The sea of motion and faces was easy to ignore.

Except for *that* guy's face.

One glance at him, and thank God I'd been between songs, or I'd have forgotten what I was doing.

And it didn't help at all that he'd been looking right back at me as if I'd caught his eye the way he'd caught mine. Not just like people casually watched a performer onstage, but like something I'd done had made him stop dead and stare. He was still, his eyes wide and his lips parted as he stared at me. I couldn't tell if it was a trick of the lights, but I swore he blushed too.

As I played on, I kept my gaze down, or at least tried to only let it drift toward the side of the room where he wasn't sitting. Otherwise I was going to go blank on every note and every lyric.

But then I was far enough into the music that I forgot, and I glanced in that direction again, and there he was, still looking right at me, and—

What song is this?

I only missed a beat or two, fortunately, and I recovered quickly. I doubted many people noticed, if any of them did. In a venue like this, a lot of people were only half-listening, as opposed to during an actual concert when they were all focused on me. I was background noise for most, even those who applauded between songs. Just as well when I was this distracted.

By some miracle, I made it through my set, and people didn't mutter things like, "Oh my God, finally," or "One more and I was going to stab my own eardrums" as I left the stage. Given that this hadn't been my best or most focused performance, I'd take it.

In the back room, where overflow books and promo items from the bookstore were kept, I put my guitar in its case and downed the rest of my water bottle. That had been, hands down, the hardest set I'd done since I'd started singing here. The first few had been tough because the emotions had been a lot more raw—because I'd been *real* smart, singing what I'd *just* written about my painful divorce-in-progress—so it had been rough for a while. But even during that period, I'd never actually struggled like I had tonight to remember lyrics and chords, or to keep my fingers from slipping or my tongue from getting tied.

And now I needed a drink. Not just water this time, either.

So, I left my guitar and jacket in the back where they were safe, and then headed up to the bar for a glass of wine. Only one, since I was driving. I'd probably have a couple more when I got home. Maybe not the healthiest thing in the world, but I'd been in a shitty place all day, and singing about my divorce poured some salt in wounds that hadn't closed yet. I wasn't apologizing for numbing that with a little alcohol once in a while.

"The usual?" Rainn asked over the bar.

I shook my head. "Glass of pinot blanc."

Our eyes met. Then Rainn nodded and stepped away to get the wine. He knew me and what I'd been through the last several months, so he didn't question me. He just didn't need to know that my ex-wife wasn't the one screwing with my concentration tonight.

He handed me the glass, and I thanked him before taking a sip. I wasn't much of a drinker, but I had to say, I loved the wine they poured in this place. One of these days, I'd buy a bottle or two to keep at home. Maybe after I finished redoing the kitchen and had a place to put a wine rack.

That was another depressing thought that didn't need to take hold tonight, so I focused on enjoying the amazing wine while I wound down after my set. My son was at his mom's tonight, so I didn't need to rush out of here to pick him up from the babysitter. I preferred the evenings where he was with me, but when he wasn't, I couldn't complain about relaxing here for a little while.

Someone stepped up to the bar beside me, and as I moved aside to give them some room, I glanced up and—

Oh. God.

Him.

Up close, looking right at me with those crystal blue eyes…*him.*

From across the room, he'd been hot. Up close, he was gorgeous. A little taller than me—*maybe* six foot—with lips that made me think all kinds of impure thoughts. There were a couple of scars on the left side of his face, each better than an inch in length, but they mostly faded into his fair skin except when the light caught them just right. His light brown hair was short and had that look like he'd finger-combed it into place, which probably meant he'd spent half an hour in front of a mirror getting it precisely right. Whatever. All I knew was I wanted to run my fingers through it.

Dude. Jon. Get a grip.

It wasn't like I'd never been face-to-face with someone hot before, and I'd checked out a few people in the eighteen months since my wife—ex-*wife, Jon*—had dropped the divorce hammer. But I'd never really been able to muster up more than an appreciative look or two. I hadn't felt a damned thing beyond "ooh, they're hot" since I'd found myself unexpectedly single.

Not until tonight.

I took a quick sip of wine, then managed, "Hi."

"Uh, hey." He smiled nervously. "That was… That was a great set." Instantly, he blushed, as if he were mortified by his choice of words, or he thought they were cliched small talk. I didn't care if they were—he was talking to me, and that was all I could process.

"Thanks." I smiled back. "It's nice to not get booed off the stage."

"Booed?" A laugh burst out of him, the smile cracking the shy façade just enough to make my heart race. "I can't imagine anyone booing you."

"Oh, put enough wine in someone who doesn't like country music, and I promise you, it happens."

He rolled his eyes. "Nothing like drunk fans, am I right?"

Oh, so he was a performer too? "You've had some experience with them?"

With a shy laugh, he said, "You could say that, yeah."

He didn't seem inclined to elaborate, so I just said, "Well, I don't know if I'd call this particular variety 'fans'." I extended my hand. "By the way, I'm Jon."

He shook my hand. "Brent." He shifted just slightly, and a faint wince tightened his features for a split second. And in fact, now that I was paying more attention, his entire stance held some tension that I was familiar with—the tightness that came with trying to look relaxed while something hurt. I'd seen it in patients with back or neck injuries, leg injuries, core injuries—really anything that made standing, sitting, moving, or breathing uncomfortable.

I didn't know him, never mind well enough to ask about it, so instead I went with, "I haven't seen you here before." Immediately I was cringing. Good God. Was I so out of practice with flirting that this was the best I could do? Maybe I did need to start using apps.

Brent didn't seem to mind, though. "It's my first time here."

"Like, first time at Vino and Veritas? Or in Burlington?"

Please be local. Please be local. Please be—

"Oh, I grew up here. Just moved back a few months ago."

"You moved in the winter?" I chuckled as I brought up my wineglass. "I thought I was the only one who did masochistic shit like that."

He laughed with a hint of uneasiness. "Well, it wasn't really the way I planned it. Just kind of the way things worked out."

"Yeah. Same."

Our eyes met again. There were questions in his, and I had no doubt he could see questions in mine, but he didn't seem any more inclined to offer up information than I was. Maybe this was a subject better left untouched for the moment.

Clearing my throat, I put my glass down. "Well, if you end up here again"—I gestured at our surroundings—"I play on Wednesday and Saturday nights, and whenever Tanner needs someone to fill in."

"Oh. Good to know." Thirty seconds in this man's company, and that smile was going to be the death of me. "I'll, um… I'll have to stop in again." A lot of people said that with zero intention of ever darkening the wine bar's doorway a second time, never mind when I was playing, but somehow, I believed him. Wishful thinking, maybe? Whatever. I liked it, so I ran with it.

Except then I remembered he hadn't been here alone. Though my attention had been almost entirely focused on Brent, there had been someone else at his table. Another guy.

"I, um… I should let you get back to your…" I nodded toward the table where he'd been sitting and the man he'd come with.

Brent glanced over, and his shy smile came back as he shook his head. "Oh, no, he's busy flirting with that guy in the corner, so…"

"The—" I blinked. "*Oh*. So he's not your… You're not on a date."

"Oh God, no." He waved a hand. "He's a friend. Dragged me out tonight because he thought I've been spending too much time at home."

"Dragged you?" I brought my wine to my lips. "Don't like places like this?"

"It's not that. I…" He chewed his lip. "I just haven't been out much lately. Like at all. And it turned out he was right." Brent gave me a not-very-subtle down-up, and he grinned. "It was a good night to get out."

I gulped. Something that brazen coming from someone that shy was…whoa. "Was it?"

"Yeah." His brow pinched subtly, as if that was as bold as he could get, and he was nervous about pushing any further.

"Well," I said. "Since you're not here on a date, is there any chance I can get your number?"

His eyes lit up. "You—really?"

"Well, yeah." I smiled, but hesitated. "How else can I text you after tonight?"

"Oh. Oh, right." Fuck, that blush was cute. He reached into his back pocket and took out his phone. After he'd brought up his contacts, he handed it to me. I gave him mine too, and we entered our numbers into each other's phones, then traded them again.

I had to fight hard against a big ridiculous grin. This was the first time I'd even tried to connect with someone in over twenty years, and I'd made it this far? Mental fist pump.

He shifted his weight, a hint of a wince flickering across his expression. "So, um…" He gestured toward the stage on the other end of the room. "Do you have another set?"

I shook my head. "No, I'm done for the night."

"Oh." Shyness and boldness seemed to be vying for dominance in his expression as he studied me. The former won: "I guess I should, uh, let you get back to…"

I tried not to let my disappointment show, and I gestured toward his friend. "Yeah, your friend is probably going to be looking for you."

"Right. Right." He blushed again, eyes flicking away from mine for a second before he looked at me again through his lashes. "But you have my number. Let's… Let's text. See what happens."

I smiled. "Good idea. I'm looking forward to it."

That brought his smile back to life, and I thought for a fleeting moment his boldness might find a second wind, but instead, he murmured a good night, and I turned back to the bar while he headed back to his friend.

Damn. Talk about mixed feelings. I was disappointed we hadn't made more than a brief connection, but I had his number, and anyway, it was encouraging to know I could catch someone's eye like that. For that matter, that someone could still catch *my* attention like that. I'd been so low and miserable since my divorce, I hadn't felt anything for anyone, and I hadn't wanted to.

But tonight, I had.

One glance, and I'd instantly remembered what chemistry was and what it felt like, and I'd remembered how good it felt to *want* that chemistry. To want more of it.

This was all I'd get tonight, but I could live with that. Especially since I had his number. If he wanted to move slowly, we'd move slowly. I was just glad to be moving at all.

In the meantime, I finished my wine. Then I went to get my jacket and guitar so I could call it a night.

3

BRENT

Well, that went better than I thought it would.

I mean, okay, I'd lost my nerve and hadn't tried to go any farther than just making a connection and exchanging numbers, but considering it was the first time in a year that I'd even thought about connecting with someone, I'd call it a win.

With Jon's number in my phone and butterflies in my stomach, I went back to the table.

I hadn't even pulled out my chair before Ethan's eyes widened and he squeaked, "What are you doing?"

"What?" I shrugged and gingerly sat down.

"You walked away from him?"

I shrugged, folding my arms on the edge of the table. "I didn't want to push my luck. He seemed—"

"*Honey.*" Ethan stared at me. "He's obviously into you. You had him undressed with your eyes before he'd finished his first song, and there is no way that man wasn't mentally fucking you the whole time you two were standing there."

My face burned and I laughed nervously. "Oh come on. I think he's kind of into me, but—"

"Kind of?" Ethan tsked and rolled his eyes. "*Girl.*" He gestured at the bar where I'd been chatting with Jon. "What the hell are you waiting for?"

I avoided his gaze as I went for my drink. "Look, I'm just not sure I'm ready for this."

"For *what?* You're hooking up, not eloping."

That should've made me laugh, but instead it kind of made my skin crawl. "No, we're not eloping, but hooking up is..." I grimaced. "Dude, no one without a medical degree has seen me naked in almost a year. And I am *not* what I was a year ago."

"Mmhmm. And?" He inclined his head. "You're hot and he's into you, sweetie." He reached into his pocket, pulled out a condom, and tossed it on the table between us. "Screw him in the dark if it makes you feel better, but seriously—what are you waiting for?"

My first instinct was to flick the condom back to him and tell him to back off. He didn't know how rough this had been on me. How my worry over my body—both the way it looked and the way it felt—had put me off even thinking about sex for the foreseeable future, regardless of what my libido had to say about it.

Except...I'd made that connection with Jon. And I did want to see if there really was some chemistry there or if it was all in my head. The way he'd been looking at me, I had no doubt that if we reconnected tonight or another night, sex would be on the table, and...I wanted it. With him. It wasn't like he knew who I was, so he wouldn't spend the whole time comparing me to what I used to be.

And maybe this would be like the first time I'd returned to the ice after recovering from a bad knee injury—a whole lot less of an ordeal than I'd made it out to be in my head. I'd been terrified to get back to skating, never mind playing hockey, because I was sure I'd destroy my knee all over again. That first practice session had been a huge relief, and it made me feel like a dumbass for worrying so much to begin with.

It was entirely possible that was what would happen here. I'd get into bed with someone—with Jon—and he wouldn't even notice all the scars or the fact that I wasn't as fit or acrobatic as I used to be, and we'd have some amazing sex, and I'd feel like a relieved dumbass for ever thinking we wouldn't.

So really—what *was* I waiting for? I hadn't felt this good since before I'd gotten hurt. And if we did end up in bed, we didn't have to leave the lights on. What kind of idiot was I to let that good feeling leave with the man who'd been into me?

"Okay." A rush of nerves made me shiver, and I tried to ignore the way that jarred my sore hip. "All right. I'll—"

"If you're gonna grab him, you better do it now." Ethan nodded toward the door.

I looked just in time to see Jon and his guitar case slip out. "Shit." I faced Ethan again. "But I came with you. I don't want to ditch—"

"*Go!*"

I went. I stepped back to snatch up the condom, and *then* I went.

In my past life, I'd have sprinted across the wine bar and caught him before he'd made it a few steps, but speed wasn't in the cards for me anymore. When I stepped outside… Damn it. Which way had he gone?

I looked up and down the street, frantically searching for his black leather jacket and his gray hair and the guitar case and—

There.

Through the throngs of people, I caught a glimpse of him heading toward what I thought was the parking garage, and I called out, "Jon!"

He halted and turned, and just seeing his eyes in the streetlights almost made me stumble as I started toward him. The heavy foot traffic on the road between us was a blessing in disguise—I had to dodge people, which meant I couldn't walk very fast, which meant he had no way of noticing how hard I was trying not to limp.

When I reached him, we stepped out of the flow of traffic, which meant slipping into a narrow and mostly deserted street between some shops. There, our eyes met in the glow of a streetlight, and my heart was racing the way it used to after I'd done an intense shift on the ice.

"Hey, I, um…" I gulped. "On second thought, instead of texting later…" *Come on. Just say it. What are you waiting for?* I moistened my dry lips, and finally managed to blurt out, "Can I buy you a drink? Like, now?"

He straightened, eyebrows jumping, and the little upward twitch of the corner of his mouth had my heart going wild all over again. "What changed your mind?"

"I…" My face was on fire. I was never this ballsy with someone in person. Not even in my cocky life-of-the-party heyday. But Jon had almost slipped through my fingers, and I was more afraid of watching him walk away again than I was of tripping over my own nerves, so I said, "I was having a good time in there. Guess I'm not as ready as I thought I was for that to be over."

Holy fuck. That smile.

Calling on every bit of courage I had, I said, "I kind of want to… I mean, I'm not new to this, but it's been a while, and I'm—"

"Oh, I can relate." It was a safe bet we weren't talking about the same thing, but the mix of sincerity and empathy in his dark eyes made my knees shake.

"You can?"

"Uh-huh. I'm single again for the first time in a long, long time. So this is all new. Well, new again."

Okay so we weren't talking about the same thing, but we could both relate to getting back into this particular saddle.

"I'm not new to being single." Was I out of breath from walking across the street? Or from him? "Just, um… A lot of things have been in flux, and I've…" I didn't know how to finish that. Not without making things awkward again. Clearing my throat, I put on a smile and hoped it didn't look as nervous as it felt. "I wasn't planning on meeting anyone any time soon. Definitely not tonight. But…"

Jon's smile turned into a grin, and if I hadn't been out of breath already, I would've been now. "So." He inclined his head a little. "I got the impression you wanted to move slow in there." He motioned toward the wine bar. "But now…"

I swallowed. "I thought I did. Then I saw you leave, and I had second thoughts."

"So you want to shift gears in the other direction?"

"Accelerate instead of tap the brakes?" I nodded. "Yeah. Yeah, exactly."

His lips curled into an even more spine-melting grin, and I was so fascinated by his mouth, I almost didn't catch it when he said, "Question is, how hard do you want to hit the gas?"

"Um." I blinked. "I…"

"We could go have another drink." He swept his tongue along the inside of his lip. "Or we could go someplace else."

Oh dear Lord.

We were moving at warp speed, and that was terrifying and exhilarating at the same time. Like diving right into the swimming pool instead of easing in one toe at a time to get used to the temperature. With as nervous as I'd been lately? With as scared to death as I was of getting physical with someone? With as much as I desperately wanted to push past that fear and prove to myself I was overreacting? Oh yeah, warp speed was absolutely okay with me this time.

The upward flick of his eyebrow asked what it was going to be.

Well, Brent—a drink, or someplace else?

I cleared my throat. "I mean I'm happy to buy you a drink, but I'm game to skip that part if you've got something else in mind."

Jon straightened a little, obviously surprised, and I was about to mumble a flustered "Or we could just get a drink, that's cool," when he put his guitar case down by our feet. Then he rose, and I'll be damned if he didn't step closer.

"I think I've had enough to drink tonight," he said in a low growl as he reached for the back of my neck. "I'm a little more interested in what happens next."

And then…

Oh. God.

This was every kiss that had ever stopped my world on a dime. The first time I'd kissed a boy in high school. That stolen kiss with a college teammate after we'd spent two hockey seasons circling each other. The time I'd found out in no uncertain terms that a rival player shared my secret attraction.

One kiss under the Marketplace streetlights, and I was putty in Jon's hands. The way his fingers slid up into my hair, he might as well have been dragging a live wire across my nerve endings. The soft brush of his lips, the scrape of his unshaven chin, the other hand sliding under my jacket and pulling me closer to him. Everything about him and his kiss was beyond sexy, and any fear I had that we were moving too fast went up in smoke. If anything, I wanted to move faster. I was still terrified of letting him or anyone else see me naked, but I was determined to push through that so I could see and feel *him* naked.

He drew back, and our eyes met under the blanched glow of the streetlight, and I swear his face was filled with as much surprise as mine must have been. As if he hadn't expected something so intense. Oh, but there was more than surprise. If he'd been hungry before, he was ravenous now, and when he pulled me back in, he growled, "Jesus fuck," just before our lips collided again.

As he held me close, his hips brushed mine, and he was rock hard through his jeans. I…wasn't. But I was still nervous. When we got our clothes off and I knew how stupid I'd been to worry this much, then my dick would get onboard. I just hoped he didn't notice right now that my body wasn't quite responding the way it should be.

Just give me a little time, and don't be an asshole when the clothes come off, and we'll be good.

I hope.

I banished that thought as I ran my fingers through Jon's hair. I was just overthinking things. I was nervous. Once we found our stride, I'd be fine. The pain I was in tonight—I was used to that. As long as we didn't get too rough, I'd manage all right.

I broke the kiss, and when our eyes met this time, we were both breathing hard.

"So," I panted, "about that stepping on the gas thing…"

"My house is about fifteen minutes away," he murmured. "But there's a few hotels like two blocks from here." Sliding his hands into my back pockets, he purred, "What do you say we get a room?"

Oh my God, the way he said it sounded so dirty, and I was nodding even before I'd found enough air to whisper, "Fuck, yeah."

"Want to follow me there?"

I thought about it, and it took me a moment to remember that my truck wasn't here. "Actually I rode in with my friend. You mind if I ride over with you?"

Jon smiled. "Not at all. Let's go."

He picked up his guitar, and we continued toward the parking garage.

As we walked, I gritted my teeth and tried to keep walking as fast as he did. He wasn't speed-walking or anything, but I had to walk slower than most people. It wasn't far, though. I'd be *fine*. When he pressed the key fob in his hand, lights flashed and a trunk opened about half a dozen cars up. Not far at all. My hip and back hurt, and now so did my knee, but I didn't want to bring things to a screeching halt by launching into a speech about my recent medical history. That would be a hell of a mood killer. I'd just let this be a reminder that, once we got into the room, I had to be careful.

We made a quick stop at a drugstore. Jon went in to get lube and condoms while I, under the pretense of saving time and absolutely not in the name of staying off my leg, stayed behind to make a hotel reservation on my phone. When he came back, I had us a room, he had a plastic bag of essentials, and the wicked grins we exchanged said that, oh yes, tonight was the right night to jump back into this pool. And this was definitely the right man to jump in with.

The hotel had valet parking—which hadn't factored into me choosing the place, no, not at all—and the check-in desk was right inside. It took about thirty seconds to check in, and the elevator was mercifully close to the desk, so we didn't have to walk far. Would we also score a room near the elevator? Not have to walk eight miles to our room? Please?

The elevator opened. We stepped out, and our room was one, two, three—*score*.

Heart racing, I grinned as I touched the keycard to the door. This was my lucky night.

As soon as we were inside, Jon tossed the bag of condoms and lube on the table, and he faced me, his eyes full of need that matched my own. "All right. Where were we?"

"Mmm." I slid my hands around his waist. "I think we were making out by the wine bar."

"I think you're right." And then he kissed me again, and oh dear God, this really was my lucky night.

I leaned on the door, and he moaned softly as he leaned into me. A few joints and muscles protested, but I ignored them because damn, it had been so long since I'd felt the solid presence of another man pressed against me. Now that I remembered how much I liked sex and being touched, I was hungry for him. Greedy for him. There was no telling how much I could handle in this not-quite-healed body, but I was definitely ready to take whatever I could get. And give whatever I could give, because holy hell, how had I gone this long without feeling a man's breath hitch like that? Or hearing him groan low in his throat as his hands slid all over me?

I wanted more. I wanted *skin*. I wanted us naked, and—

And getting naked meant letting him see and feel me. The not-quite-healed me that I barely recognized.

"Hey." He broke the kiss and touched my face as he looked right into my eyes. "You okay?"

Damn. Apparently I'd tensed up.

I tried to force a laugh. "Nerves, I guess."

"That all?"

Oh God. Could he feel it? Could he feel how I still hadn't gotten hard? Because, son of a bitch, my dick was *still* soft.

What the fuck?

Okay, maybe if we just took off the clothes and got that part over with, then I could finally get in the game. But I wasn't quite ready to just strip and hope for the best.

"Listen..." I shifted my weight, trying not to wince. "I've been through a lot the last year. Physically. So I might not look... I mean, there's scars, and I've lost a ton of muscle tone, and I'm just starting to get some of it back, and—"

"Brent." He stroked my cheek with his thumb, his eyes and voice as gentle as his smile. "I'm in my forties. My weight's gone up and down over the last twenty-some-odd years and my hairline is receding. Unless you've got *'Hey Jon, your music sucks'* tattooed across your chest, we'll be fine."

A laugh burst out of me. "Okay, I don't have that. I promise."

"Then don't worry about it." He drew me in for a light kiss. "This isn't Hollywood. Bodies don't have to be flawless."

As he kissed me again, I relaxed and wrapped my arms around him. I knew how easily comments like his could turn out to be lip service once the clothes actually came off, but his sincerity gave me the boost of confidence I needed to keep going.

Riding that boost, I tugged his belt. He slid his hands under my shirt. Little by little, everything came off. Shoes. Jackets. Shirts. Pants. We left a trail of clothes between the door and the bed, all of which I stepped over *very* carefully to make sure I didn't trip and turn this night into a disaster.

Needless to say, I was beyond relieved when we got into bed. No more tripping hazards. No more hiding. He could see me and feel me, and as we made out under the sheets, his hands roamed my body without even a hint of disgust at my less-than-fit physique.

His fingers brushed over the big scar on my hip, and though they didn't pause, I cringed a little. He had to have noticed it. But he didn't react. He didn't pull back. He kept on kissing me and touching me, and one by one, my doubts and worries went away. I relaxed into his embrace, and into his kiss, and I was going to start getting hard any minute now.

Any minute.

Any. Minute.

Um. Hello? Anybody home down there?

For fuck's sake…wake up!

"You like to top or bottom?" Jon asked between kisses.

"Either." I shifted a little and tensed as the twinge in my hip grabbed my focus for a second. "Might need to go kind of slow. Still, um, still recovering a bit. From a surgery I had a few months ago."

"Okay," he said without missing a beat, and he started on my neck. "I can definitely do slow."

I bit my lip and shivered. Hell, even if I wasn't in pain, I'd want him to go slow tonight, because he made it sound so incredibly sexy.

So why am I still not hard?

Probably because I was still pressed up close to him. Close enough he'd be able to feel my lack of a hard-on if either of us moved just right. Maybe that meant too much pressure. Maybe I needed to try a different approach. A subtler one.

I broke the kiss and panted, "Turn over. On your back."

Jon grinned. "I like the sound of that."

He turned on to his back, and I shifted so I could go down on him. This I could definitely do—sucking his thick, fully-hard cock while he moaned and swore. He just didn't need to know that while I licked and teased him, I kept surreptitiously stroking myself, trying to bring my dick to attention. There was a little stirring, but not much.

Come on, come on! What the hell? What is happening? Or…not happening?

Thank God Jon was oblivious. All he knew was what I was doing to his cock, and from the way he moaned and the way *he* had no trouble staying rock-hard, he liked what I was doing. I enjoyed sucking dick, too, so I was happy to go on for as long as he wanted me to.

But seriously—what the fuck is going on with me tonight?

Jon had seen me naked. He'd had his hands all over me and he was still into me. I was a little self-conscious, but I was into this too. Why wouldn't my cock get with the program?

"Come up here," he whispered. "Want to… Want to kiss you again."

The surge of desire at the thought of making out with him some more was almost enough to drown out my internal freak-out, but not quite. Still, kissing him did turn me on like crazy, so maybe that was what I needed.

The thought made me tingle all over. *All* over.

Yeah. Definitely, more of that.

I started to sit up, and a bolt of pain in my left leg made me gasp. "Fuck!"

Jon pushed himself up on his elbow, eyes full of concern. "Are you all right?"

"I'm good," I said through my teeth as I rubbed my hip. "Just, um…"

Damn it. What was the point? What was I even doing? My dick wouldn't get hard. Now my hip wanted to act up, and once this kind of pain started, it would be a while before it eased off unless I took something strong. And neither scenario—knuckling through the pain or swallowing something that strong—boded well for that elusive erection.

"Brent?" He touched my shoulder. "What's wrong? You okay?"

Why fight it? Why lie? Why embarrass myself any more than I already had?

Shoulders drooping, I shook my head and avoided his gaze. "No. I, um… I thought I could do this. But it's just not working."

"What's wrong?" He looked me up and down, and embarrassment made my stomach lurch. It was plain to see that my dick wasn't into this, and now that Jon could see it—now that there was no avoiding it—that was almost worse than the physical pain. The physical pain that was putting a stop to this anyway regardless of my junk's opinion.

"I'm sorry." I put up my hands. "I'm not as ready as I thought to…" To what? To have sex with an incredibly hot man after a year-long dry spell? All I could say was, "I'm sorry."

Jon didn't speak. The silence hung between us for a while before I finally looked at him, and I hated myself for the mix of hurt and concern in his eyes. The unspoken *Did I do something wrong?*

"It's not you," I whispered. "It's… I can't even explain it. But it's not you."

"Then what… Can we talk about this?"

"I'd rather not. I just… I need to go. I'm sorry."

I started to get up, and he didn't try to stop me. Neither of us spoke as I got dressed. He pulled the sheet over his lap, but he didn't seem to be heading out with me.

As I reached for the door, though, he said, "Wait."

I turned, my heart in my throat.

"How are you getting home?"

Oh, son of a *bitch*.

"I'll, um…" Did Burlington have Uber? Hell, it was a college town. It had to. If Uber didn't exist here, then I'd call Ethan, and he'd know better than to ask questions. Meeting Jon's eyes, I said, "I'll be fine. Don't worry about me."

His expression said he would worry about me, which did nothing to soothe my wounded ego or my throbbing conscience.

"The, uh… The room's paid for, so…" I gestured around but didn't finish the thought.

Mute, Jon nodded.

There was nothing left to say, so I just muttered, "I'm sorry," and then I got the hell out of there.

In the elevator, I leaned against the wall and rubbed both hands over my face. I had never been this mortified in my life. Not even after that missed shot on an empty goal had cost us a championship my junior year in college.

I was twenty-nine. I'd already lost my career. I was already living in a body that didn't feel like my own.

And now *this?* Fucking *seriously?*

I'd been terrified of getting back in the saddle. Of being naked with someone now after the toll the last year had taken on my body.

I just hadn't bargained for my body failing me like this.

So much for my lucky night.

4

JON

The door shut behind Brent, and I stared at it.

Sitting on the edge of the bed, my clothes and shoes still littering the carpet between here and the door, I just…stared.

What the hell? Because I had *no* idea what had just happened.

I ran through everything from the parking garage to now, and… well, maybe I did know what had happened. From the first moment I'd met him, it had been clear he had—but was trying to hide—some pain. I worked with too many pain management patients to miss those subtle signs. The slight hitch in his gait when he moved. The way he always seemed to stand with his weight on his right leg. Even before he'd mentioned surgery and recovery, I'd suspected it wasn't a new injury or an acute one, like a pulled muscle or something. Not when he'd had the vaguely tense posture that came after someone had learned to constantly—almost unconsciously—adapt in order to accommodate pain.

I knew chronic pain when I saw it, and that was what I'd seen in Brent. More than once, I'd considered asking, especially as we'd started on the trajectory toward the hotel room, but I'd erred on the side of following his lead. He was clearly self-conscious about the injury and—I'd found out later—his body, and I hadn't wanted to embarrass him about it. The best thing was to take my cues from him, and that was what I'd tried to do.

But then…

Alone in the enormous, silent room, I sighed.

Damn it. I should have asked. Instead of trying to intuit when he was uncomfortable, I should have had him guide me so I didn't hurt him. I should have just hit the pause button, asked him to level with me so I knew enough to not cause him pain, and—

And it didn't fucking matter, because he was gone.

He was gone, and that bothered me a lot more than it should have. Not because I'd had stars in my eyes or thought this was more than a one-night stand, but because I hadn't been with anyone since my ex-wife. I hadn't wanted to. Tonight, I'd finally felt something, and I'd thought someone else felt it right back, and…now this. Some amazing kissing, the promise of some damn good sex, and then out of nowhere, he'd bolted like the room was on fire.

Whether it was because he was in too much pain or because he'd decided he didn't want me after all, the bottom line was that he was gone, and his absence made me realize it wasn't sex I'd needed tonight. Not *just* sex, anyway. It was *touch*. My ex-wife and I had barely touched in the months leading up to the separation, and our sex life had turned distant and disinterested long before that. I literally couldn't remember the last time she'd touched me in a way that said *I want you*.

And then Brent had. The way he'd kissed me outside the parking garage? The way his hands had roamed all over me? We could have just made out with our clothes on and I'd have been thrilled because I hadn't even realized how hungry I'd been for someone to *touch* me and *want* me.

I'd had a taste, and now it was gone, and I craved that contact more than I'd ever craved sex. Given the high libido I'd had for years, that said a lot. Hell, maybe that had been what I'd needed all this time. Maybe sex had always been a means of getting that contact I needed. I loved sex, and I missed it, but damn, what I wouldn't have given tonight for everything *else*. Just lying here with Brent and touching, even if we weren't doing anything, would have been amazing for me.

And for that matter, if he were here—if he'd just given me a minute to get a word in—I wanted to tell him there wasn't a damn thing off-putting about his body, and that we didn't have to fuck or do anything if it was painful for him.

Just...don't leave.

But he had left, and now I had the room for the entire night. I kind of felt like a dick, staying here on Brent's dime, but it wasn't like he'd kicked me out. And as he'd said, the room was paid for. The alternative was going home to the house that was empty except for all the reasons I regretted buying the place and the bedroom that was vacant every other week while my son stayed at his mom's.

I scrubbed a hand over my face and swore. I was in a *great* mental place when going home sounded worse than staying in the room where I'd been with a man who'd gone from blowing me to bailing on me in a matter of seconds. But home was full of all the reminders of the other failures in my life, and I wasn't sure I could face any of that tonight.

Might as well stay here, and I had come here intending to get off, so...why not get off?

I closed my eyes, wrapped my fingers around my dick and tried to think of anyone except the man who'd bailed unexpectedly.

But all I could think of was Brent.

And thinking about Brent just made me think about how hungry I was for human contact. How things had suddenly taken a sharp turn into *what the hell?* How embarrassed he must be right now, not to mention in pain, since something had clearly hurt when he'd called this off.

Okay, so much for taking care of myself. My desire for anything sexual had left with Brent.

With a heavy sigh, I got up and went to grab a shower. No real reason. Just something to do. After that... I didn't know. Maybe I'd stay here. Maybe I'd go home.

I just knew that wherever I went, I'd still feel like shit.

5

BRENT

I sat back and stared at my laptop screen, jaw slack and stomach sick.

I'd been to a dozen different websites, including three articles in medical journals. They'd been a nightmare to parse when I was simultaneously this exhausted and freaked out, but I'd managed, and no matter how many times I said, "That can't be right," and looked up another article, they all said the same thing. There was no denying it. There was no pretending it wasn't there in peer-reviewed black-and-white on all the tabs I still had open on my browser.

This…this wasn't real. No way. It had just been nerves last night. Jon was the first guy I'd been with since before I'd gotten hurt, and I was painfully self-conscious about what the last year had done to my body, so yeah, it made sense that I'd had trouble keeping it up.

Except…

With a sinking feeling, I thought back to the times I'd tried to jerk off in recent months. It had taken a long time for me to even work up the desire—never mind the energy—to rub one out, and my stomach curdled as I thought about how many times I hadn't finished. How I'd barely been able to get started more often than not. How that hadn't been getting better even as time went on and my body healed. I'd chalked it up to being depressed, or not in the mood, or tired, or…

Why the fuck hadn't anyone warned me that a broken pelvis could lead to erectile dysfunction?

My doctors and physical therapists had told me all kinds of ways this injury was a gift that kept on giving, but no one had ever mentioned *this*. Or had they? Had I just brushed it off as one of those things they warned about to cover their asses? Like how drug companies listed four million side effects for each drug, but it was more to prevent liability than anything?

No, I was pretty sure I'd have remembered if someone had mentioned that, on top of fucking over my career, hobbling my mobility, and leaving me with chronic pain, my injuries could also *screw with how my goddamned dick worked*. Or *if* it would work *at all*.

I put the laptop aside on the couch and leaned my head back. Staring up at the vaulted ceiling, I didn't know if I wanted to cry or throw something or just...sit here and be a step up from catatonic, same as I'd been every time another bad news bombshell had landed.

I hadn't thought it was possible to feel lower than I had yesterday, but here I was. Ethan had wanted me to get out last night so I could break this funk, and oh. Yeah. *That* had worked. I felt *so* much better now that I'd had a taste of normal life again, only to get bitch-slapped back down by my battered body picking the worst possible time to say, "But *wait!* There's *more!*"

Ugh. This was some bullshit right here.

I took a deep breath and tried to pull myself together. I needed to figure out how to deal with this. That meant I needed to find out how bad it actually was, if anything could be done, or if erectile dysfunction—*oh my God, really?*—was something I should learn to live with.

First things first, I called my doctor's office. When the receptionist answered, I said, "Hi, this is Brent Weyland." I swallowed. "I, um... I need to make an appointment with Dr. Marks as soon as possible."

"Is this a medical emergency?"

"No, no, it's not an emergency."

She ran me through a battery of questions that I knew were meant to triage me. Though I desperately wanted to tell her this was of critical importance, I wasn't going to elbow my way to the front if someone else had something more urgent. So I was honest—I had some concerns, but there wasn't an emergency and there were no symptoms that warranted a fast pass.

"Okay, well, I can get you in..." She paused, murmuring something to herself. Then, "Looks like the first appointment I have is August fourteenth at three. Will that work for you?"

I blinked. "*August?* But that's..." I mentally ran the numbers. "That's like four months away!"

"Yeah," she said apologetically. "He's been booked solid lately. I can put you on a list in case something opens up sooner, but unless it's an emergency, this is the earliest I can get you in."

Closing my eyes, I exhaled. In my mind, it *was* an emergency, but of course I knew it wasn't. "No. No, August will work."

"All right. And what are we seeing you for?"

I gulped. "Uh...just some ongoing issues with my injury." It wasn't a lie. I could have told her the whole truth, but I was still so fucking embarrassed and horrified that it was even a thing, I couldn't make myself say it out loud. Not yet.

After we ended the call, I pressed the heels of my hands into my eyes and cursed. Four months until I had an answer. Awesome. Did it even matter what the doctor said, though? Because I was pretty sure I'd gotten the message in big neon letters last night. Or...little flaccid letters. Fuck.

How was this real? I was twenty-nine years old, and both my career and my sex life were over. Son of a *bitch*.

And of course I'd just had to find out like that—in bed with a hot guy. Oh God, I desperately wanted to scrub last night from my memory, but that was about as likely as pretending I'd never gotten hurt. It was there, and the best I could do was adapt to it and move on.

For that matter, I didn't want to forget Jon. He hadn't just been hot, he'd been really sweet, and I'd been a little starstruck even though he was just singing in a wine bar. I'd been a little dizzy over him too, and damn it, I'd wanted to spend some time lying in bed and talking after we'd fucked. When we were past all the games people played to figure out if they were into each other, and we knew we were into each other enough to get naked, and we'd gotten off, and we could just talk about whatever. Maybe see if we were interested enough to meet again for more than just sex.

I hadn't felt drawn to someone like that in a long time. Even before I'd gotten hurt, I'd loved the relative anonymity of no-frills Tinder hookups. But man, once in a while, there was that instant connection. Sometimes it got off the ground, sometimes it didn't, but if nothing else, it was fun to talk in between getting physical.

But we hadn't gotten far before my body had said, "LOL no," and I'd wanted to be anywhere but there. I couldn't even look him in the eye, never mind lie there and talk as if I didn't want to crawl into a hole and die.

Though, it occurred to me now that Jon probably thought I was a complete asshole. I'd flirted and probably made him think I was interested in *him*, not just his body, and then we'd barely started fooling around before I'd freaked out and bailed.

Fuck. I'd been so caught up in being mortified, I hadn't thought about how it must've made *him* feel. And I mean, I didn't believe it was love at first sight or anything, and I had no illusions that he was pining after me. He'd probably just muttered, *"Well, fuck you, asshole,"* while he blocked my number, and then he'd jerked off and gone to sleep with that huge bed all to himself and never gave me another thought.

But it bugged me. I wanted to at least try to tell him what really happened last night. That it hadn't been because I didn't want him. Maybe he wouldn't believe me. Maybe he didn't care. But it was worth a try, if only to dislodge this knot of shame and guilt in my stomach.

He might've worried he'd done something wrong, too. Especially with the way I'd suddenly called time and bailed with no explanation. After I'd been the one to chase him when he'd left the club. *After* I'd awkwardly said we'd do this another time. He must've had whiplash from me changing my mind so abruptly. If I were him, I probably would've blocked me and avoided any future drama too.

Still, it *was* worth a try.

With my heart in my throat, I pulled up his contact and tried to figure out what to say. I finally settled on: *Last night could have ended better. Can I buy you a drink to make up for it?*

Then it was sent. No taking it back. No calming down until I got an answer one way or the other, even if that answer was to go fuck myself.

And what if he accepted the drink, and I explained everything, and he reacted the way some other people had? My dad was convinced I just needed to work harder, do more physical therapy, and get back on my skates.

"Come on, Brent. Your grandfather recovered faster than this from a broken hip, and he was seventy.*"*

Yeah, okay, except Grandpa had broken his hip, not his pelvis. I'd broken *both*. Plus one of the surgeries had actually made a few things worse. Oh, and for good measure, a few tendons had decided not to heal properly, even after the surgery that everyone insisted fixed the problem in eighty percent of people (cold comfort for those of us in that other twenty percent). Between all the injuries from that night and the rest of my ages-old hockey injuries (some of which had flared to life later), I'd been pretty well fucked. My doctors and physical therapists hadn't minced words from day one: my body would never be the same again. Pain would, to some degree, be a constant companion for the rest of my life, and the best I could do was adapt and mitigate.

Now everyone my own age treated me like the old man I felt like most of the time. Everyone who was older seemed mystified that I wasn't bouncing back the way a twenty-something should.

You *fuckers take a hit like that after a lifetime of hockey wear and tear, and* then *tell me how* you *bounce back.*

So how would Jon react? He was easily a decade older than me. Probably more. How weird would it be for him to hook up with a younger dude, only to have that dude's performance get torpedoed by a broken hip and some surprise ED?

Apparently I was going to find out, because my screen lit up:

I'm free after 4. When/where?

Oh God. We were doing this.

As I wrote out the name of a coffee shop I knew, I prayed he wasn't an asshole about this. I deserved it if he was, since I'd taken off on him the way I had.

But I hoped like hell he wasn't.

Sitting in a coffee shop not far from the wine bar where we'd met, I tried not to liken the way I felt to when I'd been waiting for the doctor to tell me how bad things really were. When the drugs had worn off enough for my head to be clear, and the nurses wouldn't tell me anything but also couldn't *quite* look me in the eye, and all anyone would say was that the doctor would be along soon. I'd known then that it wouldn't be good news, and I'd spent hours—felt like hours, anyway—both wishing she'd just show up and rip off the metaphorical bandage and silently begging her not to come and tell me what I was pretty sure I already knew.

It didn't help that right now, I was hurting all over. The hip replacement had been a game-changer but not a magic bullet. My pelvis and left hip always hurt—sometimes just a dull ache, sometimes bad enough to make my breath catch—and today my back and left knee were joining the party as they often did. There were already low-grade twinges in my right knee that meant it wouldn't be long before I was paying for favoring the left. I'd been rubbing my neck off and on all day, trying to keep that telltale tightness from turning into something miserable. Every twinge and throb was another reminder that my body was royally jacked up, and that some level of pain would always be my reality.

I really could have done without that reminder while I was trying to fight off a *this conversation is going to be awful* feeling. Even pausing on the way in to pet someone's deliriously excited husky puppy couldn't shake me out of this *oh shit* state of mind.

Whatever happened today, whatever I said to Jon and however he reacted, it wouldn't be nearly as catastrophic as everything the doctor had told me almost a year ago. I knew that. It just gave me the same feeling, which made me wonder a million times over if this was even a good idea and if there was still time for me to bail. I could ghost him. Never show my face at that wine bar again. Hope we didn't run into each other (lots of luck in a town of under fifty thousand unless I really kept up the hermit thing, which kind of didn't sound like a bad idea). I wasn't usually a coward or an asshole, but last night had been so mortifying and this conversation didn't promise to be any better, and yeah, being a cowardly asshole kind of sounded like a good idea except oh, God, there he was.

Jon walked into the coffee shop, and my heart jumped into my throat.

He acknowledged me with a nod, gesturing at the counter. I nodded back, and I took a sip of my coffee while he stood in the short line to get his.

From across the shop, I looked him up and down. Goddamn. Why did my body have to fail on me *with him?* Why did I have to fuck up *with him?* Because even through my dread and embarrassment, I couldn't ignore the same thing that had forced its way past my stubbornly shitty mood last night: Jon was *gorgeous*.

He had on jeans again, this time with a pair of rust-colored hiking boots. The jeans sat just right on his ass, and I had no idea if they fit better than what he'd had on last night or if I was just mesmerized because I knew what he looked like with nothing on. Ditto with the way that familiar black leather jacket hugged his shoulders. I'd thought it was sexy last night. Today, it made my mouth water.

Oh yeah, now that I'd seen the hot, powerful body he was hiding under denim and leather, everything about him was a million times sexier.

Or maybe that was just because I knew last night would be the last time I saw him naked and today would probably be the last time I saw him at all. What a shame, because he was easy on the eyes, and he also seemed incredibly sweet. Would've been fun to get to know him.

A moment later, coffee in hand, he sat down across from me. "Hey."

"Hey."

We exchanged looks. Then he focused on stirring something into his coffee, and I stared into my own. Not awkward at all. Not even a little. Nope. No awkwardness here.

Jon was the first to break the silence. Clearing his throat, he shifted in his seat. "So, you wanted to talk."

"Yeah. I did." I thumbed the edge of my cup. Fuck. I had to be the one to do this, didn't I? Wasn't like I could expect him to start this conversation. "Listen, I freaked out last night. And I, uh…" I swallowed. "I wanted to apologize for that."

I kind of thought his expression would harden and he'd call bullshit or something.

What I didn't expect was the way his brow creased with concern, or how gentle his voice was. "Did I do something to make you freak out?" He inclined his head. "Did I hurt you?"

I almost choked. "What? No! No. Oh God. No." I shook my head. "No, it wasn't you at all."

He watched me, the creases in his forehead deepening.

I dropped my gaze as heat rushed into my face. "So, um… I guess do you want the long version or the short version?"

"Why don't we start with the short version?" He didn't sound suspicious or irritated. If anything, it felt like he was going with the option that was less stressful for me, which made me feel like an even bigger asshole for last night *and* for expecting the worst from him today.

"Okay. Um." I wrung my hands and stared into the coffee I wasn't drinking. "I guess the short version is that last night was the first time I've been with anyone since…" I hesitated, my throat tightening from just *thinking* about discussing the injury that had turned my world on its ass. Taking a deep breath, I met his eyes across the small table. "I used to play hockey professionally, and I got hurt last year. Ended my career, and… Anyway, it took a long time to recover. I'm *still* recovering, actually. Last night, I finally felt like I could handle…" Was I blushing? Was I a damn teenager? Fuck. Clearing my throat, I shifted, pretending not to notice how that aggravated all the annoying and ever-present aches or the angry twinges in my back. "The punchline is that I found out the hard way—" I winced. "I found out at the worst possible time that one of the possible long-term effects of my injury is ED."

Jon's lips parted, and he jumped like I'd kicked him under the table.

"That's why I couldn't relax, and why…" I rubbed my stiffening neck and tried not to look at him. "And I just… I'd never had that happen, and between that and the pain…" I sighed with frustration and forced myself to lift my gaze. "I mean, the bottom line is I just wanted you to know I didn't run out because of you or because of anything you did."

He tilted his head, a pair of crevices deepening between his eyebrows. "Were you… Were you in pain last night? While we were in bed?"

"I'm always in some kind of pain."

He didn't seem at all surprised, but he softly asked, "Why didn't you tell me?"

I laughed bitterly. "What difference would it have made?"

"Well, for one thing, I could've been careful, so I didn't make anything worse."

Shaking my head, I avoided his eyes. "I don't want to be handled with kid gloves. Especially not in the bedroom."

"But I don't want to be causing you pain. Not unless you want me to."

I looked at him again, startled.

He shrugged. "Look, I'll get as rough as someone wants. You want it to hurt, I'll make it hurt. But I don't want to make it, you know, *hurt*."

I swallowed. "Goddamn. Why couldn't I have met you before…" I huffed another humorless laugh. "I used to *like* it rough. I just don't know if I can handle it anymore." Heart sinking, I added, "I don't know if I can do a lot of things anymore."

He studied me for a long moment, his thumb tracing the rim of his coffee cup and his expression unreadable. "*Did* I hurt you at all? Because I mean, I saw the scars, but I—"

"No. No." I shook my head, trying not to be nauseated that he'd noticed my scars, even though they weren't exactly inconspicuous, and I *had* told him about them. "I was hurting before we even left the wine bar, but I—"

"Shit, I'm sorry. Everything we were doing, that had to have been making it worse."

"It was my fault for not telling you. You couldn't have known." Ugh, this constant feeling of shame and embarrassment was getting more nauseating by the minute. I stared into my coffee. "Things were so hot and amazing between us, and I just wanted to feel normal, you know? Feel like me again? I mean, the way you kissed me by the wine bar…" I whistled. "I guess… I mean, I was afraid it would kill the mood. If I called timeout to give you the rundown of…" I gestured at my defective hip.

"No." Jon shook his head. "To tell you the truth, I wanted you so bad last night, we could've had the entire conversation we're having right now, and I still would've wanted you."

"That's easy to say now," I whispered.

"Yeah. It is." He looked me right in the eyes. "Because we're having this conversation, and I still want you."

My heart stopped. My lips parted.

Jon didn't look away. He didn't take it back.

"Are you..." I cleared my throat, just trying to get my breath moving. "Are you serious?"

"Yes," he said without hesitation.

I shifted, wincing at the bolt of pain that shot down my thigh. "But what about everything I just told you?"

"What about it? Now that I know, I can make sure I'm not making your pain worse. It's not a deal-breaker for me if it isn't for you."

"Okay, but what about the *rest* of it? The part where... you know..." I was a grown-ass adult, but hell if I could say the words out loud.

"Brent." Jon slid his hand over the top of mine on the table, sending electricity all the way up my arm. "We can work around it."

I stared at him.

He smiled, running his thumb alongside my wrist. "If you want to pick up where we left off last night, there's plenty we can do to have a good time that won't cause you pain. As for the rest... Oh, we can definitely work around that." The way he said it made me shiver. The words were so full of promise—*dirty* promise—that I suddenly wanted to suggest we go someplace else so he could put his money where his mouth was.

"Wow," I whispered. "I was totally expecting you to tell me to go fuck myself after last night. I really didn't see things turning out like this."

"I wasn't thrilled, but now that you've explained it..." He just smiled, but it faded. "I'm more concerned about your pain. As long as we can work around that, the rest is no big deal to me."

"Really?"

Jon nodded. "If you're game, so am I."

"Yeah. Yeah, I am. Just, um..." I laughed dryly. "Probably not up for much today. My leg is..." And my back, and my neck, and my knee—fuck my life. Clearing my throat, I shook my head. "It's probably not a good idea today."

His eyebrow rose. "How much pain are you in these days?"

"Oh, it varies. There are some days where it's just annoying. Others, I can barely move." I paused, then decided to test the water a bit more. "Sometimes I use a cane to get around."

He didn't even miss a beat. "So, there's always pain, but the intensity varies?"

I nodded.

Studying me, Jon said, "You know, I might be able to help with some of that."

"Can you?" So help me, if he was about to suggest some kind of miracle vitamin supplement or magic CBD healing crystal suppository that he was selling via multi-level marketing, I would have to—

"I'm a massage therapist."

I blinked. "You are?"

He nodded. "I work with people recovering from all kinds of injuries. And I've worked on hockey players before." He half-shrugged. "I'm not promising I can make the pain disappear, but pain *management* is pretty much what I do."

"Oh." Well, fuck if this conversation hadn't taken another unexpected turn.

"For what it's worth," Jon continued, "the other issues you're having? Those aren't uncommon at all in people with chronic pain. Just getting a handle on your pain could help. And even if it doesn't, I mean, if there's something I can do so you don't have to live in that much pain, then by all means, I'm in."

My throat was suddenly tight. I'd come here expecting the worst, fully prepared for him to tell me to kick rocks or to insist like everyone else that I was young and couldn't have fucked myself up *that* much. Of all the scenarios I'd imagined on the way here and while I'd waited, I hadn't even considered he might not only be compassionate about it, and he might not only take it seriously… he might also offer to *help*. And he accepted without hesitation that I had problems with no easy fixes, and he still thought it was worth looking into solutions to make my situation more bearable.

Wow. Maybe I had gotten lucky last night after all.

"Okay. Okay, yeah. I'll keep that in mind. Thanks."

Jon's smile came back. "As for the rest?" He shrugged. "I mean, I don't want there to be any pressure here, okay? On either of us."

"On either of us?"

"Yeah. This is…" He laughed self-consciously. "I'm just now getting my toes wet again, too. Figuring out how to date and hook up and all that shit. So the less pressure, the better."

"Oh. Right. You said you're newly single."

"Eh, I don't know about newly." He chuckled with a hint of bitterness. "My ex-wife dropped the divorce bomb about a year and a half ago, and this is the first time I've even thought about connecting with someone. For a hookup or…" He waved his hand. "For anything, to be honest."

"Really?"

"Yeah. It took a while to come to terms with things. Then I was getting my own place, trying to get on my feet, sorting out the divorce, helping my son deal with it."

"You have a son?"

Jon nodded, a slight smile forming. "Cody. He's ten. Lives with me half the time and his mom the other half." Smile fading, he said, "The divorce was rough on him. His mom jumped right back into dating, and that was hard for Cody, so I held off on it. I didn't really want to isolate myself, but I also didn't want to overwhelm him."

"Wow," I said.

He picked up his coffee, and his lips quirked as our eyes met. "So now I'm a forty-one year-old single dad who hasn't had to so much as think about dating since college. It's been, shall we say, an experience."

"I can imagine."

He grunted in acknowledgment. "Which I guess means… I mean, full disclosure—I'm still figuring out which way is up after my divorce. About the best I can offer anyone is friends with benefits."

"Well, I'm not sure how many benefits there'll be with me involved."

"That's all right." Jon paused, and damn if he didn't blush as he softly added, "Last night, it just felt good to be touched again."

"Yeah," I said with a nod. "Now that you mention it, me too. Guess that's the downside of isolating myself—being so isolated I missed human contact."

"Exactly. I mean, I touch people for a living, but it's not the same. It's not intimacy." He absently opened and closed his fingers as if the lack of contact made his hands itch. "And I think that's what I need more than sex."

I chanced a smile. "So we'd almost be more cuddle buddies who might fuck when bodies cooperate?"

Jon laughed. "When you put it like that…" He seemed to consider it. "Actually, that sounds pretty damn good."

"Huh. It kinda does, doesn't it? Friends with benefits, but the benefits don't have to be sex? Or at least don't *always* have to be sex?"

"Exactly," he said quietly. "I won't say no to sex, but even if it's not an option, I'm still game."

Our eyes locked, and a warm feeling I hadn't known in a long time went through me. Just being with someone who didn't expect sex every time we touched? Someone who was down with, well, cuddling when sex wasn't in the cards?

Oh hell. This is sounding better and better.

"So, um, with that out of the way..." I shifted a little. "You want to get out of here?"

Jon grinned. "Yeah. Let's get out of here."

As we left the coffee shop, Jon walked fast. As fast as I had before I'd gotten hurt. I tried to keep up with him, and I tried not to limp, but the pain was making my eyes water. "I'm sorry." I dropped back a little. "I can't walk this fast."

"Oh. Jesus, I'm sorry." He let me catch up, then fell into step beside me. Slowing down helped, but the pain wasn't letting up. By the time we reached where I'd parked, there was no pretending I was fine.

I stopped beside my truck, and I grimaced. "Shit."

"You okay?"

I nodded. "Just..." I gestured down at my hip. "Believe it or not, it's better than it was pre-op, but..."

"I'm sure. If you're still in this much pain after that surgery, I can only imagine what it was like before."

I shuddered. "You're not wrong. I, um... I definitely don't think today's going to be a good day to get back in the saddle." I cringed, irrationally sure I'd just knocked over the entire house of cards we'd been putting together.

"Brent." He smiled as he touched my arm. "That's fine. We just talked about everything else we're game to do."

"So you're... You're really sure about that?"

His eyes widened. "Well, yeah. Do you think I'd say all that, and then insist you have to put out when you're in pain, or else forget it?"

"Uh. Okay, when you put it like that..."

Jon smiled, sliding his hand around to my lower back. "Relax. You can follow me back to my place, and we can just chill on the couch or in bed and watch movies."

"You're sure?"

Jon didn't say a word. He just smiled again, drew me in a little closer, and—

Oh.

Fuck.

Me.

If I'd thought that first kiss under the streetlight had been amazing, this one stopped the world beneath my feet.

Jon knew.

He knew I wasn't going to be the acrobatic and fit younger guy who'd probably wear *him* out. He knew that if sex ever happened, every roll in the hay with me would be a threesome with pain I'd never fully leave behind. He knew there was no guarantee I'd be able to get hard, stay hard, or get off.

And he was still…

Kissing me…

Like *this.*

His kiss didn't miraculously heal my longtime pain or make my newly-discovered ED go away, and it wouldn't instantly bring back all my confidence about my body, but it was the best thing I'd felt in a long, long time. After last night and today, it was the reassurance I'd desperately needed that someone could know all this about me and still find me attractive.

He drew back just enough to speak, and with his mouth still so close his breath warmed my lips, he whispered, "Let's go. I think we can do this someplace a lot more comfortable."

I nodded. "Okay. Yeah. That, um… That sounds good."

"Uh-huh." He brushed his lips across mine again before pulling all the way back. "I'll text you the address in case we get separated, but you can follow me."

"Perfect. Let's go."

He grinned. "See you soon."

We shared one last lingering kiss, and then he headed for his car while I unlocked mine.

As I got into the truck, my hip and my back were fucking killing me.

But that couldn't quite distract me from the way my lips still tingled.

Everything was out on the table. Cuddling, I could do. Sex, we'd have to play by ear.

And all I could think was…

Oh my God. He still wants me.

6

JON

All the way out of town, I kept glancing in the rearview, sure each time that Brent wouldn't be there. I had to be imagining things. The ridiculously hot man who'd bailed unexpectedly had then reappeared unexpectedly, and he didn't think it was stupid that I was game to just touch without sex? This sounded way too good to be true, so clearly I was imagining the whole thing. Any second now, I was going to wake up alone in that hotel room, and I'd feel like an idiot for believing my own hallucination.

But I didn't wake up. Before long, we were outside of town, following North Avenue past neighborhoods of varying affluence. My heart beat faster with every cross street and landmark that went by.

We were really doing this. I was really taking Brent back to my place. Was he serious about just indulging in some physical contact together? Because holy hell, I hoped he was. It sounded ridiculous even to my own ear. Cuddle buddies? Really? We were grown men.

But I was painfully lonely, and he seemed to be too. I really wanted his touch more than I wanted sex. Especially with sex being such an enormous challenge for him thanks to everything his body had been through, maybe it wasn't so ridiculous after all. Sex would still be there if and when he was ready for it, and in the meantime…

I shivered just thinking about having him close to me. Just kissing him in the parking garage had been enough to leave me hungry for more.

So going someplace to curl up together with no expectation of screwing around? Hell yeah. Sign me up.

Still, I was admittedly nervous about bringing him to my place, especially after he mentioned he'd played hockey professionally. I didn't know the sport very well, but I was pretty sure players made some serious money, and I…did not. My divorce had done a number on my finances, and I didn't exactly live in an upscale neighborhood. In fact, I lived about six miles north of town in a rundown house in an equally rundown neighborhood. It was closer to the wastewater plant than anything, though fortunately that didn't mean my house and neighborhood *smelled* like the wastewater plant.

The neighborhood was comprised of several houses in various states of repair tucked into the trees at the end of a dirt road. It wasn't a fancy neighborhood, but it wasn't a shitty one either. The people were nice. My son had plenty of kids to play with and plenty of adults to keep an eye on them when they played outside. The homes ranged from a pair of single wides—one kept pristine with a lovingly decorated yard, the other falling apart—to some houses built in the 1960s or so.

Mine was at the far end of the road, and…quite frankly, it looked like shit. I cringed a little as I parked in the gravel driveway and Brent pulled in beside me. The exterior was okay. The siding was the color of creosote—not quite black, but close—and the roof had seen better days. The basement windows were still boarded up because I hadn't had a chance to replace them, and the back deck was one heavy snow away from crumbling. The fence around the property consisted of moss-stained lattice panels that looked like they'd lost a fight with a windstorm.

The building itself was sturdy, but it definitely looked old and in need of some attention, especially compared to the front porch and steps, which were brand new. That was about as much as I'd accomplished on the exterior since I'd bought the place.

I got out of my car, and Brent carefully stepped out of his truck.

"So, um." I gestured at the house. "This is the place. Fair warning —I bought it with every intention of renovating it, and…it still needs work."

He nodded as we started toward the house. "I lived in fixer uppers when I was a kid. I know how it goes."

"Did you?"

"Oh yeah. My dad was flipping houses before flipping houses was cool. Which meant every time we moved into a new place…" He grimaced.

I chuckled, relaxing slightly. "Okay, so you know the drill."

"Totally."

We continued up the walk. He was moving carefully, and I was quietly glad the path had been one of my first projects. All it had taken was my son turning his ankle one time to make me leave the front porch half-finished, rip out the path, and replace it before my next custody week.

The porch was also finished now, including non-skid on the steps. Good thing, too—it had rained recently, and the last thing Brent needed was to slip on the way up.

"Are these steps all right?" I asked. "The side door is at ground level if—"

"Nah, these are fine." He held the handrail and followed me up. "My place has a few steps here and there too. I'm good." He limped a little, but he made it.

I let us in, and we both toed off our shoes by the door.

Every time I walked into this house, I was a little more discouraged and demoralized. There was so much work to be done. And now there was a new degree of *oh God, why did I do this to myself?* as I brought Brent into my partly-gutted kitchen.

"So, um." I cleared my throat. "Like I said…work-in-progress."

He nodded, looking around, and there didn't seem to be a hint of judgment in his expression. "Looks like you've made progress, though."

"A little. Mostly out of necessity." I thumped my knuckle on the gas stove. "The one that was here when I moved in was so old and fucked up, I'm pretty sure it was a safety hazard. I've been replacing the appliances as I go, since that's not too difficult aside from the price, but the cosmetic stuff?" I made a face and gestured at the backsplash, which was a mess of crooked and oddly-shaped tiles in avocado and orange like something straight from the 1970s. "That unholy thing has *got* to go."

Brent chuckled. "Old owners really liked old school colors, didn't they?"

"God, you have no idea. There are some rooms with wallpaper that's so ugly, it's actually improved by the water stains."

He barked a laugh. "Oh, I've lived in a few places like that." He rolled his eyes. "My dad bought this one house when I was in… I don't know, sixth grade? Anyway, whoever had it before thought wallpaper was the greatest invention in the world. I swear to God, we spent two weeks before we even moved in just tearing wallpaper off walls and scraping away the adhesive so we could paint. It literally took less time to paint."

"Ugh. That's going to be my son's room and the den, definitely." I looked around, mostly to give me an excuse not to meet his eyes. "I really thought this would be something to focus on and keep me busy while I was moving on after my divorce, you know?"

"Yeah, I get that. I considered buying a boat or a car to fix up for the same reason after I got hurt, but…" He gestured at his hip.

"Right? Sometimes you just need to keep busy. But I think I bit off more than I could chew." I leaned against the island. "I jumped on this place because it seemed like something to distract me from my divorce. Plus it was cheap as hell and I didn't have a ton of money." I rolled my stiff shoulders. "My ex and I were actually stuck living together for ten months after she told me she wanted a divorce."

"No shit?"

"No shit. Neither of us could afford to leave. And of course that was confusing and miserable for our son, and…" Sighing, I shook my head. "It wasn't a great time for me to be buying a place, but I needed to get something sooner than later, ideally one big enough for him and me, and this place was decent-sized and in my price range. I was about to rent, but then I saw the listing, and it was only a little more expensive than a small rental. It needs a lot of work, but I figured, hey, I can focus on that."

"Didn't work out?"

"No. I mean, I know how to do everything the house needs. The problem is…" I put up my hands and wiggled my fingers. "I kind of neglected to think about the part where home improvement means using your hands. And so does my job. The first time I spent a day ripping up tile, I paid for it with every client the next day."

"Oh. Fuck." Brent grimaced.

"Right? But that's what I get for biting off more than I could chew."

He gave a quiet, sympathetic laugh, but didn't say anything.

Silence hung between us, and it threatened to get awkward, so I gestured around the kitchen. "Anyway, yeah, it needs work. And it's probably bigger than I needed, too. Even when Cody is here, it's just the two of us. Instead of giving me a lot of projects to keep me busy, it's given me a lot of empty space so I can't forget I'm alone." I faced Brent and put my hands on his waist. "But I don't need to worry about all that now."

He grinned, pulling me in closer. "Oh, we did come here for something else, didn't we?"

"Mmhmm. We did." I lifted my chin, and the instant our lips met, I forgot all about… About whatever it was we'd been talking about. It was entirely possible this was just new and novel because it had been so long since I'd been kissed—like *really* kissed instead of just a disinterested good-night peck—but I was pretty sure I'd never met anyone who kissed like Brent did. As soon as his lips touched mine, my entire focus was concentrated into that perfect, soft point of contact. One kiss, and he made time stop.

I don't give a damn if we do anything else.

And I didn't. Good God, I didn't. We could stand here in my ugly kitchen and make out all damn night for all I cared.

Except that might not help Brent's pain.

I drew back and met his gaze. "There are much more comfortable places in this house than the kitchen. If you'd rather not stand here, I mean."

He swallowed, nervousness radiating off him. "Like, the bedroom?"

"Or the living room." I shrugged. "Somewhere we can take a load off."

He looked at me through his lashes, and that nervousness didn't ebb in the slightest.

"Hey." I touched his face. "There's no pressure. Relax."

"I'm trying." He laughed nervously as he scratched the back of his neck. "Just…after last night…"

"Don't worry about last night."

Brent closed his eyes and sighed. "That's easy to say. But it fucking sucks, realizing my body doesn't work the way it used to." He looked at me again, forehead creased. "I don't even know why I'm surprised, though, you know? Just walking or sitting is a fucking nightmare." With a bitter laugh, he said more to himself than me, "What kind of idiot was I, thinking sex would be different?"

"You're not an idiot." I slid my hands up his chest. "You're healing, and you're getting used to your new reality. That doesn't happen overnight."

He dropped his gaze, and I swore I could feel the frustration and fatigue radiating off him. God knew I'd met plenty of patients in the same boat. Adapting after a life-altering injury was not an easy process, and it was not a fast one. I was pretty sure the theory of the five stages of grieving had been debunked, but I'd absolutely seen denial, anger, bargaining, depression, and acceptance in plenty of pain management patients. Sometimes in that order. Sometimes over and over. Sometimes all at once. Resignation, defeat, more denial, more anger—no wonder the guy was wrung out.

"Listen." I touched my forehead to his and smoothed his hair. "I don't want this to be stressful for you, okay? We already took sex off the table for tonight. No pressure. No stress."

Brent hesitated. "Are you sure?"

"Yes, I am."

He exhaled, and I could feel his entire body relaxing. "Okay. Okay, cool. I can work with that."

"I'll follow your lead." I paused for another soft kiss. "If this is all you can handle, it's more than enough for me. If you feel like more, say so. Just tell me what I need to know so I don't hurt you."

He relaxed a little more, and he nodded. "Okay. This is just, um, the first time I've tried to navigate any of this since I got hurt." With a quiet laugh, he broke eye contact. "I mean, I've always had some kind of pain going on since long before I lost my virginity. Just not as much as I do now."

"Ah, that part of being a professional athlete no one likes to talk about—the toll it starts taking on your body long before you actually go pro."

"Exactly," he whispered.

"Well, for starters, we could probably find a place that's more comfortable than my kitchen." I met his gaze. "What's better for you? Couch? Bed?"

He considered it, and when he spoke, he sounded as shy as he had when he'd approached me at Vino and Veritas. "Lying down is actually a lot more comfortable. Sitting is okay, but only for so long."

"All right." I gestured past him. "This way."

In the bedroom, Brent hesitated, his cheeks coloring a bit as his eyes darted toward the bed. "Should we... Do you want to..." He gestured at his clothes, and I made the connection. He was nervous with me and probably would be for a while. About pain, about his appearance, about his limited mobility and flexibility. I didn't take it personally. He wasn't assuming that I specifically would be an asshole about his injuries or his scars. He was probably just self-conscious about them, and he didn't know me well enough to know that it was going to take more than some surgical scars to scare me away.

"We don't have to," I said. "Maybe nix our belts so the buckles aren't getting in the way, but everything else?" I shrugged.

"Okay. Okay, good idea." He paused, and with a soft smile, added, "Probably don't need shirts either, do we?"

The thought of being skin to skin with him gave me goose bumps, but I managed to keep my cool. "Your call."

"Shirts can go."

We stripped off our shirts and belts then started to get into bed, but I hesitated. "What's comfortable for you?"

He considered it. "On my side or on my back is fine."

"On your side?"

"Well, the right side. I mean, as long as I can put a pillow between my knees." He blushed as if that was somehow an embarrassing request.

I smiled. "Fortunately, I keep tons of pillows around. Be right back." I got up and went to the linen closet for a pillow, and when I came back, Brent carefully situated it between his knees. Once he was settled, I joined him, lying on my back right beside him. Just the warmth of his chest against my arm was soothing in ways I hadn't known I needed.

"Comfortable?" I asked.

He inched a little closer and nudged my arm. I took the hint and wrapped it around his shoulders, and he settled with his head on my chest. "Mmm. *Now* I'm comfortable."

"Me too." For a while, I just lay there and savored the heat of his body. The faint, unfamiliar scent of his shampoo—hell, just the unfamiliar scent of him—was heady, a reminder of how long it had been since I'd been this close to anyone, never mind someone new. Arousal was absolutely stirring, and I could think of about a thousand different ways I wanted him right then, but I had no complaints about this. Why the hell did nobody ever talk about how good it felt just to be touched? And how much it sucked to go for long stretches without feeling this, and without even knowing what was missing or how to put it into words?

I'd thought it was ridiculous when someone had suggested I must be touch-starved. I was a massage therapist, for fuck's sake. All I *did* was touch people.

But holy crap, I understood now. There was nothing I could do in a professional session that held a candle to the gentle comfort of being wrapped up in someone. Right then, as far as I was concerned, it didn't matter if Brent and I ever had sex. This was what I'd been craving, and I hadn't even known it until we'd been in bed last night. Until he'd left, and I'd been naked and cold and alone.

"In case it's not obvious," I said softly. "This is perfect."

Some tension melted out of him, and his fingertips absently trailed along my skin. "Yeah. It is. I've, um… I've never done this before. Not with a guy I just met, I mean."

"Neither have I. But as long as it's been since I've touched anyone…"

"How long *has* it been? Since you've done this?"

"Been in bed with someone? Without sex?"

"With. Without." He shrugged. "Either or."

I thought about it. "It's been… Wow. It's been at least a year and a half, I know that. Probably longer. Definitely longer since I've done, you know, *this*." I stroked his hair for emphasis.

"Really?"

"Yeah. The divorce came out of the blue, but I mean, looking back, I should've seen it coming."

"How do you figure?"

"Because all the physical intimacy had basically come down to sex." The memory still hurt. Damn. I wondered how long that would last. Sighing, I went on, "We'd fuck every once in a while, because why not? But it felt completely impersonal. Like we were going through the motions. Cuddling? Just being affectionate? I couldn't even tell you when that stopped."

"Wow. Sorry to hear it."

"It is what it is, unfortunately." I trailed my fingertips up and down his arm, just savoring being able to touch someone. "Nothing to do now but move on." Our eyes met, and we both smiled faintly.

After a moment, Brent cautiously said, "So, you were married to a woman, but now you're..." He gestured at himself, then me. "You're bi, then?"

I nodded. "Funny thing is, when Ashley and I were going to high school together, I was out to her as gay. She was one of the few. But then I got to college, realized I was into women, and after I broke up with my first girlfriend halfway through my freshman year, Ashley and I started dating."

"Oh really?" He studied me. "So you thought you were gay?"

"Yep. I didn't actually know what bisexuality was. I mean, this was twenty-plus years ago." I sighed heavily as I shrugged. "People were just finally starting to think about queer people outside of discussions about AIDS. There wasn't a lot of conversation beyond that, you know?"

"Wow. Different world."

"Seriously." I shook my head. "My parents actually thought it was an act of rebellion for a while. That I was calling myself gay to get a rise out of people. Which only made me that much more determined to not give them a reason to believe I might actually be straight." With a soft laugh, I added, "Then I got to college, fell in love, and decided that was more important than what my parents thought."

"What *did* they think of it?"

"They figured they were right." I sighed heavily and rolled my eyes. "And my mom said she was relieved now that I wouldn't get AIDS."

"Oh, for fuck's sake."

"I know, right? They're both more open-minded now, but back then..." I grimaced.

"I can imagine."

I watched myself running my fingers through Brent's hair. "So that's me in a nutshell—thought I was gay until college, married the second woman I ever dated, and twenty years later, I'm single again. I'm no virgin when it comes to guys, but this is the first time I've touched a man since I started college."

Brent laughed softly. "No pressure?"

"Nah." I leaned in and kissed his forehead. "No pressure on either of us. It's all good."

He relaxed a little.

"And by the way, last night?" I said. "I'm sorry. I could've handled things better."

"No." Brent shook his head, his chin scuffing gently across my skin. "That was on me. You were great."

"But I knew you were hurting even before we got into the room."

He tensed. "You did?"

"Well, yeah. I told you—I work in pain management. If there's one thing I recognize from a mile away, it's someone who's in pain."

"Oh." He shifted a little, cheeks coloring. "I didn't realize it was that obvious."

"Hey," I whispered, stroking his hair. "It's probably not obvious to most people, and even if it was, it's nothing to be ashamed of. I'm just in tune to it because of my job. Which is why I should've been more careful. Maybe asked you what was going on, so I didn't hurt you."

"No, you were fine," he whispered. "The pain wasn't the biggest problem. It was that sudden rude awakening that, well, something *wasn't* awakening." He made a miserable sound. "I mean, I've had whiskey dick before, but this? Fuck."

"I can imagine." I ran my palm down his arm. "Talk about adding insult to injury."

"Right? First I broke my hip and pelvis. Now my dick doesn't work." He tsked and probably rolled his eyes. "Intelligent design, my ass."

I snorted. "Shame there's no warranty or returns."

"No kidding. Playing hockey my whole life would probably disqualify me from any warranty anyway, but…"

"Hmm, probably." I paused, then cautiously said, "So, in the interest of not hurting you…"

He shifted onto his elbow so we were looking in each other's eyes. "How did I get this colossally fucked up?"

"I was going to ask how you got hurt, but okay." I studied him. "Hockey mishap?"

Shaking his head, Brent sighed. "Car accident. There's actually a video out there somewhere, but I've never seen it, so I couldn't tell you how much it shows, only that it was enough to prove that the other driver was at fault." He shifted again, though I couldn't tell if it was to get comfortable or if the memory was making him squirm. "I was on my way home after a game, and someone T-boned me in an intersection. At that speed and with the damage my car took, I heard later that the paramedics were surprised I was alive."

I grimaced. "Jesus. How fast was he going?"

"They told me, but hell if I can remember. I just know he was drunk and blew a red light." He huffed with annoyance. "And would you believe the fucker and his passenger actually tried to claim I ran a red and caused the crash?"

"Of course they did," I muttered.

"Right? Fortunately there were witnesses who called bullshit, plus the car behind me had a dashcam that caught everything." With a humorless laugh, he met my eyes. "The guy who hit me was a fan, too. He'd been at the game that night, got hammered, then went out and got even more hammered to celebrate us winning."

"And then he celebrated even harder by crashing into you and killing your career."

"Pretty much," Brent whispered. "Fortunately, I don't remember anything after the initial impact. I woke up in the hospital feeling like shit, and long story short, on top of some other injuries, I broke the fuck out of my hip and fractured my pelvis in two places."

"Whoa."

"Yeah. It was bad." He absently ran his fingers up and down the middle of my chest. "The really shitty part is that recovering from the accident meant I couldn't do much physically, so everything started to atrophy. And like, I'd been playing hockey for twenty-plus years. I've had knee surgeries, hip injuries, back injuries, you name it."

Nodding slowly, I said, "And staying in tip-top shape kept the injuries stabilized after you recovered."

"Exactly. My physical therapists had been telling me for years that

I would need to stay in the best shape I possibly could, even after I retired, because that would keep everything from coming back to haunt me later." He wiped a hand over his face. "They were right."

"No wonder it's been such a painful recovery."

"Yep. Prior to the accident, I think I spent a total of like ninety days of my pro career on the injured list because of hip problems. I was in physical therapy already to try to unfuck my pelvis, which was twisted thanks to favoring my right knee after an injury in high school, and there'd already been some talk about doing surgery after the season was over to clean up the hip joint a bit." Brent shuddered. "My doctors had been telling me for a while that I was probably going to need a hip replacement at some point in my life, but we all figured I had plenty of years left in me. Then the accident trashed my hip, and..." He laughed bitterly. "How many people do you know have hip replacements before *thirty*?"

"Given some of the athletes I've treated," I said, "nothing really surprises me anymore. Did the replacement help?"

"It helped, yeah. But the pelvis fractures—those were a bear. And you're supposed to get up and move around with a hip replacement, but with a fractured pelvis?" He shook his head. "Not happening. So they had to pin it together as much as possible, then wait until the fractures had healed enough for me to have the surgery to replace the joint." Brent exhaled. "The surgeons fixed as much as they could, and it's *way* better than it was, but it's only been the last four or five months I've even been able to lightly work out and try to get the muscles reconditioned. They think it'll be better as I build up the muscles to support everything, but that's a long fucking road when you're working against this much pain and damage."

I nodded as he spoke. "Yeah, I've treated a lot of people on that road."

He seemed to relax a bit more, as if he'd needed the reassurance that he wasn't the first person I'd seen go through this.

After a moment, he said, "Of course, I also had a ton of soft tissue damage. I had tendon problems already, and my doctors had been working with me on some tendinosis issues. After the accident, they figured it would be a good idea to go ahead with surgery as long as they were fixing everything else. Everyone was optimistic because it fixes the problem for like eighty percent of people." He scowled.

I cringed. "Let me guess—you're one of the lucky twenty percent?"

"Yep," he grumbled. "It's… Ugh. It's just been one thing after another. Like once the muscles started atrophying, it turned out they really *had* been stabilizing a bunch of my old injuries and fucked-up joints, so everything else started saying 'hey we want to play too.'" He rolled his eyes. "It didn't snowball, it avalanched, and this ride is bullshit, and I want my fucking money back."

I leaned in and stroked his cheek. "I bet."

He sighed. "I'm sorry. You just wanted the rundown, and I'm giving you the full bitch session." With a humorless laugh, he added, "Our second night together is going almost as well as the first."

"No, it's fine. And honestly, the more I know, the more I can avoid making things worse for you."

He looked at me, brow pinched. "So it's not off-putting? Even when I can't…"

Shaking my head, I whispered, "Of course not. This is more human contact than I've had in over a year, and I'm really enjoying it. So you're going to have to try a lot harder to scare me off."

That made him laugh softly, and he slid his palm up my side. "Good. Because this really is nice."

"Yeah, it is." I ran my fingers through his dark hair. "If this is all we ever do, you won't hear me complain."

Brent just smiled. Then he bent and kissed me softly.

And I meant it—if this was all we ever did, then that was fine by me.

But if he ever wanted more? Sign me the hell up.

Our schedules didn't make it easy to see each other again. Or, well, my schedule didn't. Brent had dinner with his family every Sunday, and he had physical therapy a few times a week. Otherwise, he was pretty free, especially in the afternoons and evenings.

Me? I had daily appointments at the clinic and at people's homes, plus my twice-weekly evening performances at Vino and Veritas. That would be simple enough to work around, but the day after Brent and I had cuddled together was the start of my custody week with my son.

When Cody was with me, he was my primary focus. Homework, eating dinner, spending time together—if I could only be a dad half the time, I wasn't going to half-ass the effort. As it was, it annoyed the shit out of me that he had to spend so much of his time (whether he was with me or his mom) on homework. Who the hell had decided fourth graders needed that much work? Jesus.

He needed help on some of it, especially when it came to spelling or vocabulary words, so of course he had my full attention when he worked on those. For his other subjects, he was much happier if I left him to it, and then just checked it over when he was finished. If I hovered, it would stress him out, so I didn't, and I was secretly glad—I really didn't want Cody to see my math incompetence in all its glory.

Throughout the week, I still texted with Brent, especially between appointments or when Cody was doing his homework on his own. It was fun, and it was a nice switch, but I had to admit that I was quietly worried he'd lose interest in me. What was the point of a booty call (if one could call me that) who was completely unavailable every other week and had obligations the rest of the time?

But to my surprise, we kept up a steady rhythm of texting. Sometimes it was flirty. Sometimes it was small talk. We occasionally kicked memes back and forth—I quickly learned that he loved cat memes, and he caught on fast that nothing cracked me up more than kitchen fails.

OMG look at this, I sent him one night. *Do cats even have spines?*

LOL Wish I could bend like that.

I know, right? Weird critters.

Not long after, he sent me a shot of a half-melted bowl on a burner surrounded by the charred remains of whatever someone had been trying to make.

Not gonna name names, he texted along with it, *but I'm pretty sure this is one of my teammates.*

Haha! Really?

Uh-huh. On the road, he wasn't allowed to cook anything more complicated than a Hot Pocket.

Probably smart.

In the evenings, after Cody had gone to bed, the tone of our texts shifted. Still fun and playful, but a little less focused on cat memes and kitchen fails.

Kinda feel like if we meet up in public, he said at one point, *we'll get arrested.*

Biting my lip, I wrote back, *How do you figure?*

You think we're suitable for polite company? After making out in a parking garage last time?

LOL Good point. So yeah, maybe not in public.

My place?

I'm looking forward to it. Tomorrow night?

Fuck yes, tomorrow night.

I can't wait.

And I couldn't, but until then, my priority was my son.

The next morning was, as Friday mornings usually were, bittersweet. Cody and I sat down to breakfast together, and despite my excitement about seeing Brent later, there was the usual heavy sadness of knowing my week with Cody was over.

"So what have you been doing in school this week?" I asked over cereal and toast.

Cody pushed his glasses up on his nose. "We're reading some really dumb stories in English."

"Dumb stories? How are they dumb?"

He shrugged in that animated way kids did. "One is just about this kid with a paper route. And it's so boring."

"That's it? He just has a paper route?"

"Yep. And his friends keep trying to tell him to come play with them, but he has to deliver his papers first." Cody groaned dramatically before scooping some more cereal out of his bowl. "I get it—do your chores and then play. Ugh. Same thing you and Mom tell me all the time."

I had to suppress a laugh, wondering what his teachers (or my ex-wife, for that matter) would think if I told him that kind of literature was meant to indoctrinate kids with a capitalist work ethic so they'd be good little workers in the future. Maybe that could wait until middle school. "Tell you what—when we're done with the book we're reading together now, we'll find something with kids going on adventures and quests instead of delivering papers."

Cody sat up straighter, eyes widening. "Can we read *The Grand Gates of Hemmingsworth*?"

I blinked. "Uh..."

"It's about these kids who have to get a magic sword to this warrior who's been imprisoned, and Caden and Zoe both said it was really good!"

"Okay, okay." I nodded. "I'll take a look at it."

Jesus. That cute smile. I'd been accused by my mom and ex-wife of being wrapped around this kid's finger, but seriously—who wouldn't be?

I made a note on my phone to pre-read his request. He was a voracious reader, and he loved fantasy, but especially for the book we read together before bed, I liked to make sure there was nothing in it that would give him nightmares. Fortunately, there wasn't much that would.

We put away our breakfast dishes, and Cody gathered his things so we could head out.

As I pulled up in front of the school, I glanced at him. "Remember, I'll be here to pick you up tonight, not Mom."

Cody nodded. "Okay."

"Have a good day, kiddo."

"Thanks, Dad."

Our custody agreement technically required Ashley to pick him up after school. Whoever had him the night before dropped him off in the morning, and whoever was taking him home for the night picked him up in the afternoon. But her work schedule could be unpredictable, and her boss wasn't even a little bit flexible. So if she was stuck working until five or six like she was sometimes, I'd pick him up, have dinner with him, and then drop him off at her place. It wasn't her fault, and it meant a little more time with my son, so I didn't complain.

So, that afternoon, I picked him up, and we had a quick dinner at one of the sandwich places he liked. Then I took him to his mom's.

Dropping Cody off at my ex-wife's apartment was never easy. I hated that he and I lived apart half the time.

This week, I felt seriously guilty because I had something to look forward to after Cody went to his mom's. I didn't want to rush him out the door, and I didn't want him gone, but I was excited about where I'd be going after the custody switch. That was a weird mixed bag of emotions. Was this what dating (or "dating") was going to be like now? Constantly wishing I could be with someone who wasn't there, whether it was my son or the person I was seeing? How was I supposed to feel about that, and why did none of the "how to scrape yourself up after a divorce" books mention it?

The best I could think to do was make peace with the idea that sometimes I'd be with Cody, and sometimes I'd be with Brent (or whoever I was dating as time went on). There'd probably always be some guilt over being happy to see one of them when that meant *not* being with the other. To some degree, this was probably my new normal, at least until I settled down with someone. Assuming anyone wanted to stick around long enough.

Huh. Maybe that was why my older brother had started drinking after his first divorce. The stress, guilt, and loneliness of single parenthood were *not* for the faint of heart.

Hopefully it wouldn't come to that—self-medicating had never done much for me—and I would just learn to live with it. For this evening, that meant hugging my son goodbye, exchanging some frosty looks with my ex-wife, and then texting Brent as I headed back to my car.

Still on for tonight?

7

BRENT

"Son of a bitch." I squeezed my eyes shut as my physical therapist eased my leg back down to the table. "Tell me again that it won't hurt forever."

"It won't hurt forever." Robin released my knee. "And it's better now than it was, right?"

"Mmph. Fine. Yeah. It is." I wiped sweat off my forehead. "Still sucks."

She patted my arm. "Yeah. It'll do that. But you're done for today."

"Thank *God*." I groaned as I sat up. Robin was an evil physical therapist who always left me feeling like I'd just played an entire period on the ice with no break, but she was helping. My range of motion was getting better. The muscles in my lower body were getting stronger. The process just *sucked*.

And it said a lot about her personality that we could still shoot the breeze whenever she wasn't torturing me. For a long time, she'd been one of the only people I talked to besides Ethan and my parents. Once our sessions were over, we usually chatted for a while about whatever. It probably wasn't the most professional thing in the world for her, but she seemed to enjoy it and so did I. Especially when I'd been a recluse on self-imposed lockdown for what felt like years, I'd craved the kind of interaction I got from her.

Her intimate knowledge of my fucked-up body seemed like it

should have made things awkward, but it had the opposite effect. There was no embarrassment or shame about my injury. She knew how bad it was. She knew how much it had improved and how far it still had to go.

After we'd caught up, she tilted her head and studied me. "You seem a little different lately. Kind of…happier? Have you been getting out and socializing or something?"

Damn, she was good.

"Well, I did start seeing someone recently." Kind of? Maybe? What *was* I doing with Jon?

Her eyes lit up. "Oh my God, you did? Really?"

I laughed. "Is it that much of a surprise that someone would be interested in me?"

"Pfft. You know that's not what I meant." She gave my arm a playful smack. "I meant you actually stuck your neck out far enough to *find* someone."

"To be fair, I was dragged out into public because my friend wasn't going to leave me alone until I came out for an evening."

"Yeah? Where'd you go?"

"That wine bar in the Marketplace. Vino and Veritas, I think?"

"Oh, I've heard about that place. How was it? Did you have a good time?" Beat. "Well, you must have if you met someone."

"Yeah, it wasn't half bad. And the guy who was singing that night…" I whistled, goose bumps prickling to life at the memory of the first moment I laid eyes on Jon.

"Nice." She fist-bumped me. "That's great. I'm really glad you're finding your stride again. That's hard to do after a life-altering injury."

"It is. And, um…" My good mood faltered. Being with Jon was great, but it hadn't been *all* great. "About that…"

Her smile turned to an expression of concern. "Hmm?"

"Listen, speaking of me seeing someone…" God, was I really going to do this? Except I needed some answers. I didn't want to be in limp-dick limbo for the next few months. I wanted to know if I had a fighting chance of a sex life again, especially now that I had met someone I really, *really* wanted to have sex with at some point. But who the hell else could I ask, other than the doctor who couldn't see me for months? Clearing my throat, I met Robin's gaze. "How much do you know about this kind of injury and, um..." My face heated up, and I lowered my voice. "Problems with, uh..." I gestured downward.

"ED?" She didn't sound surprised. Concerned, but not at all surprised.

Cheeks on fire, I nodded.

"It's not uncommon after a pelvic fracture, I know that."

"Yeah, so I'm learning. But is it... I mean, is it permanent?"

Lips quirked, Robin thought for a moment. "Well, it depends on a lot of things. Soft tissue takes a lot longer to heal than most people realize, and between the injury, the surgeries, the tendinosis, and your recovery, you've had a *lot* of trauma to your lower body. Particularly the pelvic area. So it's entirely possible things are just healing and taking their sweet time about it." She put up a finger. "*But* there could also be some actual damage."

"*Permanent* damage?"

"Your doctor will know better than I do, but basically it depends on what's causing it. Do you have any loss of sensation?"

I shook my head. "No. Just can't, uh, stay up."

"Can you get erect at all?"

My cheeks burned. I wasn't used to talking about this with her or anyone. I wasn't used to needing to. "I, um... Sometimes, yeah. I can't get as hard as I used to, and I can't *stay* hard, but...yeah."

"So probably not nerve damage, which is good." She folded her arms loosely. "Could be a circulatory thing. Pelvic fractures are notorious for messing up nerves and circulation, and you had a few surgeries, so there could be scar tissue, adhesions—any number of things."

I arched an eyebrow. "Is that something that can be fixed?"

"There's no way to tell until someone who knows what they're looking at does an assessment. Sometimes it's a surgical fix. Sometimes it's medication." She shrugged. "There are a lot of different things they can do."

Releasing a breath, I sat back. "Okay, I'm not thrilled about the idea of more surgery, especially not on my junk, but at least there's a possibility I'm not stuck this way forever."

Robin nodded. "There are also non-invasive solutions. Medications, for one. I also had a patient a couple of years ago who had some

ED because of some circulation issues after an injury. His doctor had him try a pump, and he said it worked wonders."

I blinked. I was used to her being blunt and even crude sometimes, but this still caught me off guard. "Like a…penis pump?"

Okay, that was a dumb question. What else could she mean? A gas pump?

Without giving me shit for the stupid question, Robin said, "Look, I know people make fun of them, but they exist for a reason. Not one of the ones people use to try to make their dicks bigger—those will just cause all kinds of damage. There are medical grade pumps that are specifically designed for this." With a shrug, she added, "You're not on any blood thinners or anything, so after you've been checked out by a urologist, it'll probably be perfectly safe to give it a try."

"Not really sure how to work that into foreplay, but…"

She seemed to consider that. "I mean, you might want to try it on your own a few times until you get the hang of it. I hear they're a little awkward at first."

"Awesome," I muttered.

"And hey, if you're in bed with someone who makes you feel embarrassed or awkward about something like that, is that really someone you want to be in bed with?"

"Hmm, okay. Good point."

She smiled, then turned serious again. "And I mean it—*medical* grade. One of the good, safe ones that require a prescription."

"A prescription?" I laughed humorlessly. "Great. A year ago, I was playing hockey. Now I'm getting prescription penis pumps so I can have a sex life again."

"Hey, just be glad we live in an era when there are options like that."

"Okay, true."

Robin needed to get to her next patient, so I went to the locker room, changed out of my gym shorts and into my regular clothes, and gathered my phone and keys.

When I checked my phone, I had a text from Jon.

Still on for tonight?

A little thrill zinged through me. Tonight? Oh, right! His son was back at his mom's today, which meant Jon and I could meet up, and he was free for the day.

But I paused mid-reply, thumbs hovering over the keyboard on my screen.

I debated telling him I was too sore and tired for anything after my appointment. That much was true—even if I had a dick that was in working order, sex was *not* an option after today's torture session with Robin. Not that Jon and I had actually done anything beyond kissing, failing to fuck, and cuddling up in his bed, but still.

I wasn't too sore or tired to spend an evening like that with him. Hopefully he was still game when there wouldn't be anything sexual. I wanted us to get there at some point, but it wouldn't be this evening. There wouldn't be much of anything tonight—cuddling was great and all, but it was possible that by the time I saw him, I'd be too sore for even that much.

Was this really enough for Jon? Or was he going to bail once he realized that patiently waiting for more might not actually pay off? And if he did, would the next guy? The one after that?

Well. I guess time would tell.

God, please let me be enough for someone.

8

JON

Heart going wild, I entered Brent's address in my navigation system. I was so looking forward to seeing him after spending a week apart—all the while feeling guilty that I was finding *any* silver lining in my custody week being over—and I was also curious to see where he lived.

The directions started with heading south on North Avenue. Not really a surprise—North Avenue was kind of the main drag leading in and out of downtown, and a lot of neighborhoods branched off in various directions along the way.

The GPS told me to turn at the elementary school that Cody would have been attending had Ashley and I not agreed to keep him at Edmunds Elementary. Flynn Elementary was much closer to my place, but letting him stay at the other school meant less upheaval for him. It just meant I had to drive him to and from school during my custody weeks, which was fine with me if it meant less stress for him.

A ways down the road, I passed Starr Farm Park, where I sometimes brought Cody to play with the other kids on the ballfields and playground equipment. Seeing the place made me miss him. What didn't make me miss him? I tried to shake it off, though. I'd see him again next Friday, and there was nothing wrong with finding a way to enjoy the weeks I *didn't* have custody. In fact it was probably healthier if I *did* enjoy our time apart instead of moping about him not being there. I was bound and determined to learn to do that.

Starting with seeing the man I'd been texting with for the past week.

The road split, and as I followed it to the right, a handwritten sign advised people this was a private road reserved for residents and guests only. Above that was a sign announcing I was entering the Sunset Cliff neighborhood.

Oh. Wow. This was supposed to be a super nice area. Like, houses-in-the-seven-figure range super nice. Which… Okay, he *had* been a professional hockey player. Hockey players made bank from what I'd heard, and he'd had a few seasons under his belt before his accident had taken him out of the game. So it made sense for him to be able to afford something like this. Though he drove a fairly modest pickup truck. Maybe he had a weekend car that was fancier and more expensive. I had a client who was a retired football player, and when he was picking up his kids from school or running errands, he drove an SUV that was nothing to write home about. When he took his wife out for an evening or they were attending some charity event or another? That was when he broke out the candy apple red Porsche.

Now I was curious if Brent had something else in the garage. Maybe I'd find out.

Or maybe, given what had happened to him, he'd *had* a fancy weekend car in the not-too-distant past. Probably best not to ask about it.

As I drove down the private road, I passed a solar array with High Voltage signs all over the tall chain link fence. I wondered for a cynical moment if the power from those solar panels was solely for this exclusive neighborhood, or if it also powered the homes of lesser mortals like me.

I kept driving.

The navigation system told me to turn right, and when I did, it announced that I'd arrived at my destination, and—

Whoa.

That wasn't a house. That was a *palace.*

It was huge, and it sat right on Lake Champlain. He probably had a private boat dock and everything—including a boat—but of course I couldn't see any of that from here. Not with the sprawling home blocking the view. The front yard was meticulously landscaped, and Brent's familiar truck was parked outside the closed three-car garage. Yeah, there might be a weekend car in there. Or three of them. Or two, if he hadn't replaced the one that had been destroyed. Definitely a subject to leave alone unless he wanted to bring it up.

I parked, got out, and followed the concrete pathway to the front porch. I was just clearing the top step when Brent opened the door, and I damn near tripped on that last step because… Fuck. Those eyes. That smile.

"Hey," he said with a grin.

"Hey." As soon as he was in reach, I wrapped my arms around his waist. "It's been a while."

"Mmhmm, it has." He pulled me close and kissed me, and just like that, the entire week we'd been apart evaporated. Was it ridiculous that I'd missed him so much? We'd just met. How were we already at best friends with sort-of-benefits?

Well. Whatever. I couldn't get enough of him and I wasn't going to apologize for that.

After God knew how long, Brent drew back, and we exchanged grins.

"I should probably let you in," he said, sounding breathless, "instead of just spending the whole night in the doorway."

"I mean I won't object to the doorway if this is what we're doing."

He laughed, sending a ripple of desire right through me. Then he loosened his embrace and nodded inside. "Come on in. I'll open the wine."

"Wine sounds good." So did getting indoors where none of his neighbors might accidentally catch a glimpse of us. Not that I cared if someone saw me with a man, but if he'd kept kissing me like that much longer, that accidental glimpse might have made things awkward with his neighbors.

Inside, I left my shoes beside his, and we headed into the kitchen. And holy shit, I'd thought this place was gorgeous on the outside.

Enormous windows let in the late afternoon sun, which illuminated vaulted ceilings, a huge, open plan kitchen with brushed stainless appliances, and a living room with a comfortable-looking gray sofa and a flat screen TV. The TV was probably some absurd size, somewhere in the ballpark of seventy-plus inches, but it was on such a big wall with such high ceilings that it looked perfectly modest and average. There were some boxes and some empty shelves, so I suspected he hadn't lived here long.

"Wow." I looked around. "This place is nice."

Brent smiled, though he didn't sound overly enthusiastic as he said, "I like it. Still kind of settling in, but…"

"How long have you been here? Wait, you said you moved back six months ago, right?"

"To Burlington, yeah. The house?" He paused like he needed to think about it. "Three months? Maybe four?" He shrugged and continued toward the kitchen, adding over his shoulder, "I lived with my parents when I first came back to town. I was still recovering, and I hadn't closed on the house yet."

"Looks like it was worth the wait."

He stopped beside the counter and picked up the corkscrew he'd left beside the bottle and glasses. With a somewhat more genuine smile, he said, "Yeah. It was. It's nice to be settled again."

"I can imagine."

Brent poured us each a glass of wine. We clinked them together, then each took a sip.

"So, um…" He absently swirled his wine. "We can hang out in here, or since the weather's holding this evening…" He nodded toward the deck. "I've got a hot tub."

"Ooh, a hot tub? That sounds tempting."

"Yeah?" He grinned nervously. "Because physical therapy was a bear, and the tub might give my muscles a chance to loosen up."

"Or it'll give us both a chance to drink a glass of wine and relax."

"So, win-win?"

"Exactly."

We exchanged smiles, then shared a long kiss before we took our glasses out to the back deck. We stripped out of our clothes and left them folded on a shelf next to the hot tub where they wouldn't get wet.

Then Brent got in, moving slowly and carefully as he stepped over the side.

"The massage therapist in me wants to remind you you're supposed to use ice, not heat." I eased myself into the bubbling water. "The rest of me says, 'fuck yeah, hot tub.'"

Brent laughed as he got situated. "My physical therapist is always yelling at me about using ice, and I do ice everything a lot, but you know what?" He leaned back, resting his arms along the edge of the tub. "The rest of me gets tired and sore from limping around, and hot water is exactly what Dr. Brent ordered."

"No judgment here." I sat beside him. "One of the houses I looked at had one of those big Whirlpool tubs, and I seriously did some calculating about how much ramen I'd have to eat in order to pay that mortgage. Sometimes I think it might've been worth it." I glanced down and prodded at the seat between us. "And there's even padded seats?" I whistled. "Damn, this is nice."

"I know, right? I wouldn't be able to use it if it didn't."

"Well, I'm glad you can use it." I slid a hand over his thigh. "Especially since that means *we* can use it."

Brent's grin made goose bumps prickle to life all over my skin beneath the hot water. I took that as an invitation, and I moved closer to him. The arm he'd draped along the tub's edge wrapped around my shoulders, and we came together in a lazy, wine-sweetened kiss. Just like the night we'd met, when we'd kissed for the first time under that streetlight, I'd have been perfectly happy to do this and nothing more. I loved the way his lips moved with mine, and I loved the way his hands roamed my body while I slid my fingers and palms all over him. It was lazy and sexy and easy, and I'd have been hooked on him and on this even if he hadn't been the first person to touch me in the better part of two years. The fact that he was the one to break that frustrating dry spell? Even better.

Abruptly, Brent flinched, then fidgeted on the seat, his breath hitching with the movement.

I drew back. "You okay?"

"Yeah." He laughed self-consciously. "Something's always sore, and I guess my back doesn't like this position."

"Might be better if I sit over you." I started to get up, but hesitated. "Is that comfortable for you?"

"Definitely. Just don't put your weight on my left hip, and we're good."

"I can handle that." I turned around, and as I straddled him on my knees, his hands slid up my sides. I'd barely situated myself on his lap before our lips met again. Between kisses, I murmured, "This better?"

"Mmhmm. Much." We both grinned, then kissed again, and the heat of the water had nothing on the warmth of Brent's body and the tightness of his strong arms around me as we explored each other's mouths. My knees probably wouldn't put up with this for too long, but the padded seats helped, and anyway, I loved this too much to worry about what my knees had to say about it.

Neither of us was hard, and I didn't mind. In water this hot, there was no danger of me getting hard, but the heat felt good, and so did making out with Brent.

I leaned down to kiss his neck, and Brent swore softly, his wet hands sliding up my back. When he dragged his nails down, I grunted, which drew a laugh out of him, so I bit his shoulder. The laugh instantly changed to a moan, and he arched under me.

"Goddamn," he ground out.

I kissed the spot I'd bitten, and he shivered as I started back up his neck.

"You know what we should do one night?" he murmured, hands sliding softly over the burning lines his nails had left.

I let my lips skate along his throat. "Hmm?"

"Bring some condoms and lube in here with us."

Goose bumps sprang up across my back and shoulders, and I lifted my head to meet his gaze. From the hunger in his eyes, he wasn't joking. I was out of breath as I said, "Yeah?"

"Uh-huh." He licked his lips, sliding his hands up my chest. "You could probably get some good leverage if you bent me over the side."

Oh. *Fuck.* We hadn't done much more than cuddle and kiss, and now he was talking about me bending him over the...

Oh my God, yes.

"You, uh, think you can..." I swallowed. "You think that's comfortable enough for you to bottom?"

"It's worth a try." He shrugged. "Not tonight, but when my body wants to cooperate?" His eyes gleamed with a hunger that made me wish we could do it now. "Yeah, I want to give it a try."

Nodding, I moistened my lips. "We'll have to turn the temperature down a bit if we want to fool around in here." I kissed him softly, and broke away just enough to murmur, "But hell yeah, I'm in."

Brent moaned, sliding his hand into my hair and pulling me in for another kiss. From the way he held me and pushed his tongue into my mouth, he wasn't kidding—he wanted to try. Just thinking about it turned him on.

And goddamn, I couldn't wait.

You want me to ride you over the edge?

Say the word, baby.

9

BRENT

As soon as I dropped the gauntlet, Jon and I weren't just lazily making out anymore. We'd both been restrained and cautious so far. Now? With that green light so close he could probably taste it as much as I could? Oh, it was game on. We wouldn't get to anything anal tonight—my hips weren't going to tolerate it—but I was pretty sure there was still plenty we could do.

"You know what we should do?" I murmured between kisses.

"Hmm?" He bent and started kissing his way along the side of my throat. Holy fuck, his lips and stubble felt so good, I would've lost my train of thought had it not been directly related to what we were doing.

"We should go upstairs." I dragged my fingers up his back. "Cool off from the hot tub a bit. Maybe… Maybe see what happens."

The sexiest groan I'd ever heard emerged from Jon's throat, and he nipped my shoulder. Then he met my gaze. "You want to?"

I nodded, licking my lips. "Yeah. I've, um… I've been wanting to, but now…" I couldn't finish the thought. Not with him looking so hot and needy like that. "Upstairs?"

"Good idea."

We grabbed the towels I'd left beside the hot tub, dried off enough that we wouldn't track water through the house, and went inside.

Despite his eagerness, Jon let me ease myself into bed first, and then he carefully joined me. He even grabbed a pillow for me to put between my knees—it probably wouldn't stay there, but it would appease my idiot leg for a while.

Once we were situated, we picked up right where we'd left off in the hot tub, and as we tangled up in a long, promising kiss, I tried not to notice my own nerves. Unfortunately for me, that was like trying not to notice my ever-present pain. It was there. It wasn't going anywhere. Might as well make peace with it and figure out how to work with it.

Please don't kill the mood this time, I begged my lemon of a body. *Just let me enjoy this. Please?*

Jon met my eyes. "Hey. Relax." He grinned. "I don't bite."

I laughed, which didn't mask my nerves *at all.* I really needed to learn to keep it on the down-low when my brain started being ridiculous like that. "What if I like biting?"

Jon's eyebrows jumped, but then his eyes narrowed, and he slid his hands up my back. "Pretty sure that can be arranged. But you know what I mean."

"Yeah. I do. I just, um..." My voice came out shakier than I expected as I said, "I wasn't this nervous my first time."

Jon smiled and kissed me softly. "You weren't recovering from an injury your first time."

Actually it'd been two months after I'd had knee surgery my sophomore year in high school, but that hadn't been as debilitating or life-changing, so close enough. "True."

"We'll just go slow." He grinned against my lips. "Which is fine with me—I *love* it slow and easy." He didn't sound the least bit patronizing. In fact, he sounded like he really meant it. That taking things slow really did turn him on.

So I stopped overthinking it as much as I could, and I got lost in what we were doing. We got rid of the pillow I'd been keeping between my knees, and Jon gently rolled me onto my back. I had a flicker of *oh shit* at the thought of trying to straddle him—there were tendons that took exception to that particular position—but Jon must've remembered what I'd said in the hot tub, and he straddled me instead.

"This all right?" he asked against my lips. "I'm not putting too much weight on—"

"You're good." I lifted my head and kissed him again, sliding my hand up into his hair as we made out in this new and surprisingly comfortable position.

I wasn't hard, which was irritating if not surprising, but the friction felt good. Like...really good. I pressed my heels into the mattress and experimentally pushed my hips against his. It didn't hurt (well, it didn't hurt *more*), and it drew a throaty groan out of Jon as we rutted together, so I did it again. He kissed me harder, and we rocked together, and—

A red-hot shard of pain in my hip made me gasp.

Jon tensed, pushing himself up. "What? Are you okay?"

"Yeah. Yeah. I'm good." I winced and rubbed my hip.

"You sure? If you're in pain, we don't have to—"

"I'm always in pain." I pulled him back down. "There's no such thing as a pain-free day. Probably never will be." I slid my hands up his back. "But it does ease off sometimes. Like...now."

"Yeah?"

"Mmhmm. It was just a little spasm. Startled me more than anything." I kissed him lightly. "I just have to be careful moving like that. It's all good."

"You sure?"

"Oh yeah," I purred. "I want this."

"Mmm, me too." Jon combed his fingers through my hair. "But tell me if something hurts, okay? If we need to change something, or stop, or whatever?"

I swallowed. It still stung, having to be this careful with things I'd taken for granted for so many years, and it was a blow to my pride—rational or not—when someone fell all over themselves to accommodate me. I hated it. At the same time, I knew I needed it, and I was grateful that Jon was careful not to hurt me. Ignoring my ego, I nodded.

"Okay. I will." Licking my lips, I trailed my fingers through the thin hair on his chest, and I tried not to let it show that my heart was still pounding with nerves. There was no hiding that I wasn't getting it up. I reminded myself over and over that Jon knew this was a thing, and it wouldn't be a surprise to him, but it was impossible to shake off that mortified feeling.

Years ago, a case of whiskey dick had left me with some hardcore performance anxiety for months. I'd known then that it was the alcohol that had done it, but that didn't stop me from being irrationally afraid it would happen again even while I was stone-cold sober.

Now? I was as drunk as I was hard. Which is to say…not even a little. And I still couldn't get it up.

I wasn't surprised. Robin and I had talked about it, and I couldn't even get it up most of the time when I was alone. Something was wrong, and I wouldn't know *exactly* what until I could finally get in to see my doctor. Did I even want to know? Because I was terrified the answer would be that, much like my career, my ability to get an erection was a permanent casualty of my accident. Because goddammit, I wanted Jon, and I hated that my body didn't show it.

Just climbing under the covers with Jon, both of us naked and turned on, would normally have had me steel-hard in no time. I was definitely turned on, though, especially as Jon kissed up and down the side of my throat, and I closed my eyes, tilting my head back into the pillow. I tried to enjoy it and ignore the way my body was—or wasn't—responding. It was the same as when I'd tried to jack off recently. The desire was there. The need for friction and an orgasm was there. The hard-on? Not so goddamned much.

This injury really is the gift that keeps on giving, isn't it? Fuck.

Jon met my eyes. "You good?"

Oh. Shit. So much for keeping my internal freak-outs on the down-low.

"Yeah." I ran my hands up his back. "Just, um… I'm…" I nodded downward. "Still getting used to the idea that things don't work quite right."

He nodded. "But I'm not hurting you?"

"No. Definitely not. I just hate that I don't know if this is… Like if it's a permanent thing, or… I mean, I've gotten hard a few times on my own, but full disclosure, even if I *can* get hard, I don't know if I can come."

"Okay. Duly noted." He kissed me lightly. "Is coming the only part of sex you enjoy?"

I blinked. "Well, no. Of course not."

Jon smiled, caressing my cheek. "Then it's all good. No pressure."

"Easy for you to say." It came out with more bitterness than I'd intended.

"No pressure from *me*," he clarified. "There's plenty of ways I can make your toes curl whether you're hard or not." He grinned. "I mean, I don't know about you, but I can almost never stay hard when I'm bottoming. I still enjoy the hell out of it, though."

"Oh. Yeah. I guess I hadn't thought of it that way." But then I tensed and looked in his eyes. "What if I can't top you, though? You said you like bottoming, and I can't—"

"Brent." He brought my hand up and kissed the middle of my palm. "I was happily married for twenty years to someone who wasn't equipped to top me or anyone else, and she wasn't at all interested in pegging, either. I assure you, I can live without bottoming."

Well, damn. I hadn't thought of that either.

"Honestly," he whispered, combing his fingers through my hair, "when we met? When I kissed you outside the wine bar?" He squirmed. "I decided right then and there that if we just found a place to make out all night, I'd be happy."

"You… Really?"

"Are you kidding?" He drew me in closer. "With the way you kiss?" And then he kissed me, and goose bumps sprang to life all over my skin.

It was impossible not to believe him, and anyway I *wanted* to believe him, so I wrapped my arms around him and let his lips and his hands assure me everything I brought to the table was enough.

As we touched and kissed, I slid a hand between us. He broke the kiss with a gasp, and when I closed my fingers around his cock, just watching his face and stroking his thick erection had me turned on as all hell, even if my body didn't show it.

"God, yeah…" He squeezed his eyes shut as his lips parted. "That feels so good." The arousal in his voice made me hot, and I stroked him a little harder. He rocked his hips, pushing himself through my fist, and when he found my mouth with his, his kiss was deep and demanding.

To hell with caring if I was hard or if I could come. I hadn't realized how much I'd missed feeling like this. Like someone could be that turned on and out of his mind because of me. I wanted more, so I pumped his cock the way I'd done with myself and with guys in the past, and every time Jon moaned or shivered, the rush made me dizzy with need.

"Goddamn..." He pushed himself onto his forearms and thrust into my grip, and the way his breathing sped up, he was close. Letting his head fall beside mine, he whispered, "Oh God. Keep..." He trailed off into a moan, rocking his hips harder as he fucked my fist. "Mmph, Brent..."

I bit my lip, mesmerized by him. He was so damn sexy already, and when he was on the edge, he was smoking hot. The deep crevices between his eyebrows, the way his lips pulled tight across his teeth, the flush in his face and his throat—I could watch that all night long. The fact that I was doing this to him? Wow, that was heady as hell.

He gasped, and his spine straightened as he thrust into my fist, and then with a harsh, *"Fuck!"* he came, shooting all over my hand and stomach as his breathing became a mix of sharp gasps and ragged exhalations. My God, he was gorgeous, and getting him off like this was...holy fuck.

Then he sighed, shuddered again, and relaxed, eyes still closed as he panted and trembled. "Whoa."

I laughed softly. "You okay?"

"Uh-huh." His eyes fluttered open, and he grinned drunkenly. "I'm good."

I returned the grin, and he kissed me softly before he rolled away to reach for the tissues on the nightstand.

My grin faded. The pang of disappointment was as tough to ignore as the ever-present ache in my hip. Making him come had been fun, but...now what? Was this the part where his head cleared and he remembered I was, uh, limited?

Jon tossed the tissues. Then he rolled over to face me, and he snaked his arm over me. "There. Now there's no need to worry about either of us getting off," he whispered against my lips. "We can just do what feels good in the moment."

He kissed me again, and I had to agree—this did feel good in the moment. I wished like hell I could get it up and get off too, but if lazily making out with Jon was the consolation prize, I could live with that. How had I gone so long without being touched and not completely lost my mind?

Okay, the jury was still out on whether I'd lost my mind. The last year had been...rough. But this? This was *good.*

Jon met my eyes, brow furrowed slightly. Stroking my hair, he asked, "You all right?"

Shit, had my somewhat-lost mind been wandering again? "I'm fine." I licked my lips. "I'm good. Just…" It was hard not to keep the disappointment out of my voice, so I stopped fighting it. "Just wish I could do more, you know?"

"I know. But for what it's worth, I can get off with my hand and some lotion. This?" He slid his palm up my chest and brushed his lips across mine. "*This* is what I'm here for."

And then he claimed another kiss, and insecurities and performance anxiety be damned, I melted into his arms all over again. If he was faking it, if he really did think I was more trouble than I was worth because of my newfound limitations, he was damn good at convincing me otherwise. That, or I just needed it to be true too much to catch on that it was all lip service.

More and more, I didn't think it was fake. After all, he'd already gotten off, so he could easily roll over and go to sleep. But no, he held me against him, and he kissed me lazily. *Decadently*. Like he really meant it when he said that with the urgency to come out of the way, we could finally relax and *enjoy* this.

And oh my God, I *was* enjoying it. *Really* enjoying it.

It turned out to be surprisingly relaxing to just fall into the moment and enjoy touching and kissing without any pressure. We weren't just cuddling in bed, and we weren't having wild and acrobatic sex, but this happy medium? Oh, I could live with that. I could barely handle what it felt like to be in my own body, but I loved being tangled up with his.

I looked in Jon's eyes. "Are you sure this is enough for you?"

He didn't even hesitate: "Definitely."

"What about when I can't do anything? Like, when my dick is the least of my problems?"

He ran his fingers through my hair. "Same as before—we just watch a movie or relax. There's no pressure. At least, none from me."

"But we're still friends with benefits?"

He seemed to think about it, then shrugged. "I know this isn't how friends with benefits usually works, but after going from being married to being alone, I think this is what I need the most. Just being with someone without all the issues and tension."

I was curious about his divorce, but it seemed like a raw wound, so I left it alone for now. He'd bring it up when he was ready to, and until then, it was none of my business. We could both show cards later if we were ready.

For now, I was just going to enjoy this. Being such a recluse for so long, I'd forgotten how much I loved being close to someone. Jon was right—this part *was* good, and it wasn't something I could do alone. The hard-on was optional. The touch of another person? Not so much.

Sex was going to be different now than it was before I got hurt. It was probably going to be different for the rest of my life.

But maybe it wasn't so hopeless after all.

10

JON

After decadently sleeping in until almost ten, Brent and I pulled ourselves out of bed, took a shower, and headed downstairs for some much-needed coffee. I had no appointments today and didn't need to be at Vino and Veritas until tonight, and Brent's schedule was wide open. There was no hurry to be anywhere but here.

Now that the sun was up and we weren't so focused on getting into bed, I could actually look around and take in Brent's house. All that had really registered last night was that it was huge, and it seemed even bigger with late morning light pouring in through enormous windows along one side of the open plan kitchen and living room.

The place was sparsely furnished and even more sparsely decorated. There were some bookcases with a few books on the shelves, and boxes beside them with *books* written in Sharpie. Some items of varying shapes and sizes were on the top shelves, still wrapped in brown paper as if he hadn't had time to do more than that.

Brent cleared his throat, gesturing at everything as he headed toward the kitchen. "Sorry for the mess. I've been a bit slow about unpacking."

"Nothing to be sorry for." I followed him into the kitchen, wincing on his behalf as I noticed his subtle but unmistakable limp. "You've seen my place. I've still got boxes everywhere and the house is a construction zone."

"You're renovating, though. I'm just..." He made a sharp gesture at our surroundings. "Not getting anywhere."

"And you're also still healing." I rested a hand on the small of his back and kissed the side of his neck. "No one's going to judge."

"I am," he muttered. Then he sighed. "I'll get there. I know I will. It's just frustrating."

"Yeah, I get that."

Brent poured us some coffee and we went out onto his back deck. The sight of the hot tub gave me goose bumps, but the view of Lake Champlain was breathtaking, especially on a clear morning like this. The waves were rolling gently, not a whitecap in sight, and the distant New York shores were perfectly visible.

"Wow," I said. "Between the house and the view—man, this place is *amazing*."

Brent smiled, a hint of shyness in his eyes as he handed me a cup of coffee. "I like it. One of these days I might even finish unpacking."

"I know the feeling. I figure I'll be done right about the time I go to move out."

He laughed softly. "Yeah, me too." Leaning against the counter, he looked around. "There've been some days where I think I can tackle it, but then my hip says no. And then there are days where I can handle it physically, but my brain won't let me get up off the couch." Some unspoken thought made his eyes go unfocused for a moment. Then he sipped his coffee and said, "I, uh... I think the house is bigger than I needed."

"Yeah?"

He nodded. "It was available, and it was tucked away so I could basically hide from everyone and everything. But when it's just me, it feels so....empty."

"You wanted to hide?"

Some color bloomed in his cheeks. "Yeah. When I lost my career, I guess I kind of lost my identity too. So I came here and bought this place." He pressed his hands onto the railing and stared out at the lake. "I didn't care about anything except that I wanted to hide from the world, and this seemed like a good place to do it. Except instead of feeling like home, it feels like a stadium after all the fans have gone home. It's just a big, empty place to sit in alone and lick my wounds."

Blushing, he laughed almost soundlessly and shook his head. "It sounds so stupid when I say it out loud."

"Not really. I can kind of relate."

He turned to me, eyebrows up. "Can you?"

"When it comes to buying a place based on your state of mind in the moment, and then realizing you might not have thought it through? And that maybe it's really not what you want?" I laughed dryly. "You saw where I live." Shaking my head, I sighed. "I can't believe I didn't even think about what renovating would do to my hands and arms."

Brent nodded. "It's funny how you don't think about physical limitations even when you know you have them."

I turned to him, eyebrows up, not sure if or how to ask him to go on.

He gestured at my hands. "You bought a place to renovate, but you didn't think about how you have to be careful with your hands, arms, back..." He sighed, looking back at his house as if he were taking it in for the first time. "And my dumb ass... I mean, one of the first places I had the real estate agent show me was amazing, but it was three stories with like two mezzanines. There were stairs *everywhere*. Even the living room was two steps down from the kitchen, and one of the lofts was only accessible by a *ladder*. On paper, I loved it, and it didn't even dawn on me until I tried to tour the place that there might be a reason it would be a disaster for me." He laughed bitterly. "I seriously felt like someone who was deathly allergic to cats, but asked to tour a house full of cat trees, and then acted surprised when I started sneezing."

I chuckled. "That's one way to look at it. But you ended up with this place, which is seriously nice."

"It is. It's just, um...big. What the fuck do I need a three-car garage for?"

I studied him, then cautiously asked, "How many cars do you have?"

Facing the lake again, he gestured over his shoulder. "Just the truck."

"Oh."

"I had more." He sipped his coffee. "Thought I was hot shit with a Ferrari and a Maserati."

I whistled. "Wow."

"Yeah." He laughed, but he didn't seem to feel it. "The Maserati… There's nothing left of that thing. People who've seen the video and the pictures still say they can't believe I survived." With a quiet shudder, he added, "I just take their word for it."

"You really haven't seen it?"

Grimacing, he shook his head. "No way. My head's fucked up enough trying to deal with…" He gestured at himself. "I don't want to know how bad the car was."

"Hmm, I can understand that."

"Yeah. And then the Ferrari…" His shoulders slumped, and he absently kneaded one as he gazed out at the lake. "I wish I could have kept it. That was a sweet, sweet car. But it's too low to the ground for me to get in and out comfortably, and even if I could, I can't drive a manual anymore."

"Oh. I hadn't thought about that."

He nodded, gaze still fixed on the water. "So, I sold it, and then I bought the truck. It's not fancy, but it's an automatic, I can sit comfortably in it, and I can get in and out. Selling the Ferrari hurt, though." He turned to me, eyes sad. "I loved the car, but selling it mostly sucked because it meant admitting I couldn't drive it anymore."

"Damn," I whispered.

"Yeah." He paused, then shook himself and cleared his throat. "Anyway, that's a depressing train of thought." He took another sip of coffee. "You hungry? I suck at unpacking my house, but I do have a decently stocked kitchen, and I can cook."

"Can you?" I grinned.

"Better than my teammate, that's for sure."

"Isn't that setting the bar kind of low?"

Brent chuckled, and he motioned for me to follow him inside.

As he went about making us some omelets—he was right, he could cook—I thought about our conversation and what we were doing. Being with him was easy, and it felt right, but there was a nagging little voice in the back of my head that warned me against getting too attached. This was, after all, friends with benefits. And anyhow, I hadn't been able to keep my own wife happy. Our marriage had been holding her back from everything she wanted in life. I was kidding myself if I thought I was enough for a man who'd had a taste of having the world at his feet.

Besides, our backgrounds couldn't be any more different. I was a single dad starting over in my forties after being married for twenty years. Brent was a young athlete recovering from a serious injury that had cost him the only career he'd ever known. I lived in a place held together by moss and prayers. Brent had an enormous lakefront house in an exclusive neighborhood. He'd downgraded to a modest pickup he could drive comfortably from a Ferrari I could never dream of affording.

The only things we really had in common were that our lives had been upended around the same time, and we were both still dealing with our respective aftermaths. We both needed some human contact and, bodies permitting, sex.

So I had no illusions that this was forever. Even if one or both of us was ready for something more than sex and mutual affection, we were too different to pull it off together.

But I was absolutely going to enjoy it while it lasted.

I'm here whenever you're ready.

I read the text as I was leaving a client's house and breathed a sigh of relief. Brent had had physical therapy earlier, but thank God, he was still in the mood to meet up. The longer we'd been…well, for lack of a better phrase, seeing each other around my custody schedule, I'd started to get a feel for how his pain affected him. Sometimes he was too sore after he'd had these appointments, which on the worst nights meant breaking out the heavy duty painkillers. Those nights, he spent alone, which I understood. When the pain was less intense, we'd spend the evening together, and we'd play things by ear. Sometimes he was game to cuddle up on the couch or in bed. Sometimes he couldn't handle being touched at all. I just followed his lead.

I was always relieved whenever he was still game to see me. For one, because it meant he was feeling all right. For another, because I got to see him. I always wanted to see him, and I'd also have taken any excuse not to go home to an empty house. It was probably going to take me years to get used to only having my son half the time.

Living alone? I had literally gone from living with my parents to moving in with Ashley. I was forty-one years old, completely on my own for the first time in my life, and I could *not* get the hang of this.

Tonight, I didn't have to, because after I'd again dropped Cody off at his mom's for the start of her custody week, there was a gorgeous former hockey player who wanted my company.

When I arrived, though, and Brent opened the door, alarm surged through me. From the tightness of his features and the uncomfortable way he was leaning on the cane he rarely used, he was in some serious pain.

"Hey," I said as I stepped inside. "Are you okay?"

He grimaced, hobbling a bit as he shut the door. "I was fine earlier. Kind of sore after physical therapy, but then I stumbled bringing some groceries in from the truck, and..." He gestured down at himself and made a frustrated face.

"Oh, shit. How bad is it?"

"I'll be fine. It just fucking hurts." Leaning hard on the cane, he led me into the living room, and as he sat down, he added, "I took a pain pill, but so far, it hasn't done a goddamned thing except make my head fuzzy."

I chewed my lip as I followed him and watched him moving like every twitch of every muscle hurt. I'd seen him in pain before, but not like this.

So why don't I help him?

I'd always assumed I'd never do therapeutic massages for people I was involved with. It was just too easy to blur professional and personal lines. I'd done them for Ashley after she'd hurt her back and when she was pregnant, but casual hookups and friends with benefits? Not a good idea.

Still, I couldn't just sit back and let Brent be in this much pain if there was something I could do about it. And I *had* offered in the beginning, hadn't I?

I joined him on the couch, I touched his face, and looked in his eyes. "Let me help."

His brow pinched. "Do you think you can?" He paused, then quickly added, "I mean, I'm not saying what you do doesn't help. I'm just not sure it can help with *this*."

"It's worth a try if you want to. It's musculoskeletal pain, so if I can relieve some tension in the soft tissue, it might at least take the edge off."

Brent exhaled. "At this point, I'll try anything. Just, uh, go easy. My physical therapist already tortured me today, and I've had some massages before that hurt like a motherfucker."

"Oh, don't worry about that." I put a gentle hand on his thigh. "Some massages can be painful for a little while, but I'm not going in for a deep tissue massage on something that's this tender. Especially when I don't have a file on the specifics of your injuries." I ran my thumb alongside his thigh. "If anything I'm doing hurts, we can stop."

He studied me, then swallowed. "Where should we do this?"

"Wherever's comfortable. My table is in the car, but for this, I think you're fine just lying on your bed. The couch could work too, but the bed will give me a bit more room to maneuver."

His forehead creased. "And you really don't mind?"

I touched his waist and kissed him softly. "This is literally what I *do*."

"But you're off work."

"Uh-huh. And you're in pain."

He winced, avoiding my gaze. My years of experience with pain management patients was definitely serving me well now. Prior to that, I might not have understood the uneasiness and embarrassment. A lot of people—especially athletes—struggled to admit even to healthcare professionals when pain was too much because they were convinced it meant they were weak. They were ashamed of being a burden or a downer. That aspect of society had been a source of tremendous frustration for me throughout my career. It was heartbreaking, how people were conditioned to think they needed to push through pain—and, ideally, *smile* through it—so that others wouldn't be disappointed or inconvenienced.

I found his hand and laced our fingers together. "Everything you're feeling—physically and otherwise—is completely normal for someone recovering from an injury like yours." Squeezing his hand, I whispered, "There's no shame in asking for relief."

He swallowed hard. Finally, he looked at me, and he nodded. "Okay. Yeah." With a weak smile, he added, "Thanks."

I leaned in and brushed my lips over his. "Let me get a bottle of oil out of the car." Sitting up again, I patted his leg. "Meet me in the bedroom."

I helped him to his feet. While he headed for the bedroom, I stepped out to grab the massage oil out of my trunk. I paused, then grabbed a large sheet and a waterproof liner to put under it, since most people didn't like massage oil getting into their sheets and blankets.

When I joined him upstairs, he'd pulled off his T-shirt, and he gestured down at the gym shorts he was wearing. "Should I, um…"

"Leave them on for now." I doubted we were in any danger of this turning sexual, but I preferred to keep the lines distinct. For that matter, even though we were intimately acquainted, being in pain made people feel vulnerable in ways that weren't welcome in the bedroom. Keeping his shorts on would hopefully make him feel less exposed.

I held up the sheet and liner I'd grabbed from the car. "Let me put these down over your sheets. The oil tends to stain."

He helped me put everything in place. Then he leaned his cane against the nightstand, and he swore as he lay back on the bed. "Is this okay?" His voice was taut with pain. "Or should I be on my stomach?"

"This is fine. Especially to start with." I paused. "Let's put a pillow under your knees, though." I picked up one of the other pillows, then slid my hand under the knee closest to me and gently eased it up. He winced, but sighed as I carefully let his leg settle back on the pillow.

With both knees situated, he exhaled and wiped a hand over his face. "Damn. That feels better already."

"I'm sure it does. Where's the pain?"

"Everywhere," he grumbled.

I raised my eyebrows. "Okay, where's the worst of it?"

"My left leg. It's all fucking with my back, and my right knee and hip hurt now too."

"Hmm, yeah, that makes sense. Especially when you have to favor the left, it's going to take a toll on the right." I nodded toward his right leg. "Is your physical therapist keeping an eye on it?"

He nodded.

"Okay." I uncapped the massage oil. "I'm going to start slow, and I'll go easy." I poured the oil on my hands, and as I started rubbing them together, met his gaze again. "Like I said, if anything I'm doing hurts, say so."

Another nod, but he didn't speak.

If I were his massage therapist, and if I were more well-versed in the specifics of his pelvic injury and prosthetic hip, I might have done some techniques to actually move his leg around and release the joint. But without a working knowledge of all the damage and repairs I couldn't see, I erred on the side of extreme caution—gently prodding the muscles in search of spasms that I could carefully work out with my fingers.

I put the oil aside so it was in reach but wouldn't spill. Kneeling beside him on the bed, I started midway up his left calf. This was partly to feel for tightness in case the spasms were affecting his whole leg. It was also to give him a chance to get used to my touch and be sure I wasn't going to dig my fingers in painfully.

Little by little, I worked my way up to his knee. Pain flickered across his face, and the muscles in his abs and thighs tensed. I didn't linger on the joint—it was undoubtedly tender, but I had no way of knowing if he had ligament damage, arthritis that wasn't visible, a torn meniscus, or any number of things I should know about before messing around with it. I'd stick to muscle spasms for now. Better to avoid causing him more pain or injury than he already had.

I moved on to his thigh, and the soft but firm tissue started to take on a distinctly more rigid texture. His lips also pulled into a tight, bleached line, and his eyes were squeezed shut, confirming what I could feel beneath my fingers.

"I think I found part of the problem."

He opened his eyes and grimaced as he asked, "Yeah?"

I nodded. "Your quads are seriously tight."

"You don't say," he ground out.

"I can work at them and see if they'll loosen up," I said. "But it'll probably feel worse before it feels better."

He exhaled through his nose. "Fuck."

"It's your call. Do you want me to leave it alone?"

Eyes closed and lips still tight, he seemed to think about it for a long time. Then his Adam's apple jumped, and he shook his head. "No. Don't leave it alone."

"You sure?"

He hesitated, but nodded. "Yeah."

"Okay. If it gets to be too much, say so."

I kept working at the cable-tight muscles. With a normal client, I'd be more aggressive about loosening the spasm, like pressing a thumb hard into the belly of the muscle and working at it until the tension released. This time, I took the frustratingly slow approach of just gently kneading the muscle, steadily encouraging it to relax. From the hitches of his breath and the occasional muttered curse, it wasn't comfortable, but he didn't ask me to stop, so I kept going.

After a while, I moved away from his quads and started on the other leg. Unsurprisingly, his calf and quads were painfully tight on that side too. I worked on them until they weren't quite so rock-hard, then moved back to the left thigh. I kept my hands extra gentle as I felt for lingering tightness.

Little by little, his muscles relaxed, and soon, so did he.

"Oh my God." He closed his eyes and sighed. "Everything still hurts, but…fuck, that's better."

"Good. Glad to hear it." I stopped, hand still resting on his thigh. "I probably shouldn't do too much more, or you'll end up sore."

"No, it's great." He looked up at me with a drowsy smile. "I feel a lot better. Thank you."

I squeezed his leg. "Why don't you stay here, and I'll go grab you some—do you have icepacks in your freezer?"

His eyes widened. "Icepacks?"

"It'll help keep the muscles from tensing back up."

"Ungh." He made a face and melodramatically whined, "I hate icepacks."

Chuckling, I patted his leg and rose. "I know. They suck. But they help."

"Says you."

"Uh-huh. Anyway, do you have icepacks? Or a few bags of frozen peas you're willing to sacrifice?"

He motioned toward the bedroom doorway. "Freezer in the kitchen has some icepacks."

"Okay. I'll be right back."

His freezer was well-stocked with icepacks in different sizes. I picked three, grabbed a couple of bottles of water from the fridge, and took some dishtowels off the counter too. As much as Brent obviously didn't care for ice—I couldn't blame him—he didn't argue as I put the towel-wrapped packs over each thigh and tucked another under his right calf.

Once all the icepacks were situated and Brent had had some water, I lay next to him on my side. "How do you feel?"

"Better. A lot better." He laced his fingers between mine. "And thank you. I'm sorry I'm not up for anything tonight."

"It's all right." I brought his hand up and kissed his knuckles. "I'm glad I could help."

"You did. You're *really* good at this."

I felt myself blush. "I better be good at it if I'm going to charge people for it."

"Okay, true, but I've had some massage therapists who were…not as good." He rubbed his thumb along mine. "It really did make a difference."

"Just let me know if you need it again."

His smile was enough to nudge away my worries about blurring personal and professional lines. Regardless of the other things we did in this bed, I didn't see myself ever saying no if he was in pain and I could do something about it.

Brent reached down to adjust one of the icepacks. Then he turned to me. "So, um, two or three weeks ago—around the time we first started doing this—I talked to my physical therapist about the issues I've been having." He swallowed. "In bed."

I slid a hand over his stomach just to touch him. "Yeah?"

Color bloomed in his cheeks. "She said she's going to make some calls about getting me in to see a specialist, but she doesn't think it's completely hopeless. In fact, she, um… She said some guys have luck with…" The color deepened, and he looked at me through his lashes as he said, "Penis pumps."

"Yeah? They help?"

"They can. If it's not nerve damage."

"Oh." I couldn't quite read his expression, so I cautiously asked, "Do you want to give it a try sometime?"

Brent searched my eyes. "You mean… You mean, like together?"

"Sure."

"You wouldn't…" He moistened his lips. "That wouldn't bother you?"

"Of course not. Especially not if it means you might enjoy things more. I'm game for anything so we can both have a good time." I smoothed his hair. "Do they actually work?"

"She said the medical grade ones do." He ran his hand along my forearm. "The specialist she wants me to see can check me out and maybe prescribe one." He laughed dryly. "Figures she can make a call and get me in, but I have to wait *months* to see my own doctor."

"How long does she think it'll take to get in to see the specialist?"

"Don't know." He sighed. "She was still working on it when I saw her today, so I guess we'll find out."

"I guess we will."

Silence fell, and I didn't know how to fill it. After a while, he said, "So when did you start singing?"

I ran with the subject change, since he clearly didn't want to discuss his ED more than we already had. In fact I was surprised he'd brought it up tonight, since he was probably feeling vulnerable already. "At the wine bar? Or in general?"

"In general." He adjusted one of his icepacks, then looked up at me. "You're really good, so I'm assuming you didn't just pick up a guitar and start killing it."

Laughing, I shook my head. "No, I didn't. I started playing when I was…nine? Ten? Around Cody's age, I know that. My grandpa had an acoustic guitar, and he'd teach me some chords whenever I came over. Then I talked my parents into letting me take lessons, and I was in choir all the way to graduation, so I learned to sing."

"Apparently you stuck with it after graduation."

"I…" I avoided his gaze. "Well, kind of."

Brent watched me for a moment. "What do you mean?"

I thought about it, wondering if I wanted to get into the whole story right now. Finally, I took a breath and met his eyes. "My friends and I started a band in high school. We… I mean, we weren't great, but we had some potential. And we'd *all* had record deal dreams since forever, so we were bound and determined to *get* one. We even managed to get some local gigs, and the summer between our junior and senior years, we played a couple of festivals."

"Wow," Brent whispered. "That's impressive, especially for a high school band."

"Yeah, we did all right." The memory hurt, but I continued

anyway. "Toward the end of our senior year, though, the band voted to boot me out and replace me with our drummer's girlfriend."

Brent's lips parted. "Whoa. Seriously?"

"Yep." Bitterness crept into my voice. "I was so pissed off about the whole thing, I pretty much put the guitar away and wouldn't pick it up for love or money. It wasn't until Ashley and I separated that I needed an outlet, and pouring it all into music seemed healthier than any alternatives I could think of." I laughed dryly. "My ex isn't thrilled about me singing about our divorce onstage twice a week, but it's not like I name names, so..." I shrugged.

"Well, and your style is country. Do people really assume everything you sing is about you?"

"They might. They might not. But she's pretty sure the songs are about her. Or, well, about us. I finally told her that the divorce was her decision, not mine, and how I deal with that is *my* decision, as long as I'm not actually calling her out by name or explicitly saying, 'hey, this is about my ex-wife.'" I paused, then admitted, "It might not do much toward smoothing things over with her, but by that point, I think I'd just burned out on trying to be the bigger person."

"Can't imagine why."

"I know, right? So that's how I got into music. And got *back* into it." I laughed humorlessly. "It's kind of poetic, if you think about it."

Brent tilted his head. "How so?"

"I ditched music because I got dumped. Then I got dumped again, and picked up the music to deal with it."

"Huh. Yeah, I guess that is kind of poetic." He smiled sweetly, sliding his hand over the top of mine. "For what it's worth, I'm glad you got back into it."

"Well, yeah." I grinned. "We wouldn't have met otherwise."

"Okay, true. But I meant it sounds like something that was really important to you. And I know what it's like to lose something like that. So, getting it back is... That's really great, you know?"

"I hadn't thought of it like that, but...yeah. You're right." I smiled, and I actually felt it this time. "It is great to have it back."

"And the part where it caused us to meet?" He chuckled. "I can't really argue with that, you know?"

"Hmm, no. Neither can I." We exchanged grins. Then I cleared my throat and, admittedly sounding a little shy, said, "I'm, uh, performing at Vino again tomorrow. If you want to come down, we could grab dinner afterward."

"Really?"

"Sure." With a slightly self-conscious laugh, I added, "I mean, my singing hasn't scared you off yet, so..."

"Oh please." Brent grinned. "Nothing about your singing is going to scare anyone off."

"You'd be surprised."

"Uh-huh. And I've also heard drunk hockey players sing karaoke. Trust me—nothing you do onstage is going to scare me away."

"Awesome," I said with a laugh. "I'm better than drunk hockey players doing karaoke. That's a high bar."

Brent tsked and pulled me in closer. "Shut up. You know what I mean. And yes, I'd love to join you tomorrow night."

Then he drew me down and kissed me.

And good God, I couldn't wait until he felt good enough to fool around again.

11

JON

I had no idea if Brent would actually show up at the wine bar the next night. A lot of people said they'd come to performances, but it was rare that they actually did. I'd mostly given up on asking people, but I'd suggested it to Brent after the massage last night because if he did show up, then we could spend part of the evening together.

There was always the possibility he was too sore, though. He'd told me as we'd texted throughout the day that the massage had helped, but he'd still been in rough shape. And anyway, pain was an unpredictable thing for him. If he was anything like some of my pain management patients, all it would take was sleeping wrong, stumbling like he had yesterday, or just plain bad luck for his entire day to be derailed again.

He'd either be here or he wouldn't, and I was way early anyhow. I just hoped I'd see him later this evening. In the meantime, I hung around the wine bar, waiting until it was my time to go onstage.

Not five minutes later, though, while I was at the bar getting a bottle of water, the door opened, and I looked without really thinking about it.

Oh my Lord. There he is.

He was wearing a gray T-shirt and jeans, plus a flannel overshirt that he'd left unbuttoned. He walked a little gingerly, his limp as inconspicuous as the way his features twitched when he put weight on his left leg. That could just as easily have been a result of the walk from the parking garage or because he was having another bad pain day.

As he came over to where I was standing at the bar, it occurred to me that inviting him to listen to me sing probably hadn't been a good idea while I could still get tongue-tied and stupid just glancing at him. Too late now—couldn't exactly tell him to wait outside until I was done. And I didn't want to.

Instead, I smiled, and when he was within earshot, I said, "Hey! You came."

"Well, yeah. I said I would." He tensed. "You…wanted me to, right?"

"Definitely!" I touched his waist and kissed him lightly. "It's just unusual for someone to actually show up, even when they say they will."

"Oh. Huh. Okay, well, if I say I'll be somewhere, I'm there." He smiled sweetly. "So here I am."

"Great! And, um, it's crowded as hell, and…" I checked my phone. "We've still got a ton of time. We don't have to stick around here."

Brent shrugged. "Okay. Any ideas?"

We bounced a few thoughts back and forth. Since Brent was less sore than he'd anticipated today, and he'd been told repeatedly by his physical therapist that he needed to move as much as possible, he was okay with a short, easy walk before he'd be sitting for an hour. Market Street was somewhat crowded, and the bricks were uneven enough to make them difficult for him, plus the street was on a gentle slope. So, we decided to go someplace else. It was a beautiful night—spring was definitely on a fast-track to summer—so we went down to the waterfront. It was technically walking distance from Vino and Veritas, but it was steep in places, which didn't bode well for Brent. Even if he hadn't been physically limited, I doubted we could walk down there and back in enough time for me to get onstage.

Instead, we drove and parked across from the ferry terminal and the ECHO center, the science center I'd brought Cody to a number of times. From there, we walked across the train tracks and the multi-use trail, then strolled along the boardwalk in the direction of Battery Park. A short ways down, Brent stopped and rested his forearms on the railing. Gazing out at the water, he said, "Man, I always loved coming down here when I was a kid."

"Me too."

A mischievous grin tugged at his lips. "Was any of this even here when you were a—"

"Shut up."

We both laughed, and I folded my arms on the railing beside his. The sun was beginning to sink behind the New York side of Lake Champlain, warming the sky as daylight steadily dimmed.

Brent exhaled. "It really is gorgeous out here. I mean, the whole area is..." He laughed softly and shook his head. "There are a lot of things I miss about my career, but it's nice to be home again."

"I can imagine."

He turned to me. "You ever lived anywhere else?"

I shook my head. "Born and raised here."

"Really? You didn't even go away for college?"

Chuckling, I gestured over my shoulder. "Did you miss the university that's right here in town?"

He laughed softly and shrugged. "Yeah, but I think half my classmates were itching to go someplace else."

"What about you?"

"Hmm?"

"What about you?" I studied him. "Did you want to get out of here?"

"I..." Brent's humor faded a little, and he stared out at the lake and the setting sun. "My university decisions weren't about Burlington or Vermont. They were just about the shortest distance between me and a professional hockey contract."

"Oh. Okay, yeah, that makes sense. What was your major?"

"Business." He shrugged. "I just went for something kind of generic that didn't seem like it would require the shitloads of reading and writing other majors did." He chuckled softly. "That makes me sound a lot lazier than I am. I really did study and everything, but for a good chunk of the academic year, hockey had to be my priority. I had some teammates who were majoring in shit like English and history, and..." Whistling, he shook his head. "There was no way I was writing a huge-ass term paper or reading a whole stack of books on the bus between games."

"Ugh, that sounds exhausting even without the bus or hockey."

"Right?" Brent laughed, unaware of how gorgeous he was in the warmth of the fading day. "I had a couple of teammates who were in the same class, and they had to read…" His brow furrowed, his gaze turning distant. Then he shook himself. "I don't remember what the book was. One of those really dense classics they use to punish high school students for existing."

I snorted. "Pretty sure I've read a few of those."

"Uh-huh, exactly. Anyway, they both had to read this book, and they hated it. I mean…*hated* it. One of them started ranting and raving about it on the bus, so we were all like, *'Dude, how bad can it be?'*" He laughed again, blue eyes sparkling. "The next thing we know, the book is getting passed around from one player to another, and we're all doing dramatic readings and falling all over ourselves laughing. The coaches legit thought we were drunk."

The thought of a busload of hockey players dramatically reading a classic made me chuckle. "I mean, I could think of worse ways to get through a dry read."

"Exactly! It was stupidly fun, and they both got A's on their papers, so it worked out." He clicked his tongue. "Too bad I couldn't get them to do it for Intro to Business Law."

I made a face. "Ugh. My eyes are glazing over just thinking about that one."

"You have *no* idea."

We both chuckled and gazed out at the water for a moment.

My phone vibrated, and when I checked it, I had a message from Cody. It was a picture of the stack of books he'd brought home from the school library. I laughed softly and wrote back, *Those will keep you busy!*

Pocketing my phone, I glanced at Brent. "Sorry. My son went to the library, and he was all excited to show me what he'd checked out."

"Yeah?" Brent smiled. "Bookworm?"

"Oh yeah. He loves to read." I couldn't help beaming. "He's a boy after my own heart—all about fantasy and sci-fi. In fact, he's been after me to read this one fantasy book with him. I really need to give it a quick read and make sure it's okay for him."

"So, appropriate for his age?"

"Basically. I do the same with movies. As he gets older, I'm less strict about it, but there are some things he just doesn't need to see, you know?" I scowled. "I would love to watch *The Neverending Story* with him, but..."

Brent and I glanced at each other, and we both said, "Swamps of Sadness."

He shuddered. "I swear, that scene traumatized me."

"I think it traumatized a couple of entire generations." Blowing out a breath, I shook my head as I gazed at the water again. "With as much as Cody loves horses? No. Way."

"Oh yeah, if he's into horses, forget it." He paused. "But I mean, if there's a fantasy movie or something you want to pre-screen for him, I won't be upset if you want to do it while we're hanging out."

I turned to him, the innocent look on his face making me laugh. "To help me check them for age appropriateness for my son?"

"Well, yeah. Two sets of eyes are better than one, you know? Like if you want to show him *Willow*, or *Labyrinth*, or *The Dark Crystal*..."

"He loves *The Dark Crystal*."

"Damn."

I slid my hand over the small of Brent's back. "But I haven't watched it in a while. It probably wouldn't hurt to give it another look. Just in case I missed something."

"See? Now you're thinking."

Chuckling, I lifted my chin and stole a quick kiss. "I'm sure we can work something out."

"Awesome." We exchanged grins.

"I really should pick up that book soon. He wants me to read it to him when we're done with the one we're reading now."

"You still read to him?" Brent studied me, his expression curious but not judgy. "That's really cool. I think my parents stopped when I was like five."

"Truth be told, I think he wanted to stop around the time he was eight or so, but then the divorce happened, and he suddenly wanted it religiously." I paused, debating if I should say more, and decided to add, "I'm glad he did. I think it's been good for both of us."

"Oh, I bet." Brent straightened a bit and leaned over his hands on the railing. "That's great that you guys have something like that. To help you both adapt."

"I'll take every little bit of help I can get, believe me."

He just nodded. After a moment, he glanced at his phone, then sighed as he pocketed it and turned to me. "I guess we should get back to the wine bar. You're supposed to go onstage soon."

"Yeah, probably." He was right, but he was also fucking gorgeous in the light of the setting sun, and I…couldn't quite make myself leave yet. We still had time. Not much, but time. Sliding my hand over his lower back, I quietly said, "We don't have to rush."

Brent moistened his lips, eyes flicking toward my mouth as he faced me. "But you'll be late."

"Nah." I pulled him in a little closer. "We won't be that long."

"We won't?"

We exchanged grins, and we were still grinning when our lips met, but only for a second. Lips softening, we wrapped our arms around each other. I forgot all about the lake and the view and the sunset. I was vaguely aware of the rattle of a bicycle flying past us, but I didn't even open my eyes. Brent's long, gentle kiss pulled my focus away from anything and everything, though I did keep an ear out for anyone who might want to harass us. A couple of queer guys being affectionate in public couldn't be too careful.

Mostly, though, I was just lost in Brent. On some level, I knew this probably wasn't in line with everything we'd agreed to be, but was anything we'd done? I was pretty sure we were friends with benefits. Maybe a slightly cuddlier version of fuck buddies.

But the way we were kissing right then? The way my heart was going wild as Brent cradled the back of my neck and gently explored my mouth?

It sure didn't feel casual. It just felt like…*us*. And I loved it.

Brent was the first to pull away. "We should…" He licked his slightly swollen lips. "We should get back to the wine bar. You're supposed to be onstage soon."

"Right. Yeah. We should go."

"We should."

"Mmhmm. We will."

And we would.

In a minute.

By the skin of my teeth, I made it onstage in time. Tanner looked mildly annoyed when I came through the door in a flurry of apologies and explanations. When he saw Brent coming in behind me, though, he just chuckled and rolled his eyes, and he didn't say a word.

I quickly tuned my guitar, took a few swallows of water, and went up to the stage to start my set.

The crowd had thinned a little in the time we'd been gone, and I didn't mind. I just liked playing here, and as a bonus, the people who did come usually tipped well. It was rare for someone to get drunk enough to heckle. And hey, with a small audience, there'd be fewer people to notice if I tripped over my own lyrics or forgot how to play guitar.

I had enough songs in my repertoire that I rotated some in and out. That way the regulars didn't hear the same set every night and I didn't get bored repeating the same lyrics ad nauseam. A few, though, were crowd pleasers, especially the ones that dug down and scraped raw nerves, and I always sang them, even on nights when it was hard to get the lyrics past the lump in my throat.

Tonight, the lump wasn't there. The songs didn't sting like they usually did.

"The river runs; doesn't ask for more," I sang for the millionth time on this stage. "Doesn't ask for the rain to fall."

Usually it was like prodding at a bruise—not excruciating, but definitely painful. Tonight, it felt more like I was telling the story of a breakup that had happened in high school. I knew it had hurt in the moment, and it had taken a long time to get over, but the pain was as distant a memory now as the breakup itself.

"A steady pace can break through stone," the song went on. "Gentle water's gonna bring you home."

The divorce had barely been finalized, and part of me was still reeling from being blindsided. Tonight, though, all of that felt as far in the past as our wedding. The hurt and confusion of the last eighteen months seemed as distant as the nerves and excitement of that day.

Was I finally starting to get over Ashley for good? Or was I just distracted by Brent? It could have been a little of both, but whatever it was, it beat the hell out of that shitty feeling that had been a constant companion ever since the words *"I want a divorce"* had turned my world on its ass. I'd take it.

After a few more songs, I wrapped up my set, and the small crowd applauded politely as I stepped off the stage. I gave Brent a "just a minute" gesture, then went into the storage room to put my guitar in its case. With my instrument safely stowed, I joined Brent at the bar.

While I took a swig from a bottle of water, Brent swirled his wine and tilted it toward the stage. "I never did ask you before. Those songs—Are they covers?"

I shook my head. "No. I wrote all of them."

His eyebrows rose. "Really? Wow." He sipped the wine, then put down the glass. "Usually when I hear people perform in places like this, all they're doing is covers."

"Oh, I've done my share of covers. This stuff"—I gestured over my shoulder at the stage—"is mostly what I wrote while I was going through my divorce."

"Wow. You ever thought about recording them?"

My face heated up, and I shrugged. "I don't know. Maybe someday. Right now, it's just nice to be singing again."

Brent opened his mouth to say something, but right then, someone appeared beside us. I looked up, and I grinned as I shook hands with Colin, a semi-regular I'd quickly become friends with since starting at Vino.

"Hey," I said. "How's it going?"

"Good, good." He turned to Brent and extended his hand. "Colin. Hope I'm not interrupting."

"Nah, you're fine." Brent shook his hand. "I'm Brent."

"Nice to meet you." Colin gestured over his shoulder toward the seating area. "I'm hanging out here with some buddies. You guys want to join us?"

I turned to Brent and silently asked what he thought.

Brent tensed a little, looking uneasy as he glanced back and forth between us. I was about to say never mind, we didn't have to, but then he shrugged. "Sure. Yeah. We can do that."

I arched an eyebrow. "You sure?"

He considered it for a second, then nodded. "Yeah. I'm down." He looked at Colin. "Where to?"

"Awesome! Come on." Colin led us toward a table where he'd been sitting with four other guys, two of whom I didn't recognize.

Voice low, I asked, "You don't mind if we stick around for a while?"

"Nah, I'm good." Brent smiled, though there was a hint of nerves and shyness in his eyes. "Just, uh, haven't socialized in a while. But I'm good."

I was hesitant, but I trusted his judgment, so we followed Colin. At the table, everyone made room as we pulled up a couple of chairs. I introduced him to everyone I knew, and Colin filled us in on everyone else.

As Brent sat down, I stayed standing. "I'll go get us drink refills and something to eat."

"Okay, perfect."

"What do you want to drink?"

His lips quirked. "You know what? Just a Coke, since I'm driving."

"Yeah, me too." I leaned down to kiss him lightly, then headed up to the bar.

I gave the order to Rainn, and as he poured our Cokes, he dropped his voice to a conspiratorial whisper. "So when did you start seeing him? He's *cute*."

"I, um..." Why was my first instinct to say we weren't seeing each other? I wasn't embarrassed of him, and even if we weren't, strictly speaking, boyfriends, we *were* seeing each other. So I smiled. "Not too long ago. It's kind of a new thing."

"Well done." He winked as he handed me our glasses. "Food will be out in a few."

"Thanks."

I returned to the table, and I was just sitting down beside Brent when Colin wagged a finger at him. "Wait, I recognize you. Aren't you Brent Weyland? The hockey player?"

Brent smiled, if a little halfheartedly. "Yeah, but I don't play anymore. Had to retire last year."

"Oh, right! I heard about that." Colin cringed. "Car crash, wasn't it?"

Brent nodded. "Drunk fucking fan, ironically."

"Jesus." Ian said. "Does that count as a hockey-related injury?"

With a bitter laugh, Brent shrugged. "I mean, it ended my hockey career, but an actual hockey injury probably wouldn't have hurt quite as much." He paused. "Well, maybe it would have, but…"

Colin gave an amused huff. "It probably would have, with the way you boys play. I mean, no offense, but I think you hockey players are nuts." He shook his head. "Going a million miles an hour, on ice, wearing skinny little blades under your feet? *No,* thank you."

Brent snorted. "Okay, when you put it like that, we do sound crazy. But you kind of have to be to play hockey, so…" He half-shrugged. "I guess the shoe fits. Skinny little blades and all."

Everyone at the table laughed, and Ian raised his glass and said, "You're braver than I am."

"I gotta ask." Colin put down his drink. "You guys are wearing tons of pads out there, but I mean… That shit still has to hurt, right? When you get hit by pucks or each other or whatever?"

"Eh, depends on what hits you, where, and how hard. Like if some asshole hits me in the shin with his stick, I feel it, but it doesn't hurt *that* much. If he hits me in the mouth?" Brent grimaced.

"In the *mouth*?" Ian put a hand to his own mouth like he had sympathy pain. "Tell me you don't have experience."

"I do." Brent pointed at his front teeth, which looked flawless to me. "Took out two on the top and one on the bottom."

We all shuddered, and I couldn't help pulling my lips between my teeth as if that could ward away the mental image of having three of them knocked out.

"You lost *three* teeth?" Colin whistled. "Whoever fixed it did an amazing job. I'd never have guessed."

Brent laughed. "We had a pretty fucking good dental plan, let's put it that way."

"God, I hope so," Ian said. "Man. Getting teeth knocked out…" He shuddered.

"It's a rough sport," Brent said with a quiet chuckle. "Shit happens."

"Not wrong," Colin said. "You ever seen the video of that guy who took a skate to the throat?" He rubbed his neck and grimaced. "That was horrible."

"Oh yeah." Brent made a face. "Our goalie said he had nightmares about that."

Ian squirmed, looking a little green. "I don't even play hockey, and *I* had nightmares about it."

That got a laugh out of everyone.

Right then, Murph, the adorable twink who worked at the wine bar, sauntered up with the nachos I'd ordered for Brent and me. As we dug in, the conversation kept wandering, and I couldn't remember the last time I'd been this content.

Vino and Veritas had been an escape for me in the first months I'd lived alone after the divorce. The atmosphere was warm and relaxing, and on nights when I didn't have Cody, staying here after my set meant I didn't have to be alone in the construction site I called home. Chilling with some friends—old and new—was always a welcome change, and having Brent here? Bonus. Especially the more he relaxed into the conversation. Maybe he just had a shy streak. Hadn't I noticed that the night we'd met?

As the evening went on, he was still kind of shy, but he was peeking out of his shell. And he didn't seem to mind talking about hockey; I'd worried that would be a raw nerve for him, but at least for tonight, it wasn't. He laughed easily, and he listened more than he talked.

At one point, I leaned over. "You having a good time?"

His smile sent a rush of heat through me, and he slid his hand over my leg. "I'm having a great time."

I put my hand over his.

I was having a great time too, and even though I knew it would, I hoped this evening wouldn't end.

Later on, as we settled onto my couch, I asked, "Was that story about your teeth true?"

Brent nodded. "Yep. I think there's a picture floating around out there somewhere of me spitting blood and teeth on the ice."

I shuddered and made a strangled noise. "Oh God."

He chuckled. "Yeah. That was a shitty night. At least he waited until *after* I'd scored before he hit me in the face."

"You scored that night?"

"Mmhmm. First pro goal and first time losing teeth, all within about half an hour of each other." He laughed with some actual feeling. "It was a hell of a night, let me tell you."

"Jesus. No kidding." I squirmed in my chair. "I think the threat of losing teeth would've scared me away from hockey if I'd ever thought about playing."

"Eh, it's not that bad. I mean, I played with a *lot* of guys who have gold teeth, gaps, snaggle teeth, or suspiciously perfect teeth from having work done. And I've chipped teeth, bitten my tongue, cracked a filling. So yeah, it's a thing, and it's a risk when you play. But I didn't *lose* any teeth until I'd been playing…" His eyes lost focus as if he were doing the math. "Twenty years? Something like that?"

"And then you lost three in one go." I gave him a thumbs-up. "Really selling the sport, Brent."

He snorted.

"Don't you guys wear mouthguards?"

"Oh yeah. But if someone hits you hard enough in the mouth…" He shrugged.

"Christ. What did that do to the rest of your face?"

He tilted his head back and gestured below his lip, and for the first time, I noticed the barely visible scar extending down the side of his chin. Lowering his chin again, he said, "It was a lot worse for a while, but I had some plastic surgery done during the off season." He blushed, and sheepishly added, "Every time I saw it in the mirror, it made my teeth hurt all over again."

"Can't blame you." I caressed his cheek, and my fingertip ran over one of the two more prominent scars on his face. "Are these from the accident?"

Swallowing, Brent nodded. "Yeah. I might get rid of those eventually too, but they're less visible than the one by my mouth was. And the ones in my hair pretty much don't show up at all."

"In your—Oh, from the glass?"

Another nod. "I'm kind of surprised the hair didn't come in white, but I'll take it."

"Yeah, they're not noticeable at all."

"Unlike these two." He gestured at the ones on his face. "At least they're not as dark anymore."

"No, they're barely noticeable unless the light hits them just right."

"That's encouraging." He paused, then shook himself. "Anyway. Enough about all my hockey tattoos." Our eyes met, and we both chuckled.

The conversation wandered, and we talked a bit more about my music, and about Brent's plans to unpack his house one of these days, and about Murph, who we both agreed was cute as fuck. Now that it was just us, Brent was looser and more talkative, as if the crowd had intimidated him, but he was more comfortable with me. He'd peeked out of his shell with my friends, though.

After a while, we went into the kitchen to find something to eat. As I rummaged around, Brent said, "So, hey, I was thinking about what you said about your house. How you haven't had time to work on it."

I looked over my shoulder. His gaze was fixed on the hideous backsplash. As I pulled a couple of beers from the fridge, I said, "Yeah?"

"Yeah, and…" He looked around the room for a moment, then cleared his throat and turned to me, his expression a little shy. "I, um…I actually know how to do a lot of that stuff. From when my dad flipped houses—Anyway, I have a fair amount of time on my hands these days."

"But what about…" I hesitated. "Your hip? And your back? And you're still moving into your place, aren't you?"

"Yeah, but helping you out would get me *out* of my house, which I think I would do me a ton of good." He pursed his lips. "Okay, there's a lot of stuff I can't do, but…" He motioned toward the ugly backsplash. "I can help with some of the lighter things. And as long as you're not in a huge hurry, I can pace myself. In fact, it'll probably help me with my conditioning anyway. My physical therapist has been after me to move around more and push myself a bit. So…" He gestured around the kitchen.

I thought about it. As much as I didn't want to admit that I was in over my head and needed help, my ego wasn't going to fix this house. Letting someone else take over a few of the minor, tedious projects would get me closer to finished, and I might actually have a home instead of a construction zone with furniture.

Meeting his gaze, I took a deep breath. "You wouldn't mind? I could use the help, and I'd be happy to pay for—"

"Nah." He shook his head, looking around. "Like I said, it'll get me out of my house and give me something to focus on. Maybe that'll break me out of my funk enough that I can make some progress on my own place." He turned to me, and there it was again—that shy smile that made my knees weak. "Money's not an issue."

I laughed dryly. "Must be nice."

"Eh." He shrugged, the smile fading as he looked away. "At least I still have *something* besides interesting X-rays."

"Oh. Yeah. I can imagine." I paused, debating if I really wanted someone else to take over the projects I'd intended to get done myself.

Reality check, Jon: if he doesn't get it done, will you?

I turned to him. "If you do have the time and it won't cause you more pain..."

"I'd be happy to do it."

Our eyes met, and we both smiled.

"Just tell me what you need done, and..." Brent shrugged. "I can help you make some headway."

"Great. Thanks." I opened the beers and handed him one. After we'd clinked the bottles together, I said, "It would be really helpful. And by the way, thanks for indulging me tonight. Hanging out with my friends, I mean."

"Nah." He smiled, sliding his free hand around my waist. "It was nice, to be honest. Being social again. I mean, you wouldn't know it, but I used to be the life of the party. I'm not quite there yet, and I don't know if I'll ever be again, but tonight, I felt a bit more like my old self." He looked in my eyes. "So, thanks for letting me tag along."

I leaned in for a soft kiss. "Tag along? I was spending the evening with you one way or the other."

He just smiled, then curved his hand behind my neck and kissed me again.

And as we sank into each other, I tried not to think about how we didn't feel like friends with benefits tonight.

12

BRENT

Ever since the first night I'd slipped into the hot tub with Jon, I could not stop thinking about doing it again. And we had a few times, but that conversation we'd had about him fucking me over the edge? I couldn't get it out of my head.

I also couldn't think of many other places that would be as comfortable to cautiously experiment and see what kinds of sex I could handle in this new body. The seats were cushioned and didn't slide. The bottom was textured so feet wouldn't slip. The hot water—even if it wasn't cranked up *too* hot—relaxed my muscles and tendons.

If there was anywhere we could try pushing the envelope and seeing what I could handle, that was it.

Today, I'd been feeling pretty good. Pain was a steady two or three, which was about as good as it ever was.

I want this. Tonight.

Especially since his custody week had just ended again, and I hadn't seen him in several days. Now that he was on his way over, I was restless with hunger. Hopefully he'd be game, because hell if I knew when my pain would let off enough for us to try again. We'd been exchanging flirty and even downright racy texts all day, so I was pretty sure he'd be in the mood. I hoped he was.

Please…

When I opened my front door and met Jon's gaze? Oh, those

prayers had been answered. One look in his dark eyes, and my knees went weak. And that was before he stepped inside, wrapped his arm around my waist, and claimed a deep, hungry kiss as he kicked the door shut behind him.

"Do you have any idea," he murmured between kisses, "how hard it is to concentrate or drive when I've got a phone full of dirty texts from you?"

I laughed, sliding my hands into his back pockets. "Does that mean you want me to stop sending you dirty texts?"

"You better not." He kissed me again, letting it linger.

"Mmm, well, as long as you're horny..." I gestured over my shoulder toward the back deck. "Pain isn't too bad tonight. And I turned the temperature down on the hot tub."

Jon's eyes widened, and I swore I could feel the ripple of arousal go through him. "Oh yeah?"

"Uh-huh." I kneaded his firm ass through his jeans.

He didn't argue, and when he kissed me this time, he left no doubt that he was completely onboard.

After one more long kiss in the hallway, we crossed the living room and went outside to the back deck. Neither of us wasted any time getting out of our clothes, and I couldn't help grinning when his gaze landed on the condoms and lube I'd left within reach. Meeting my eyes, he licked his lips, and without a word, we both slipped into the hot water.

As eager as I was to live out that fantasy of letting him fuck me over the edge of the hot tub, I didn't want to rush this. I just loved making out with him. Every time we were together, I was amazed all over again at how much I'd missed being touched by someone who wasn't trying to analyze or repair my injuries. I'd been touched a lot in the last year if you counted EMTs, doctors, surgeons, and physical therapists. Touched intimately? By someone who wanted me? That had become one hell of a novelty, and I hoped Jon didn't get bored with my need to draw out foreplay for ages.

If he did get bored, he didn't let it show. We made out in the hot water for what felt like hours, hands sliding all over skin while we kissed like this was the first time. It went on until I was so relaxed I was nearly boneless.

Eventually, Jon broke the kiss and looked in my eyes. "So, you want to try it? Over the side?"

I nodded vigorously, my whole body tingling with the anticipation of being fucked for the first time in forever. "Yeah."

Jon grinned and leaned in for another kiss. "Turn around," he murmured. "I'll get the condom on."

I bit back a whimper. It was tempting to jump up and get into position, but I moved slowly and carefully, not wanting to jostle some bitchy joint or tendon out of whack and ruin our evening.

He stood, and then I did, and I paused just in time to meet his eyes as he tore the condom wrapper. My heart was going a million miles an hour now, and the sight of his hard cock made my mouth water.

God, please, don't let my body fail me now.

Moving carefully, I put my left knee on the seat. Then I leaned over my forearms, keeping as much weight as I could off my bad leg, and pulled the other knee onto the seat. The padded seats were soft, and they also had some tooth, so I wasn't worried my knee would suddenly slide out from under me, and after a little shifting and adjusting, I found a comfortable position. With any luck, it would stay that way.

He cupped my ass. "You good?"

"Uh-huh."

The water moved around me, probably from him coming closer, and he ran his hand up my spine. "You sure this is comfortable for you?"

I nodded. "It's good. Just, um, don't grab on to my hip or anything."

"Noted." His palm slid down my back. "Now the fun part—getting you ready for me."

And holy hell, Jon did not fuck around when it came to prep. After spending so much time kissing him, I shouldn't have been surprised that his tongue was magic at this too. Or that he'd use his fingers to tease my balls while his tongue made dizzying circles around my hole. I kind of wanted to tell him we shouldn't spend a ton of time on prep because I didn't know how long my hip would hold out, but damn, this felt so good I didn't want him to stop.

"Jesus, Jon," I moaned. "That feels so…" Eh, fuck words. He knew what I meant. He kept at it too, and I had to really hold on to the side of the tub to keep from melting into the water.

After ages, he stopped what he was doing, and I almost whimpered in protest, but then the lube bottle clicked. Oh. *Oh*. Right, the whole point of this was so we could fuck, and yeah, he could do that. Like now.

Except he wasn't done teasing me. His finger made the same little circles his tongue had, then pressed in gently. I was so relaxed, it didn't take much for him to press inside, and goose bumps prickled my skin as I closed my eyes and pressed my forehead against my arm. I hadn't been penetrated in so long, the sensations were overwhelming and so damn good, even from a single finger. If his finger had me this turned on, I could only imagine how amazing his cock would feel.

C'mon, I wanted to say. *Hurry up and* fuck *me.*

Oh, but he wasn't in a hurry to do anything. He kept teasing me with his finger. Then he added a second and kept right on teasing, sliding his fingers in and out and crooking them just right, and…

"Fuck," I breathed.

"Something wrong?" From his tone, he knew there wasn't a damn thing wrong.

I moistened my lips. "I've… bottomed before. You don't…" *Oh fuck, touch that spot again.* "You don't have to go this slow."

"Oh, I know I don't." There was a wicked grin in his voice, and his breath cooled my shoulder just before he planted a soft kiss on my skin. "We both know you're ready for me." He paused as he slowly withdrew his fingers, and as he pushed them back in, he purred, "But half the fun is teasing you."

I moaned with both arousal and frustration, pressing my forehead harder into my arm as he kept fingering me. This was so damn good —the slow strokes, the gentle stretch—and I couldn't decide if I wanted him to keep doing it, or if I wanted him to fuck me already.

"Jon…"

"Hmm?" The grin in his voice was so, so evil. "Something wrong?"

I moaned. "Nothing… Just…" I rocked back against him, careful not to aggravate my hip but also eager for more penetration. "*Fuck.*"

"Mmm, this your way of saying you want more?"

More? Yes. Yes, more. I nodded and made a sound that I hoped conveyed the same.

Jon's fingers slid free. I swore, gripping the tub's edge as anticipation threatened to shake me to pieces. The click of the lube bottle and the sound of him stroking some onto his dick had my head spinning and my heart racing. God, yes, I needed him. Like right now.

He didn't keep me waiting. He'd barely put the lube on the edge of the tub before he rested a hand on my uninjured hip and guided himself to me. By this point, he had me so slick and relaxed, he pushed in easily, and the long, slow slide of his cock along with his low, throaty groan had me holding on to the side of the tub so I didn't melt right then and there.

"How does this feel?" he panted.

"Good." I struggled to speak. "Just... God, like that."

He moaned, and he kept riding me just like that—deep, slow, perfect. In my past life, this was when I'd have begged a man to start going fast and hard, but I couldn't handle that anymore. And this was... This was sexy as hell. Not just because it was what my body could handle. Even if I were still in peak hockey condition, this would have been amazing, and the fact that I could handle it—could enjoy it—despite my ever-present pain? God, I kind of wanted to cry from pure relief.

There are things I can do that don't feel like someone's handling me with kid gloves.

I can still enjoy sex.

I can enjoy a whole new level of sex that—Jesus Christ, how have I never had anyone fuck me like this before?

I didn't even care that I wasn't hard right now. I was so deliriously turned on, and so mesmerized by Jon's long, fluid strokes, that nothing else even registered. Nothing except the addictive slide of his cock and the warmth of his hands on my skin. I'd always loved bottoming, but it had never turned me on like *this*. Because it had been so long? Because I'd convinced myself I'd never do this again? Because Jon really was *this* good? Oh, who cared?

Jon held on to my waist as he picked up just a little bit of speed. "This okay?" He sounded like he was speaking through clenched teeth.

"Yeah. Yeah, it's good."

He moaned softly, fingers twitching against my sides. "Jesus…"

"You gonna come?" Just the thought sent electricity right through me.

"Uh-huh," he panted. "Oh God, you feel amazing." Yeah, he was close, and I could almost *feel* his impending release, and I had the space of a heartbeat to remember that a lot of guys I'd been with tended to lose control when they came, thrusting deep and hard as their orgasms took over.

Oh no, what if Jon—

"Fuck!" His hips jerked and his hands tightened on my sides, but he didn't slam himself into me or pull me back on to his dick. He gasped, and I thought he swore again, and his whole body jerked again. Then he relaxed, leaning over me and resting a hand on the edge of the tub beside my elbow. "Oh my God."

"Uh-huh. Seriously." I hadn't come, and I didn't care. I felt amazing.

I didn't know how he'd stayed in control like that, especially not in the throes of an orgasm, but he had, and that gave me a whole new rush of exhilarating relief—I could enjoy bottoming, and I could trust Jon to be mindful even while he was coming. I hadn't even realized I was worried about it until just before Jon had come, and I could only imagine how much more relaxed I'd be next time.

And dear God, please let there be a next time.

We left our towels in the bathroom and lay in the middle of my bed as we tangled up in a long, lazy kiss.

"That was fun," he murmured.

"Uh-huh. We should do it again."

"Yeah, we should." He drew back and met my eyes. "It wasn't painful for you, was it?"

"No. It was really good. Especially the way you were going slow, and…" I shivered.

Jon grinned. "Good, because that was seriously hot for me too. Especially after I didn't see you for…" He kissed me again, and I couldn't remember the last time I'd been this blissed out. I hadn't come, but I'd been fucked, and I'd been fucked *good*, and the warmth of Jon's skin and the gentleness of his kiss made me dizzy.

In the hot tub, there'd been some pain, but that was to be expected. When *wasn't* there pain? What mattered was that I'd bottomed for him, and it had been amazing. He'd been careful and gentle. My body had held out instead of deciding to throw a pain tantrum at an inopportune moment. It was as close as I was probably ever going to get to the sex I remembered from my past life, and I… really couldn't complain. Different? Yes. Satisfying? *Hell* yes.

Still kissing me, Jon nudged me onto my back. Then he slid his hand down my chest and my stomach, and when he started stroking me, I broke the kiss with a gasp. Only for a second, though—I found his mouth with mine again, and we kissed lazily but hungrily as he kept teasing me with his hand. I wasn't hard, and I doubted that was going to change, but what he was doing felt good. He wasn't stroking the way he would if he were giving me a handjob. More like massaging. And…fuck. It felt good. Really, really good. I was too turned on to even be self-conscious about my inability to get it up, and I lost myself in his gentle touch and his long, mind-bending kiss.

"Like that?" he asked, lips barely leaving mine.

"Yeah." I carefully rocked my hips—not enough to aggravate my injuries, but enough to push my cock against his palm. The gentle friction, the long, sexy kiss, just being touched and wanted and not worrying that my body was going to scare him away—this was all heady and dizzying and seriously amazing.

Jon broke the kiss and started on my neck.

"Mmph." I bit my lip. "Fuck…"

"That good?" His breath was hot against my throat, and I couldn't help rubbing my cock harder against his hand.

"Y-yeah. It's good."

His lips curved into a grin, and then he nipped the side of my neck before he continued kissing his way up toward my jaw. "I could do this all night."

I closed my eyes and arched under him. "Me too."

And I didn't think he was kidding. I had no idea how long we went on, his lips on my neck, my mouth, my neck again, all while he rubbed my cock and drove me wild. I even got a little bit hard. Not nearly enough to do anything with—sure as hell not enough to top him—but more than before.

Jon started getting hard too, so I stroked him, and we fell into a rhythm—hands moving in unison on each other's dicks while we made out. Nothing rushed. Nothing frantic. Just touch and heat and sensation, and the longer we went on, the higher I was. I lost track of time, and I forgot to be self-conscious about my body and my mostly soft dick, and I just surrendered to this hot, decadent thing we were doing in my bed.

And then…

Oh God.

It took a minute, but I recognized the feeling. Was it… Oh fuck, was I going to come? Because this was how I'd felt in my old life when an orgasm was in sight. Not quite inevitable yet, nowhere near the point of no return, but heading that way, and fuck, it felt amazing.

My breath came out in a ragged sigh. "Keep… Oh fuck. Keep doing that, and you'll… You might make me come."

"Yeah?" The interest and excitement in that single syllable made my toes curl.

"Yeah, I…" I closed my eyes. "Oh God… I think I'm gonna…"

"Me too," he murmured, thrusting into my hand. "Ungh, you feel so…" He let his head fall beside mine, and the hot huffs of breath against my shoulder drove me almost as high as the delicious friction on my dick. We were still slow, still languid, so we didn't get tired as we went on and on and he took me higher and higher. I was dizzy and shaking and so, so close, and—

"Fuck!" I gasped, my hips jerking, and even the sharp bolt of pain wasn't enough to distract me from the rush of pure ecstasy as I came for the first time in I didn't know how long. I hadn't even *wanted* sex in months, and now it was like releasing a whole year's worth of pent-up stress and need.

With a blissed-out sigh, I relaxed back onto the bed, and Jon grinned down at me. "That was hot."

"Uh-huh. You're telling me." I glanced down. I'd definitely had an orgasm—a strong one, too—but there was no cum. Hadn't I read somewhere that that was a thing? Guys could come without being hard and without ejaculating? Apparently so. Fine. Whatever. I felt too good to care.

"Damn," I panted. "I guess I *can* come without getting hard."

He kissed me gently. "I guess so."

I realized I'd stopped stroking him, and when I started again, he gasped, a full-body shiver running through him as he closed his eyes and whispered, "*Jesus*."

I bit my lip and kept jerking him off, still flying high from my own climax and eager to give him the same release. His cock thickened in my hand, and his breathing fell to sharp, shallow gasps, and as the crevices between his eyebrows deepened, I held my breath and pumped him for all I was worth.

"Don't stop," he murmured, fucking into my fist. "That's it, baby. Don't… Don't stop. I'm…" A shudder jolted his whole body, and he gasped as cum landed on my hand and stomach.

With a sigh, he slumped over me, trembling and panting. I kissed his temple, and for a moment, we just lay there, basking in the heat of each other's bodies and the satisfaction of our orgasms.

Eventually, we separated long enough to clean up and, while we were at it, we got ready for bed. After all, I doubted either of us was staying awake much longer. Might as well brush our teeth and turn off the lights as long as we were up.

"So," he said, "any chance you'll keep the hot tub at that temperature?"

I laughed, ignoring a twinge in my hip and cuddling closer to him. "If it means you'll fuck me like that, you better believe it."

"Any time." He pressed a kiss to my forehead. "Just say the word."

I smiled into the darkness and closed my eyes. "I'll keep that in mind. And you know, the more we do this—even if we're just fooling around like we did in here—the more I feel like my sex life isn't completely doomed." I ran my fingers down the middle of his chest. "It'll probably always be different from what it was before, but it's not over."

He smiled, caressing my cheek. "No, it's not over. I'm sure there's going to be a learning curve where we figure out how to do this without hurting you. I'm game to learn it if you are."

Warmth rushed through me, and I lifted my head to kiss him softly. I didn't know what to say, but I hoped I was conveying how excited I was that we *could* do this, and how grateful I was that he wanted to.

I could so get used to this. Not just sex that was more pleasure than frustration, but the relaxed, playful banter. Being comfortable together. As much as it could be under the circumstances, sex with Jon was *easy*. Everything with Jon was easy.

Pain was going to be a part of my reality forever. Hockey was now relegated to my past.

But tonight, I had a little more hope that there would be a lot more to my future than living in pain and grieving the past.

13

BRENT

The last couple of nights had been amazing. Just amazing. Last night, there'd been the hot tub. Before that, there'd been Friday night at the wine bar, and I'd sat with his friends during his performance, and then we'd all hung out after, and I'd been among people who were laidback and chill and knew who I was but didn't give me grief or pity for my hockey career being over. It was exactly the kind of socializing I'd shunned in the months before Ethan had dragged me out to Vino and Veritas the first time, followed by more quiet downtime with Jon and a blissful night of sleeping beside him. It had been exactly what I'd needed.

And on the heels of an evening like that, Sunday was a bigger gut punch than it usually was.

Because Sunday meant my non-negotiable weekly obligation: dinner with my parents.

They'd been out of town the last couple of weeks, so I'd been off the hook. Now they were back, and I was expected as always, and… ugh. An hour after leaving Jon's place, and with all my usual trepidation, I parked in my parents' driveway, and I let the engine idle for a moment while I debated backing out and bailing on dinner. I knew I'd eventually cave and go in, but that didn't stop me from having this internal *what if I didn't?* debate every single time.

I could barely stomach Dad's criticism and Mom's pity, but the two of them had been lifesavers during my recovery. They'd been awesome when I'd been selling my old house and moving back to Vermont, and they'd let me stay here with them until I'd closed on the new place. I was grateful for all of that and didn't want them to think otherwise.

But goddamn, these dinners could be an *ordeal*.

I glanced at the cane leaning against the passenger seat. Today was one of those days when I really, really should have been swallowing my pride and using the damn thing, especially since my parents had stairs and a couple of rambunctious dogs. Even without the stairs and dogs, my hip was killing me right now. Had been since I'd gotten out of bed. If I tried knuckling through and hobbling around on my own, I'd be sore as hell tonight. *Extra* sore if I stumbled over a step or a dog, or my knee or hip just gave out on me like they sometimes did. Yay for tendon damage and all that other bullshit.

But I'd only recently made peace with even needing the cane. It had taken a long time to understand that it was a mobility aid, not a sign of weakness or surrender, and I still had a ways to go in that department. I hadn't quite learned how to stomach being seen with it, and more than anything in the world, I *hated* letting my *dad* see me with it. This evening was going to be miserable enough as it was. So which was the lesser of two evils—pretending I wasn't in pain and praying I could move around unaided, or giving my dad more ammunition to criticize me?

With a sigh, I shut off the truck. I continued my internal debate for a few more seconds, but then the front door opened, and my dad stepped out onto the porch.

All right. No cane.

I sent up a little prayer, took the keys out of the ignition, and carefully stepped out of the truck.

As I headed up the walk, Dad eyed my truck, the faintest smirk appearing on his lips. When he met my gaze, he sighed and shook his head.

God. We weren't even in the house and it was already starting?

Apparently so, because as I came up the steps, he motioned toward my truck. "You really like that thing? It's a hell of a downgrade, don't you think?"

I was seriously getting good at not rolling my eyes even when I desperately wanted to. Keeping my voice even, I said, "It's fine. And it'll be a lot better in the winter than the car was."

He glanced at me, his eyes snidely suggesting I was probably too scared to leave the house during the winter anyway. I swallowed my frustration. Oh, he was right—the thought of venturing out when it was icy scared the hell out of me. But I really hoped he wasn't going to give me more shit about being a hockey player who was suddenly afraid of the ice.

You'd be afraid of it too if you'd seen my X-rays.

Fortunately, he just quietly continued into the house.

My stomach turned. More and more I was convinced that my body would return to normal long before my dad ever stopped getting on my case about all the ways I'd adjusted my life to accommodate the injury. And my body was *never* returning to normal.

I focused on carefully climbing the stairs to the top floor of my parents' split-level house. I refused to let them see how much it hurt, though I couldn't hide how much it made me sweat. Dad sometimes gave me grief about how that meant I clearly wasn't training hard enough, which was why I was still hobbling around instead of playing hockey.

Not now, Dad. I really don't have it in me to explain that the sweat is from pain, not exertion.

Well, not just *exertion.*

Damn it, why didn't I buy them that ranch-style house Mom wanted instead of this one? No good deed goes unpunished, does it?

I hadn't even cleared the top step before Dad said, "I still think you should've kept the car."

I gritted my teeth. At least he wasn't harping on me about the stairs, but apparently I needed to be specific in the future when I asked the universe to keep him off a particular subject. "Why?" I asked as coolly as I could. "So it could collect dust in my garage?"

Ah, there it was—the disappointed Dad sigh. I was pretty sure I'd heard that more in the past year than I had in my entire life, and that said *a lot.*

He looked at me, head tilted just right to make him look extra condescending. "You invested a lot of money in that thing. I'm sure you sold it at a loss, didn't you?"

"Would've been a bigger loss if I'd bought that Lambo," I grumbled.

We scowled at each other. We'd both had opinions about which car I bought, and even though it was my car, he'd never missed an opportunity to give me crap about the Ferrari. Who knew I could disappoint my father by spending my own damn money on the over-priced sports car I wanted instead of the one he thought I should have?

In the end, it turned out Ferraris held their value better than Lamborghinis, even if it did depreciate a little, so at least I hadn't lost quite as much money when I'd sold it.

And really, it didn't matter which car I'd bought or how much I'd sold it for. Thanks to what happened to my Maserati, I couldn't have driven the Lamborghini any more than I could drive the Ferrari, so what was there to argue about?

He took a breath, clearly about to say something, but I put up my hand.

"Dad. The car is sold, okay? It's done."

"Honey, leave him alone." Mom appeared in the kitchen doorway. "Honestly, you two and cars." She rolled her eyes the way I wished I could. "Would you go check the grill, please?"

Dad huffed quietly and headed for the back deck.

Relieved by the interruption, I hugged my mom. "Hey, Mom."

"Hey." She kissed my cheek, and as she let me go, she looked me up and down. "How are you feeling today?"

"I'm good." It wasn't a lie. I was stressed about being here, but the pain was a bearable dull roar.

"Can I get you a drink?"

"No, no. I'm fine. Thanks."

And thank God she'd derailed my dad. I was so tired of having these conversations with him. I was exhausted just thinking about explaining—again—that no amount of grit, determination, sweat, or hard work would change the fact that my body was never going to fully recover from my injury.

No, I wasn't thrilled about trading a pristine Ferrari 488 Spider for a Chevy S10 pickup. Yes, I missed the hell out of my old cars just like I missed the hell out of playing hockey and living in a body that didn't hurt all the time and functioned the way it was supposed to. But this was the hand I'd been dealt. I needed a vehicle that didn't sit quite so low to the ground, and I couldn't comfortably drive anything with a clutch anymore. Keeping the car had made about as much sense as keeping my stick and skates, and Dad hadn't forgiven me for jettisoning those either.

The sliding glass door opened again, and some shrill yaps and the skitter of claws on linoleum made me smile. I turned to see my parents' three papillons stampeding across the dining room toward me.

"Hey, guys!" Using the back of a chair for support, I leaned down as much as I could, petting the tops of their heads and letting them lick my fingers as they bounced and spun at my feet.

"Why don't we all sit down?" Mom suggested. "I'm sure you could stand to give that hip a rest."

Thank God one of my parents understood. We headed for the living room, but before I could get to the couch, the dogs launched themselves onto it and started bouncing and running in excited circles on the cushions.

Laughing, Mom ordered the dogs to the floor. They all obeyed, sitting on the carpet and wagging their tails so hard their tiny bodies were vibrating.

I sat down, and once I was situated, she said to the dogs, "Okay!"

Immediately, all three of them flew onto the couch and started jumping all over me and the cushions. I laughed, trying not to get slurped in the face as I petted all of them. They were small and lightweight, so especially on a relatively low-pain day, I could handle them jumping on me.

Coming to my parents' house wasn't all bad. My dad's constant criticism was depressing and demoralizing as all hell, but it was a little easier to swallow when these three were so happy to see me. They were happy to see everyone, but whatever. I loved it.

In fact, maybe I needed to get a dog of my own. That would definitely break up the silence and make my house feel less empty. Not something quite as hyper as these three, but some company would be nice. Especially when Jon was at work or with his son.

Jon. Just thinking about him made me smile again. It would be a few hours before I saw him again, but I was already counting down. Wow. Something to look forward to? Damn. That was a weird feeling at Sunday dinner. Usually I left here feeling like utter garbage after my dad reminded me how many ways I'd failed at life and disappointed him. It was hard to be optimistic or enthusiastic about anything after that.

But later this evening, I'd see Jon. And that made today... Well, it was kind of like the ever-present pain. Sometimes it was awful. Sometimes it was bearable. With Jon on the horizon, being in the same room with my dad seemed like when my leg was just aching and annoying instead of those times it hurt so bad I could barely breathe and wanted to throw up. It still sucked, but I could get through it.

The dogs got over their initial excitement at "OMG person!" and finally settled down. Daisy curled up on my lap. Rosie flopped down next to me on her back. Pepper joined my mom in her chair. Dad came in and sat down too, but the dogs didn't really acknowledge him.

Petting Pepper, Mom asked, "How are you feeling these days? In general?"

I shrugged. "Better than when I woke up in the hospital."

"That's good. Right?"

"Definitely."

"How's the pain?"

"Eh. There's good days and bad days. Something always hurts, but my physical therapist is helping a *lot*."

My dad grunted. "Got news for you, kid—pain is part of life. My back never stops hurting after everything my job put it through."

I scowled. Funny how he could still golf and roughhouse with his grandkids. I'd had to give up golf and playing with my nieces and nephews. Quite possibly forever.

Dad went on, "You know, Mario Lemieux's back hurt so bad he couldn't even tie his skates, and he still played." Sighing that disappointed sigh, Dad shook his head. "If your doctors and physical therapists are telling you to give up, then you need to find new ones who will actually *help* you."

I tongued the back of my teeth as I tried to fight back my frustration. "They *are* helping me."

"They're obviously not doing enough. You need a second opinion."

Ugh. I was so tired. Like literally exhausted. Going around in these circles with my father always left me completely drained and ready to collapse, and why the hell hadn't I come up with an excuse not to come over tonight?

Keeping my tone and voice neutral, I said, "I *had* second opinions. And third and fourth opinions. Everyone said the same thing, which is that there is *no way* I'm playing hockey again."

Don't you understand how much it hurts every time I have to say that out loud?

I wasn't even surprised Dad was harping on me about it. I expected it every time I came over. What *did* surprise me was the way my throat ached and my eyes kept threatening to sting. What was wrong with me today? Why was I so damn raw?

Oh. Right. Because this was the first time I'd sat through Dad's disapproval after I'd added "jacked-up sex life" to the list of ways this stupid injury had turned my world on its ass. Thinking about Jon was keeping me afloat and giving me hope that I'd feel better than I did right now, but being with him had also revealed some things about my recovery that I still didn't quite know how to cope with.

As my parents and I carried on talking, and Mom mercifully diverted the conversation to what my brother and sister were up to, I smiled politely and tried to stay engaged. It was tough, though. Yeah, I should've bailed tonight. I tried not to do it too much because it always meant an extra helping of grief and guilt the next Sunday, but it would've been worth it tonight.

I'd spent my entire life, from the time I started skating as a damn toddler, working toward a professional hockey career. I'd pushed through injuries, busted my ass when coaches said I wasn't good enough, and I'd made it. I'd fucking *made it.*

One split-second impact. One perfect storm of angles and speed and someone else's blood alcohol content. One crash. One horrifying realization that something was wrong.

And now my entire world had changed.

Nothing had gone unscathed, from my sex life to my ability to sleep, to being able to drive a manual transmission. Out of all of that, few things hurt like realizing how much my relationship with my dad had soured and how little I could do to fix it.

I looked at Daisy, and her tail started thumping as she wiggled and smiled up at me in that way dogs did. I petted her, which made her tail wag even harder, and she rolled over in my lap, paws flailing and tail going wild. As little as she was, she wouldn't aggravate my injuries. Right then, I kind of didn't care if she did.

At least someone still likes me without my skates on.

14

JON

Brent was someplace else.

We'd been in his bed for a little while, mostly relaxing after we'd spent God knew how long making out and Brent had given me a long, amazing blowjob. I'd thought he was drifting off, but now I realized he was awake. He just...wasn't here. Was he disappointed that we hadn't been able to do more earlier? That I'd gotten off and he hadn't? I'd have been happy to do anything he wanted, whether it got him off or not, but he'd been too sore to continue. So instead, we'd just been lying here. Or at least, I had. There was no telling where he'd been for the last however long.

"Hey." I nudged his arm. "You still with me?"

Brent blinked a few times. Then he met my gaze with a puzzled expression. He must have seen the concern in my eyes, because he sighed and shook himself. "Yeah. Yeah. I'm...yeah." He slid a hand up my side under the covers. "Mind was wandering a bit."

"So I saw. Where was it wandering to?"

He avoided my gaze and gnawed his lip, and I wondered if he wanted to talk about whatever was on his mind. If it was even appropriate for us to be talking about things besides sex and small talk, though that seemed stupid since we'd had plenty of conversations about all kinds of things. Still, this might not be a nerve he wanted to expose right now.

Before I could take the spotlight off him and change the subject, though, he took a deep breath and gazed up at the ceiling.

"So I told you I had dinner at my parents' house tonight. Just like I do most Sundays." He deflated. "And every time I leave, I feel as low as I did when I first got hurt."

Alarm straightened my spine. "Why's that?"

"Mostly because my dad won't let it go."

"Let… Let what go?"

"Hockey." Brent rubbed his eyes. "I swear my dad's having a harder time letting go of my career than I am, and he never lets me forget it."

"Seriously?" I shifted onto my elbow. "If my son were injured so badly he had to stop playing a sport, I'd be more concerned with him being in pain and losing mobility."

"Your son's lucky. My dad…" Brent sighed. "The thing is, he's always wanted a pro athlete in the family. He wanted me to be a pro hockey player, and he had visions of me retiring after like fifteen or twenty seasons with all kinds of championships and records under my belt."

"He's…aware that hockey is physically brutal, right?"

"Yeah." Brent gave another dry, humorless laugh. "But he just always assumed players who retire because of injuries are weak."

"And he hasn't changed his tune about that? Not even after you got hurt in a car crash that could have killed you?"

Shuddering, Brent exhaled sharply. "Are you kidding? I can still walk, so obviously I didn't fuck myself up *that* bad."

I groaned, suppressing the choice words I had about his dad. "He… I mean… It doesn't work that way. I had a patient whose hockey career ended his junior year in college because of a shattered knee. There's… Even if the mind is willing, sometimes the body really can veto things."

"Right? But Dad had a dream, and…" Brent waved a hand. "He had me skating as soon as I could walk and using a stick as soon as I could hold it upright. He literally doesn't know what to do with me if I'm not playing hockey. Especially since it wasn't a hockey injury that ended my career. As if that should matter."

"Wait, you were skating as soon as…" I raised my eyebrows.

"Wow, I knew hockey players usually started young, but were you really that little?"

"Yeah. I actually don't remember learning to skate." He laughed. "My mom sometimes jokes I was skating the day after I took my first steps, and… I mean, she might be right for all I know."

"When did you start playing hockey?"

He seemed to think about it. "My first team was in the Mites league, which is eight and under, and I think I was… five? *Maybe* six? I'd have to ask my parents, to be honest."

"So you learned to play hockey when you were in kindergarten?"

"Oh God, no." He shook his head. "By the time I actually joined a team, I already knew how to play."

I stared at him. "Really?"

"Mmhmm. In fact my mom still has an old picture on the wall of me pushing a puck around when I was… I want to say three." Brent chuckled. "It's kind of a cute picture. That stick must've been like this long." He held up his hands about a foot apart.

I laughed softly too, but couldn't quite mask my uneasiness.

Brent apparently caught it because he tilted his head and asked, "What?"

"Just, um… When exactly did you decide you wanted to play hockey?"

"I couldn't tell you. I've been playing as long as I remember."

Nodding slowly, I asked, "Okay, but when did you decide you wanted to play? And make a career out of it?"

Brent's eyes lost focus for a moment. "I don't remember, honestly."

"Did you ever think about doing anything else?"

He exhaled. "No. And maybe that's why I'm struggling so hard now. I've literally never thought about doing anything except playing hockey. I have a degree just because I needed to go to college to play hockey, and I had to keep my grades up and all that, but there was never any question that I was going to play. If I hadn't made it into the pros, then I'd have coached or something."

My uneasiness didn't budge, and apparently it showed.

"Why?" Brent asked.

"I'm just…" I chewed my lip. Sliding my hand up his arm, I

looked in his crystal blue eyes. "Did you *want* to play hockey professionally? Or did your parents want you to?"

He opened his mouth like he was about to insist that of course he'd wanted to play professionally. Closing his mouth again, he stared up at the ceiling, eyes fixed on nothing before he finally whispered, "I don't know. I don't remember a time when hockey wasn't..." He paused, then added, "I don't remember a time when hockey wasn't my life."

"Or when your dad wasn't expecting it to be your life?"

Brent nodded.

"That explains why he's struggling to let go of your career. It kind of sounds to me like he wanted to live vicariously through you."

"Huh. You're, um... You're probably right, now that you mention it." Brent scratched the back of his neck and sighed. "I've never thought about it before. But now that I am... I mean, my parents pushed my sister into gymnastics too, and my brother was signed up for football and baseball as soon as he was old enough."

"Did they go pro?"

He shook his head. "By the time my sister was in sixth grade, she had stress fractures in her spine. Her doctor told my parents that if she continued with the sport, she was going to do permanent damage to her body. She still has back problems to this day, and she's had like four surgeries on her shoulder."

"And your dad still can't accept that you did permanent damage to your body?"

"Not when I was the last hope for a pro athlete in the family," he grumbled. "And because I did make it after my siblings failed, he figured I'd retire after an awesome career." I laughed humorlessly. "Never even got close to winning the Stanley Cup, and I don't think he's over that."

"Are you?"

He didn't seem to have an answer.

I tilted my head. "What about your brother? You said you were the only one to go pro."

Apparently grateful for the slight shift of topic, he said, "Brian got busted smoking pot in high school. My parents fought like hell to keep the school from kicking him off the teams, since it was just a dumb mistake."

"They kicked him off anyway?"

"Oh, no, the school backed down and let him keep playing on a probationary basis." Brent winced. "His junior year, *right* before the state championships?" He put his fingers to his lips as if he were smoking an invisible joint.

"I bet that went over well."

Grimacing, he said, "*Real* well. My brother spent the entire rest of his junior year grounded, and I'm pretty sure he decided to go to college out of state just to get away from my dad for four years."

"Did it help?"

"Eh. Not really. Dad and Brian always butted heads anyway, and they never quite resolved things after that." Brent sighed. "The shitty thing is that Brian and I *were* pretty close, but we aren't now. When I got my full ride hockey scholarship, and when I was one of the top draft picks, my dad threw it in my brother's face. Brian's always kind of resented me since then."

"Damn." I whistled. "Your parents really wanted athletes, didn't they? Whether you kids wanted it or not?"

"Yeah, I guess they did. Growing up, I always thought they were really supportive of us doing sports. But man, now that I think about it..."

"No wonder it's so hard to move on. It's practically all you've ever known."

"Exactly," he breathed. "I really don't know how to let it go. I don't know who I am without hockey."

Those words were heartbreaking. Jesus. What kind of parents pushed their kid into a sport so hard he had no identity without it?

"I can't even imagine. Leaving something like that has to be hard, and adapting to life after an injury sucks." I smoothed his hair. "But maybe this is your chance to decide who you are instead of being who someone decided you were before you had any say in the matter."

"Maybe. I mean, it isn't like I have much choice." He exhaled, deflating again. "The thought of trying to play hockey right now literally makes my entire body hurt, but I miss it. I really, really miss it."

"Of course you do. And of course you're still going to grieve. It's a huge change, and it sounds like you did love hockey, regardless of who decided on your career path."

"True. I did. And…yeah, grieving actually sounds like the right word. Feels like that's what I've been doing ever since they told me I'd never play again." He ran his hand through his hair, then kept it behind his head on the pillow. "I'm really trying to move on, you know? Figure out who and what I am without hockey. But the minute I go to my parents' house…"

He fell silent, and I watched him for a long moment before I cautiously said, "I have a question you don't have to answer."

His eyebrows rose. "Go for it."

I held his gaze as I carefully searched for the words. "If your family makes it so difficult for you to move forward, why do you keep subjecting yourself to that?"

He deflated a little, breaking eye contact. "They're my family."

"Right. And?" I paused. "Look, I don't know how close your family is, and I could be totally out of line here. But if they're making you—or, well, if your dad is making you feel this awful when you're dealing with something this big? I'm not suggesting you necessarily cut them off, but can't you take a break from them? Bow out of dinner once in a while?"

"I can, yeah." He avoided my gaze. "They're, um… They helped me after my accident. A lot. They came and stayed with me, and when I moved back here, I lived with them. I don't know how I would have gotten through all that shit without them, and… I mean, this probably sounds pathetic, but they're kind of all I have these days."

"Really?"

Brent nodded. "My social circle now that I'm living here is pretty much you, my best friend, and my parents. Which is partly my fault for being a recluse for so long, but I went from constantly being around a ton of people to…not."

"Like your teammates?"

"Exactly. And I mean they're still in touch. We email and I've FaceTimed with them occasionally. But we're not as close as we used to be. We can't be when we're this far apart. So I had this really tight group of people when I played hockey, and the minute I got hurt, that was just… It was gone. They didn't abandon me or anything, but they were on the road playing hockey while I was home or in the hospital. When I moved back here…" He flailed a hand. "They were most of my social life. Now I don't have that many people left."

"Damn. I never thought of that."

"Funny thing is, one of my doctors warned me about it. He said long term injuries and chronic pain tend to mean isolation, too. I didn't believe him because at that point, I was seeing so many doctors, union reps, people from the team—I kind of liked the idea of being isolated because I was overwhelmed by people. Especially people telling me that life as I knew it was over. As soon as I was released and came back to Burlington?" He shook his head and didn't finish the thought. I supposed he didn't need to. After a while, he said, "I guess this has all just been a huge adjustment. Like, a bigger one than I expected, because it's not *just* that my career is over. I mean, that sucks, and I miss it like crazy, but the worst part is that it's like my body isn't mine anymore, you know?"

I nodded. "I get that."

"You do?"

"Definitely. Quite honestly, it's probably the most consistent thing I hear from my pain management patients."

"Really?"

"All the time." I trailed my fingers up and down his arm. "Especially when it's chronic pain. It's one thing when you sprain your ankle or something, and you know it'll heal. When you realize the pain isn't going anywhere, and the best you can do is mitigate it as much as possible and adapt? When you have to revamp your entire life for it? That's a huge thing."

Brent nodded slowly. "Yeah. Exactly. And then there are people who insist it can't possibly hurt all the time. Like, since they can't wrap their head around the idea of being in some kind of pain 24/7, then it must be bullshit."

"Or since they can't fathom enduring it, obviously it isn't possible."

He laughed bitterly. "Right. Like I have any *option* besides enduring it. I can't exactly cry 'uncle' and turn it off, you know?"

"I have a *lot* of patients who wish that was an option."

"Right? It's better now, I'll give you that. The hip replacement was like night and day. I was still in a ton of pain, but I went into the OR with pain at a twelve, and woke up at a seven. And it's been consistently better since the surgery than it was before. Still hurts, and I still have days where I can barely move, but it hasn't been *that* bad again."

"That's good," I said with a nod. "I was surprised when you said they did a hip replacement at your age, but if it made that much of a difference, then it sounds like it was the best decision."

"It's..." He studied me. Then he laughed again, a soft, bitter sound. "You'd be surprised how many people don't think that way. My dad..." Brent sighed, wiping his hand over his face. "No joke, I've been defending that surgery to him ever since the day I told him my doctor was suggesting it."

"*Defending* it?" My lips parted. "Why the hell would you have to defend it? Did he... Did he *want* you in pain?"

"He thinks I can work through it and get back on the ice, and getting that surgery would fuck me out of any hope of getting my career back." Brent rolled his eyes. "I've never been able to get it through his head that my career was over before the hip surgery ever entered the equation. I guess he thought I was... I don't know. Giving up. I just know I've spent a lot of time explaining to him that, no, I'm not too young to need a hip replacement because my hip really was that messed up, and yes, my doctors really thought it was necessary." He met my gaze again. "So it's kind of a novelty when someone accepts it, you know?"

"Wow. It shouldn't be, but I get it."

A smile flickered across his lips before his expression darkened again. "He's not the only one who's thought I was too young to have it done. Some of the doctors weren't even sure about it. But the orthopedic surgeon basically said it was either do it now or spend the next five or ten years in horrible pain—which would just fuck up all my other joints, not to mention my back—and *then* replace it."

"That was my thought too. If your hip was in that bad of shape, then you were going to destroy your knees, your back, your ankles... Sounds like the surgeon did the right thing."

"Exactly. And I mean, my knees, back, and ankles are already fucked up, and losing all that muscle tone after I got hurt just meant all those old injuries coming back to haunt me."

"Because the joints weren't as stable anymore?"

"Yep." He pushed out a long, tired sigh. "So doing a hip replacement in my late twenties was my best bet for actually rehabilitating everything else. As much as it can be rehabilitated, anyway."

"And with all that, your dad still thinks hockey is in the cards?"

"If I just worked hard enough and conditioned myself, yep." Bitterness dripped from every word, and Brent laughed humorlessly as he rolled his eyes again. "He really doesn't get it. I don't think he wants to."

"Hopefully one of these days he'll get it through his head that his opinion doesn't change the facts."

"Yeah. Hopefully."

I watched Brent, and my heart ached for him. It was getting a lot easier to understand why he was so down and depressed these days. That was par for the course with a life-altering injury and with chronic pain (especially when someone was still adjusting to the idea that their pain *was* chronic), but so many people had little if any support. The people in their lives who were supposed to be there for them got tired of the constant pain and limitations, and treated the injured person like an inconvenience. People tried to convince them the pain couldn't be that bad, couldn't be that constant, and would get better if they stopped complaining and bought into whatever miracle cure was being sold through the latest pyramid scheme. A lot of my pain patients had people who were frustrated because they were tired of the patient being hurt or sick, and it really just needed to go away. Others handled them with kid gloves, or kept them at arm's length out of fear. And then there were patients who shut themselves away so they didn't annoy people, inconvenience them, or get accused of being a downer. The results were incredibly lonely.

And Brent had the added insult of his father pressuring him to continue a high-speed, high-contact career that probably would have ruined Brent's body if a drunk driver hadn't gotten to him first.

No wonder the guy was struggling.

After a while, Brent shook himself, and as he met my gaze, he touched my face, his expression soft. "I'm sorry. We were having a good time earlier, and then I had to be a downer."

"No, you're not." I covered his hand with mine and kissed his palm. "Not at all."

"I kind of killed the mood, though." Something in his eyes told me he didn't want to talk about things anymore, and that he wanted to go back to the way we'd been before he'd zoned out. So, I ran with it.

"Nah, you didn't kill the mood." I leaned in. "I'm pretty sure we can bring it back without too much trouble."

He grinned, his features relaxing. "Yeah?"

"Uh-huh." I kissed him, and this time when he sighed, it wasn't out of frustration or sadness. Not with the way he wrapped his arm around me and pulled me in close.

I was right—we brought back the mood without any trouble at all.

Brent and I spent most of our free time together. Sometimes fooling around. Sometimes talking. They say time flies when you're having fun, though, and sure enough, before I knew it, another Friday had come around again. I was looking forward to seeing Cody, but admittedly, I was disappointed that I wouldn't see Brent for another week.

For the next week, my evenings were focused on spending time with Cody and helping him with his homework (aside from my twice-weekly performances at the wine bar). Fortunately, that didn't mean Brent and I were completely cut off from each other. We texted a lot, and if Cody was asleep and the two of us weren't ready to crash for the evening, we'd squeeze in a FaceTime call. It was nice, having some adult interaction on those nights. Prior to Brent and during my non-custody weeks, I'd usually lingered for a little while at the wine bar to chat with the regulars and employees who I knew, but I never liked leaving Cody with the babysitter later than I had to.

The rest of the time, it was just me and Cody after work and school were out, and I loved spending time with him. I always made a point of having a sit-down dinner so we could catch up, and I tried to make sure we always had some downtime to watch TV together or go out for a little while. That was a challenge, given the amount of homework he had every night (seriously, what the fuck?) but I did the best I could.

I'd text occasionally with Brent during that time, but he understood I was with my son, and I didn't feel too guilty about taking a minute here and there to read and reply to a message.

When my custody week came to an end on Friday afternoon, I

drove over to Ashley's place to drop Cody off. I helped him get his things out of the trunk, then followed him up the stairs to her second floor apartment.

He keyed himself in. "Mom?"

Ashley appeared in the living room doorway as Cody and I were stepping into the hall. Annoyance flickered briefly across her face when she looked at me, but she quickly schooled her expression and smiled as Cody went to hug her.

After he'd hugged his mom, he toed off his shoes and took his schoolbag from me. His expression was a little sad, which brought that familiar lump into the back of my throat. This would get easier eventually, wouldn't it? For both of us?

The best I could do now was not let it show that this was a struggle for me, so I just smiled, gave him a quick hug, and said, "Okay, buddy. I'll see you in a week."

He smiled shyly and still a bit sadly, then headed into his bedroom, probably to do homework or play before dinner. Dropping him off wasn't as bad these days. I hated only having him with me half the time now, but the first few weeks after I'd moved out had been rough on him. He'd had a hell of a time with the divorce anyway, and for a long time, he'd freak out every time one of us left him with the other because he was sure we weren't coming back. After eight months of Ashley and me picking him up like clockwork on alternating Friday afternoons, though, he'd accepted that neither of us was going to ride off into the sunset without him. Maybe one of these days my conscience would stop needling me for putting him through that, but I didn't see that happening any time soon.

Right then, Ray, the man I told myself she hadn't started dating until *after* we separated, strolled into the living room. One look at me, and his whole demeanor darkened, same as it always did. I at least tried to keep my expression neutral, though sometimes I wondered how successful I was. He was a big guy, both in height and in the shoulders. Younger than both of us—maybe even younger than Brent, though I'd never asked—with angry eyes and a perma-scowl. Or at least, that was how I always saw him. He might've been a perfectly pleasant guy the rest of the time.

The three of us stood in tense silent for a moment, and I was glad

Cody had gone to his room. We all did the best we could to keep all this animosity out of his sight.

Without a word, my ex's boyfriend left the room.

Yeah, keep walking, asshole.

Ashley watched him go, then shifted her weight and looked at me with no shortage of irritation in her expression. She was probably ready to kick me out, but I put up a hand.

"Listen," I said, "before I go, we should touch base about his schoolwork..."

Ashley fixed an impatient look on me. She obviously wanted me to get out of here sooner than later, and her boyfriend probably did too.

Sorry, you two. Ash and I still have to be parents, so suck it up.

I pretended not to notice her attitude. "I've started doing his spelling and vocabulary when he first sits down to do his homework. He seems to struggle less when he's not already tired from going through everything else."

She frowned. "But he's still having a hard time with it?"

I nodded. "I copied you on the email to his teacher. Maybe she has some other ideas. But doing it first seems to help him concentrate on it."

"Okay. I'll keep that in mind."

"Okay."

Our eyes met. God, I hated how awkward this was.

"Anyway." I took a step toward the door. "I'll, um—"

"Actually, before you go." She folded her arms. "Just FYI, Ray is moving in at the end of the month."

I blinked. "Oh. Uh. Does Cody know about this yet?"

"No." She tightened her arms across her chest. "We're going to tell him this weekend. I just wanted you to know."

"Okay. How do the two of them get along?"

She narrowed her eyes. "Do you really think I'd move someone in if he didn't get along with my son?"

I glared right back, swallowing a retort about other decisions she'd made about living situations and how those had affected *our* son. Instead, I went with, "I trust your judgment, okay? Cody just hasn't said much about him, so I have no idea how he feels about him."

She held my gaze, clearly annoyed. This was getting far too familiar. In fact, lately it had been getting harder and harder to remember a time when the air between us wasn't this cold.

Didn't we smile when we said our vows?

With an annoyed sigh Ashley broke eye contact. "They get along fine, okay?"

"All right, but I—"

"He's moving in," she snapped. "I'm letting you know, not asking your opinion on it."

I stared at her, taken aback by the hostility. "Yeah, I appreciate the heads up. I'm just making sure our son is going to be okay with it. He's had a rough year, you know?"

She winced, and I realized the comment had probably come across as more barbed than it was intended. As if the past year-plus had been her fault. I didn't take it back, though. I tried—really, really tried—not to be petty and snide with her, but yes, I *did* blame her for the hell Cody had been through. This had been her choice, not mine. She'd decided to leave instead of fixing or even addressing whatever had gone wrong with us, and it would be a long, long time before I thought about forgiving her for it.

Neither of us pressed the issue any further, and I got the hell out of there. As I took the stairs down to the parking lot, my heart felt like lead. I could make peace with us no longer being together. I could move on. In fact, I was already making progress in that department. I had been since before I'd met Brent. I could live with the idea that Ashley had a new boyfriend now, and that there was no going back.

It was the frost between us that didn't sit right. We were civil enough to get through our weekly custody exchanges, and when there was something we needed to discuss or if she needed help financially, we could talk about it without involving lawyers. I wouldn't say we were cordial, but we weren't cursing each other out or devolving into screaming matches. Not bad for a relatively newly divorced pair.

But this wasn't *us*. Or, well, it shouldn't have been. It didn't make sense. Neither of us had cheated (though I wondered exactly when Ray had entered the picture). There'd been some heated arguments after she'd announced she wanted a divorce, but that was to be expected with all the stress and with emotions running hot. Now that it was all settled, though, and we were moving on and didn't have to live together anymore, where the hell was this hostility coming from?

Walking away from Ashley's apartment, I had to fight back a familiar surge of emotion.

What happened *to us?*

We'd been through a lot as a couple, but we'd always leaned on each other. We'd had rough spots, and we'd been in a rut, but I'd never had a clue she was looking for greener pastures. For the life of me, I didn't know if I'd been that oblivious or if she'd been that good at keeping it out of sight. Or both.

I gave her credit—she tried as much as I did to keep things civil within earshot of our son. The minute we were alone, though? The ice set right back in.

I hated these encounters with her. I still didn't even know what happened—one day, everything was fine. The next, she was distant and cold toward me. Even then, it still came out of the blue when she said she wanted to find herself, starting by divorcing me.

I could live with us being divorced, but I didn't get why we had to be like this.

It didn't matter, though. We were like this, and she quite obviously wanted me to leave, so I'd gotten out of her hair.

And I wondered again if this new normal would ever *feel* normal at all.

15

BRENT

Today, I felt good enough to get to work on Jon's house. We'd texted back and forth about what I'd need and where to start, and he'd promised to leave a key under the mat for me.

Sure enough, there it was.

I let myself into the house. There was a list on the kitchen island of the various projects we'd discussed. All fairly light stuff—I wouldn't be doing any major demolition or construction. There was no way my body would tolerate that, at least not any time soon. And I was damn thankful my father didn't know about this project—the last thing I needed was him giving me grief for not doing the literal heavy lifting.

But there was a lot I could do, and it felt amazing to be out of my house and *doing* something besides staring at the lake and wondering who I was.

Today was a decent day as far as pain. It kind of reminded me of how I'd feel the day after a hard game—tired and sore, but mobile. These days, that was nothing to complain about. After a couple of anti-inflammatories, and with a more hardcore pain pill in my pocket in case I needed it, I was as good as I could expect to be. I didn't want to overdo it and send myself into a world of hurt, but I cautiously got to work on Jon's list.

Fortunately, instead of having me carry things in from the garage, he'd left tools and such in the rooms where they were needed. Paint and gear in the rooms that needed painting. Tools and a power sander for the kitchen backsplash. Fittings in the bathrooms (those would have to wait until I had a bit more strength and flexibility than I had now). I was especially grateful he'd thought to put the heavier things where I wouldn't have to move them, and he'd gone for gallon-sized paint cans rather than the less expensive but substantially heavier buckets. I hated *needing* that kind of accommodation, but I was seriously grateful for it.

I started in the empty downstairs bedroom, which needed to be painted. There was already some plastic down to protect the carpet and some more taped over the windows, and Jon had taped the molding around the floor. I cautiously ventured onto the stepladder, and once I was sure my hip and knees were stable, I started taping the crown molding. Aside from a little fatigue in my arms and shoulders, that wasn't so bad.

Once the molding was taped, and I'd made sure the plastic around the floor and windows was secure, I poured some paint into the paint sprayer and got to work. Thank God he'd gone with the sprayer. I wasn't so sure I could do a roller or a brush, though I was pretty sure I could handle them if I needed to do some small touch-ups.

By the time I'd finished two even coats, I knew without a doubt I'd be feeling this tomorrow, but that was okay. It felt like something I hadn't experienced in a long time—good pain. The pain that came from a satisfying workout or doing something like helping a friend move. A year ago, I'd have barely felt a job like this, but today I would, and I had no complaints. I'd go a little easy tomorrow. Pop a few extra anti-inflammatories. Feel more hopeful than I had in a long time because *I could actually do things*.

While the bedroom's paint dried, I cleaned out the sprayer. Then I went into the kitchen to tackle another task.

The backsplash behind the stove turned out to be as cheap as it was ugly. The tiles popped off without much encouragement, and the power sander chewed through the grout like it was nothing.

When I was done, I took off the respirator and stood back, and I couldn't help grinning a little at my handiwork. Yeah, all I'd done was get rid of an old shitty backsplash in my booty call's kitchen, but after months of doing more staring at walls than anything, I'd take it. Especially when I pulled this off the same day I'd painted a room.

Man, it really did feel fucking amazing to be able to *do* something. Yeah, I had to be careful, and yeah, there were some things I couldn't do, but I wasn't as useless as my injury had left me feeling lately.

With the Shop Vac that Jon had left in the kitchen, I vacuumed up the dust and pieces of tile, then wiped down the stove and counters to be sure I hadn't missed any. I was just washing my hands when Jon's key clicked in the door.

He came in a moment later, and his gaze went right to the bare wall where the backsplash had been. "Oh. Wow. You've been busy."

"Yeah." I smiled as I started washing the remaining dust and paint off my hands. "Got the downstairs bedroom painted too. I'll check tomorrow to see if it needs any touch-ups, then get rid of the tape and plastic."

"Awesome. Thanks!" His brow furrowed. "And you're not too sore?"

"Nah, I'm pretty good, actually." I shut off the faucet and flicked some of the excess water into the sink. "Probably won't do anything tomorrow beyond finishing up that bedroom. Or, well, I might have to wait a day to do that. We'll see how I feel tomorrow. But yeah, I'm good."

"Good, good." He looked at the wall behind the stove again, and he chuckled. "You know, it says a lot when it looks better like that"—He gestured at the remnants of paint and grout—"than when it was tiled."

I laughed. "You said it, not me."

"Hey, I didn't install that mess. You can insult it all you want."

"Fair enough." I wiped my hands on a shop towel. "So, what do you want to put up instead?"

He gazed at the empty space, lips quirked. "I don't know. I do like the look of tiles, but I don't know if I want big or small, or what color, or…" He waved his hand. "I have no idea."

"Well, if you want to, we could always hit up the hardware store and see what they have. I think they're open until like nine."

He looked at me through his lashes. "You want to?"

"Why not? We could grab something to eat while we're out and still have plenty of time." I paused. "I mean, you just got home, so if you don't want to, that's—"

"It's fine." His smile made my skin tingle. "But we have time to eat here before we go." He gestured toward the bedroom. "Let me just change clothes, and we'll figure something out."

It didn't get much more domestic than cooking together before heading to the hardware store to pick out kitchen tiles. I wasn't sure where that fit into being friends with benefits, but I liked it, and Jon seemed to like it too. Maybe we weren't playing by fuck buddy rules. In fact that ship had probably sailed the first time we'd gotten into bed together with no intention of having sex. If there was a rulebook for this, we'd ditched it at the start, and I had no idea how anyone else would have defined what we were doing. Or how I defined what we were doing.

I just knew I didn't want to stop.

At the hardware store, we wheeled a shopping cart to the tile section. Pushing it gave me something to lean on subtly, which my tired joints and muscles appreciated.

Jon perused the gigantic selection of tiles that could feasibly replace the monstrosity I'd removed earlier. Halfway down the aisle, he pointed at a display. "What do you think of this one?"

I studied it. It was pretty—varying shades of blue with some black tiles and the odd silver accent—but we were under bright fluorescent lights. "I think it might be a little dark. The kitchen doesn't have a lot of natural light, so unless you're going to put in some brighter fixtures, this could make the whole room seem a lot darker." I paused. "I think that's part of why it looks so much better now that the old backsplash is gone—the wall behind it is way lighter than the tiles were."

Jon turned to me, eyes wide. "Wow. You really do know home renovation, don't you?"

I laughed quietly and shrugged. "It's about the only thing I know besides hockey. At least this is still useful."

"You're better at this than I am." He rolled his eyes. "Says the guy who bought a house to renovate."

"Eh, a lot of it sounds complicated and like a giant pain in the ass, but once you actually start doing it, it's pretty straightforward."

"Is it?"

I nodded. "I mean, don't ask me to lay a hardwood floor or install electrical shit. But like tilework? It's just messy and tedious. And I doubt I could do a tile floor anymore, because…" I gestured at my leg. "But a backsplash? Pfft. Easy."

"I'll take your word for it." He gestured at some more tiles. "What do you think of these?"

We went up and down the aisle several times, fending off salespeople as we debated between abstract designs, different color palettes, and various shapes and sizes of tiles. Jon finally settled on some small tiles in an assortment of white and two shades of yellow. We did the math to figure out how much he needed—thank you, smartphone calculator apps—and he put four boxes in the cart.

As he set the last one down, he eyed me. "These aren't exactly light. Are you going to be able to pick something like this up if I'm not at the house?"

My first instinct was to insist that I wasn't going to have my ass kicked by a box of kitchen tiles, but my pride was slowly making peace with reality. "Just leave them on the island the day you want me to put them up. Then they'll be where I can get to them."

"Okay, sure. I can do that. And the grout too."

"Oh, good idea. In fact, let's grab that and everything else I need while we're thinking about it."

At the house, I carried in some of the bags of tools, shop towels, tile spacers, tile mesh, and whatever else wasn't heavy enough to fuck up my balance. Jon left the tiles in the garage for now along with the grout, which he stacked next to the paint cans he'd bought on a previous trip.

"Okay." Jon put his hands on his hips and looked over everything we'd brought in. "Looks like we're set to make my kitchen look less trashy."

I chuckled. "No pressure, right?"

"No, none. And thank you." He met my eyes with the sweetest smile on his lips. "You're doing me a *huge* favor."

"Don't worry about it." I wrapped my arms around his waist and pulled him in closer. "I'm not home trying to motivate myself to get up off the couch for anything besides doctor's appointments, so this is great for me."

"I can imagine." He slid his hands up my back, and a twinge in the muscles made me flinch before I could stop myself. He noticed, too: "Back hurt?"

Nodding, I reached back to rub the annoyed muscle. "I guess that's to be expected."

"Is it just muscle fatigue? I can probably relax some of it."

"Yeah?"

He smiled. "Home renovation is easy for you. Getting rid of muscles spasms?" He held up his hands and wiggled his fingers. "That's my specialty."

"Well, I won't say no to having your hands on me."

Jon kissed me softly, then nodded toward his kitchen table. "Can you sit backwards in one of those chairs without making your hip hurt?"

I looked at the chairs. The backs tapered downward, and near the seats, they were narrow enough that I wouldn't have to really straddle to sit. "Yeah, I think so."

"Okay. Take off your shirt and have a seat. I'll go grab my oil."

While he went upstairs, I took off my shirt and left it on the table. Then I carefully sat down and folded my arms on top of the chair back. Funny how just thinking about having his skilled hands working at my muscles made things start to relax. Was there a massage therapy placebo effect? Hell, who cared? As long as I felt better—especially without the haze and side effects that came from taking a pain pill—I wasn't looking any gift horses in the mouth.

Jon returned a moment later, and the sound of him rubbing oil on his hands made me shiver.

"Cold?"

"No, no." I glanced back at him. "I'm good."

"All right. Just say so if you're not."

"Will do."

He got started, his hands warm and slick, and the slow, firm slide of his palms along my skin was hypnotic. Whenever he found a particularly tight muscle, he pressed his thumbs in harder, which always made me wince, but before too long, the tender muscle would loosen up and he'd go back to gentler strokes.

Jon's hands were amazing when we were fooling around, and they were unreal when he was doing what he was trained to do. It wasn't comfortable, especially not when he was working at an especially tight spot, but the results… Oh my God.

I pressed my forehead against my folded arms, arching my back a little and pushing against his hands. I closed my eyes and just enjoyed what he was doing. I lost track of time. I lost track of where I was. I lost track of literally everything except his touch and the sound of him breathing.

After a while, he asked, "Doing all right?"

"Mmhmm."

"How's the pain?"

Pain?

Oh. Right. He'd started doing this because my back was tight. Was it still?

Huh. No. It wasn't. Some muscles were vaguely achy and would probably be tender if he worked at them again, but for the most part, my back felt great and my head was floaty.

"It's good," I murmured. "Thanks."

"Don't mention it." His touch was extra light now, his palms and fingers barely grazing with the slow, circular motions. They slowed, slowed, slowed, and finally stopped, and he softly said, "Why don't we go up to the bedroom so we can relax?"

I nodded, and managed to lift my head. "You're um, not expecting…"

"Baby." He touched my chin and leaned down to kiss me. "You know me better than that."

"Okay, true."

He did have a point. For all I worked myself up about sex these days, he was about the least demanding and most patient man I'd ever met. I'd been with guys who'd expected me to put out right after I'd played hockey (hahaha *no*), but Jon was all, "Your back hurts? Not feeling it? Cool. Let's just chill."

When the time came for us to move on from each other, he was going to be a hard act to follow.

I shook that thought away as Jon and I headed upstairs. Since it was late, we got ready for bed, but we didn't turn off the light yet.

I tucked my arm under the pillow as I faced him on my side. "So what made you become a massage therapist?"

He propped himself up on his elbow and rested his other hand on my waist. "You want the honest answer or the one I give my clients?"

"They're not the same?"

Chuckling, he shook his head. "Clients want to hear that I wanted to help people."

"And the real answer?"

"My plans to become a professional musician had gone down the toilet, and everyone was telling me to get a real job. As long as I had to do that, I at least wanted to help people, but I couldn't afford to go to medical school and didn't want to be drowning in student loans for the rest of my life. So—massage therapy."

"And in the end, you're helping people."

"Exactly." He slid his hand down my arm. "I always knew that if I couldn't swing music, I'd want to do something in the medical field. It really just came down to what I could afford and what I thought I'd be good at."

"Yeah? What else did you look into?"

"Physical therapy. Occupational therapy. Acupuncture."

"Acupuncture?" I raised my eyebrows. "Really?"

"Mmhmm. Sometimes I still think about learning, but it's a lot of intensive schooling. Maybe when Cody is in college."

"Does that stuff actually work?"

"It can." He watched his fingers trailing up and down my arm. "I mean, I know some patients and practitioners who think it's like a cure-all for everything, and I don't buy that. But it's great for pain and inflammation."

That got my attention. "Oh, really?"

He nodded. "I mean, it's not going to repair damage, but it can help with pain management."

"Hmm. I might have to look into that." I squirmed, grimacing. "The needles, though…"

"Eh, they're not so bad. They're super thin and they barely go in."

"Have you had it done?"

"Yeah, one of the other therapists in the clinic where I work recommended it when I was having some sinus problems a few years ago."

"Wait, it helps with that?"

"Uh-huh. Though..." He made a face. "That particular treatment hurts."

"Why's that?"

"When the sinuses are all fucked up, the nerves in the face get touchy too." He gestured at his face. "Poke a needle in, and it stings. But it sure does clear the sinuses."

I shuddered. "So, fucked up and touchy—are those actual medical terms?"

"Absolutely," he deadpanned. "Straight out of the secret dictionary that only healthcare providers can access."

I laughed. "Uh-huh. That's what I thought."

He chuckled. Sobering, he looked me up and down. "Seriously, do you feel better now than you did earlier?"

"Yes." I took his hand and brought it up to press my lips to his knuckles. "I still think it's witchcraft, but whatever you did, it worked."

"Good." He kissed me softly. "I'd be kind of an asshole to leave you in pain, especially after you worked on my house."

"Oh, I see." I tsked melodramatically. "It's just because I worked on the house."

He rolled his eyes. "Shut up. You know what I mean."

"Yeah, yeah." I cuddled closer to him and rested my head on his shoulder. "Mmm, I really do feel so much better. Whatever you did, it's fucking magic."

He laughed. "Nah. But I'm glad it helped."

"It did." My eyelids fluttered. My whole body was relaxed thanks to him, and now my brain was quickly following suit. Voice a little slurred, I murmured, "Man. I think I'm gonna fall asleep."

Jon pulled me closer and kissed my forehead. "Then sleep."

16

JON

"Let me know if you need help, okay, kiddo?"

Sitting at the kitchen table with some worksheets and a textbook, Cody nodded. "Okay."

We'd already been through his spelling words, which was where he struggled the most, and he'd have me look at the rest of his homework before he put it away for the night, but he could usually handle other subjects on his own. In fact, we'd learned early on that the worst possible thing I could do was hover over him while he was trying to do his work. If he needed help, he'd ask.

So I left him to it and went upstairs.

With the bedroom door open a crack—I'd hear if Cody came up the squeaky stairs—I lay back on my bed and texted Brent.

FaceTime?

Then I put the phone down on my chest and waited.

My life was oddly divided lately. It had been since Ashley and I had finally sold our house and didn't have to be under the same roof anymore, but it seemed even more divided now that Brent was in my world. My days were more or less the same—massage appointments at the clinic or in people's homes, depending on the day—but once I was off the clock, I was either picking up Cody from school or heading out to meet up with Brent. Which was definitely better than when it was either picking Cody up or going home to the empty house I wasn't getting anywhere with renovating. And in fact, the house was already looking a lot better now that Brent was making headway, which motivated me to tackle some of the bigger projects. I'd started looking up articles and ideas for how to replace the backyard fence (which was secure, just fugly) and the back deck (which was one windstorm away from turning into a pile of kindling).

I'd get to those at some point. Mostly I was just alternating between spending time with Cody and with Brent. I had a week with Cody. A week with Brent. A week with Cody. During my custody weeks, there was still texting and FaceTime with Brent. When I was with Brent, Cody and I still texted now and then.

Unsurprisingly, I missed my son when he was with his mom. More and more, I was missing Brent too. I tried not to read too much into that. He was adult, human contact outside of work, and on good nights, being with him meant some *literal* human contact. Even when sex was out of the question, just being close to him was more than enough for me. What could I say? Loneliness fucking sucked.

My phone vibrated, making me jump. It was a FaceTime request, and my heart sped up as I accepted the call.

On the screen, Brent smiled, though his features were tight. "Hey."

"How's your day going?"

"Eh." His expression tightened a bit more. "Physical therapy was rough, so I've mostly been lazy today."

"Lazy is good if you're sore. How sore are you?"

"Enough that I'll be popping a pain pill before bed, that's for sure."

I grimaced. "Damn."

"It is what it is." He shrugged minutely, as if that was all his overtaxed body could do right now. "My bad days now are better than the good days last year, so I'll take it."

"That means you're improving, right? Steadily?"

He wobbled his hand in the air. "Kind of."

I nodded. "I'm glad you're on a positive trajectory, though."

"Me too." Brent shifted a little, a wince flickering across his face. Settling back against his couch, he said, "So what about you? How was your day?"

"Not bad. Just the usual—work, then making dinner for Cody and helping him with his homework."

"Homework?" He wrinkled his nose. "I thought he was like ten?"

"He is," I grumbled. "And someone somewhere decided they should have mountains of homework starting in kindergarten."

"*Ooh*, yeah. I remember that bullshit. What a pain in the ass."

"It is, and it's so stupid." Rolling my eyes, I rested my free hand behind my head. "I've flat out told him it's not the end of the world if he doesn't finish all of it. I want him to put in a good faith effort, and I'm not letting him slack off, but he still needs to be a kid, you know? Once he's in ninth grade and it counts, well, we'll cross that bridge when we get there, but I'm not going to punish a fourth grader because he occasionally doesn't have it in him to do spend three hours on homework."

"That's such bullshit," Brent muttered. "What does a kid that age even get out of doing that much work?"

"No idea. But I think it takes some of the pressure off him, knowing that if he's really burned out and tired, I'll err on the side of letting him rest over making him grind through it. Or if there's a family thing, or some special occasion he shouldn't have to miss, I'll write his teacher a note and not even feel bad about it."

"Good. You don't need him burning out in elementary school, for fuck's sake."

"Right?" I blew out a breath. "One of his teachers got pissy with me over it. She acted like I was letting him skate and not making him do any homework, all because he said his dad told him he didn't have to finish one assignment. It was literally *one* assignment after he'd finished everything—and done well on everything—for the entire school year."

Brent scowled. "I hope she got over it."

"She did. And my ex-wife did too. She doesn't like the leeway I give Cody." I rolled my eyes again and laughed. "To hear her or the teacher tell it, I don't make him do any homework, and I tell him he doesn't have to finish any of it. Uh, no, I basically just tell him that as long as he's done his best, and he doesn't take advantage of it, he can say, 'Dad, I don't think I can finish this' without getting in trouble." I half-shrugged. "He's literally done it like twice in the two years since I implemented that."

"So he's not just using it as an excuse to skate."

"Not at all. In fact, I think he's a lot more relaxed and focused without that pressure. He doesn't fight me over homework like he does with his mother."

Brent's lips quirked and his eyes unfocused as if he were considering what I'd said. Then he nodded. "That makes sense to me. I mean, I'm not a parent, but I remember being a kid. The more pressure there was to get something done, the less likely I was to *get* it done because of that pressure."

"Exactly. I'm pretty sure that's how Cody works. And I mean, his report cards are all glowing and he takes all his work seriously. A little breathing room when he needs it doesn't seem like too much to ask."

"No kidding."

I started to speak, but hesitated. "You probably don't need to hear all about homework and kid stuff. I'm sorry."

"It's fine." He smiled, though obvious pain still kept his features taut. "Don't worry about it."

"Okay, but say so if I'm ever rambling on forever about him."

He just laughed.

I cleared my throat. "So, um, I still have him this week, but tomorrow's Wednesday, so I'm on at Vino and Veritas. If you want to come…"

His eyes lit up. "Oh. Yeah. That sounds like fun."

"I can't stay too late, since Cody will be with his babysitter, but it would be great to see you."

"Definitely. Sure." He hesitated. "I mean, I'll see how well I'm moving. If tonight's any indication, I might have to bring the cane."

I wanted to tell him I'd make sure the staff reserved a seat for him so he wouldn't be stuck standing, but I'd gotten the impression things like that made him uncomfortable. He didn't like needing accommodations for his pain or mobility, and he probably wouldn't like me assuming he needed one.

"There isn't usually a huge crowd," I said. "Especially during the week. So you shouldn't have any trouble finding a place to sit."

Brent nodded. "Okay, perfect." And there was that smile—so sweet and adorable even when it was tempered by his physical discomfort. "I'm looking forward to it."

Cody left for the babysitter's shortly after I'd brought him home from school. He stayed with a neighbor on my nights at Vino and Veritas, which meant he could play with their two boys. Plus the neighbor had a couple of cats. He was hardly heartbroken whenever he stayed there, and since he went early, I left early too.

Brent and I met up at Vino and Veritas shortly before I was supposed to be onstage.

I flagged down Rainn at the bar. He responded with a nod, then came over after he'd finished with his current customer.

Brent ordered some wine, thanked Rainn for it, and took a sip. "Damn. They have really got some good wine here, don't they?"

"They do. If I ever get that wine rack in place at home, I'm buying a few bottles."

"I think I might do that too. I'm not much of a drinker, but I do like a good glass of wine sometimes."

"Me too." I paused. "And, um, are you sure you don't mind hanging out again tonight?"

"Mind?" Brent grinned at me over the rim of his wineglass. "I get to have a drink and listen to you sing. What is there to mind?"

"I, um…" I cleared my throat. "You'd be surprised. A lot of people really aren't into…" I motioned toward the stage.

He put his glass down, and his smile was sweet. "I don't know if you remember, but that"—he gestured in the same direction I had—"is what you were doing the first time you got my attention. So you don't have to twist my arm to watch you again."

"Well, thank God for that." I put a hand on his waist and kissed him softly. "I really am glad you came."

"Me too."

We didn't have time for much more conversation than that—minutes after Brent walked in, I was due to start. He joined Colin at one of the tables while I went onstage.

And as I sang, I felt…different than I had in a long time. Or at least, different than I had when I'd first started singing here.

In the beginning, these performances had been therapeutic. There was nothing lonelier than singing alone about heartbreak, and having a small audience made a big difference. Then it had become something to look forward to. Something to keep me moving when the divorce made me want to give up on everything.

Years ago, I'd seen a particular country singer in concert. A lot of his songs were just gut-wrenchingly sad, and he always poured his heart into them and made them sound like the pain was happening right then. Except by the time I'd gone to that concert, he'd met his wife, and they were happily married. In fact, I was pretty sure that had been when they were expecting their first baby.

But he'd still gone onstage and ripped every last audience member's heart out as if he'd been singing about fresh wounds.

I'd wondered back then how he managed to dredge up those emotions even while he was blissfully happy offstage. Was he just that good at putting on a show? That good of an actor? Or did he know how to pull open his own wounds long enough to give us our money's worth before he walked back to his happy life?

Tonight, I felt like I was a step closer to understanding how he did that. Because I was happier than I'd been in a long time, and the man who was responsible for a lot of that newfound happiness was sitting in the back of the room with a wineglass in his hand. It wasn't that I was in love with him—I just felt more like I was putting the past behind me and moving on to better things.

Even with that newfound optimism, it didn't take much to dredge up all the emotions from my failed marriage. They weren't far beneath the surface anyway, so it wasn't hard to call them up and pour them into a song I'd written about how much I missed Ashley, about how it had been a special kind of hell to live separate lives in the same house before I'd been able to move out, about how hard it was to swallow that what I'd thought was a quiet, content life had been a boring, miserable hell for her.

But every time I finished a song, the emotions trailed away like a fading echo. They'd been here and they'd been real, and now they were gone. One look at the man in the back who was applauding with everyone else, and all those emotions went right back to being a distant memory.

As I went into the next song, I had to dig a lot harder to summon up those feelings.

Because here and now?

Life was pretty fucking good.

17

BRENT

I went to Jon's performances more often than not. Pain permitting, I was there, especially during his custody weeks, since then I'd get to see him—however briefly—before he went home to his son.

Tonight, after another Saturday night at Vino and Veritas, we relaxed together on my bed. Neither of us was ready to call it a night, but my back voted for not sitting up anymore. Fortunately, Jon didn't seem to mind, especially not as we lounged together in the middle of the mattress.

"I think I might've mentioned this before," I said, draping my arm over his stomach, "but your songs are amazing. And there were some tonight I hadn't heard before—I loved them."

He smiled. "Thanks. The divorce was hell, but I sure got a lot of music out of it."

"Silver lining?"

"Something like that."

We lay there in silence for a while. I was sore as hell—my hip and back had decided to get pissed off for no apparent reason while I'd been sitting in the wine bar—but an anti-inflammatory had reduced the pain to a dull roar. Enough to be annoying, enough Jon and I hadn't been able to have sex, but not enough to keep me from enjoying this warm closeness with him.

He finally spoke out of the blue. "It's weird, you know? Starting over in my forties. I was with Ashley for pretty much my entire adult life. Longer than that, really."

"You were?"

Jon nodded. "Like I told you before, we knew each other through high school and started dating in college. We got married before we graduated." He sighed. "I got married when I was twenty. Signed our divorce papers when I was forty. It's weird to hit the reset button like that, let me tell you."

"I bet."

"And I mean, it wasn't all bad. The end sucked, but we had a lot of good years together. And I still have Cody, so I really can't complain."

"He's, what—ten?"

"Yep." He met my gaze, and he must have seen the curiosity in my eyes, because he went on, "We wanted kids right from the start, and we were too stupid to listen to anyone who said we should wait, establish ourselves, buy a house." He waved his hand. "But biology kind of stepped in and made us wait."

"What do you mean?"

"I mean it was a long time between when we decided to start trying and when Cody came along. Almost eight years, all told."

"Wow."

He laughed dryly. "It's funny—we both lost our virginities in high school, and we had classmates who wound up having kids before graduation. It was like every girl could get pregnant standing downwind of a boy. By the time I slept with a woman for the first time, I was seriously paranoid about it, and Ashley and I were *obsessive* about being careful. Then when we actually *wanted* a kid, it just...didn't work."

"Damn. I never slept with a girl, so I can't imagine, but that must've been frustrating as hell."

"It was an experience." Jon sighed. "It was hell on our sex life, too. We tried to keep things fun and interesting, but it was always there in the back of our minds. There was just so damn much pressure." He wiped a hand over his face. "In fact, about four, five years into it, we were coming up on a three-day weekend. I suggested we go out of town somewhere, and that we bring condoms this time."

I cocked my head. "Condoms?"

"Mmhmm. I knew if we did the 'stop trying and just relax' thing, we'd both be secretly hoping—and stressing—that it would happen now that we weren't trying. So this time, I figured if we actively *didn't* try, and we just spent some time together and had sex because we wanted to instead of to get pregnant, it would help."

"Did it?"

"It did," he said with a subtle nod. "We had a great time. Probably some of the best sex we had in our whole marriage." His shoulders slumped. "But a few days after we got back, her chart said she was ovulating, and it went right back to being something we *had* to do. It was hard. Really hard. It stressed both of us out, especially her. I suggested adoption or fostering, but..." He shook his head. "I think it became a thing she wanted to overcome. Like she felt defective or like a failure because every woman she knew was getting pregnant and she couldn't."

"I get that."

"Do you?"

"Well, yeah." I carefully propped myself up on my elbow and met his gaze. "When your body refuses to do what all your peers' bodies are doing like it's nothing?" I huffed a humorless laugh. "Kinda fucks with your head."

He studied me.

I went on, "I've always hated running. I did it because it helped with conditioning. But one time in college and once after I got signed, I got hurt and *couldn't* run. I was chomping at the bit to get back out there. Every five minutes I was asking when someone would clear me to run again. And when they finally cleared me, I still hated it, but I needed to do it so I didn't feel *broken* anymore."

Jon's eyes lost focus. "Wow. I never thought of it that way."

"It kind of comes with the territory when your body fails on you."

"Yeah, I guess it would. Huh." His eyes stayed distant for a moment. "I mean, I guess I get it. And I definitely get why she said we were stopping at one. Going through all that again..." He shook his head. "I don't blame her."

"I don't either. It must have taken a lot of pressure off her once that was finally over."

He nodded slowly. "She did seem a lot happier after that. And she said a number of times it was worth it when Cody came along." He smiled. It was so cute, the way his face lit up whenever he mentioned his son.

"Glad it worked out in the end," I said softly. "Even if things, uh, didn't work out...in the end..."

He shrugged. "It's life. Not everything works out the way we think it will." He met my eyes, and his smile warmed. "That's not always a bad thing."

My heart sped up. "No, I guess it isn't." I ran my hand up his chest. "Hard to believe we both went through some shit, and now..." I gestured at us.

"I know, right? Life is strange."

"It really is.

We were quiet for a long time, just lying there together. It wasn't an uncomfortable silence; I was enjoying the warmth of him being this close to me, and he seemed to be lost in thought.

After a while, he said, "Is there anything you've always wanted, but couldn't have because of your career?"

I studied him. "What do you mean?"

"Well, I mean..." He shifted onto his side and rested on his elbow. "Now that you're moving on after hockey, is there anything that hockey kept out of your reach?"

"Hmm." Eyes unfocused, I thought about it. Then I looked at him. "A dog."

"Yeah?"

I nodded. "I love dogs. Always have. But from the time I moved out of my parents' house, I've been traveling constantly because of my job. Couldn't really justify having a dog if I was just going to leave it behind all the time."

He smiled. "Well, what's stopping you now?"

"That...is a really good question." Huh. It really *was* a good question.

Jon covered my hand with his. "There's a shelter in town. Go have a look. See if someone wants to come home with you."

I couldn't help smiling, and I squeezed his hand. "I think I will." I paused, then cautiously asked, "You want to come with me?"

"Sure. I've got time if you want to go tomorrow."

"Really? You'd... I mean, you'd want to?"

"Of course." He ran his fingers through my hair. "We should probably take my car. Your truck might get a little crowded with us and a dog."

"Oh, good point. We can put some towels down so hair doesn't get—"

He cut me off with a gentle kiss. "I've got a blanket in the trunk. Relax."

I...relaxed. And damn, I was excited about this. A dog? And spending more time with Jon? There was literally no downside to this.

"You're, um, welcome to stay here tonight." I paused. "I can pretty much promise there won't be anything, uh, physical happening, but if you want to stay..."

Jon smiled, and he leaned in to press a soft kiss to my lips.

We settled in to go to sleep, and man, I would never get tired of this. I loved the feeling of someone beside me, even when pain or body heat meant we drifted apart during the night.

For once, it wasn't pain or anxiety that wouldn't let me sleep. Yeah, my hip and back hurt, but even if they didn't, I was pretty sure I'd still have been wide awake. Except this time, the thing keeping me awake was something I hadn't felt in so long I couldn't remember the last time: *excitement.* I had something to look forward to.

I'd always joked about visiting friends and family just so I could get my critter fix, but it wasn't entirely a joke. If not for my parents' dogs, I probably would have come up with more reasons to skip Sunday dinner. One of my teammates had had a couple of huskies, and whenever he had barbecues, I spent more time playing with the dogs than anything.

A dog would make this huge place a hell of a lot less empty. And my doctors and physical therapists had been encouraging me to get out and walk more. I had enough of a yard that I could let the dog outside to play when I was hurting too much to go for a walk, but the thought of having a pup to walk instead of just limping along with my thoughts? Oh yeah. That would definitely get me out of the house more. There were dog parks and beaches—plenty of places to go on walks or throw a toy.

I wouldn't get a puppy, though. There was no way I could keep up with one. And maybe not something as wild as my parents' papillons. Something a little mellower that was past the puppy stage.

Was the shelter open yet? Could we go now?

I chuckled at my own thought. I could wait a few hours. I hoped Jon didn't mind being there as soon as they opened, though, because I couldn't wait. Getting a dog was such an obvious solution now that Jon had pointed it out, and I really had wanted one for a long time. Wow, was this a side effect of my accident that was *good*? With all the bullshit in my life thanks to that crash, was I finally going to get a silver lining?

Maybe. Maybe now I could live the life that hockey hadn't let me live. Stay in one place. Travel when I wanted to, not when someone told me to. Have a dog of my own. Maybe two. And hobbies.

I was limited by my body, but I suddenly felt like I had a lot more options and opportunities than I'd thought.

There would always be a part of me that missed the sport and the life of a professional athlete. Whether it had been my choice or not, it had been my life, and I'd loved it. Letting go of that was hard, and Jon was right—I'd be grieving it for a long time.

But maybe not forever.

Because while nothing would ever bring hockey back to me, that didn't mean my life was over.

Maybe it meant my life could finally be *mine*.

18

JON

I didn't think I'd ever seen Brent more excited about something than he was when I pulled into Chittenden County Animal Shelter's parking lot.

He left his cane in the car, and though he was walking slowly and his features tightened now and then with pain he was obviously trying to hide, he seemed to be moving more easily than he'd been last night. Whatever pain he was in now, it didn't dull the excitement in his eyes.

I didn't even try to suppress my smile. He was so cute when he was this excited.

Inside, a woman with glasses and *Taylor* on her nametag greeted us. She showed us to the kennels, and for the first time, Brent's excitement faltered a bit.

"Man," he said. "It's so sad. I wish I could take *all* of them home."

"Yeah, I know what you mean." I rested a hand on the small of his back. "But I suspect you're going to make one of them seriously happy today."

He glanced at me, and when his smile came back to life, my heart fluttered.

"Is there a particular kind of dog you're looking for?" Taylor asked. "A puppy? A hunting dog?"

"Just a companion," he said. "Something kind of mellow? Definitely not a puppy." His expression turned a little sheepish. "I'm recovering from a leg injury, so I have to be kind of careful. Probably can't take anything that'll trip me or bowl me over."

She nodded. "Okay, so you're not going to want a super high energy breed." She paused, and then she smiled. "How are you at throwing?"

"Throwing?" His eyebrows jumped, and he shrugged. "I mean, I'm not a baseball player or anything, but I can throw."

Her smile broadened. "Let's go in here where it's a little quieter, and then I think I have someone you should meet."

Brent nodded. "Sure."

She took us into a back room with some dog toys and posters encouraging people to adopt instead of going to breeders. "Okay, wait here. I'll just be a minute." She stepped out, and Brent and I exchanged glances. The excitement in his face was still very much there. I couldn't wait to see his expression when he met whichever dog went home with him.

I didn't have to wait long.

The door opened again, and Brent's eyes lit up as Taylor came in with a good size black Lab hiding behind her and carrying a big rubber toy in its mouth. The dog looked up at Brent and me, and holy shit, if Brent didn't adopt this dog, I would, because those big brown eyes *instantly* won me over.

"This is Luna." Taylor reached down to pet her sleek black coat. "She's been through a lot, and she's a little shy, but she's very sweet."

The dog's tail was partly tucked between her legs, but it wiggled tentatively, as if she really, *really* wanted to wag it, but she was scared. Brent tugged a plastic chair toward him, carefully took a seat, and then offered his hand to Luna. She was hesitant, but she stretched her neck out. He inched a little closer, which sent her back behind Taylor's legs. After a moment, though, she took a cautious step forward. Then another. Instead of sniffing his hand, she dropped her toy, letting it roll toward Brent. Then she drew back, watching hopefully and wagging her tail with a touch more enthusiasm.

Brent picked up the toy, which made her eyes widen with even more hope. He held out his other hand again. The dog leaned closer, and she took another tiny step. This time, she sniffed his fingers.

"It's okay," Brent said softly. "I won't hurt you."

Luna glanced at Taylor. Then at the toy. Finally, she gave Brent's fingers a timid little lick.

"You're so cute," Brent said, and petted her. That seemed to break through some of the worry, and Luna's tail wagged wildly now. With his other hand, he offered the toy she'd given him. Watching him intently, she delicately took the toy from him. Her ears were still down, her eyes still wide, but she seemed to be quickly catching on that Brent wasn't going to hurt her.

"Do you want to take her out in the yard?" Taylor smiled. "I'm sure she would love it if you threw her toy for her."

"Definitely." Brent stood carefully, his smile almost masking the wince. "Show us the way."

"Come on, baby." Taylor gave the leash a gentle tug. "You want to go outside and play?"

That got Luna's attention. Her tail went up, and she trotted alongside Taylor, her toy still in her mouth. Brent and I followed.

The shelter had a small yard that was partly grass, partly concrete. Luna was still timid when Taylor unclipped the leash, and she obediently dropped the toy in Taylor's hand, but she watched us all with a mix of worry and hope.

Taylor gave Brent the toy. He threw it, and Luna was immediately off and running. In an instant, she changed from the scared dog we'd met inside to the happiest creature I'd ever seen. She grabbed the toy and ran so fast back to us, she was kicking up grass in her wake.

Brent held out his hand, and she deposited the slobbery toy in it before running in circles and yipping happily. "You ready?" he asked with a big grin, holding up the toy. "Ready?"

More yipping and circling.

He threw it, and I honestly couldn't decide who was happier in that moment—Luna or Brent.

"Have you ever had a Lab before?" Taylor asked him as we watched the dog having the time of her life.

Brent shook his head. "I've had dogs before. Never a Lab."

"Okay, well, they're fairly easy. She'll need to be brushed fairly often because that undercoat sheds a *lot*. Also, Labs love water, and she is no exception."

"Oh, that's perfect." Brent smiled. "I live right on Lake Champlain."

Taylor straightened. "That *is* perfect!" She touched a hand to her chest. "Luna would be so happy there."

Luna skidded to a halt in front of us and dropped the toy at Brent's feet. He winced a little as he leaned down to pick it up, but he didn't seem to want to stop playing with her. As she chased the toy again, he said, "She's kind of timid. What's that about?"

Taylor's face fell. "We're not exactly sure where she came from, but from her behavior, I think someone was mean to her. This is *not* a dog you want to raise your voice to, especially if she's had an accident or chewed something."

He nodded, gaze fixed on the dog. "That's not really my style."

"Good. And give her some time once you get her home. She's been through a lot, and it'll be a huge change for her. It might take her some time to be this outgoing"—she nodded toward Luna—"at home."

"Oh, I can understand that." Still watching Luna, he smiled. "I've got all the time in the world."

Perfect," Taylor said. "As you can see, she's got a lot of energy and likes to play, but she's very obedient and mellow too."

"Obedient?"

She nodded. "Whoever had her before..." Taylor frowned. "Well, like I said, they weren't nice to her, but she did learn some commands that she'll still obey. I just can't emphasize enough how important it is to make sure you use a gentle tone with her."

"I can do that," Brent said. "I'm, uh, not really the type to raise my voice."

"Good. It probably won't take her long to trust you, then." When Luna came up again, Taylor requested her toy. Luna gave it to her, and Taylor said in a gentle voice, "Luna, sit."

The dog dropped onto her haunches and stared plaintively up at Taylor and the toy as if to say, *"Okay, I did the thing. Can I go back to playing now?"*

"Okay!" Taylor threw the toy. "Go get it!"

I watched Brent's face. This man was obviously in love with this dog, and the way he smiled was beyond adorable. I gave his elbow a gentle nudge. "So, you going to keep her name?"

"Oh yeah." He grinned broadly. "It suits her." There were a couple of plastic chairs in the yard. Brent pulled one closer, brushed off some pine needles, and carefully sat down. Then he leaned forward and gestured for Luna to come up to him. "Come on, Luna. I won't hurt you."

Her timidity came back, and she kept her head down and tucked her tail again as she came closer, but as soon as he started petting her, she started to relax again. She inched closer. Closer. Then she dropped onto her haunches beside him and leaned against his leg, her head on his lap as her tail thumped the concrete. God, I could just *feel* how bad she *wanted* Brent to be safe and to love her. From the look in his eyes, this pup had hit the jackpot. And so had he—with as much as he'd been struggling to find his footing after his injury, I suspected Luna was exactly what he needed too.

To Taylor, he said, "So what do I need to do to take her home?"

Taylor gestured back inside. "We've got some forms for you to fill out, and there's an adoption fee. After that, she's all yours."

"Awesome. Let's do this."

Inside, while Brent filled out the paperwork, I wandered back to where all the other dogs waited. It really was heartbreaking, not being able to help all of them. I liked dogs, and it was hard to see them living in a place like this without families.

One set of big brown eyes caught my attention. On the other side of the bars was a dog whose breed I couldn't begin to identify. A bit bigger than Luna, maybe with some golden retriever in there judging by the color and the shape of his face. I couldn't put my finger on the breed to save my life, but those eyes… Oh my Lord.

The card beside the door read:

My name is Winston. I'm about five years old, neutered, and have all my shots. I love kids and other dogs, and I don't understand why the squirrels won't play with me. I probably wouldn't be happy with cats. I'm playful, know basic commands, and will con you out of anything you're eating.

Below that was the date he'd arrived at the shelter, and doing the math quickly in my head, I realized he'd been here almost two years.

I looked at him again, and my chest ached.

In two years, *nobody* had taken him home?

I crouched in front of his door, and he came right up and pushed his nose between the bars. I petted his snout, and he tried to lick my fingers as his tail went wild, and I'll be damned if he wasn't looking at me the same way Luna had looked at Brent. He wasn't timid, but he had that same hopeful expression that melted my heart right then and there.

I rose, and I could feel his heart sinking as hope dimmed in favor of disappointment. Disappointment that probably wasn't a new feeling for this poor guy.

"Don't worry," I told him. "I'll be back. I'm just going in the next room."

Of course he didn't know what I was saying, and damn if he didn't have that same look in his eyes that Cody had gotten the first few times Ashley or I had dropped him off for a custody week. That absolute crushing certainty that I was leaving and never coming back.

Aw, dude. You're killing me.

"I'll be right back," I whispered again, and hurried back to the lobby. Leaning in the door, I cleared my throat and gestured over my shoulder. "Could I, uh, visit with Winston in the yard?"

Taylor's already bright expression brightened even more. "Winston? Oh sure! Let me get a leash."

As she went into the back, Brent looked up from his paperwork, a sweet smile on his lips. "I didn't think you were looking for a dog."

"I wasn't."

He grinned. "You big softy."

"You're one to talk."

He just chuckled and continued with his paperwork.

Taylor returned a moment later with Winston on a leash, and he wasn't timid in the slightest. His tail was wagging, and his face said nothing if not *"Where we going? What we doing? Is it playtime?"* When he saw me, he barked excitedly and started tugging at the leash, his expression full of, *"You didn't leave? You're not leaving?"*

Not without you, little buddy.

Brent and I followed Taylor and Winston out into the yard, and she handed me a ball to toss for him. He tore after it.

Luna was in a pen beside the yard, and she bounced and yipped, wagging her tail. Winston ran up to the pen and dropped his ball, and they sniffed each other's noses through the chain link.

"Do they get along?" Brent asked.

"Oh, yeah." Taylor nodded. "They both love other dogs as long as they're not aggressive, and neither of these dogs has an aggressive bone in their bodies."

Brent and I exchanged looks.

To Taylor, I said, "Any chance we can let them out together?"

"Sure!" She went over to the pen, opened the gate, and Luna burst out of it. Immediately, she and Winston were zooming around the small yard, tongues hanging out and tails wagging furiously as their feet kicked up grass and gravel. They wrestled. They chased toys we threw for them. They chased each other. Both just looked deliriously happy, and I could have watched them all day.

At one point, Luna whipped Winston in the nose with her tail, and another time, Winston bowled Luna over and sent her sprawling, but neither seemed particularly upset. They recovered immediately and continued playing.

"They're just like kids," I said with a laugh. "They bounce right back."

"And they'll both probably be dead asleep this evening," Taylor said.

Just the thought of Winston sprawled on the couch or on the floor made me smile. To Taylor, I said, "How in the world has he been here this long?"

She sighed, watching Winston galloping around the yard. "He hasn't actually been *here* all that long. He came from one of the over-crowded shelters in Georgia—we take some of their overflow sometimes. But someone's always looking for something different. They want a puppy, so he's too old. They want a senior dog, so he's too young. Then some movie comes out with this or that breed, and everyone wants that one." She shook her head. "There's not a thing wrong with him as long as you don't have cats. He's just the sweetest boy, but someone else always catches people's eye."

"Poor dude," Brent said.

I frowned. "No kidding."

Taylor sighed. "And I wish we had more space than this." She looked around. "Not just living space, but so they can get out and run around. You know—be dogs."

"They'd probably love that," Brent said, almost more to himself.

"They would. I mean, the best case scenario is they all get adopted out to forever homes. But some of them are with us for a while." Gaze fixed on the dogs, she said, "The least we could do is give them more than…" She waved a hand at the small enclosure. "*This.*"

I felt bad for all the dogs we couldn't take home today, and she was right—they'd be a million times happier with more space. Especially outdoor space.

But for today, two dogs—including one who'd been here for way too long—were coming home with us. Luna and Winston's days of cages and too-small yards were definitely over.

I turned to Taylor. "So, any chance you have another one of those forms?"

"Okay, looks like you're both set." Taylor smiled up at us. "Let me grab the papers that go with their rabies tags, and then we'll be done."

"You hear that?" Brent said to Luna, whose leash he was holding. "We're going to go home!"

Her ears were still down, her posture still timid, but she wagged her tail and gave his hand a tiny lick. He smiled and petted her, and she leaned against him as her tail wagged faster. Oh, yeah. Those two were going to be a great pair.

And I still couldn't look at Winston without my heart melting all over again. He'd sat beside me while I'd finished filling out the paperwork, his chin on my lap, and though he couldn't have known what any of us were saying or doing, I think he knew good things were happening.

I tousled his ears. "It's a shame you were stuck here for so long, but I'm glad you're coming home with me."

He just wagged his tail.

"How about a picture, huh?" I took out my phone, snapped a quick selfie with him, and sent it to Cody with, *Look who's moving in with us.* He wouldn't get the message until lunchtime, but I couldn't wait for the excited response.

The shelter hooked us up with a doggy necessities shopping list, plus some car restraints so the dogs could travel safely. Once we had Winston and Luna buckled into the backseat of the car, we left the shelter.

Brent looked over his shoulder. "I guess we should go get everything on our list." He turned to me. "Do you want to?"

"Sure." Glancing in the rearview at the happy pups, I said, "Petco lets dogs into the store, don't they?"

"If they don't, I think there's a PetSmart in Williston." He took out his phone. "Let me check."

At the pet store, we went inside with Winston and Luna in tow. Brent couldn't walk very fast, but the dogs didn't mind. Luna stayed right next to him—she didn't even need to be told to heel. Winston pulled at the leash and tried to encourage me to walk faster, though he wasn't unruly.

Brent chuckled. "Looks like we got the right dogs, didn't we?"

"I guess we did." I gave the leash a gentle tug. "Winston. Heel." He did, but he gave me a pitiful look. "Oh dear God." I tousled his ears. "My son gives me that look when he doesn't want to do something. Not you too!"

Brent just laughed. He got a shopping cart, and we started toward the dog aisles. Someone else had a German shepherd puppy who was beside herself to see a couple of dogs, and the owner didn't mind them socializing, so we let Winston and Luna visit with her for a minute.

"Taylor's right," I said to Brent. "They're going to sleep like the dead tonight."

He nodded. "Assuming they make it that far. They're probably going to be exhausted before we get back to the car."

The puppy's owner moved on, and we continued toward the dog aisles.

"Oh, hey, check this out." Brent stopped the cart and picked up a long plastic thing with a claw at the end. He opened and closed the claw a few times, then looked at me. "I could use this to pick up her toy so I don't have to crouch down."

"Good idea." I chuckled. "Though she seems pretty eager to put them in your hand."

"True. But just in case…" He put the claw thing in the cart, and we continued through the store, the dogs walking happily beside us.

I was surprised he'd gone for the claw that enthusiastically. He was usually so self-conscious and embarrassed about his injuries and about admitting he had limitations. Which I got—that was a tough thing to adapt to. But he actually seemed excited to find something that would help him work around those limitations so he could play with his dog. Not frustrated that he needed something like that, but excited that something existed to make a task easier, especially when that task was playing with his newfound four-legged friend.

That had to be a good sign. He'd been struggling so hard to make peace with how his body and his life had changed, and instead of seeing things like this as a sign of defeat—something he'd only accept with a lot of resignation and self-loathing—he was seeing them for what they were: something to help him do things that were otherwise difficult.

After we'd each picked up some dog food, dishes, brushes, and a few other things on the list Taylor had given us, we turned down the toy aisle. Immediately, both dogs' tails started wagging.

I gestured at some stuffed squeaky toys. "You want one?"

Winston seemed puzzled for a moment, but he sniffed the toys. Looked at me. Sniffed them again.

"It's okay." I patted his hip. "Go ahead."

After another tentative moment, he nosed around and picked up a stuffed alligator, which he immediately thrust at me.

I laughed. "You want this one?" I tugged on it. He growled and pulled back, but his tail was still wagging, so this was clearly a game. Chuckling, I gave it another pull, and he growled again as he shook his head. His tail nearly knocked over a few more toys.

Luna was, unsurprisingly, not sure about taking a toy. She looked at some of the toys, but then turned to Brent and lowered her head as she put her tail between her legs again.

"Man." He gently patted her side. "Someone really worked you over, didn't they?"

Luna watched him.

He watched her for a moment, then reached for the shelf. "How about this one?" He held up a large bone made of braided rope. Her ears perked up, and her tail wiggled. "You want it?" He pushed it toward her. "We can take it home if you want it."

She sniffed it. Then, nervous eyes fixed on him, she delicately closed her jaws around the toy.

"That's it," Brent said with a smile. He gave it a little tug. She cautiously tugged back. "That's a good girl!" Her ears perked up. Her tail wagged. When he pulled the toy a bit more firmly, she tugged back with some enthusiasm this time. No growling or dangerous tail like Winston, but she definitely wanted to play.

"Oh my God." He looked up at me as he gave her a gentle pat. "She's so cute."

"She is."

And so are you.

Because good Lord, he was. The look on Brent's face every time he smiled at his new dog had my heart doing things I didn't think it had ever done before.

He glanced at my dog. I glanced at his. Then we looked at each other, and we both smiled.

The four of us had been down some rough roads to get here, but now here we were. Our houses would be a little less empty and lonely. Winston and Luna wouldn't have to spend another night in a shelter.

Hopefully that meant things were going to get better for all of us.

19

BRENT

As I led her from the truck into the house, Luna was back to shy and timid like she'd been when Taylor had first brought her out. She kept her head down, and her tail was tucked between her legs even as it wagged cautiously.

"It's okay." I held open the front door. "Come on."

She glanced at me. The door. Me again. Finally she crept into the entryway and looked around.

I unclipped her leash and hung it on the coat rack. She was obviously curious, peering at the living room and the stairs, but she didn't move.

Hoping to distract her from her nerves, I opened the bag and pulled out the rubber toy she'd had at the shelter. Instantly, her eyes lit up. She was still unsure, but she was full of hope, and her rump wiggled as her tail wagged faster, even while it was still between her legs.

"You ready?"

Her ears perked up.

I gave the toy a gentle toss, sending it bouncing down the hall.

Instantly, Luna tore after it. The toy banked off a wall, and as soon as she'd caught it in midair, she scrambled back toward me. About halfway back, though, she slowed down. As she approached me with the toy in her mouth, she ducked her head and tucked her tail again.

I reached out to pet her, but she flinched away. "It's okay," I said as softly as I could. "Relax."

The fear in her eyes made my chest tight. Hadn't we broken through that at the shelter? Except I reminded myself that Taylor had told us it would take Luna a while to settle in. She *had* been through a lot.

Okay. Okay, so it would just take time, and that was okay. I had all the time in the world, and Luna gave me something to focus on besides all the things that sucked in my life.

Maybe she'd be more relaxed if I got another dog. She'd seemed totally happy with Winston. I could ask Jon to bring Winston over to play with Luna, but… No, not today. They were probably getting settled in too. Another time.

I gestured at the sliding glass door. "You want to go outside? Check out the yard?"

That seemed to add a hopeful little spring to her tail, and her ears lifted slightly.

"Come on." I pulled the toy picker-upper out of the bag and stepped outside onto the deck, out of the way of the open door. "It's okay. Come on out."

Luna approached the door slowly. She sniffed. Looked up at me. Sniffed some more. Taking small steps and keeping her head down and her tail tucked, she ventured out uncertainly.

She stood in the doorway for a moment, front paws outside and back paws inside, ears up as she looked around and sniffed. I worried she might duck back into the house, but surprisingly, she continued across the deck and down the steps. I followed her, keeping a safe distance so she could explore without me right on her heels. She sniffed along the deck and the fence, and she trotted right up to the water's edge, but she didn't go in. Hadn't Taylor said Labs liked water?

"You can go in," I called to her as I came closer. "It's okay."

She looked at me, a mix of hope and uncertainty on her face.

I picked up a stick and tossed it a few feet out. She bounced like she wanted to go get it, but she just couldn't make herself go past the surface. With a frustrated little whine, she stared at the stick floating on the surface.

Well, damn. I didn't want her to be upset. That water was also fucking cold, so I wasn't going in after the stick. Instead, I found another, got her attention with it, and tossed it toward the deck.

That brought her to life. She transformed into the dog I'd seen at the shelter—running around, happily chasing anything I threw for her, whether it was a stick or her toy.

At one point, a fat gray squirrel sauntered across the deck railing, and Luna about lost her mind. She dropped the toy in her mouth and started barking, chasing the squirrel despite him being well out of her reach. When the squirrel disappeared up a tree and chittered. Luna barked and pawed at the grass.

I laughed. "Luna!" I held up a stick. "He's gone. Come on!"

The stick distracted her from the squirrel, and she was once again tearing around the backyard. She gave the water a few longing looks, but didn't quite go past the edge. Maybe she needed to work up to that.

I let her run around for a while. Thank God for this claw thing—otherwise I'd have had to call time on this long before she was probably ready. Without having to stoop and bend every time I wanted to get her toy or a stick, I held out for a long time and didn't even think I'd regret it later.

While she was running after the toy, I quickly checked the time on my phone. Almost four. Damn. I'd need to head over to my parents' house soon.

Luna came galloping up and dropped the toy in my hand. She yipped happily and ran in circles, tail wagging furiously until I threw her toy again.

It occurred to me that she was starting to relax with me. Would I be restarting her anxiety if I took her to my parents' house? She'd probably be okay with the dogs, but with new people? Another strange place?

It was rare for me to bail on Sunday dinner, but for Luna's sake, I called my mom this time.

"Hey," I said when she'd answered. "Listen, I'm sorry for the short notice, but I need to bow out tonight."

"What?" She sounded so disappointed. "Are you all right?" Because God knew that was the only reason I could usually bail, and it better be some sickness, not my hip or back acting up again.

"Yeah, I'm fine. But I, uh, I just got a new dog, and—"

"Ooh! You did? What kind?"

I smiled as I took Luna's toy and threw it again. "Black Lab. She's super cute, but she's also really nervous. I guess she came from a bad home."

"That's such a shame." She tsked. "I'll never understand people who treat animals badly."

"I know, right? But I really don't want to leave her alone, and I think bringing her to the house right now would just make her nervous."

Mom was quiet for a moment, then sighed. "Well, we'll certainly miss you, but I understand not wanting to stress out your pup."

But you won't understand not wanting Dad to stress me out.

I kept that to myself, though. Mom and I ended the call, and since Luna was starting to get a little tired (though she probably didn't agree), I took her inside. In the kitchen, I put down a water dish for her and filled up her food dish. She approached them cautiously but kept glancing at me.

Maybe she'd be less nervous if I wasn't in the room. Then she could eat and probably explore a little on her own.

So I left the kitchen. I'd barely stepped into the living room before she started crunching on her food. That was a good sign.

While she ate in the kitchen, I sat down on the couch with a relieved sigh. The day had been a good one, a really good one, but I'd done a lot of moving around, and this new body was tired. It was getting harder to imagine the days when I could play back-to-back hockey games and still have enough left to celebrate a win with my teammates.

More and more, though, I didn't think this slower, quieter life was as terrible as I'd made it out to be in my head. The pain and fatigue sucked, but they would improve (to a point) with conditioning. Without the frenetic pace of regular season hockey, I could slow down. I could relax and spend time with my new dog. And with Jon. I could absolutely have done without everything that had yanked my life out from under me last year, but the slower pace of my new life really *wasn't* so bad.

I wished Jon was here now. I could have used the encouragement that I wasn't doing anything wrong with Luna, that she was just getting used to me and the house and her new life. Plus she'd probably be happier to play with another dog right now. But I also kind of wanted him here now because I always wanted him around. I liked being with him more than I liked being away from him.

Which…set off all kinds of alarm bells in my head. We were just friends with benefits. Yeah, we had fun in bed together despite my shortcomings, and yeah, we now had a couple of dogs who would probably love some playdates.

But at the end of the day, we were fuck buddies. I would be wise to remember that, even when it didn't feel like we were just fuck buddies. We were, weren't we? Yeah, we were close, but that didn't mean anything, did it?

Just means you're an idiot for getting this attached.

I closed my eyes and sighed. I *was* getting attached. I couldn't even deny that.

So was I latching on to Jon because I really felt this connection with him? Or because of my deep fear that I'd never find someone for a relationship? Especially not someone my own age who was as gentle and accommodating as Jon was without making me feel embarrassed of my body and my struggle to perform?

Ugh. When did life get so complicated?

Oh. Right. When some asshole got drunk at a hockey game and decided to drive home.

The click of claws on hard wood pulled me out of my thoughts, and I turned as Luna came around the couch. She stopped and looked at me for a moment, poised like she was ready to scurry away from me if I moved suddenly. I didn't move. I let her get used to me being in the room, and once she'd apparently decided I wasn't going to do anything, she started tentatively exploring the living room. She still seemed scared—her head was down and her tail was low—but she was exploring a little more. She sniffed around the TV stand. The fireplace. The bookcases. The boxes I still hadn't unpacked.

She kept an eye on me as she made her way to the coffee table, and the whole time she sniffed all the way around the top and bottom of the table. Then she moved to sniff the couch. One end. Then the other. Around the back. The front.

As she did, she inched closer to me until she finally put her chin on the cushion beside me. Her ears lifted ever so slightly, and little creases appeared above and between her eyes, as if she were nervously asking if this was okay.

"Good girl." Remembering how she'd flinched when I reached for her before, I moved slowly this time. I offered my fingers first, which she sniffed, then shyly licked. From there, I worked up to the side of her neck, and when I scratched her gently, her tail wagged with a touch more confidence.

"That's a good girl," I said. More wagging. It was hard to imagine anyone ever being mean to her. I couldn't imagine being mean to an animal anyway, but I couldn't comprehend anyone raising their voice or their hand to this sweet, timid dog.

Moving carefully, I sat back and patted the cushion.

She looked at my hand, then at me.

"Come on." I patted it again. "You can sit up here."

She hesitated. For a moment, I thought maybe she didn't understand. But then she crouched on her haunches and tentatively put a front paw on the cushion.

"That's good!" I said, and patted the cushion a third time.

She still didn't, and I wondered if she'd gotten in trouble before for being on the furniture, but then she jumped onto the cushion beside me. At first she seemed nervous again, but only for a second before she turned in a small circle and laid down, her paws folded over the edge, and she looked up at me as the very tip of her tail moved with the most uncertain little wag.

I carefully reached over to pet her side. "Good girl."

And with that, her tail finally came to life, thumping on the cushion.

I smiled. Yeah, she'd need some time to settle in, but I had a feeling we were on the right track.

My phone chimed, startling Luna.

"It's okay." I gave her a gentle pat as I took my phone out of my pocket. "Relax."

The chime was a FaceTime request from Jon, and when I accepted it, Luna rested her chin on my leg.

"Hey," I said. "What's up?"

"Just kicking back. How's Luna settling in?"

"She was pretty nervous for a while, but…" I turned the phone so he could see her.

"Aww. She really looks like she's calmed down."

I turned the phone back to myself again. "She's still really nervous, and she's going to need time to really settle in, but I'll call this progress. How about Winston?"

"He found a stick in the yard." Jon turned his phone, revealing Winston going to town on a stick and making a mess of bark and wood chunks on the floor. Jon appeared on the screen again, and with an exasperated sigh, he said, "Good thing I bought a decent vacuum cleaner."

I laughed, glancing down at Luna as I ran my thumb along the silky black fur of her ear. "Maybe we should let them play together again. Let them wear each other out."

"I think they'd love that."

"Definitely. Bring him over next time you're here. We can see how they like the lake."

Jon laughed. "I'm looking forward to that. And hell, at least we don't have to worry about what to do with our dogs when we're having sleepovers."

My heart fluttered. I couldn't explain it, but there was something ridiculously sweet about imagining the two of us and our dogs hanging out together. It was almost domestic, and it was adorable, and it definitely pushed the bounds of friends with benefits, but whatever. I wanted more.

We chatted for a while, mostly about what the dogs were doing and how much they'd probably love splashing around in the lake together. I had a feeling Luna would actually go in if Winston went first.

Eventually, we ended the call and said good night, promising to meet up tomorrow after he was done with his appointments. Now that we were off the phone, some worry worked its way back into my otherwise good mood.

It was fun to talk about puppy playdates and all that, but how long were we going to do this? And if we stopped with the benefits, would we still be friends? That seemed like something we should talk about. Something we *would* talk about if at least one of us wasn't a gigantic coward.

Though I thought I was justified in being afraid to think about the post-Jon future. What happened after we moved on from each other?

It would suck, I had no doubt about that, but it was inevitable, so... when that time came, where did I go from there? I mean, how exactly was I supposed to word my Grindr profile? Was there a way to disclose upfront that even though I wasn't thirty yet, I had the body of a sixty-year-old and the dick of a ninety-year-old?

I cringed. Maybe that was why I was letting myself get so into this thing with Jon. Why, when it felt like we were getting closer than we should, I kept making excuses to tweak the rules rather than saying, *"No, this wasn't part of the deal."*

I liked Jon a lot, but I was also terrified I'd never find someone after him. I didn't delude myself into thinking we were in for the long haul, but I could sure see me doing this for as long as Jon wanted to simply because I was afraid of life after him. Someday I'd move on and so would he. In the meantime, I'd enjoy it and maybe try not to think about the future.

It was hard not to think about it, though. I didn't know how to date now. I missed the days when I could have my pick of men on apps (and if I couldn't find someone one night, chances were I'd be in another city before too long) and when I could go to a club and dance my way into someone's bed. Or a men's room. I wasn't picky.

What would dating look like post-accident and post-Jon? I supposed I'd find out soon enough. Tonight, I still had Jon, and I had this adorable dog settling into the house.

Petting her back, I looked down at her. "Think we should get some sleep?"

She still had her chin on my lap, but her eyes were fixed right on me.

"You want to go to bed?"

Her tail wagged.

Man, with everything that was fucked up in my world, I had this ridiculously cute Lab who I hadn't even met until this morning. I really couldn't complain, could I?

With a gentle nudge, I encouraged her to get down, and then I rose. I let her out in the backyard for a minute to do her business. Once she was done and I'd scooped it so neither of us stepped on it in the morning, she followed me upstairs.

I put her bed by the footboard so I wouldn't trip over it if I got up during the night, and I put a couple of toys and a dog biscuit in it along with a blanket she'd had in her kennel at the shelter. She sniffed it tentatively, glanced at me with a face full of uncertainty, and stepped into it. After a moment, she turned in a small circle and dropped onto the bed in a tight ball.

"Good girl." I kept a hand on the footboard to steady myself as I reached down to pet her, which got her tail wagging again. "I know you're nervous, but you're home now. Nobody's going to be mean to you anymore. I promise."

Her tail kept wagging and she licked my fingers. I had no idea if she had a clue what I was saying, but she seemed happy.

I got myself ready for bed. As I came out of the bathroom, she had her chin between her paws on the edge of her bed, and she gave one of those big sighs that I recognized from the dogs I'd had as a kid. That sound that meant she was relaxed and ready to call it a night.

I tousled her ears once more, then climbed into my own bed and shut off the light. Once I was situated on my side with a pillow between my knees, I closed my eyes and sighed, probably not sounding much different from my new dog. It was a good day.

I was starting to drift off when I heard Luna get out of her bed, and I opened my eyes and listened in case she needed to go out. Her tags jingled quietly, her paws padding on the carpet, and I realized she was right beside the bed.

I pushed myself up on my elbow and turned on the bedside light to find her beside me, gazing up with her ears down and her tail wagging. "You need to go out?"

She stood up on her haunches and put a paw on the bed, just like she'd done on the couch earlier.

I smiled. "Want to come up?"

Her tail wagged faster.

I scooted over and patted the mattress. It was higher than the couch, but she hauled herself up with no trouble and flopped down with a groan.

Chuckling, I patted her side. Okay, so now dog hair in my bed was going to be a thing. Eh, that was what laundry detergent and lint rollers were for. I could live with it, especially with my new dog snoring happily next to me. Hopefully Jon didn't mind. Though I had a feeling, softy that he was, he had a certain dog occupying real estate in his bed tonight too. With both dogs, one of us was going to need to get a bigger bed.

That thought sobered me. No, we didn't need to get bigger beds to accommodate our dogs and each other for something this casual and temporary. No matter how casual and temporary it *didn't* feel.

Absently petting Luna, I sighed. It *was* temporary. It was *meant* to be temporary. That didn't mean I couldn't enjoy it for what it was right now, including the part where we were probably fighting two large dogs for mattress space.

The thought made me laugh.

Luna snuffled and shifted a little. Then she sighed again.

I smiled in the darkness. With her, the house didn't feel so huge and empty, and I focused on that instead of the things that tried to pull me down. Like the part where, despite everything that had derailed it a year ago, not to mention my fear of being alone, my life didn't feel so empty anymore either.

Life was different now, and there were going to be ups and downs.

But maybe it would be okay after all.

20

JON

Do you mind if I swing by and show Cody his new dog?

Staring at my phone, I waited for Ashley to respond. She probably had no desire to see me today, and she would be well within her rights to tell me this could wait until next Friday. Still, I hoped she'd be willing to indulge me this one time. Cody had already messaged me a dozen times about how excited he was to meet Winston.

Don't do it for me, Ash, I thought. *Do it for him. Come on.*

To my surprise, while I was following Winston around the backyard as he sniffed everything, my phone buzzed.

We're home, so whenever.

My heart sped up. "Hey, Winston?"

He looked at me, tail wagging and ears perked up.

"You want to go for another ride?" I patted my leg and started walking. He trotted behind me as I said, "It's not just me. You get a kid to play with too." I tousled his ears. "Let's go meet him."

I knew Winston had no idea what I was saying, but I didn't care. It was great to see him this happy, and I had a feeling he was going to lose his mind when he met Cody. In fact, they probably both would.

I clipped Winston's harness to the seat belt, got in the driver seat, and headed into town. When I reached Ashley's apartment, I texted her, *In the parking lot.*

Winston's paws had barely landed on the pavement before my son came running down the stairs. "Is that him? Is that our new dog?"

I smiled. "Yep. Slow down—remember, this is a parking lot."

He skidded to a halt at the curb, looked both ways, and then hurried toward us. Winston had already noticed him, and he lit up like he had when Luna had been turned loose to play with him. He'd had a toy in his mouth, and it dropped as he woofed happily at the excited little boy jogging toward him.

"He's so cool!" Cody held out his hand, which Winston immediately started slobbering all over. "He's big!"

"Yeah, he's a big boy." I patted Winston's side. "You like him?"

"Yeah!" He was grinning so wide, it was ridiculously adorable. "I didn't know we were getting a dog."

"I didn't either," I said as I took out my phone. "But I went to the shelter with a friend so he could get one, and when I saw Winston..."

Cody nodded, still grinning. I felt a little guilty that I'd gone and gotten a dog for us without bringing him along. He'd have loved to pick one out. And maybe once Winston was settled in, we'd go get a second dog. One Cody picked out.

I just hadn't been able to walk away from Winston, and Cody didn't seem the least bit upset about his new yellow-haired friend.

"Hey guys." I held up my phone. "Smile!"

As if I even needed to tell Cody. Or Winston for that matter. That picture was going to be my lockscreen until the end of time.

"He looks thrilled." Ashley's voice made me jump. When I looked up, she was watching our son with his new dog, a fond smile on her lips.

I cleared my throat. "Cody? Or the dog?"

Turning to me, she shrugged tightly, though her voice and her expression were soft. "Both."

We exchanged smiles for the first time in a long time and watched quietly as our son got acquainted with his new dog.

As we did, I couldn't help noticing how alien and how familiar this was. Our marriage was dead and gone, but for a moment, if I didn't look too closely, we resembled an actual family again. Not enough to make me want to go back—there was no going back and we'd clearly both moved on from each other—but enough to give me a pang of sadness about what we'd left behind.

"Now that we're standing on the ashes," part of me wished I could say to her, *"was it really worth burning us down?"*

But there was no point. If she did regret it, I'd just be pouring salt on her wounds, and no matter how much bitterness I still carried, I wasn't feeling particularly vindictive right now. I didn't want to start anything in front of Cody, either. The more he saw the two of us coexisting peacefully, the better we would all be in the long run.

Ashley had Ray. I had Brent, even if I doubted we were playing for keeps. Life was going on, and today, I felt a little more hopeful that we could eventually move past all the anger and resentment, and just be Cody's mom and dad.

Standing here watching Cody play a gentle tug-of-war with Winston and a toy, things with Ashley felt less adversarial than they had in a while.

Maybe that meant there was hope for us yet.

Maybe I should've gotten Cody a dog sooner.

"It's really too bad they don't like each other," Brent mused as Winston and Luna thundered up and down his hallway.

"Right?" I laughed. "Think we should let them out in the backyard so they don't destroy your house?"

"Probably not a bad idea." He headed for the back door, calling over his shoulder, "Luna! Come on!"

The noise changed direction, and about two seconds after he'd opened the sliding glass door, the dogs shot through it in a black and yellow blur. We'd barely followed them out onto the deck when, without slowing down or hesitating, they both ran and took flying leaps into the lake.

"Ha!" Brent grinned. "She finally went in!"

"She wouldn't before?"

"Nope." He was smiling like a big kid as he watched the dogs splashing around. "She wouldn't go in the water by herself." Gesturing at them, he added, "Guess she just needed someone to go in with her."

"You didn't wade in with her?"

"Uh, no." He shot me a look. "That water is cold."

"Pfft. It's not that cold."

An eyebrow flicked up. "Okay. Fine." He motioned toward the water. "Go get in with them."

"Yeah, maybe not."

"Uh-huh. That's what I thought."

We exchanged playfully challenging looks, then chuckled and turned our attention back to the dogs, who were having the time of their lives. The water near the shore was fairly shallow, and both dogs were obviously strong swimmers. I had to keep reminding myself they were dogs, not toddlers, and they didn't need me to stay within two inches of them at all times to avoid disaster. What could I say? Old habits died hard. And even now that my son was older and had a few years of swimming lessons under his belt, I still worried when he went near the water. Sometimes he said competitive swimming sounded fun, and if he was still interested in that by the time he got to high school, I might have to look into some Xanax. Or at least keep some paper bags handy to breathe into.

Winston, though, was probably fine. He and Luna splashed and swam and chased each other, and one of them found a stick that they suddenly both needed to have right now. They argued over it, but even as they growled, their tails were wagging, spraying water all over the place.

We let them play for a while but didn't want them getting too cold, so as the daylight was starting to fade, Brent whistled. "Luna, time to come inside!"

"Winston!" I called. "Come on!"

Both dogs exploded out of the water and galloped toward us, water flying off them as they ran up onto the deck. When they skidded to halts, nearly crashing into us and each other, I had a split second to think, *Oh shit*, and shield my face before—

"Oh my God!" Brent cried as both dogs shook, showering us with lake water. "Fuck, that's cold!"

They looked up at us, smiling the way only dogs could smile with their tails still wagging and still flinging water everywhere.

Brent grabbed a couple of towels from beside the sliding glass door and handed me one. As he carefully crouched, Luna sat down and put up her paw. "Good girl," he said, and started drying off her paws while her tail thumped on the deck.

I did the best I could to dry off Winston. He was furry as hell, and he also liked being dried, so he wiggled and squirmed the entire time.

Brent chuckled, looking up from wrapping the towel around Luna. "You've been spoiled with clients that stay in one place, haven't you?"

I laughed as I tried to hold Winston still and dry him at the same time. "Yeah, they're a lot easier than this." I glanced at Luna, who sat patiently while Brent dried her sides and back. "How'd you get her to sit like that?"

"Years of training?"

"Uh-huh."

He laughed and put an arm around his damp dog. "Nah, she's been good about it every time she's come in from the yard with wet paws. Whoever had her before was a dick to her, but apparently she remembers how to do this."

"Poor girl."

"Right?" He patted her gently and smiled at her. "Nobody's gonna be mean to you anymore, though, are they?"

Her tail thumped harder and she licked his chin. He chuckled, kissed the top of her head, and hugged her against his chest.

God, he was cute. And so was she. I'd already been stupid over Brent, but ever since he'd adopted Luna, he'd become even more adorable. She was pulling him out of his funk, and she also brought out this utterly loving and tender side of him that made me weak in the knees.

Do you have any idea how sweet you are?

But I kept that to myself. Eventually, I managed to get Winston dry enough that he could go in the house.

Of course, now Brent and I were drenched, not to mention covered in dog hair and the odd leaf they'd dragged in from the lake.

Brent tossed the towels into the laundry room. As he came back out, he grinned. "Well, as long as we're soaked… You feel like spending some time in the hot tub?"

"Ooh, that sounds good." I glanced at the dogs, who were playing in the living room. "How do we keep them from joining us, though?"

Brent laughed. "Well, so far, Luna doesn't know the hot tub exists. Or that it's anything other than a big mystery box on the deck. So I say we give them some chew toys and leave them in here."

"Good plan."

He'd bought some large bones at the pet store, and he pulled out a couple for the dogs. Luna already had at least two that I could see, but I supposed he didn't want her to get jealous if he gave something to Winston and not to her. He was such a sucker for her, it made my heart melt all over again.

While the dogs gnawed happily on the bones in the living room, Brent and I slipped out onto the back deck. He put a couple of condoms and some lube beside the edge of the tub, and we exchanged glances. Oh, hell yeah. Anal was a rare thing for us, given Brent's hip, but with just a look and some strategically placed supplies, he'd all but said, *"Fuck me."*

Say the word, baby. Anything you want.

First things first, we stripped out of our damp clothes and got into the tub. Once he was situated, I joined him, and he wrapped his arms around me as we came together in a languid, unhurried kiss.

As eager as I was to be inside him, I was in no rush. We'd get there. I was having way too much fun making out with him and running my hands all over him. Especially since I couldn't get over how much this man enjoyed kissing. I'd always loved kissing, and with him, it was just intoxicating. The fact that he was never in any rush to stop? Jackpot.

Christ, I really had hit the jackpot. The way I felt every time we touched, the way my heart went wild every time those blue eyes landed on me…

We were supposed to be friends with benefits, but that wasn't what this felt like. Not at all. And it hadn't felt like that for a while.

Alarm bells should've been clanging inside my head, reminding me not to get too close because neither of us was ready for more than sex and friendship. We weren't in it for *this*. But I couldn't hear any alarm bells over the soft sounds of us kissing and breathing and my heart pounding in my ears. Maybe later, I could wring my hands and worry about us getting too close. Right now? We couldn't get close enough.

"God, I want you so bad," he murmured, stroking me slowly beneath the water.

"Yeah? What do you want me to do?"

"Fuck me," he whispered, his hand tightening around my cock.

I shivered just thinking about doing as he'd asked. "How's your hip tonight?"

He licked his lips, that hungry gleam still in his eyes. "I think it'll cooperate if I bend over the side."

"Mmm, you *want* to bend over the side?"

Brent grinned. "Kind of feel like if I do, you'll make me really glad I did."

I laughed and leaned in for another kiss. Barely breaking that kiss, I murmured, "Turn around."

He shivered.

We separated, and while he got situated over the edge, I put on the condom and some lube, and I stole a moment to rake my eyes over him. He was so self-conscious about his scars and his changed physique, but he didn't see what I saw. He couldn't have understood how beautiful he was, bent over and offering up that gorgeous ass as his back and shoulders rippled with anticipation. He couldn't have imagined how long I could have watched him like this, or that I could spend half the night chasing every drop of water down his skin with my tongue.

Or how much I wanted to have my hands all over him while my cock slid in and out of his tight hole.

Which was exactly what he was waiting for me to do.

I ran my palm down his back, and his arm almost muffled a soft moan as he shivered beneath my touch. I grinned. Then I got to work.

I always took my sweet time prepping him. Long after he was relaxed, I kept on rimming him just because I wanted to, and I did the same when I was fingering him. I wasn't worried about hurting him —he could take me easily enough—but teasing him like that was so damn fun. Nothing turned me on like watching him tremble and squirm or listening to him beg for my dick.

"Jon." He rocked back against me, driving my fingers deeper. "Just fuck me already."

"You want me to?" I purred. "Because I'm enjoying—"

"*Jon,*" he pleaded. "Please. Now."

I slid my fingers free. "Let me put on some more lube."

He made a frustrated sound, and while I slicked myself up again, he kept rocking a little as if he just couldn't wait to have me inside him.

I can relate, baby, I thought as I guided my cock to him. *I can't wait to... Oh God.* I closed my eyes and moaned as he took the head, and he swore.

"This good?" I panted. "Not hurting—"

"It's good," he said. "Oh my God, Jon..."

I eased in deeper, moving slowly and carefully as he yielded to me. The condom dulled the sensations just enough to keep me from going off too soon. Turned on as I was, I needed all the help I could get, especially since I wanted this to last. I wanted to savor every stroke and every moan until neither of us could take any more.

With one hand on his right hip to steady myself, I slid the other up and down his back as I slowly rode his perfect ass. "You are so fucking hot," I ground out. "Jesus, Brent..."

He moaned something I didn't understand. It might've been perfectly clear English, but my brain was so scrambled at this point, so focused on how good it felt to be moving in and out of him, I couldn't make sense of anything else.

I wrapped my arm around his waist and leaned down to kiss the back of his neck as I kept slowly rocking my hips.

"Oh my God, you feel good," he moaned. "Ungh..."

I nuzzled the side of his neck. "So do you."

I didn't ask if he was in pain. We'd been doing this long enough that I knew he'd tell me if he was hurting too much to continue—either he'd say it out loud, or the tension in his muscles and the hitches of his breath would give him away. Asking would just draw his attention to his pain, and I didn't want to ruin the mood he was obviously enjoying.

Instead, I just kept slowly fucking him, and condom or not, it was genuinely a miracle I hadn't come already. With Brent, I had to be more careful than I'd been when I'd topped anyone in the past, and the accidental side effect of that was the most deliciously sensual sex I'd ever had. Thrusting deep and hard was fun and all, but taking forever to complete a slow slide in and back out? Oh my God.

Burying my face against his neck, I inhaled deeply, catching his familiar scent over the chlorine smell, and I kept rocking slowly in and out of him.

"Jon."

I lifted my head a little. "Hmm?"

He didn't say anything. He just twisted around slightly, and I got the message—leaning forward, I found his lips with mine, and oh, yeah, adding his languid kiss to what we were doing was *perfect*. It was a little harder to move my hips while still being mindful of his, but it was enough. It was amazing. It was hot, and sweet, and decadent, and…

Right.

This was *right*. This was what we were supposed to be doing together.

Except this wasn't how friends with benefits had sex. This wasn't how it felt to be with a casual fuck buddy. I hadn't felt this close to someone, this intimately tangled up with another person, since long before the end of my marriage, and I wanted to just get lost in it. Get drunk on it. Drown in this and in Brent and in all the intimacy I'd been craving for the past few months. Or years.

Brent broke the kiss and let his head fall forward, and I buried my face against his neck again. My head spun. I was supposed to be driven by the need for friction and release, and the need to give him the same. This insatiable hunger to be as close to him as I could get? That wasn't what I'd signed up for. It wasn't what we'd agreed to.

But damn if I could resist.

A shudder went through me, and I had just enough presence of mind not to thrust into Brent. It was a struggle, not losing control when I was so close to coming, but I was always careful.

"You getting there?" he asked over his shoulder.

"Uh-huh." I picked up a little speed—not enough to hurt him—and groaned as my orgasm closed in fast. "God, yeah…"

Brent moved in a way I couldn't quite define, and oh, God, I couldn't take anymore. I dug my fingers into his shoulder, buried myself inside him, and came, and he kept moving, kept driving me on until my knees almost went out from under me.

Slumping over him, I exhaled. "In case I didn't mention this the first time?" I kissed the back of his neck. "Fucking you is *amazing*."

21

BRENT

I wished I could say nights like the one we'd spent in my hot tub were a regular thing, but such was life. Pain was what it was, and I was glad Jon still didn't mind hanging out even when sex was off the table. As much as I'd gotten used to my reclusive existence, I was definitely starting to like getting out of the house more, especially when that meant spending time with him.

Tonight, we sat on his couch, bingeing a series of true crime shows. I sat on the recliner end with an icepack pressed to my left hip, and Jon carefully sat against me on the other side. Luna was beside Jon with her head on his leg, and Winston looked like someone had thrown him onto the loveseat.

As much as I could have done without the pain in my hip, leg, back, and the handful of other body parts that had decided to join the party tonight, this was nice. There were worse ways to spend an evening than relaxing with Jon and our dogs.

"Do these people actually think they won't get caught?" Jon sipped his Coke. "Because I feel like they don't plan very well."

"Right? And cleaning up the blood never works." I gave a haughty sniff. "At least put a tarp down or something first."

He turned to me, eyebrows quirked. "Should I be sleeping with one eye open?"

"I don't know," I deadpanned. "Should you?"

We both laughed, and he elbowed me playfully. He opened his

mouth to say something, but right then, a ringtone I didn't recognize started playing.

"Oh for fuck's sake," he muttered, gesturing past me at the end table. "Could you hand me my phone?" I passed it to him. "Thanks." He put it to his ear. "Hey, what's up?"

His eyes lost focus. I could hear the voice on the other end but couldn't quite make out what she was saying, only that she didn't sound thrilled. Not angry, just…upset?

Jon sighed. "Sure. Yeah. I'll, um…" He hesitated. "Do you need me to come get him, or can you drop him off?" Beat. "Okay, I'll be there as soon as I can. Sure. See you in a bit." Then he put the phone down, and he tapped his nails on the darkened screen.

Heart sinking, I cleared my throat. "Do you, uh, need to…?"

He turned to me, forehead creased. "Long story short, my ex-wife's boyfriend's car broke down near Manchester, so she needs me to come get my son for the evening while she goes to get him."

"Oh." I tried not to let my disappointment show. I was enjoying our evening, but of course his son came first. "Okay. I'll get out of your hair, then."

Jon studied me. Then he cautiously said, "Do you, um… Do you want to come with me?"

That was unexpected. "You…want me to meet your son?"

He seemed to consider it for a moment before he nodded. "Yeah, I do. If you want to, I mean."

"Sure. Yeah." I shrugged. "Why not?" I wanted to ask if that would be too weird or if we were crossing any lines, but Jon didn't press. And anyway, if Ashley needed him to come get Cody, we probably needed to get moving. We could dissect this in the car.

So, we collected our phones and jackets, and Jon grabbed his keys. The dogs followed us to the door, tails wagging but faces full of confusion.

"We'll be right back," Jon told Winston. "No parties, okay?"

I tousled Luna's ears. "Winston's in charge. Got it?"

They both stared at us like we were idiots, and we chuckled as we headed outside. I always hated leaving Luna alone, especially since she used those big brown eyes to guilt the hell out of me whenever I tried to go, but I didn't feel so bad when she had Winston for company. They'd probably forget all about us in like five minutes.

As Jon drove out of his secluded neighborhood, I turned to him. "So, um, you really don't mind me meeting your son?"

He shook his head. "No. In fact, now that it's on the table, I'd really like you to meet him."

"Why's that?"

"Quite frankly, because meeting you might counterbalance the guy my ex is seeing. I know that sounds kind of dickish, but the dude is..." He stared at the road for a moment. "The thing is, you're mellow and easygoing, and I think Cody will be more comfortable around you than he is around Ray."

"Oh." I had no idea what to say to that.

"I guess I just want him to know that not everyone his parents date post-divorce will be...like *that*." He paused, and in a low growl, he added, "That, and I just have a gut feeling that Ray isn't exactly the type who'd be caught dead with a rainbow flag in his hand. Ashley assures me he doesn't let anything homophobic slip out around Cody." Jon tapped his thumbs on the wheel and glanced at me, his forehead creased. "But I don't trust him."

"So having Cody see us together will make him see what a same-sex couple really looks like."

"Bingo." He stole another glance at me in the low light. "Are you okay with that?"

"Yeah, I am. Honestly, I'd have sold my soul for a queer role model at his age."

"Really?"

"Are you kidding? I was a senior in high school when I figured out same-sex couples weren't some weird anomaly or deviant thing." I rolled my eyes. "My dad would probably prefer I still thought that, but..."

"Your dad's a homophobe?"

"My dad's..." I stared out at the headlight-illuminated road as I tried to figure out how to explain it. "Like, he accepts that I'm gay. And I've brought boyfriends home before. But he still has this hang-up about like letting kids see us together, or whether it's appropriate for me to bring a boyfriend to this or that family thing. I'm pretty sure he still hasn't gotten over me bringing a boyfriend to my grandma's funeral when I was in college."

"Did he say anything at the time?"

"He didn't make a scene, but he told me in private that he didn't think it was the time or place to be flaunting my relationship."

"Oh for fuck's sake," Jon muttered, and I thought he might've rolled his eyes too. "Because showing up in public is 'flaunting.'"

"I know, right? But my dad thinks that way. And I kind of did too when I was younger. So, help a kid see that two guys can be together and it's no big deal?" I nodded sharply. "Definitely. I'm there."

Jon smiled. "Awesome. Just, uh, don't freak out when I call you my boyfriend."

I laughed. "Well, I assume you haven't explained the concept of friends with benefits to your son, so…yeah, don't worry about it."

"Yeah, no, definitely not having that conversation with a ten-year-old."

"Can't blame you." I pressed my elbow into the window and watched him in the darkness. "And he knows you date men?"

Jon nodded. "Oh yeah. I told him a couple of years ago that I dated boys before I dated his mom. And that wasn't much of a shock to him, because the first time he noticed two men holding hands, his mother and I explained that sometimes boys like boys and girls like girls."

"How old was he when you had that conversation?"

"Four, I think?"

I whistled. "Damn. Lucky kid."

Jon glanced at me. "Yeah?"

Scowling, I nodded. "My dad was really vocal about not allowing gay kids to do sports. They're wimps, they'll be in locker rooms with straight boys…" I waved a hand. "He was really loud about it when he found out the kicker on my brother's football team was gay."

"For fuck's sake." Jon shook his head. "Like being gay means you can't kick a football."

"Right? Joke was on Dad, too—the kid moved to another school his junior year, and he helped his team win back-to-back state championships." I laughed, but then sighed. "Anyway, yeah, my dad wasn't thrilled about it. I didn't come out until college because of him, and he didn't like that. Then I got a bunch of attention for coming out publicly after I'd started playing professionally, and me and a few other gay players were featured in a bunch of publicity. Everyone was really positive about it, and suddenly Dad was proud of his out gay hockey player son." I rolled my eyes. "He still didn't want me bringing boyfriends to things like funerals, but he was happy to wave that rainbow flag when it was the appropriate time or place."

Jon grunted in quiet amusement.

I studied him. "How did your parents take it when you came out?" I paused. "Wait, didn't you say your mom was worried about you getting AIDS?"

"Yep, and they thought it was a phase and an act of rebellion. They definitely weren't happy. Then I started dating Ashley in college, so they figured I'd just stopped being queer. Clearly it *was* just a phase, right? I don't know how many times I explained bisexuality to them, but as far as they were concerned, I had a wife, so I was straight. End of story." His jaw worked and he glared at the road ahead. "At least until we had problems when we started trying to have kids."

I blinked. "Seriously?"

"Yep." He sounded more bitter than I'd ever heard him. "They were… I mean, they were as tactful as anyone can be with an accusation like that, probably because they didn't want to actually say, 'Are you sure you're not using up all your energy screwing dudes behind your wife's back?' but it was there."

"Wow. They really thought…" I pressed back against the seat and exhaled. "That's messed up."

"It is. And that's also why Ashley and I were determined to explain queerness to our son as soon as he was old enough to understand it. Age-appropriately, of course, but we wanted him to hear it from us and know that there's nothing wrong with it." He tapped his thumbs on the wheel again. "So he knows I'm queer, but this will be his first exposure to me actually dating a man."

"No pressure, right?"

Jon chuckled and patted my leg. "No pressure."

About twenty minutes after we left Jon's house, he pulled into the parking lot of an apartment complex and took a vacant guest spot. At the front door of what was apparently his ex-wife's unit, Jon took a deep breath. Nervous? Maybe.

Then he knocked.

The woman who answered was white with her blonde hair pulled into a messy ponytail, and she had on an oversized Moo U hockey jersey. Her eyes went right to me, then flicked to Jon. "Um..."

"Brent, this is Ashley. My ex-wife." Jon gestured at me. "Ash, this is Brent. My boyfriend."

Okay, he'd warned me, but I had to admit—it definitely sounded strange to hear him refer to me as his boyfriend. I didn't let myself linger on it, though. I knew why he was telling her that. It didn't change the arrangement we had.

The suspicion in Ashley's face intensified even as she and I shook hands. "Boyfriend? I didn't realize you were seeing anyone."

"It's kind of a new thing."

Narrowing her eyes, she released my hand and looked at him. "So you're going to bring our son over with your *new* boyfriend?"

"Ash, you asked me to come pick him up. Brent was with me."

She pressed her lips together and pushed out a breath through her nose. Then she shrugged tightly. "All right. I can come get him around eleven, but—"

"He'll be asleep by then," Jon said. "Let's just let him sleep over, and we'll make up the day some other week."

For a second, she looked like she might argue, but she finally said, "Okay. Whatever. Let me go get him—I need to take off."

She left the front door open and stepped away, but she didn't invite us in. Somehow I wasn't surprised.

Under my breath, I said, "I'm totally killing this. She loves me."

Jon snorted, and we both laughed quietly.

A moment later, Ashley returned with their son. Cody was super cute. He was small for his age—I thought, anyway—with platinum blond hair and glasses, and he was wearing a Captain America T-shirt. I could definitely see the resemblance to both of his parents. He had his mom's hair color, and I suspected as he got older and lost some of the roundness in his face, he'd be the spitting image of Jon.

"Cody," Jon said, "this is Brent. He's going to be hanging out with us tonight."

Cody looked up at me and offered a shy, "Hi."

"Hey." I smiled. I wasn't quite sure what to say; I hadn't had a lot of experience with kids aside from my nieces and nephews, and they were younger than Cody. Plus I didn't want to say or do the wrong thing while Cody's mom was still standing here glaring at me like she was just *waiting* for me to give her a reason to say, *"Nope, he can't be around my kid."*

To Jon, Ashley said, "He hasn't had dinner yet." Instantly, she shifted to a defensive expression and tone. "Ray called right before I called you. This came up suddenly."

"All right." He put up his hand, then turned to Cody. "You have everything?"

Cody looked up at Ashley. "Am I staying the whole night?"

She glanced at Jon. Then at me. Without sounding the least bit pleased about it, she said, "I don't know how late I'll be, so you'll be staying at Dad's tonight. Is that okay?"

He nodded without hesitation, and he broke into a smile. "Yeah! I have everything I need."

"Are you sure? Did you pack your homework?"

Cody tapped the strap of the backpack he was wearing.

"Okay. I'll see you tomorrow." Ashley hugged Cody and exchanged frosty looks with Jon. She gave me a polite(ish) goodbye, and Jon and I left with Cody. On the way down the stairs, we glanced at each other over Cody's head, and neither of us had to say a word. I made a *What the hell?* face, and Jon rolled his eyes. Well, at least it wasn't just me.

Cody was hungry, so we stopped at a sandwich shop on the way, and at home, the three of us sat down to eat at the kitchen table.

That was kind of surreal. I'd come over to Jon's thinking we'd watch a movie or maybe fool around. Now we were having dinner with his son while our dogs patiently waited for table scraps. I'd introduced Cody to Luna when we'd arrived, and she hadn't been at all shy with him. That was encouraging; adults were still tough for her, but she wasn't afraid of kids, and he seemed to be as enthralled with her as he was with Winston.

While we ate, Jon asked about Cody's day at school, and all three of us talked about the dogs in between tossing them those coveted scraps, and it was surprisingly easy. I'd never dated anyone with kids. If I squinted hard enough, it almost looked like that was exactly what I was doing right now—dating a single dad, as opposed to being that single dad's booty call during his non-custody weeks.

It probably should have been weird. If anything, the weird thing was how weird this *wasn't*.

After dinner, Jon set up Cody at the table with his homework. Then he stepped into the living room with me. "Listen, I just need to help him through one of the subjects he has a hard time with. Twenty minutes, tops. After that, he prefers to work on his own and have me check everything later." Brow pinched, he quietly asked, "Do you mind waiting? And then we can watch a movie or something?"

"Sure, yeah." I shrugged. "No problem."

"Really?"

"Dude, he's your kid. I get it." I touched his cheek and kissed him softly. "We can adapt. It's all good."

He exhaled as if he'd really been worried about it. "Thank you."

"Don't mention it." I paused. "And, um, your ex-wife doesn't like me, does she?"

Jon barked a laugh. "It's not that. She doesn't like *me*. You're just guilty by association."

"Oh. But I didn't think you guys had that bad of a breakup. What's her deal?"

Sighing, he shook his head. "I've been wondering that for a while, believe me. It is what it is, though, and I mean it—thank you for being flexible tonight." He squeezed my hand. "I know this isn't quite what you had in mind for this evening."

"It's all right." I nodded toward the kitchen. "Go help him with his work. I'll peruse Netflix and see what's on."

Jon's smile made all our upended plans worth it. We probably wouldn't fool around tonight, and I'd probably sleep at home, but I had no complaints.

He went into the living room. As I browsed Netflix, I could hear the two of them talking.

"But I thought it was 'i before e, except after c.'" Cody sounded aggravated.

"I know. And it usually is."

"So how do I know when a word breaks that rule?"

Jon didn't answer right away. Then he sighed. "I wish I could tell you. The fact is, the English language is kind of a jerk, and the rules always apply right up until they don't. If it makes you feel any better, they trip me up too."

"Really?"

"Oh yeah." Jon groaned with exaggerated exasperation. "I will never in a million years spell 'definitely' on the first try, and I *still* have to stop and think about the differences between 'there,' 'they're,' or 'their.'"

Cody's giggle was soft, but made it to the living room where I was sitting, and I smiled to myself. I wondered if Jon knew how sweet he sounded. And how much young me would have killed for a teacher or a tutor who came out and said, *"Yeah, sometimes it sucks and doesn't make any sense, and you're not the only one who has a hard time with it."*

Of course I knew now that a lot of it had to do with English scavenging words from other languages, but ten-year-old me could have been spared a lot of frustration just by hearing that, as Jon put it, the English language was kind of a jerk.

I chuckled softly and kept scrolling through movies.

What does it say about me and what we're doing that listening to you with your son makes me smile like this?

22

JON

While Brent was at his folks' house for dinner on Sunday, I took Cody and Winston to one of the dog parks in town. Here, we could let Winston off his leash, and I thought Cody was going to wear out his arm throwing the toy for him. I genuinely wondered if my kid or my dog would run out of energy first, but I'd probably be worn out from watching them long before either of them were ready to call it a day.

These days, I was starting to understand why my dad used to grumble, *"If I could bottle up all that energy from you kids, I'd be a billionaire."* I wasn't exactly ready to be put out to pasture, but the endless energy of my youth was a distant memory.

And how long before my much-younger boyfriend notices?

I shook that thought away. Brent wasn't *that* much younger than me. And he wasn't even my boyfriend. Anyhow, today was about spending time with my son. Something I didn't get to do nearly as often as I would have liked.

Returning with his toy, Winston skidded to a halt but slipped on the grass and crashed into Cody. They toppled into the muddy grass, legs and arms flailing.

I was instantly on my feet, my head full of visions of my son upset and crying, but instead, Cody was giggling. He and Winston started playing tug-of-war with the toy while Cody tried to get up, and he laughed his head off while Winston's tail wagged furiously.

Watching them, I shook my head and chuckled. I really should have gotten Cody a dog sooner. He'd always been shy when he first met kids, and he didn't make friends as easily as some of his classmates, but he jumped right out of his shell with animals. With a dog as happy and playful as Winston? My God, they'd been instant best friends.

I let them play until I was amazed either of them could still move. Dusk was setting in, so I called Cody, and he trotted over to me with Winston right behind him. His clothes would need to go in the wash as soon as we got home, but whatever. My son and my dog had had the time of their lives, and a few grass and mud stains weren't the end of the world.

"Getting hungry?" I asked.

Cody nodded. "Yeah."

"Okay. Let's go home and I'll find us something to eat."

We headed for the car, and Winston looked up at me as we walked, his tongue hanging out and his big eyes bright and happy. I reached down and petted him, which got his tail wagging even harder. It still broke my heart to think about how long he'd been at that shelter. I just hoped the home I gave him had been worth the wait. He sure seemed happy these days, especially when he was playing with Cody or Luna. Hell, maybe he'd get to play with both of them more often. Now that I'd introduced Brent and Cody, there was no reason we couldn't all spend more time together, including our dogs.

Where exactly does "hanging out with my kid and our dogs" fit into friends with benefits?

Am I kidding myself if I think that's still what we're doing?

My stomach knotted.

Am I kidding myself if I think Brent will want to stick around if we're doing more than what we set out to do?

That probably wasn't a train of thought I should linger on too long. The best I could do was enjoy this thing with Brent for as long as I had it, and not think too hard about the inevitable.

In the meantime, I had an evening to spend with my son.

We left the park, and at the stop sign by the elementary school, I stopped and glanced in the rearview. Winston was sprawled across the backseat and was already snoring with his head in Cody's lap. "I think you wore him out."

Cody smiled, patting his dog's side. "I bet if I showed him a stick, he'd wake up."

"Hmm, probably. But let the poor guy take a nap." I pulled out and hung a left on to the road that would take us home. "What do you think for dinner—spaghetti or chicken burgers?"

"Hmm. Spaghetti?"

"Okay." I nodded. "When we get home, how about you change into some clean clothes, and I'll toss these in the laundry. Then I'll get dinner going."

"Okay. Is Brent coming for dinner?" He sounded hopeful.

"He's having dinner with his parents tonight."

"Oh." He sounded disappointed.

I glanced at him. "So what do you think of him?"

Cody shrugged. "He's nice."

"Yeah?"

He nodded. "Are you and Brent going to live together like Mom and Ray?"

The question prodded at some raw nerves he couldn't have known about, and I kept my tone and face neutral. "I don't know. That's the thing when people are dating. Sometimes they move in together or get married." I half-shrugged. "Sometimes they don't."

"Oh."

How was I supposed to explain to him how slim the odds were for me and Brent living together or being anything remotely serious? I couldn't explain what we were doing. Or that we had left that original friends with benefits thing in the dust and had moved on to something I couldn't define and was afraid to define because it would probably scare Brent right out the door. I was probably fine and good for a guy who was still picking up the pieces after he'd had his world yanked out from under him. Once he realized he had plenty of life left in him and didn't need to settle for someone from the bargain bin?

Unaware of my depressing thoughts, Cody asked, "Would you be sad if you and Brent broke up?"

I tried not to visibly wince. It was a struggle. "Sure, I would. He's a nice guy. I like him a lot. And breaking up with someone is always hard."

"It is?"

I nodded. "Yeah. But that's part of dating. It's why people date."

Cody watched me, confusion written across his face.

I shifted in my seat. "You date someone to see if they're a person you want to live with or marry. Sometimes you can really, really like someone, but when you live together, it doesn't work."

"Like you and Mom?"

Ouch, kid.

"Mom and I..." I thought about it, choosing my words carefully. "Well, we were together a long time. Sometimes people change, and they realize they don't get along enough to live together anymore. It doesn't mean there's anything wrong with either of them, or they don't love each other anymore." *Doesn't mean one is getting action on the side either, but we know* that *happens.* "They're just happier by themselves or with other people."

"Oh." He held my gaze. "Do you and Mom still love each other?"

It was hard not to visibly flinch. And how the hell was I supposed to answer that in a way that was diplomatic and honest?

I finally settled on, "Your mom and I had a lot of really good years together, and we have you." I smiled even though it hurt. "We realized we're happier not living together, but I'll always love her."

I wasn't sure how he'd take that. To my surprise, some tension in his neck and shoulders eased. How long had he been carrying that? Had this been bothering him all this time?

"Is Mom going to marry Ray?"

Boy, he was just full of easy questions tonight, wasn't he?

"I don't know," I said with total honesty. Then I cautiously asked, "Do you want them to?"

"I don't know." He shrugged, fidgeting. "He lives with us now."

I nodded slowly, glancing at him in the rearview. I tried to tread carefully where my ex-wife and her new love life were concerned, but I also wanted to make sure our son wasn't upset. "How do you like living with him?"

"It's okay, I guess. Mom wants to get a cat, but Ray says no."

Oh, now *she wants a cat? In twenty years, she never wanted a pet, but—*

I rolled my eyes at my own stupid thoughts. I had a dog now, and Ashley's pet preferences weren't my problem anymore. "He doesn't like cats?"

Cody shook his head. Before I could ask any further, he said, "Does Brent like dogs?"

I brightened. "He loves them. That's why he got Luna. In fact, that's how I got Winston, actually—we were at the shelter so he could get a dog." I glanced at him again. "So, do you like him?"

"Yeah, he's nice. And I really like Luna."

Chuckling, I kept following North Avenue toward home. Well, my son liked my quasi-boyfriend's dog. That had to be a good sign, right?

Cody sometimes put up a fuss at bedtime. My mom insisted that was karma for me being a pain in the ass about bedtime until I was a teenager, at which point they just gave up and said if I was tired at school, that was on me. God help me when Cody reached that age.

Tonight, though, he didn't resist much. Once he had on his pajamas and he'd brushed his teeth, and after we'd read a chapter from that book we were both loving, he faceplanted in his pillow, and that was that.

By the time I was lounging in my own bed to FaceTime with Brent, Cody was sound asleep and Winston was snoring beside me.

"Is that Winston in the background?" Brent asked with a laugh a few seconds into our call.

"Yep." I turned the phone so Brent could see the dog. "He wore himself out with Cody earlier."

"Oh, he must've had fun."

"He did." I turned the screen toward myself again. "They were both ready to collapse when we got home."

"I bet." Brent shifted his own screen, and revealed Luna flat on the couch beside him. "My parents have three papillons, and they all exhausted each other."

"Papillons? Aren't those little yappers?"

He turned his phone back to himself. "They can be, and they have a ton of energy, but they're pretty well-behaved. They're so much better than the chihuahuas my mom used to have." He groaned. "My God, those things were like what would happen if someone poured cocaine into a Five Hour Energy, and it came to life."

I laughed hard enough to startle Winston, but then he sighed and went right back to snoring. "So other than the dogs wearing each other out, how was dinner?"

Brent's humor faded. "Ugh. I swear to God, dinner with my family these days is like when my coach used to call me into the office for *a talk*."

"Shit. That bad?"

"Uh-huh. It's…" He shook his head. "It just sucks. Let's leave it at that."

I wanted to ask. It clearly stressed him out, and I was curious how bad tonight had been and why he *still* kept subjecting himself to it. He obviously didn't want to discuss it, though, so I let it be. "So, um, I still have Cody this week, but if you want to come over tomorrow night and just hang, we'll be here."

"Cool. Should I bring Luna?"

"Of course! Cody and Winston will be thrilled." I paused, thinking about what I'd said. "That, um… I mean, is this crossing a line? We're friends with benefits, but now you're hanging out with me and my son, and…" I was too nervous to finish the thought because he might catch on that, let's be real here—the "friends with benefits" ship had sailed a *long* time ago.

Brent seemed to consider it for a moment, eyes fixed on something offscreen. Probably Luna. From the way his shoulder moved slightly, he was petting her. Finally, he looked at me, and he shook his head. "I don't think it's crossing a line."

"You sure?"

"Nah." His smile was tentative. "It means I get to see you more often, so I can't complain."

"Okay. I just… I mean, some people think it's a bit intimate with a single parent. When they start meeting the kids and spending time with them. And with the way we set out in the beginning—if it bugs you, just say so. I'm not going to get offended if you want to put down some boundaries, even if that boundary is that you'd rather not spend time with my kid."

Brent was already shaking his head. "No, I don't think we need to do that. If *you'd* rather we didn't, then cool. But I'm okay with this."

"Yeah?"

He nodded. "I don't know how it meshes with our rules or what we decided in the beginning." He half-shrugged. "I just know I like it."

"Me too." God, wasn't that an understatement? "Whatever it is we're doing."

Well, that was a relief. I knew this wasn't forever, but I was so glad we had it now.

We chatted a while longer. He avoided the subject of dinner with his parents, and that was fine with me. It was clearly not a pleasant topic for him, and he didn't need to get himself wound up and tense over it right before he tried to go to sleep. So we shot the shit about our dogs and whatever else came to mind.

And even with that lingering worry in the back of my mind, chatting with him relaxed me. I loved his smile. I loved how adorable he was when he told me about Luna getting all excited when she realized she'd gotten her very own hamburger in the McDonald's drive-thru.

"She was so cute," he gushed. "That tail is dangerous, though—she whapped me in the face with it after I gave her a piece of the burger."

I laughed. "You didn't tell her to sit first?"

"I did, but she got so excited, she was trying to run in circles on the seat, and my dumb ass had unclipped her since we were just sitting in the parking lot." He sighed with playful exasperation. "Guess I know better than to do *that* again."

"But you'll probably do it again."

His lips quirked, and then he shrugged. "Yeah, probably."

We both laughed, and the conversation kept wandering until we eventually had to call it a night. As we wrapped things up, I said, "I'll see you tomorrow?"

"Definitely." He flashed me another one of those disarming smiles. "Have a good night."

"You too."

We ended the call, and I put the phone on my chest. Absently petting Winston, I stared up at the ceiling.

Brent didn't think we were crossing a line. And he was right—having him here with Cody meant we could see each other more often. A lot more often. Even if we couldn't hook up, which we frequently couldn't anyway because of Brent's pain levels, we could be together.

Friends with benefits, huh?

I didn't want to think too hard about whether there was something more between us. Or if I *wanted* there to be something more.

I'd just enjoy whatever the hell this was for as long as I was enough for Brent.

23

BRENT

Now that I'd met Cody, I saw a lot more of Jon. We mostly hung out when Cody was with us, and I didn't always spend the night, but that was fine. It meant spending more time with Jon, so I had no objections. When it was just the two of us, we fooled around, bodies permitting. When Cody was there, Jon and I were affectionate but didn't do much in bed, though I still slept over a few times a week.

At Cody's bedtime, Jon would slip out for half an hour or so to read to him, something they did religiously. Afterward, he'd join me again, and we'd watch TV or just hang out.

I was kind of surprised he wanted me to spend the night when his kid was there, but even Ashley was okay with it. After all, she and her boyfriend were living together. Having grown up as a kid who didn't understand until my late teens that same-sex couples were perfectly normal, I was absolutely onboard with Cody being ten years old and fully at ease with Dad having a boyfriend.

This week was Jon's custody week, so he'd be home with Cody later this afternoon. In the meantime, I was bound and determined to make some headway on Jon's kitchen, so I was at the house by around eleven in the morning.

Since I was planning to spend the day and part of the evening at Jon's, I brought Luna with me. No sense leaving her home alone when she'd be happy to play here with Winston. Plus I wouldn't have to worry about running back to the house to let her out, and anyway, Jon and I had dog-proofed all the areas of his house and yard that were under construction. It was already kid-proofed—Cody was careful and all, but nobody needed him stepping on a nail or something—and now we'd made sure there was nothing the dogs could destroy or get hurt on.

The dogs played a bit, then napped, while I worked on taping the crown molding in an empty bedroom. At a little after one, I made myself some lunch and sat down at the table. Luna and Winston came trotting in and sat side by side, staring intently at me as if they might will my sandwich to leap from my hand and into their waiting jaws.

Of course I shared pieces with them. I'm not an asshole.

I was just getting ready to get back to work when Jon called.

"Hey," he said. "Listen, Tanner just texted me. Whoever was performing at Vino and Veritas tonight had to bail, and they were looking at a pretty decent crowd, so he's asking me to fill in."

"Are you going to?"

"I should, but..." He exhaled. "The thing is, I can't take Cody to a wine bar, and I'd just as soon not leave him alone in the bookstore. Especially since he really doesn't need to overhear the songs I wrote about his mom divorcing me. I tried his babysitter, but she's not answering, so I'm—"

"Let him stay here." I shrugged for no one's benefit but my own. "I can get some more work done on that backsplash, and he won't be here alone."

Jon went quiet. "Are you sure?"

"Yeah, it's fine."

More silence.

I went on, "Seriously. As long as you don't expect me to help him with math homework or something, we're good."

"You suck at math too?" He tsked melodramatically. "Great. Anyway, no, I just need to make sure there's someone there with him. He handles his homework fine on his own most of the time, and I'll grab some dinner for all three of us."

"Oh, free food? Sounds good to me."

He laughed softly. "You're the best. I'll see you tonight."

Jon arrived around five-thirty with Cody and some takeout they'd picked up. The three of us ate dinner at the kitchen table, and then Cody went into his bedroom to do his homework while Jon went to change clothes before his performance.

When he came back down, he put his guitar by the front door and came into the kitchen. "So I checked with Cody, and he's fine staying with you. And Ashley knows you're here with him too." He put a sticky note on the counter. "This has her number and the number for Vino and Veritas in case you need them. Tell whoever answers that you're watching Cody and need to talk to me, and they'll grab me."

I nodded. "Okay. I think we'll be fine, but...good to know." I studied him. "And you're sure about this? Leaving him alone with me?"

"Yeah, I am. I trust you." He inclined his head. "Are *you* sure about it?"

"It's fine." I smiled, gesturing over my shoulder at the kitchen. "Like I said, I've got that backsplash to work on. I might even make enough headway that your kitchen won't be trashed anymore."

He chuckled. "I meant the part about staying here with Cody."

"Yeah, it's fine. I might be a little nervous if you left me with a toddler or something, but..."

"Oh, hell, *I* was nervous being left with a toddler, and he was mine." He squeezed my arm. "This age? They're a breeze."

"Thank God for that."

"Tell me about it. Hopefully I don't pay for him being a chill, easy kid when he's a teenager."

I grimaced. "Good luck with that."

"Yeah. Thanks." He checked his phone. "I should feed the dogs before—"

"Jon." I turned his face toward me. "I'll take care of the dogs, and Cody will be fine. *Go*."

He exhaled. "Okay. Okay. I'm going." He lifted his chin for a quick kiss. "Thank you again. You're a lifesaver."

"Don't worry about it."

He left while I took care of feeding Winston and Luna. They ate the same kind of food, which made this part easy, and both dogs had dishes at both houses. Because we totally weren't adapting every facet of our lives to the fact that we were together more nights than not.

With the dogs crunching happily on their kibble, I went back to my project in the kitchen.

As I worked, I tried not to read too much into anything Jon and I were doing. We were still friends with benefits even if we were starting to feel a lot like boyfriends who'd settled into a comfortable groove. For us, part of that meant being friends, and if he trusted me enough to leave me in his house to keep an eye on his son, then that was a good thing. It didn't mean we were getting in over our heads or that this was turning more serious than either of us had bargained for.

I wondered how many times I'd have to have this conversation with myself before I believed that.

For the moment, I focused on my task at hand. Right now, that consisted of arranging small ceramic tiles on a sheet of mesh so I could attach the backsplash. I worked at the kitchen island so I could stand, which my physical therapist had suggested as a way to strengthen some of the angry soft tissue. When my hip ached, I'd shift slightly to one side, carefully stretching the offended muscles and tendons. To my surprise, it helped. The low-grade ache in my hip and knees was annoying, and the odd twinge or spasm made my teeth grind, but compared to a few months ago, it was a hell of a lot better. I'd take it.

I was just pressing a spacer in between some tiles when Cody came in. We glanced at each other, but he didn't say anything. He was a little shy, and he might've been nervous about interacting with just me, so I said hello and left it at that. Especially since, hell, who was I kidding? I was nervous around *him*. I was okay with kids, but this was Jon's kid. And Jon wasn't here. No pressure or anything.

Cody poured himself a cup of juice, but he didn't go back into his bedroom. Instead, he climbed onto one of the high barstools on the other side of the island and peered at the tiles. "What are you doing?"

I gestured at the mesh laid out in front of me. "Putting all the tiles in place so I can put them"—I pointed at where the backsplash had been—"up there."

"How come you're doing it like that instead of putting them on the wall?"

"So they don't slide while the glue is wet." I put some glue on the back of a title and pressed it into place. As I wedged a spacer between that tile and the three around it, I said, "This way I can arrange them the way I like and make sure they're spaced right."

"And so they don't fall off?"

"Exactly." I tapped the bucket of grout sitting next to my tools. "When the glue is dry, I'll put some grout on the wall and stick the mesh to it. Once that's dry, I'll put in more grout so it looks nice."

"Nicer than the old one?"

I laughed. "Hopefully."

For a few minutes, he drank his juice while he watched me placing tiles. When he broke the silence, it wasn't about tiles or backsplashes:

"How come you don't play hockey anymore?"

The question stung, but I didn't let it show. He couldn't have known. "I got hurt in a car accident. My doctors said if I tried to play now, I'd probably get hurt again."

"Oh." Cody watched me press another tile onto the mesh. "Do you miss it?"

It shouldn't have been a surprise that he didn't try to talk me back into playing hockey. He was a kid. And maybe it wasn't a surprise, but it was refreshing. A lot of adults could learn a thing or two from him.

"Yeah," I admitted as I took a plastic spacer from the bag. "It was hard. It still is."

He was quiet again, but not for long: "My dad won't let me play hockey."

"Oh yeah?" I glanced at him before shifting my attention to the spacers I was pushing into place. "Why's that?"

"He says it's too dangerous." He kept his gaze fixed on the tiles as he absently pushed his glasses higher on his nose. "My mom's boyfriend wants me to play, though."

I raised an eyebrow. "Does he?"

"Yeah. He says he played when he was a kid and it taught him to be tough."

"Why does he want you to play?"

Cody picked up his cup and looked at me through his lashes. "So I'll be tough."

"He doesn't think you're tough enough?"

The kid shook his head.

"Why's that?"

"Because things make me cry."

I studied him, my stomach tightening as I wondered how to navigate this conversation without Jon around. Where were the lines? How did I stay in my lane? Cautiously, I asked, "Things like what?"

"Sad movies."

"Oh. So he thinks you should play hockey so sad movies won't make you cry anymore?"

He shrugged in that uncomfortable, non-committal way kids sometimes did.

I glued the tile in my hand onto the mesh and pressed in some spacers. Then I rested my forearms on the island so I was closer to eye level with him. "Guess what?"

His eyes widened behind his glasses, and he nodded.

I smiled. "I cry during sad movies."

"You do?"

"Mmhmm. Sometimes the happy ones too."

He straightened a little, his expression brightening a few degrees. "Really?"

"Yep. A few years ago, some of my teammates and I were watching a really sad movie, and we *all* started sniffling. A room full of big, burly hockey players. In fact, do you know who Reid Caulfield is?"

Cody nodded vigorously. "He went to the Olympics!"

"Yeah, he did. And he played his heart out and came home with a medal. He was on my team, and that night we were watching the movie? He had a black eye because he'd been in a fight during the last game." I snickered. "Every time he had to wipe his eyes, he got mad because it hurt."

Cody laughed. "Reid Caulfield really cried? During a movie?"

"Oh yeah." I picked up my phone off the island and started thumbing through photos. "Believe it or not, he's the biggest softy in the world. He's as tough as anyone you'll ever meet when he's got his skates on. The rest of the time?" I showed him the screen, and Cody squinted a little. Then he smiled too, because no one was immune to getting all gooey over the picture Caulfield's wife had taken of him cuddling with his daughter's kitten. "He's a tough guy, but he's soft too."

"Oh." Cody stared at the tiles, but his eyes didn't seem all that focused.

I put my phone aside and cautiously asked, "Does it bother you that movies make you cry?"

He seemed to think about it. "It does when Ray makes fun of me."

I gritted my teeth. Talk about a minefield. My first time alone with Jon's kid, and it was so hard not to throw down some trash talk about the ex-wife's new boyfriend. *That* would help smooth things over between all the adults in this situation.

I finally settled on, "There's nothing wrong with crying during movies." I paused. "In fact..." I took my phone out of my back pocket, opened YouTube, and for the first time since that fateful crash on the ice, looked up a video of myself and my teammates. I pointedly did not look at the thumbnails beside "DASHCAM VIDEO! Brent Weyland's Career OVER!" and "WATCH: violent car crash on ice leaves Denver's Weyland with a broken pelvis," and scrolled to one that was hard to watch for different reasons.

With the video cued up, I leaned over the island and held the phone so we could both see the screen. Then I hit play.

Cody craned his neck as my teammates and I battled for the puck on the ice. In a matter of seconds, the opposing team snatched the puck away and fired it at the goal. The horn sounded, the crowd roared, and our opponents hugged and back-slapped.

As the winning team celebrated on the ice, the camera panned to me and my teammates. To this day, I could *feel* that crushing defeat.

The camera caught one of my buddies wiping a towel over his face, and there was just the quickest glimpse of his eyes before he turned away.

"You see that?" I gestured at the screen.

Cody nodded, watching as one of our other teammates slung an arm around the first. They hugged and headed for the chute.

I stopped the video and put my phone down again. As I picked up a tile, I said, "We were *so close* to advancing in the playoffs, and that game was brutal. We were tied almost the whole time, and we went into overtime. And it just kept going and going, because neither side wanted to lose, you know? Then *one* goal scored on us during a shootout?" I shook my head. "That was it. The season was over. The playoffs were over."

"So you guys were sad."

"Very." I gestured at my phone. "Especially Bronson, the guy you saw. Because he was retiring, so he wasn't going to play a pro game ever again, and he definitely wasn't going to win the Cup." I smiled cautiously. "He's one of the toughest guys I've ever met. I swear I don't know any player who did more time in the penalty box for fighting."

Cody laughed, his face lighting up and reminding me so much of his dad right then. "Really?"

"Oh. Yeah." I nodded emphatically. "Our coach used to get so mad, like…" I rolled my eyes and mimicked Coach Harris's gruff, exasperated voice. "You're not supposed to fight with your own teammates during *practice*, Bronson."

Cody giggled.

"He actually had to go to the penalty box during practice a few times because our coach was just over it." I chuckled at the memory, but then turned serious. "So if *that* guy can cry because he's sad, then —" I caught myself before *"fuck anyone who gives you shit for it"* rolled off my tongue. Blushing, I cleared my throat. "Then there's no need for you to"—I made air quotes—"toughen up just because someone doesn't think it's manly." I huffed with annoyance. "Hockey won't make you less sad during movies. You'll just be sore while you're crying over the sad movie."

Cody laughed. "But it's fun, right? Hockey?"

"It is. And if you really want to play and your parents say it's okay, I can probably teach you a few things." I paused to pull some more tiles from the box. "But only if you want to, you know? Not because someone thinks it should toughen you up."

He nodded. "Okay." Silence fell again, and he watched intently as I put glue on the back of a tile. "Can I help?"

"Do you want to?"

Another nod.

"Do you, um…" I hesitated. "Didn't your dad say you're supposed to be doing homework?"

"It's done. I just had social studies and math, and those are easy."

"Math is easy?"

He grinned. "Yeah!"

"Maybe for you." I smiled. "Okay, well, as long as you're all done with your homework, sure." I moved aside and gestured at the place where I'd been standing. "Pull up a chair."

24

JON

"You sticking around for a drink?" Rainn asked after I'd left the stage.

"Not tonight." I smiled, gesturing at my guitar case. "The kid's at home, so I gotta run. Could I bug you for a bottle of water, though?"

"Of course." He handed one over the bar. "See you next time!"

I waved with the hand holding the water, then headed out of Vino and Veritas. At first, I made myself walk slow, but then it occurred to me that Brent wasn't with me. I was so used to pacing myself for him, it had become a habit. Breaking into a near jog, I hurried toward my car.

In the parking garage, I put the guitar down and set the water bottle on the roof of the car. Now that my hands were free, I texted Brent:

On my way home. Everything okay?

I was just putting the guitar in the backseat when the response came. As I settled into the driver seat and dropped the water bottle in the cup holder, I checked the message:

All good. See you soon.

I pushed out a breath, put my phone aside, and uncapped the water for a much-needed swig.

Why was I so worried? Cody's homework had probably kept him occupied most of the evening, and Brent was relaxed and responsible. The two of them got along.

But I was a dad, Cody was my son, and worrying was my natural state. Especially since this was the first time I'd left him alone with Brent. I'd been nervous the first time Ashley and I had left him with my own parents, so yeah, no shit I was going to be nervous leaving him with my sort-of boyfriend.

Were they getting along? Had Cody had second thoughts about being okay with staying alone with Brent? If Cody needed something, did Brent know how to handle the situation?

Brent said everything was fine. Would Cody have the same report?

One way to find out.

The whole way home, I drove slightly faster than usual—above the "cops might let me get away with it" range and into "probably asking for a ticket"—and prayed like hell there were no cops out tonight.

If there were any, they didn't see me. Or at least they didn't stop me. Before long, I was pulling into my driveway beside Brent's truck. Lights were on in the house, and Brent hadn't felt the need to take Cody to the emergency room or something, so I was, predictably, worried about nothing.

Luna and Winston greeted me at the door, and as I petted him and scratched behind her ears, the thumping of their tails against my leg and the wall didn't quite drown out the voices coming from the next room.

"Okay, hold it just like that," Brent was saying. "You got it?"

"Like this?"

"Yep, just like that. You good if I let go?"

"Yeah."

"All right. I'm letting go." Beat. "Still good?"

Silence, followed by a loud ka-chunk, ka-chunk, that I recognized as my nail gun.

"Awesome. Okay, you can let it go. Let me get the other one."

Curious, I followed the sounds to the kitchen with the dogs on my heels. I found my son kneeling on the counter beside the stove, holding a sheet of tiles against the backsplash, which Brent was securing with the nail gun. They both had on safety glasses, and the big red ear protectors looked comically huge on Cody. What looked like tile grout was smeared on their hands and forearms as well as a smudge on Cody's cheek.

"And"—Brent put one more nail in to the top corner of the mesh —"now it won't move."

They let go of the tiles, and as Cody sat back on his heels on the counter and took off his earmuffs, he pointed proudly at the backsplash. "Dad, look! Me and Brent put up the tiles!"

I smiled. "I see that! Good job."

He beamed. To Brent, he said, "Can I help grout 'em?"

Pulling out his earplugs, Brent glanced at me, then the clock on the microwave. "It's a bit late to start on that, but I'll wait to do it until you're here. How about that?"

Cody seemed a little disappointed. "You promise?"

"Promise." Brent gestured at the tiles. "They're not going anywhere."

Apparently satisfied, Cody went upstairs to get ready for bed. I told him I'd be up in a minute, and after he'd gone, I turned to Brent. "Sounds like the two of you had a good time while I was gone."

He laughed, but he sounded slightly uneasy. "Yeah, he really enjoyed helping out." Gesturing at the mesh, he added, "There's mastic under that so it won't move once it sets, but it kept trying to slide. So we nailed the mesh in place just to be sure."

"Smart."

He still seemed nervous, though.

"Something wrong?" I asked.

Brent chewed his lip.

My heart flipped and my stomach turned to lead. "Brent?"

He took a breath. "Listen, um." He glanced up the hallway toward Cody's bedroom, then looked at me, his expression alarmingly serious. "I don't want to butt in where I don't belong, but..."

A sick feeling coiled in the pit of my stomach. "What's on your mind?"

"So, um." He cleared his throat. "We were talking. And he asked me about playing hockey." He laughed uneasily. "Most kids do."

I nodded, but didn't say anything.

"Anyway, he says..." Brent chewed his lip, gaze flicking toward Cody's room again before he looked right in my eyes. "He told me his mom's boyfriend wants him to play hockey. To toughen Cody up. Apparently, the boyfriend says it made him tough as a kid." Eyes full of worry, he added, "That's, um... That's not a good idea."

I swallowed. I'd had no idea Ray had been pushing Cody to play hockey, never mind to "toughen him up." That left me reeling enough, and my mouth went dry as I asked, "Why isn't it a good idea?"

"Well... I mean..." Brent gestured at himself. "The car wreck wasn't my first serious injury, and I didn't start fucking myself up when I went pro. I had my first hockey-related surgery when I was twelve."

That sick feeling burned even hotter.

"It's not just the physical side," he went on, voice soft. "I'm not saying hockey players are bullies, but some are. And the way hockey makes a lot of kids tough is by not leaving them a lot of choice." He swallowed again. "Especially if Cody's—if his mom's boyfriend is pressuring him because he thinks it'll toughen him up? The kid's going to get it on and off the ice, and I can tell you from experience, that doesn't do good things to someone."

"Shit," I whispered.

"Like I said," Brent continued, "I know it's none of my business. I'm just afraid he'll go out there, and the sport will eat him alive. And at the risk of being disrespectful toward your ex and her boyfriend..." He sighed heavily. "People like him piss me the hell off."

I blinked. "Do they?"

"Oh God, yeah. Because they're everywhere in hockey, and football, and..." He waved his hand. "They say they want sons who are athletic, but what they really mean is they want their sons to be everything they think is masculine. I mean, I played hockey with a kid in high school who could absolutely skate circles around all of us because he'd been a figure skater since he was like five. But his dad didn't like him 'prancing around in sparkly shit'"—Brent rolled his eyes—"and pushed him to do hockey instead. It obviously wasn't about being athletic, because that kid was in better shape than I was at that age. I mean, he was *cut*, and he was an athlete in every sense of the word. He was just involved in the wrong sport, and I think it really fucked with his head."

"Yeah, Cody doesn't need that."

"No, he doesn't. But I think *someone* thinks he does. Bullying and all."

My hackles went up.

Brent scowled. "He said his mom's boyfriend thinks he's not tough enough because sad movies make him cry. Things like that."

Rage had my teeth grinding before he'd even finished the sentence. "That son of a bitch."

"I know, right?" Expression turning a little sheepish, he added, "I, um, I told him sad movies make me cry."

"You did?"

Brent nodded as a blush crept into his cheeks. "He seemed really embarrassed by it, and it sounds like that jackhole makes him feel like it's something to be ashamed of."

"*Do* sad movies make you cry?"

The blush deepened. "Sometimes."

Oh God, my heart. Not just at the thought of Brent being soft enough to cry during a movie (I wasn't at all surprised by that part), but at him showing that card to my son so he wouldn't feel bad.

"Thank you." I put a hand on his waist and kissed him softly. "I'm going to have to have a chat with my ex-wife about what her boyfriend is saying to Cody, but hearing that from you probably did him a lot of good."

"It did?"

"Oh yeah." I smiled. "Nothing will take the wind out of that jagoff's toxic masculinity sails like someone who has lived and breathed professional hockey admitting that he cries when he watches movies."

Brent exhaled with obvious relief. "Oh thank God. I was afraid I'd overstepped and—"

"No." I shook my head. "Not even a little. That idiot overstepped, and he's going to get a piece of my mind. Either directly or via my ex-wife."

"Good," he growled. "What an asshole."

Laughing, I nodded. "He already doesn't like me, and now he can like me a little less. But Cody is *not* playing hockey unless it's what *he* wants to do, and I will take Ashley to court over it if I have to."

Brent's eyes widened, but only for a second. "Just let me know if you need me to testify about what it's like for kids in hockey."

"I'll keep that in mind."

But hopefully it wouldn't come to that.

25

BRENT

With a stomach full of nervous butterflies, I tapped my thumbs on the wheel and followed the GPS's instructions. Was I doing this? I was doing this. Oh fuck. I was doing this.

Jon had appointments all day and an event at Cody's school this evening, so I wouldn't see him until tomorrow. I'd had physical therapy this morning, and I was planning to take Luna down one of the multi-use trails this afternoon if my hip held out (otherwise I was pretty sure she'd be thrilled just to chase her toy in the backyard).

But before I went home to pick her up, I had a stop to make.

Assuming I didn't lose my nerve, anyway.

At the GPS's instruction, I pulled into the parking lot of a strip mall, and I immediately zeroed in on the shop I was looking for. Heart thumping, I shut off the GPS, pulled into a parking space, and stared at the garish purple neon signs between the blander fronts of a chiropractor's office and a beauty supply store. It looked out of place, but I couldn't really conjure up something where it would fit better. Next to a strip club, maybe?

Well, it didn't matter. It was here and so was I.

I shut off the engine, got out, and headed inside. I was doing this now, because I'd made it this far, and if I bailed like the coward I was, God knew when I'd get myself back here again.

At the door, I didn't let myself hesitate. I pushed it open and walked inside.

Instantly, I was hit with the smells of incense and scented candles with a side of leather and latex. There was a subtler scent that reminded me of the massage oil Jon used. Did he buy it here? Probably not.

I shook myself and looked around. I'd been to plenty of shops like this in the past. One of my exes and I had been into all kinds of toys and light restraints, and God knew my teammates and I had been known to prank each other with things that could only be found in a place like this. In fact I was pretty sure my coach was still finding dick-shaped glitter in his desk to this day.

But coming in here today was weird. I wasn't just looking for something to spice things up or to play around when I was alone. This was the first time I'd come looking for something to do what I couldn't.

A woman with black pigtails leaned over the counter. "Can I see your ID?"

"My—oh. Right." I fumbled with my wallet and handed her my driver's license. I didn't imagine she actually thought I was under eighteen, but she probably had to check everyone who looked younger than Larry King.

"Cool, thanks." She gave back my license. "Can I help you find anything?"

A rush of nerves very nearly sent me bolting out the door. "Uh, no. No, I'll be okay. Thanks." I was probably blushing. Either that or it was seriously warm in here. Hmm, yeah, probably blushing.

She just smiled. "Sure. Just let me know if I can help."

"Will do," I muttered, and continued into the store.

Hands in my pockets, I wandered casually through the aisles until I found what I was looking for. When I did, when I found the racks of every size, shape, color, and texture dildo imaginable, I gulped. Fuck. Where did I start?

Swallowing my pride, that was where.

Because I wasn't here to get something to use on myself. The thing was, Robin and I had talked this morning about my problems below the belt. She'd sweet-talked my doctor's office into writing a referral without seeing me first (since my appointment was still weeks away), and she'd managed to score me an appointment with the urologist.

Next week.

Gulp.

I was thrilled we'd nailed something down. That I'd be able to talk to someone about fixing whatever was wrong with me. But I was also terrified. I wondered if this was along the lines of what it felt like to be facing down biopsy results or something. Not on the same scale by any means, but like there was serious potential for bad news *and would someone just tell me already?*

It was entirely possible that next week, someone would tell me that my days of getting hard enough to top someone were over. Hard-ons and easy orgasms were a thing of my past, and the sooner I made peace with that, the better.

Which brought me here. To the sex shop. And the dildo displays.

I flicked my gaze from one toy to the next. Maybe I should've brought Jon. The whole point of coming here was to find something I could use in place of my cock. He insisted he was fine without bottoming—after all, he'd been with someone for twenty years who didn't top—but I hated the idea that the only reason he couldn't bottom was that I lacked functioning equipment.

No, a dildo wouldn't be the same. It would be something, though. Something I could use to give him the good time he deserved.

Maybe it'll be enough, since I can't be.

I pushed that thought back and tried to just focus on finding something we could play with. Nothing gigantic or weird. Just... something dick-shaped, roughly the size I would be if I could get fully hard. We could bring in others later if Jon wanted to. This one, though—it was probably irrational, but I needed this to be something I brought to the table. Something to make up for what I *couldn't* bring to the table.

Yeah, probably irrational.

Whatever. I was doing this.

I took a deep breath and stepped a little closer so I could get a good look at some of the available toys. I felt weirdly conspicuous. Again, probably irrational—I doubted there was a question I could ask or an item I could buy that would faze the people working in a place like this. They had to have seen, heard, and sold it all. And I'd bought dildos before without so much as blushing.

But today, I was absolutely sure that the person behind the

counter would take one look at the toy and know I was buying it because I needed an inanimate object to tag in for me.

Which…fine. She could think whatever she wanted. I just… wouldn't come back here. I'd buy a toy, walk away, and never come back, and I'd hope to God she'd only looked at my birth date on my driver's license.

Christ, she recognized my name, didn't she?

And who cared if she did?

News flash, world: Brent Weyland is an out gay man with an active(ish) sex life!

I laughed at my own stupid thought. God, I was losing my mind. And the longer I stood here, the more conspicuous I would be, staring at dildos like they had all the answers to life and the universe. Maybe they did. What did I know?

I eventually settled on exactly what I'd come here for—a dildo molded from an actual dick that was roughly the size of mine. Well, a little longer than mine, since I needed to be able to hold on to it. And it had a flared base, too. Perfect.

I went up to the register. There was a woman in line ahead of me, buying several things, and I stood back a little to give her some privacy.

"Do you know when they'll get more in?" she was asking the cashier, holding up a bottle of what I thought was flavored lube. "It's been out of stock for ages, and now this is the last one."

"Ugh, I know." The cashier made a face. "We keep asking the owners for more, but they only order us one box at a time."

The customer made an annoyed sound. "I can order it online, I guess. I just prefer to support local businesses, you know?"

"We appreciate that," the cashier said with a bright smile. "I'll nudge them again." She held up a business card, then tucked it into the bag. "You can always email them too, and ask when we'll have it in stock. Sometimes hearing from customers gets the point across."

"I'll do that—thanks!"

They kept chatting, and I envied them for being so chill and casual about all this. On the other hand, if they were, then why the fuck was I so wound up? We were all adults in an adult store. I needed to calm the hell down.

The lady in front of me took her bags and left, and I put the box on the counter. The cashier cheerfully asked if I'd found everything okay and if I wanted to sign up for their rewards program (nooo, no, no), then gave me my total. After I'd paid, she slipped the box into an opaque black plastic bag—the unmarked kind that was meant to be discreet but absolutely screamed *this is 100% an adult purchase*—and thanked me for shopping.

I thanked her and left the store, walking as fast as my leg and back would allow, and climbed into the truck. I tossed my new purchase on to the passenger seat, released my breath, and gave myself another mental smack for being so ridiculous about all this. It was just a dildo. Just a sex shop. I was a few months away from thirty, not a fifteen-year-old buying condoms at Walgreens and hoping to God no one saw me and ratted me out to my parents. Why the hell did I feel like I was? Hell, maybe some old habits just died hard.

Well, whatever. It was done. I started the engine, then turned to stare at the black plastic bag riding shotgun.

I'd done it. I'd conjured up the courage, come into the store, and bought the toy.

Question was, how long would it take to conjure up the courage to show it to Jon and suggest using it?

Guess I'd find out.

"Well, hey there, stranger!" Ethan spread his arms as he stepped into my foyer later that afternoon. "It's been ages!"

"It hasn't been *that* long." I hugged him carefully.

"Girl, I haven't seen you since we went to Vino and Veritas. It's been *ages*."

"Hmm." I let him go. "Now that you mention it, it has been a while, hasn't it?"

"Um, yeah?" He tsked, but then he looked down and put a hand to his chest. "And who is *this* lovely thing?"

I followed his gaze and found Luna peeking in from the hallway, her ears down and her tail tucked like the day I'd met her. I patted my thigh. "Come on, baby. It's okay."

She hesitated, then crept closer. Watching Ethan warily, she hurried to my side and hid behind my legs. Once she was safely behind me, she looked up at him, her expression hopeful.

I scratched her shoulder. "This is Luna. She's still kind of getting used to things."

"Well, she's obviously used to you." He crouched slowly and held out his hand. "Hello there, princess. It's okay. I probably smell like cats, but I promise I left them at home."

Luna glanced up at me. Then she looked at Ethan, and she stretched her neck out to sniff his outstretched fingers.

"It's okay," he cooed. "I won't—There you go." He grinned as Luna gave his fingers a tiny lick. To me, he said, "She is *adorable*!"

"Isn't she?" I petted her, and when she wagged her tail, and when she looked up at me, I went all gooey inside all over again. She really was adorable.

As Ethan and I went into the kitchen, I spoke over the click of Luna's nails on the hardwood. "She loves playing in the lake, and you wouldn't think a dog that small could hog a bed that big."

He laughed. "I have cats, honey. I know all about how pets defy physics and hog the bed."

"Okay, true. You want something to drink?"

"Eh, whatever you're having."

I poured us a couple of Cokes, then tossed a dog biscuit to Luna because I was an enormous softy where she was concerned. She crunched happily on it in the kitchen while we moved to the living room, and then she joined us, crawling partway into my lap.

"That is so sweet," Ethan said. "My God. And you can walk her and play with her? Even with…?" He gestured at his hip.

I nodded as I petted Luna's silky black coat. "If I can't take her on a walk, I can turn her loose in the backyard and she runs around and swims. And she's really good about not getting underfoot or anything like that." I tousled her ears. "You're a good girl, aren't you, baby?"

Luna's tail thumped against Ethan's leg. He just kept his glass out of the way and looked at me. "Well, it looks like you're doing great with your new little friend."

"I am. She's awesome."

"So I see." He shot me a pointed look. "What's his name?"

"I told you—*her* name is Luna."

"Not the dog." He rolled his eyes and made an exasperated noise.

"I know her name. I'm asking what *his* name is." His eyebrow arched sharply. "You know, the guy you've been with for the last however many weeks?"

I blinked.

Another eye-roll. "Honey, please. I couldn't drag you out of this house for anything, and now you're always busy. *Clearly* you've been getting somebody's pants down."

A laugh burst out of me. Sometimes I forgot how little filter Ethan possessed. "What? You can't think of any other reason why I'd be—"

"Don't even try it with me." He wagged his finger and shook his head. "I know you. What I don't know is who he is. So…spill it, sister."

I tried to laugh it off, but I was pretty sure the heat in my cheeks was giving me away, so I gave a dramatically defeated sigh. "Okay, fine. *Fine.* Remember when you took me to that wine bar? That guy I met there?"

He blinked. "You're still banging that singer?"

Face burning, I nodded. "Yeah. I am."

"Hmm. I don't know why I'm surprised, with the way you two were eye-fucking each other." He pursed his lips, then shrugged. "Huh. Well, I'm glad you're not moping around the house anymore. And you seem a lot happier now." He smiled. "It's like he fucked you back to life."

I almost spat my drink all over myself and my dog. Still sputtering, I said, "Anyone ever told you how classy you are?"

"All the time, darling. So…things are good with him, then?"

"Yeah, they're…" My heart sank a little, and I gazed down at Luna, who was dozing off with her head on my leg. "They're good."

"You don't sound very enthusiastic. Like, at all."

I wanted to insist I was, but I couldn't quite convince myself. "The thing is, there's still a part of me that feels like my life ended with my hockey career. Like I'm nothing and no one if I can't play hockey." I shifted a little, wincing at a twinge in my hip. "And Jon even pointed out that's because I've never been allowed to be anything or anyone besides a hockey player. So I'm trying to figure out who I am now, you know?" I absently trailed my fingers along the edge of Luna's collar, watching the fine hairs bend beneath my touch before springing back upright. "But what if who I am isn't good enough?"

Ethan cocked his head. "Good enough for what?"

"For me? For anyone else?" *For sex that doesn't require an inanimate designated hitter?* "For Jon?"

He stared at me like I'd lost my mind. "Well, why wouldn't you be?"

"I..." Damn. How to put it into words. "For one thing, he's made it clear several times that we're just friends with benefits. That's all he wants from me or anyone else right now. And I'm fine with that." I paused. "I *think* I'm fine with it." Another pause. Then my shoulders sank a little. "I *thought* I was fine with it."

"So, you want to be more than fuck buddies?"

"Sometimes I think we already are, but I'm afraid he'll figure that out and want to move on. I mean, it doesn't *feel* like friends with benefits. It hasn't for a while, but I just can't make myself let go."

"How do you mean?"

"I mean..." I chewed my lip. Then, lowering my voice, I said, "You ever been in bed with someone, and it doesn't feel like you're just fooling around? Like there's something really going on between you?"

Ethan's eyes widened. For a heartbeat I thought he was going to call me out for being a sap, but instead, he said, "It was like that with Ty when we first got together. Neither of us wanted a thing, but then it became...a thing."

"So what happened when it did?" I asked. "I mean, were you like, not looking for a thing, and just rolled with it? Or did you guys fight it?"

He thought about it. "Ty really didn't want anything, but by the time we realized what it was, we rolled with it."

I swallowed as I stared down at Luna.

"Why?" Ethan prodded gently. "Do you want to keep it casual? Or do you want it to be more?"

"I..." That was a good question, wasn't it? And I'd brushed up against it in my own head enough times that I should've had an answer. Maybe I did have an answer. I just hadn't wanted to look it in the eye until Ethan had nudged me. With a sigh, I met his gaze. "The thing is, I really, really like him. And I think if we gave this thing a chance, it could really be something. But what if I'm not enough for him?"

"What in the world—" Ethan shook his head and waved dismissively. "Honey. No. You are a lot of things, but not enough for someone? Pfft."

"Dude." I gestured at myself. "*Look* at me."

He clicked his tongue. "Sweetie, you have got to quit getting so down on yourself. Yes, I know, getting hurt did a number on you. But there's nothing lacking about you."

I laughed bitterly, avoiding his gaze again. Oh, if he only knew. Losing the hockey physique I'd been so proud of? That had sucked. Losing the ability to perform in the bedroom? To the point I went and bought a toy (one I was still too embarrassed to talk about, never mind use) just so I might have a fighting chance of satisfying the man I was sleeping with? Not great on the ego.

"He's a single dad," I said. "He's trying to figure out life after his divorce. He's got a kid to raise and a house to renovate." My shoulders slumped, and I thumbed the condensation on my Coke glass. "Why the hell would he want to add me to his—"

"Brent." Ethan touched my arm. "Don't even go there. You're no one's burden. He obviously likes you if the two of you are spending this much time together."

I wanted to point out that Jon liked me as a booty call, so of course he spent time with me. But how often did we actually do anything that booty calls usually did together? Not very. And for the same reasons I was worried he'd balk if he decided things were getting too emotionally intense between us. Because he didn't want more than this, and because more than this with *me* was probably not what he'd signed up for.

I sighed. "Maybe he likes it now. But even *I* get sick of everything that comes with..." I gestured at myself. "Can I really expect him not to?"

"Yes! Because you're a lot harder on yourself than anyone else." He paused. "Well, maybe aside from your dad, but he's wrong and so are you." He smiled, squeezing my arm again. "You're a catch, and if he's smart he can see that."

"So what do I do?" I hated how pathetic I sounded. "I know what he wants out of this. I know it feels like it's turning into something else. What the hell do I do?"

"Just give it a chance. Don't push him away because you don't think you're good enough for him." Ethan patted my hand. "That car accident didn't do a thing to you that will make a good man think you're not enough."

I swallowed past the lump in my throat.

And I wanted to believe him so, so bad.

26

JON

"Before I go, we need to talk."

My ex-wife shot me an impatient look as we stood in the hallway by her front door. "Right now? Because Ray and I were going to take Cody to—"

"Yes, right now." I kept my voice firm, but tried not to be confrontational. "It won't take long, but it can't wait."

She crossed her arms, glare hardening. "Fine. What is it?"

"Is it true you and Ray are encouraging Cody to play hockey?"

She straightened, hostility faltering in favor of confusion. "That's the issue?"

"Yes. Because I don't think he should play."

"What? Why are you suddenly opposed to hockey?" She narrowed her eyes. "Is this about that guy you're seeing?"

"No. It's about the one *you're* seeing."

Her eyebrows jumped, and I could feel the *I beg your fucking pardon?* coming off her in waves.

"Cody playing hockey isn't the issue," I said. "The issue is why Ray is pushing for him to play hockey."

She folded her arms tighter. "You don't think it would be good for him?"

"Not for the reasons Ray apparently thinks it will." I made myself keep my voice down so we didn't attract Cody or Ray into the room, and it was a struggle. "Listen, I don't have a problem with our son playing sports. But if the reasoning behind it is to toughen him up?" I nodded sharply. "You're damn right I have a problem."

Ashley glared at me. "It's just a sport, Jon. Playing sports is good for kids."

"Uh-huh. So let him play basketball or baseball or something. Let him play soccer. Not something your boyfriend specifically thinks will make him tougher." Anger was getting the best of me, and before she could respond to my comment, I barreled on: "When he shames our son for crying during a movie, what do you say? What do you do?"

She pressed her lips together and looked away.

"Ashley?"

Forcing a breath out through her nose, she hugged herself tighter. "He's just trying to keep Cody from getting bullied."

"By bullying him?"

She glared at me. "Ray is *not* bullying him."

"Isn't he? Because right now, Cody feels like you and Ray think he's weak and needs to be tougher."

Her jaw worked, but she didn't speak. Then she gestured at the door. "You know what? If we're going to do this, let's do it outside. Cody doesn't need to hear it."

I didn't argue, and we stepped out into the breezeway. As soon as we were alone, I faced her. "Look, I'm not interested in dictating your love life." I had to force the anger out of my voice. "Who you see is your business. But who you see also interacts with our son, and that part *is* my business, especially when that someone is trying to turn Cody into someone he's not. So I want hockey off the table until he's older."

"What?" Ashley huffed with annoyance. "And what if he *wants* to play?"

"Even then, I'd like to let him grow a little more. If you want to sign him up for skating lessons, fine. But with him being small for his age and not very aggressive, I'm worried he'll get mowed down out there by the bigger kids."

"So you'd prefer to underestimate him?"

"I'd prefer not to let him get hurt. Skinning his knees when he falls off his bike is one thing. Maybe I've worked on too many hockey players, but—"

"Worked on?" She narrowed her eyes. "Or slept with?"

I fought back my aggravation. "Brent's not the first person I've encountered who has permanent damage from the sport. And he's not the youngest either." I hesitated, not sure if I should bring his opinion out, but I finally said, "He explained to me that the way hockey makes kids tough is by not leaving them much choice. They either toughen up, or they get crushed. I don't want that for Cody."

"We can't handle him with kid gloves forever, Jon. We—"

"He's *ten!*" I exhaled hard. "If you want to work together to figure out ways to get him past his shyness, fine, but not in a hockey rink."

"So you're just unilaterally making that decision."

I had to fight so, so hard not to let fly about some of the decisions she'd unilaterally made. "If I told you I was going to take him out this week and teach him to drive, would you veto it?"

"Of course I would. He's way too young for that."

I inclined my head.

She held my gaze, then rolled her eyes and shifted her weight with an irritated huff. "For God's sake, that's not the same thing."

"Isn't it?" I shrugged dismissively. "The only difference I can see is that it's not legal for him to drive. But if you thought it was unsafe and putting him at unnecessary risk, then—"

"Oh my God, fine!" She threw up her hands. "He won't play hockey. But if he starts asking why he can't play, *you* get to tell him."

"Fine. Send him to me if he asks."

"Fine." She shifted again, eyeing me irritably. "Are we done here?"

"Yeah, we're done." I'd already said goodbye to Cody, so after Ashley went back inside, I headed down to my car. On the way, I rolled my shoulders and pushed out a breath. As much as even the smallest battle with her frustrated me, I was relieved we'd come to an understanding on this one. It would probably come up again—Ray would no doubt push back—but for the moment, hockey wasn't in my son's future.

Now I could breathe a little easier as I headed home to spend an evening with the ex-hockey player Cody had unexpectedly opened up to. This wasn't part of our arrangement—him meeting Cody, never mind having heart-to-hearts with him while I wasn't around.

But right now, I was beyond thankful he had.

Lounging in bed beside Brent was never going to get old. Seriously. Ashley and I had, somewhere along the line, stopped cuddling unless we were going to sleep (and later, even then). Sex, when it happened, was something to do before we rolled over and fell asleep.

With Brent, though? Even if we were sleeping over and wouldn't be awake much longer, there was always this luxurious period of just basking in the afterglow and each other's body heat under the sheets. What could I say? I couldn't get enough of lying next to someone who actually wanted to be tangled up with me.

Now the cold bed I'd shared with my ex-wife—not to mention the frosty conversation this afternoon—felt like a distant memory. Whenever I was this close to Brent, it was hard to imagine I'd ever been anywhere else.

Except I *had* been somewhere else. Shifting a little, I said, "I talked to my ex-wife this afternoon."

"Did you?" He turned his head slightly. "How'd that go?"

"Well, it wasn't fun, but in the end, she agreed not to push Cody to play hockey."

"Oh, thank God," Brent breathed, sounding genuinely relieved.

"Right?" I stroked his hair. "Her boyfriend probably won't be happy about it, but she knows where I stand, and she backed down."

"Good. Fucking jackass is just setting that kid up to be bullied."

I blinked.

Brent laughed sheepishly. "Sorry. I just… I don't have any patience for people who throw their kids to the wolves like that. Especially since I know what those wolves are like."

"I get that," I said with a nod. "And I appreciate you telling me what Cody told you. I had no idea about the whole hockey issue."

"Glad I could help out. He's a good kid. Doesn't need that bullshit in his life."

God, the things it did to my heart, knowing Brent was this protective of my son…

We lay in comfortable silence for a little while, and I just enjoyed the warmth of his body as we relaxed. Eventually, though, he spoke.

"So, um." He swallowed, avoiding my gaze. "I have that appointment next week. With the, um… With the urologist."

"Yeah?" I ran my hand up his forearm.

"Yeah. My physical therapist called in some favors or something and got me in with a doctor she knows." He huffed an annoyed laugh. "Got in to see this guy before I could even see my own doctor. How messed up is that?"

"Seriously. I'm glad she got you in."

"Me too. But...I'm not gonna lie." He met my gaze, his eyes full of more worry than I'd ever seen in him. "I'm fucking terrified."

"Of the appointment itself? Or what he'll tell you?"

"Both. Mostly what he'll tell me." Brent blew out a breath. "What if he tells me there's nothing he can do?"

"Hey, don't go all defeatist." I squeezed his arm. "You haven't even heard the guy out yet."

"Okay, but with my track record, it's easy to be pessimistic. I mean, that tendon surgery?" He gestured at his hip and thigh. "They said that had an eighty percent success rate, and that was being conservative."

"All right, I get that." I laced our fingers together. "But you've been able to get hard sometimes, and you've gotten off. That has to mean *something*."

"Maybe. But..." Brent gnawed his lip. "Listen, hypothetically, if he says this is the best I'm ever going to get, what does that mean for, um..." He searched my eyes.

It took me a second, but the meaning of his question finally hit me. "What does it mean for us?"

Brent nodded.

"If nothing changes medically, then nothing changes here." I shrugged. "Why would it?"

He held my gaze. "Well, I mean, if nothing is going to improve..."

"Brent." I lifted my chin and brushed my lips across his. "I haven't been just biding my time and waiting around to see if there's a solution. You better believe I'm not going to bail if there isn't one."

His brow pinched.

I smiled, stroking his hair. "I don't know if you've noticed, but I haven't had any complaints about the things we do in bed."

"No, but we haven't been doing this very long. It's bound to get old."

"Probably more for you than me."

"I just..." He exhaled, wiping his hand over his face. "It's not just the sexual problems. It's the pain. The lack of mobility." With a bitter laugh, he said, "The sexual part is just insult to injury. Literally. And I hate feeling like I'm living in someone else's body. I want to feel like myself again." He met my eyes. "Even if I'm not playing hockey anymore, I just... For fuck's sake, living in a body that doesn't work the way it's supposed to is exhausting." He paused. "God, that sounds crazy."

"No, it doesn't."

He looked at me again.

"You sound just like the pain management clients I work with." I laced our fingers together and brushed my lips across his knuckles. "It's not easy. But you're not alone."

That seemed to relax him a little, though he was obviously still tense and nervous. He opened his mouth like he was about to say something. His eyes darted toward the nightstand, but then he exhaled as if he were letting go of whatever he'd been thinking of mentioning. Instead, he smiled, though it seemed a bit forced. "I guess we'll see what the doctor says, right?"

I was curious what he hadn't said, but I let it go and went with, "I guess we will. And I hope he has good news for you." I kissed his knuckles again. "But even if he doesn't, nothing changes here."

He searched my eyes again, and I thought he might have more cynicism, or he might bring up whatever had been on his mind a minute ago, but he just lifted his chin for a soft kiss. I held him closer as the kiss lingered. He'd been too sore to fool around earlier, and I doubted that had changed, but just kissing and touching was more than enough for me. Just being this close to him—naked and warm in bed—was all I needed.

We're casual. We're fuck buddies.

At least...we're supposed to be.

That had crossed my mind plenty of times since we'd started this, but tonight, I didn't fight the thought that we were a lot closer than we should have been.

Mostly because I didn't want to.

27

BRENT

A few hours after I'd walked into the urologist's office, I was at home. Sitting on my bed. Reading and rereading the notes he'd sent home with me. Eyeballing the box I'd picked up from the pharmacy.

The appointment itself had been…not fun. I'd never been bothered by doctors seeing or touching my junk before, but something about knowing he was prodding around because we both knew something was malfunctioning—yeah, that sucked.

Based on the physical exam, what he could glean from the X-rays I'd brought with me, and the battery of questions he'd asked about function and sensation, he'd determined that I probably hadn't damaged any nerves. That much was encouraging, since nerve damage sounded awfully permanent.

"In fact," he'd said, "I think it's quite possible this isn't a result of the pelvic fracture itself."

"It isn't?"

He'd shaken his head. "Erectile dysfunction certainly *can* be a result of a pelvic fracture, but I'd expect that to accompany urethral damage, which you didn't experience, or other signs of significant nerve damage, which you aren't experiencing."

"So, what's causing it, then?"

He'd explained that an injury like mine meant a lot of physical and psychological trauma, and sometimes that was enough to screw with hormones, libido, and mental health. Though it seemed like my injury had happened a lifetime ago, it had barely been a year, and healing from something like that continued for a long, *long* time after the worst was over. Just being in pain all the time could contribute to the ED.

Maybe that means I'm not broken. Maybe it just means I'm still recovering. Please, God, let that be what it means.

He wanted to run some more tests at a later appointment just to be sure there wasn't some minor circulatory damage, which could make it difficult for me to stay hard. Since I'd been able to get hard and get off occasionally, though, he decided it was safe for me to start trying some non-medicinal methods at home.

Hence the box from the pharmacy.

A penis pump.

An honest to God, medical grade, "Do you have any questions?" asked with a straight face by the pharmacist, penis pump.

Of course I'd had all kinds of visions of the ridiculous cartoonish contraptions people used to try to make their dicks bigger, and I'd heard about how much damage those could do, so I'd been dubious.

"Those aren't what I'm recommending for you," my doctor had reassured me, echoing what Robin had said in the beginning. "This is a medical device, and it's frequently prescribed to men with erectile dysfunction."

Those last two words had twinged like something hitting an exposed dental nerve, but I'd pushed past it and tried to grab on to the glimmer of hope he'd been offering. "So, you think it'll work?"

"I think it's worth a try. They're safe and effective, and I've had many patients report that they're quite easy to use with some practice."

Practice.

I glared at the unopened box. It was bigger than anything I'd ever brought home from a pharmacy. Just an unassuming white box with some medicalese on the side that apparently translated to "junk resuscitator."

"So using it when I'm alone, okay, I can do that." I'd struggled to hold the man's gaze. "What about when I'm with someone?"

He'd smiled warmly and not even a little bit patronizingly. "If you're not comfortable being watched, you can always step into the other room, but honestly, it's like anything—it's what you make of it, and there's no reason you and a trusted, loving partner can't work it into your foreplay."

I'd swallowed, and I did the same right now.

I did trust Jon. Maybe "loving" wasn't the right word for us, but he was gentle and sweet, and he'd been understanding from the beginning after I'd explained that I was having some problems south of the border. When I'd told him I was going to the specialist, he'd insisted that regardless of the outcome, nothing changed where we were concerned.

I wanted to believe that, and deep inside, I did. And hadn't Robin said that if I trusted someone enough to be intimate with them, I should be able to trust them with a penis pump too? Except I was still nervous and embarrassed—I hadn't even been able to break out that dildo I'd bought—and even now I could feel my face turning red just thinking about opening this new box in bed with Jon. Rational or not, I imagined him being turned off by it. By the fact that I couldn't get hard without it.

And what if I can't even get hard with *it?*

I closed my eyes and exhaled, trying to tamp down that nagging worry. The doctor had urged me to be as optimistic as he was, but he'd also warned me this would be a process. The pump might not work. They didn't work for every guy, regardless of the cause of their ED, and if it didn't, it wasn't the end of the world.

"You've been able to get erect, you haven't lost sensation, and you've been able to achieve orgasm," he'd said. "Those are good signs. If this doesn't work, there are still options. It might take some time to find the solution that works best for you, but all is not lost."

Damn, this guy really must've specialized in ED patients, because he knew exactly what I needed to hear. The fact that he didn't think I'd done irreversible damage, and that what little success I'd had by myself and with Jon were good signs—that was enough to give me the first glimmer of optimism that maybe this was temporary.

"It's also entirely possible," he'd gone on, "that there is a psychological component. Depression, anxiety, stress—those can all be contributors. Especially after what you've been through this past year, and now with the performance anxiety of being a young man facing erectile dysfunction, we would be wise to consider how much your mind is contributing."

"So it's all in my head?"

"Of course not. But you know from being an athlete that mind over matter is very real, and so this process might be a physical step forward, followed by a psychological step forward, followed by another physical one." He'd given my arm a reassuring squeeze. "Just don't give up, and don't get discouraged if the results take time."

Easy for him to say, but I appreciated the encouragement.

So now here I was, trying to work up the courage to use this thing for the first time. I wasn't sure what I was most afraid of—that it wouldn't work, or that it would be such a cumbersome thing that there was no way in hell it would lead to sex. Unless it was pity sex.

I shuddered. No. Not with Jon, anyway.

And maybe I was overthinking this. The doctor insisted he had a lot of patients who used these, and a study I'd read said the success rate was high. There was no way this thing could be as clunky and mood-killing as it was in my head if it worked for that many people.

And tendinosis surgery works on eighty percent of people, but somebody has to be the twenty percent.

I didn't let that thought linger. It was possible I could be spectacularly unlucky with this just like I had with the attempts to repair my fucked-up tendons, but I wouldn't know until, well, I knew.

And right now, I had some time on my hands. And I was curious. Might as well give it a shot. See if I could get this thing to work. See if it did the job. See if I could get off.

"What about orgasms?" I'd asked the doctor despite the warmth in my cheeks.

"You don't have to get an erection to have an orgasm," he'd replied.

I'd eyed him dubiously. "But I've *rarely* been able to get off with my…by myself or with my partner."

"Some of that may be psychological. Many men feel a lot of shame and self-consciousness if they can't get or maintain an erection, and those feelings don't really bode well for an orgasm."

Couldn't argue with that. We'd talked for a while about it, and he didn't think there was any mechanical reason why I hadn't been able to come. The fact that Jon had gotten me off occasionally definitely made the doc lean toward it being a psychological block more than a physiological one, and that actually made me feel better. A mental block sounded more moveable than a physical one.

"Okay," I said into the silence of my bedroom. "Just take it out and see what happens."

With my heart in my throat, I opened the box. Inside was a black plastic case with a latch, kind of like the ones some power tools came in. I tried not to think too hard—think too *much* about that comparison.

I unsnapped the latch and looked inside. Tucked into the foam insert were some rings, a clear plastic cylinder about the size of a Grande Starbucks cup, and some instructions.

First things first—instructions.

Fortunately, they were written in layman's terms instead of something that required a medical degree or a decoder ring. Because goddamn, I didn't need to feel stupid on top of the other flurry of emotions I had right then. Though there was probably a YouTube tutorial out there if I got really confused.

I read through all the steps, and so far, it sounded pretty straightforward. Put on some lube, put on the ring, attach the cylinder, pump it slowly and carefully, detach the cylinder from the ring, leave the ring on my dick, and ta da! Boner.

Apparently this worked better if I was shaved, so the cylinder could actually form enough of a seal to do its thing. Huh. I'd thought about shaving for aesthetic reasons in the past, but never for practical, functional reasons.

Oh hell. Why not? Nothing else in my life was normal anymore.

I left everything on my bed, stepped out to double check that Luna was good and didn't need to go out (she was happily snoozing in a sunbeam by the sliding glass door), and then went in to grab a shower. As I dried off afterward, the newly shaved skin definitely felt different, but it wasn't bad. I'd even managed to avoid nicking myself, which was kind of a miracle. With the way everything had been lately, I really wouldn't have been surprised if I'd had to put a couple of scraps of toilet paper down there to staunch the bleeding.

Freshly showered and duly shaved, I lounged naked on the bed and faced down this weird-looking piece of equipment.

"All right," I murmured as I tugged the open case closer. "Let's do this."

There were several rings in the box, and after I'd put on some lube, I tried on three before I found one that seemed to fit right. It might've even been a little loose, but erring on the side of too loose seemed like the way to go. If it was the wrong size, I could switch it out for one that was tighter. If I tried one that was too tight…that didn't sound like it would end comfortably.

The cylinder attached easily enough. I had to pause and chuckle because it was either that or die of embarrassment even though there was no one else around. This all looked so bizarre—my soft cock inside a clear plastic contraption that looked like something out of a sci-fi movie. I tried not to think about whether that movie was a slapstick comedy or some dark dystopian nightmare, and I reminded myself this was no different than putting on a brace while I'd been going through my early stages of physical therapy. It was a medical appliance. It was there to help. It had been designed by experts for people like me, and even if it looked and felt a little weird, so had some of the casts and braces I'd worn.

I glanced at the instructions.

Then I steadied the bottom of the cylinder, which was against my newly shaved skin. With my other hand, I carefully started moving the outer piece up and down. It was a motion not unlike jerking off, and the instructions were emphatic about doing it really slowly at first until I knew how much I could handle.

So I did it slowly. After a while, I could feel the suction. Weird, but not bad.

And as I steadily pumped it more, pausing now and then like the directions told me to, my dick started getting hard.

My heart sped up. For a second, I thought it might be some catastrophic cardiac disaster that meant I needed to stop this immediately, but I quickly realized that it was a surge of hope. That little rush of *maybe this* is *working*.

It *was* working.

It was a frustratingly slow and steady progress, though I held on to my doctor's assurance that I'd get faster and more adept at it with some practice, but *it was working*.

The instructions were emphatic about stopping often to let blood keep flowing. Every time I did, I cringed, expecting to lose the progress I'd made, but…I didn't. My cock stayed hard.

I let my head fall back against the pillow. Holy fuck. *This* was all I'd needed?

Okay, but there was getting hard, and there was staying hard. The moment of truth would be when the cylinder came off. The ring would stay on, which was supposed to help keep me from going soft, but the negative pressure from the cylinder would be gone.

Well, so far, so good. Might as well see what happens.

Detaching the cylinder from the ring took a little doing just because it was unfamiliar—the assembly was simple and the instructions were clear, but I was clumsier with it than I would have liked. I had a few seconds to worry that momentary frustration would kill the hard-on I finally had.

But it didn't.

With the ring still in place, I experimentally gave my cock a slow stroke. A sigh slipped past my lips as I closed my eyes and let my head fall back against the pillow again. Oh my God. I'd been thinking so hard—so to speak—about whether this would work, it hadn't even occurred to me how good it would feel when I got this far.

I wasn't losing my hard-on. I wasn't as rock-hard as I would've been in my previous life, but I was hard, and this felt fucking *good.* The ring wasn't so bad—just different. A thing that would take some getting used to. It wasn't uncomfortable, and it seemed to be the right size. It was just a little weird to have it there at all.

But even with the ring, I was hard, and every stroke made me want to moan with pleasure I hadn't experienced in way too long. I'd been too self-conscious. Too freaked out that something I'd always taken for granted was gone and seemed to be gone forever. I wasn't sure if I'd get off, but I kind of didn't care if I did. Right now, this felt so damn good, just being hard and *staying* hard and enjoying the friction of my slightly lubricated hand instead of freaking out until I lost my erection.

I closed my eyes and kept stroking myself as I let my mind wander through a few go-to fantasies. Some hookups I'd had in the past. The odd porno that I'd mentally filed away for nights when I was by myself.

Unsurprisingly, my mind kept shifting to thoughts of Jon, and I stopped fighting it. After all, he was sexy as hell, and imagining my cock between his lips or moving in and out of his ass… Oh yeah, those fantasies were a lot hotter now that I didn't have that nagging "It'll never happen" voice in my ear. Maybe it *could* happen now. Maybe I could watch Jon's head bobbing over my cock and struggle to speak clearly enough to ask him to finger me while he was at it. I probably wouldn't be able to fuck into his mouth—not because of my injury, but because he'd hold me in place, pinning me to the bed so all I could do was lie there and enjoy everything he did.

I swore into the silence of my bedroom, and I tightened my fingers around my cock as I stroked faster. I couldn't remember the last time I'd jerked off like this—relaxed, unhurried, and without fear of pain and failure trying to kill the mood at every turn. The next time? Oh fuck, the next time I wanted Jon's hand on me instead of mine. Maybe his mouth against mine too. Making out while we stroked each other—that sounded amazing. It sounded fucking hot. For once, it sounded *possible*.

And that wasn't all that suddenly seemed possible. The more I stroked myself, especially as I gave a little twist over the head, the more that intense need swelled, not just for friction but for release. Not just need...possibility. *Inevitability*.

"Oh God," I murmured, and I ignored the fatigue burning in my elbow as I kept going.

Then my hips jerked, sending a mild bolt of pain down my left leg, but that barely registered over the intense release as I came on my hand and stomach.

I collapsed back to the bed and stared up at the ceiling, my head spinning as I tried to catch my breath.

It worked.

Oh my God. It... It fucking worked!

That thought brought almost as much relief as the orgasm had, and I actually laughed, closing my eyes as I wiped my clean hand over my face. I wasn't broken. I could still have a sex life without thinking, *Goddammit, I miss being* satisfied.

I'm not. Hopelessly. Broken.

As I came back to earth and the dust settled, I looked down at my still-hard cock. The directions had been clear about not leaving the ring on for more than thirty minutes total, and I figured taking it off sooner than later was the way to go so I didn't fall asleep or something. I took it off, grabbed some tissues, and wiped away the cum and lube. Then I sprawled back on the bed, still dizzy and blissed out.

It wasn't like this had been the most intense orgasm I'd ever had, but the relief was mind-blowing. It had been *easy*. If this was the result of using the pump, then damn right I'd use it enough to get good at it.

My first instinct was to pack this thing up and take it with me next time I saw Jon. I could finally get hard for real while we were in bed. I could *come*.

But...maybe not right out of the gate.

I'd need to do this on my own a few times before I tried it with Jon. It was clunky and weird, and I was more than a little dubious of my doctor's insistence that it could be worked into foreplay.

On the other hand, maybe it would be worth it if I could get hard and stay that away while we were in bed. A few minutes of awkwardness, and then we could have something closer to *normal* sex for the first time.

Especially since I didn't imagine Jon would be weirded out by it, or that he'd make me feel self-conscious about needing one. That wasn't like him at all.

I let my gaze drift to the pump, and my heart did a little flutter that seemed out of place right now.

Then again, maybe it wasn't out of place.

I couldn't imagine bringing a medical grade penis pump into the room with any of the men I'd been with in the past. I couldn't even imagine explaining to them why I needed it, never mind them staying long enough to figure out how to work around it or incorporate a device like this into sex or foreplay. Jon, though... I couldn't see him laughing about it or bolting or making it weird. That hadn't stopped me from balking about the dildo, but that was more about me than him.

And now that I thought about it, the fact that it was a no-brainer to use the pump when I was with Jon—that it was a matter of when, not if—put an interesting light on him and on the two of us. I'd been thinking a lot lately that we didn't quite fit the mold of friends with benefits, and now that I thought about that in the context of whether he was someone I felt safe enough with to bring something clunky and awkward into bed so I could get hard, I couldn't think of him as a fuck buddy. We'd started out as strangers who both needed physical contact, even if it wasn't sex. Now it genuinely felt like *friends* with benefits. Like we'd been friends all along, and the "benefits" had just been a fun addition between two guys who trusted each other enough to get naked and not feel ashamed of what we wanted, what we needed, or what we couldn't necessarily do.

The night we'd met, we'd both been on the same page—sex. When we'd met the second time, he'd been sweet and understanding about why I'd abruptly bailed, and we'd just been getting closer ever since.

We talked. We watched movies. We texted when we couldn't see each other. I'd worked on his house and hung out with his son. We'd adopted dogs and let them play together every chance we could. The nights we spent apart, we FaceTimed.

As much as we'd both insisted all along that we were just in this for sex and maybe friendship, the fact was that somewhere along the line, no matter how much I'd told myself we hadn't, we'd quietly segued into so much more. Enough that I could bring a penis pump into bed with him and be confident he'd see it as a way to enhance the sex we had, not something to be judgy about. Same with the toy.

I wanted to try it with him. I believed he'd be sweet and patient. I believed the sex that resulted would be hot and fun.

But I wanted a little practice first. One thing at a time. I'd get used to using the pump on my own before I trotted it out with Jon.

And to my surprise, I was excited about bringing this into bed with us. Nervous, yes. Still mad at the universe because I needed the damn thing, totally. I wasn't quite ready to bring out any of the extra equipment I now had to move things along, but I'd get there. And they would give us more options when we fooled around. Time would tell if I'd be able to top him, or if my hip would make that a moot point anyway.

But I felt better about my sexual future—*our* sexual future—than I had in ages.

And I couldn't wait until I was ready for us to try it together.

28

JON

Brent had been to the specialist today, and he hadn't said anything about it in his texts. We'd gone back and forth about when he'd be coming by this evening, but he hadn't said a word about the appointment.

Was that a good sign? A bad one? No news is good news? He didn't want to talk about it? He wanted to talk about it in person instead of via text? Some clairvoyance would've really come in handy right about now, because the suspense was killing me. Mostly the part where I wanted to know how he felt about whatever the doctor had said. What could I say? I was worried about him.

At a little after six, he and Luna came to the door. So far, he seemed pretty chill, laughing as Winston and Luna greeted each other excitedly, and he wasn't moving like he was in any more pain than usual. That had to be a good sign, right? Or at least not a bad one?

Unaware of me trying to read his mind, Brent unclipped Luna's leash. Of course, she and Winston started tearing through the house.

He chuckled as he hung the leash beside the door. "I wish my friends were that excited to see me whenever I showed up."

"I know, right." I slid a hand around his waist and pressed a kiss to his lips. "I mean, I'm excited to see you, but I might pass on…" He gestured at the dogs as they darted through the entryway again.

He laughed, wrapping his arms around me. "Hmm, I think I like how you say hello."

I grinned, pulled him in, and kissed him for real. We weren't going to go tumbling into bed, but like hell was I missing an opportunity to enjoy the way this man kissed.

When I drew back, I asked, "Have you eaten?"

"Not yet." He gestured toward the sound of our dogs playing in the living room. "I was thinking we could go pick up something we can share with them." He was such a sucker for Winston and Luna, it made me smile.

"Good idea. I'll get my keys."

We secured the dogs in my backseat and headed into town. At one of the sandwich shops that we both liked near the waterfront, we picked up a couple of sandwiches for ourselves and some extra cold cuts to share with "the kids," as Brent jokingly called them before I went in to order.

So far he seemed to be in good spirits. Hopefully that was a good sign. As we unwrapped our sandwiches in a parking lot by the waterfront, I stole a few glances at him, trying to read him. I was still painfully curious about his appointment today, but it was a sensitive subject for him. If he wasn't volunteering the information, then it wasn't my place to pry it out of him. He'd talk about it when he was ready.

We ate, shared with the dogs, and laughed at a squirrel who'd outsmarted a seagull and made off with a hunk of food the bird had apparently stolen from someplace else. The seagull wasn't happy, and while I wasn't fluent in squirrel, I was pretty sure that chittering translated to *"Fuck you, feather rat."*

After a while, Brent got a little quiet. From the way he gazed out the windshield at nothing, he had something on his mind, but I couldn't tell what it was. I waited silently and didn't push—clearly he was trying to formulate some thoughts that wouldn't come easy. Which worried me, given his appointment with the specialist. Had he gotten bad news? Discouraging news?

Finally, he took a deep breath. "So, the doctor thinks there's hope for me. In the bedroom, I mean."

I sat up straighter. "Does he?"

Brent nodded. He quickly ran me through everything the specialist had said, and finished with, "He had me pick up a pump too. A, um…" He blushed. "A penis pump."

"Yeah?"

He moistened his lips. "Yeah. So I got one. And I tried it once. By myself." He swallowed, and when our eyes met, a smile slowly came to life. "It worked. Like, *really* worked."

My heart sped up. "Did it?"

"Mmhmm. It's, um, it's a little awkward. It's going to take some practice. But I mean..." Blushing deeper, he laughed. "It got me hard. And I actually got off."

"That's great!"

"Yeah. It is." Still smiling, but his expression turning shy again, he looked at me through his lashes. "Would you be willing to try it? Together?"

"Of course!" I laced our fingers together on the console between us and squeezed gently. "If it helps you and it means you can enjoy what we're doing more, hell yeah. Sign me up."

He held my gaze, and little by little, he relaxed. "All right. I, um, I want to use it a bit more on my own first, though. Kind of get the hang of it, I guess." He chewed his lip. "It's a little clunky, so..."

"Okay." I brought his hand up and kissed his knuckles. "Whenever you're ready, say the word."

"Thanks. And, um..." He broke eye contact again, and silence set in, punctuated by the quiet snoring of our dogs in the backseat.

I squeezed his hand. "What's on your mind?"

His eyes flicked up to meet mine, then darted away. "I guess, um... I don't know how much sense it makes, but..."

"Try me."

"Okay." He cleared his throat. "After the first time I played with the pump, I immediately wanted to suggest it. For us to play with, I mean. And I guess that got me thinking."

I had no idea where this was going, so I just nodded for him to continue.

Brent stared down at our hands. "I can't think of anyone I've been with in the past—hooking up or in a relationship—who I'd have been comfortable bringing something like that into bed. And I thought maybe it was just because you're the only one I've been with since I've had...problems. But I think it's more than that."

My heart was pounding now. "Do you?"

Nodding slowly, Brent took a deep breath and met my eyes. "Long story short, I trust you. Really trust you. And that made me realize…" He moistened his lips. "The punch line is that I think I'm getting in deeper than I meant to." He hesitated. "With you."

That…was not what I'd expected. At all. Talk about a flurry of emotions, too. I was thrilled that he trusted me this much. At the same time, he didn't seem entirely sure about his newfound feelings. Or about how he *felt* about those feelings.

"Oh. Um." I swept my tongue across my lips, not sure what to say, and not sure which way he was going with this. Was he in too deep and wanted to back off?

"I know we went into this looking for friends with benefits," he went on. "I know that's what we both wanted out of this. But it feels like..."

"Like we're more than that?"

Brent hesitated, then nodded as he shyly said, "Yeah. I don't know what that means, or if it changes anything." He laughed softly, shaking his head. "I don't have a clue." Sobering a little, he met my eyes. "I just know I'm a lot more invested in this than I set out to be."

I searched his eyes. Was he gently telling me he wanted to tap the brakes? Or that he wanted to hit the gas?

Cautiously, I asked, "Do, um… Do you *want* to be that invested?"

Brent held my gaze, oblivious to the way my heart was slamming into my ribs. After a moment, he nodded again. "Yeah. I think I do."

"Me too," I whispered.

His forehead creased, but then he smiled, crinkling the corners of his eyes. "Really?"

Nodding, I drew him closer. "Really."

He released a relieved sigh, and then found my lips with his. His kiss was so soft and gentle, it chased away the remnants of that worry that had been following me around all day. The doctor hadn't given him a miracle cure, but he'd given him more hope than he'd had before. That would boost Brent's confidence in the bedroom, I was sure of it. And then, as a bonus, the conversation had segued into us both admitting what I'd known all along—that we were more than friends with benefits.

He drew back and looked at me. "So does this… I mean, does it change anything? Do we…" His brow furrowed with some renewed worry.

I stroked his cheek. "It doesn't have to. We don't have to commit to anything. Let's just, you know, keep an open mind and let things evolve how they're going to evolve."

He nodded. "Okay. Okay, I can live with that. I'm definitely not in a hurry to slap a name on it or whatever."

"Neither am I." I grinned. "I'd much rather enjoy living it than worry about defining it."

"Me too." He glanced into the backseat, then gestured at the dogs. "Think we should use them as an excuse to walk off our dinner?"

"You up for a walk?"

"Yeah, I'm good. The multi-use trail is pretty level."

"Okay." I twisted around. "Winston, you want to go for a walk?"

Instantly, both dogs were wide awake and bolt upright, vibrating with excitement.

Brent laughed as he reached for his door handle. "Well, I guess that answers that."

Brent was asleep on my shoulder, but I was wide awake, staring into the darkness and replaying our earlier conversation over and over in my head.

And I wished I could say I still had that giddy feeling I'd had when Brent had first tipped his hand. Because really, what wasn't to be thrilled about when this amazing man said he felt more for me than just lust?

Well, there was the part where Brent was young. And the part where his life had been in massive amounts of flux for the past year, and he was just starting to get everything back on the rails. He was on the rebound from his old life just like I was on the rebound from my marriage, and I was terrified that wouldn't bode well in the long term.

Brent was simultaneously everything I wanted and everything I was afraid of. A man I couldn't help falling for, and a man who was clearly itching for new horizons and greener pastures. Did I really want to let myself get in this deep with someone whose foot was probably out the door just like Ashley's had been for Christ knew how long? Was there any choice? Because I *was* in this deep, and the choice was either to stay or go.

I didn't want to go. God, I so did *not* want to go.

But would he stick around?

Maybe I was more raw from my divorce than I'd thought, because I was suddenly afraid I was a placeholder for Brent like I'd been for others in my life. I'd been a good enough lead singer to keep us getting gigs until my band had found someone better. I'd been good enough at my last pre-massage job until they'd found someone with a higher degree from a more prestigious university and better experience from a bigger company. I'd been enough for Ashley until... Well, until I hadn't been.

Stroking Brent's hair, I watched him in the moonlight. I was enough for him now. How long until he realized he could do better than a forty-something single dad with a pile of debt? How long before he noticed that I was living in a fixer-upper that was a metaphor for my whole life—something I had all kinds of dreams and plans for, but couldn't quite get off the ground because of money, time, and physical limitations? How long before he wanted more than I could give and less of what I couldn't help bringing to the table?

Brent's body would never be the same as it was before his injury, but it was improving. He was gaining more strength and mobility. The specialist had given him hope that he could get back some of what he'd lost in the bedroom, and the pump had driven that hope home. His mental health seemed to be getting better too—though he clearly still had a lot of grieving to do, and his father wasn't helping him move forward, he was coming out of his shell and out of his funk.

I was thrilled for him, and I hoped this positive trajectory continued. I wanted him to be healthier and happier. I just...couldn't help feeling a little insecure. Maybe it was because he was so much younger than me. Maybe it was because of the way my ex-wife had decided greener pastures were wherever I *wasn't*. Whatever it was, I had to admit there was a part of me that worried that as Brent recovered, he'd realize he could do better. That he could absolutely have his pick of the younger guys out there who had fewer kids, less baggage, and more hair.

I closed my eyes and exhaled.

How long before you figure out you can have so much better than anything I can offer?

And this wasn't like dating when I was a stupid kid with nothing to lose. I had a kid of my own now. A kid who was affected by my decisions.

My heart sank.

A kid who was already attached to Brent. And Brent had been so good to him, too. In terms of someone I could date who I could trust around my son, and who would get along with my son, Brent was the jackpot.

So what if I had to tell Cody that Brent wouldn't be here anymore? I still hurt thinking about the moment Ashley and I first broke the news to him that we were divorcing. He was older—he'd been eight when we'd separated, and now he was ten—but he was a sensitive kid. He still struggled with the divorce sometimes.

Sighing, I held Brent a little closer, and he murmured in his sleep as I kissed the top of his head.

I wanted to be enough for Brent. I wanted this to be real. I hoped and prayed it was real.

I was just afraid of how real the inevitable heartbreak would be.

29

BRENT

"What's this?" Dad gestured at Luna as we came up the porch steps. "Still haven't gotten her an emotional support animal vest?"

"Very funny," I said through my teeth. "She's not my emotional support animal."

He made an ugly, amused noise, but at least he patted Luna. I could say a lot about my dad, but he was nice to animals. I was so not in the mood for any of his crap today. I felt like trash. The last few days had been so good, and then my pain decided to shoot up to a nine last night for no apparent reason. Jon had tried like hell to help, but no amount of massages, painkillers, or modified sleeping positions helped. Now I was exhausted, not to mention embarrassed he'd had to deal with a sleepless night like that, all because my body sucked. Literally the only thing keeping me going today was the dog my father snidely suggested was my emotional support dog.

I started up the porch steps, trying to keep my pain out of sight.

Really should've brought in my cane.

But no. Not where my dad could see it. No fucking way.

I'd grit my teeth and get through this. Just like I did every time.

I made it up the stairs to the kitchen without dying (though holy shit, I was surprised I didn't pass out from the pain). After I'd said hello to my mom, I let Luna out into the backyard where the papillons were playing. All it took was one look at the trio of tiny yappers, and she was in seventh heaven. The four of them tore around, tails wagging and tongues flapping in the wind. Luna found a stick that was bigger than all three of the other dogs, which didn't stop them from trying to take it just because she had it.

"They're all going to sleep hard tonight," Mom mused as we watched from the back deck.

"No kidding." I chuckled, watching Luna run around with her head up while the papillons tried in vain to reach the stick she was keeping out of their reach. "She's got a lot of energy, though. If I open the back door, she could be dead on her feet and she'd still run out and dive in the lake."

Mom laughed. "A Lab with lakefront property. That's a match made in heaven."

"No kidding. Plus she loves my boyfriend's dog."

"Oh does she?" There was a note of interest in her voice. I hadn't said much about Jon except to casually brush up against the fact that I was seeing someone. It never hurt to get them—especially my dad—used to the idea well before I started making noise about bringing a guy home.

"Yeah," I said. "He's got a golden retriever mix or something. They adore each other. And they can usually wear each other out if we let them play long enough. *Especially* in the lake."

"A retriever and a Lab? In the lake?" She snorted. "You don't say."

"I know, right?" I laughed, but it was difficult, mostly because I was trying to ignore the sharp, relentless pain in my hip and both knees. My back wasn't doing so hot, either. I rested my elbows on the deck railing, ostensibly to look casual as Mom and I watched the four dogs tearing around the backyard. Truthfully, the pain was so bad, my eyes were watering, and the pain in my back was steadily climbing upward toward my neck.

Any other time, I'd have been leaning hard on my cane to take the weight off my hip, but not here. And ironically, the stress of being around him at all was making the pain worse. To the point my entire left leg didn't feel stable. Like the artificial joint was going to come apart or my knee was going to buckle at an inopportune moment. All because I was too stubborn to just lean on my damn cane already.

They say pride goeth before the fall. Not sure they meant being too proud to be seen with a cane before *literally falling*. Today it didn't seem far from the truth.

"Hey, Brent?" Dad called from the house. "Can I borrow you for a second?"

I turned around and craned my neck warily. "What do you need?"

"Go ahead, sweetie." Mom patted my arm. "I'll keep an eye on the dogs."

The dogs didn't need much supervision. The fence was high and secure, and none of the four dogs was prone to taking off. It wasn't Luna I was worried about.

Guard up, I went back into the house. "What do you need?"

"I was going to refinish that dresser in the back bedroom and give it to your sister. The girls need something bigger." He gestured down the hall. "How about giving me a hand moving it into the garage?"

I planted my feet. "Uh, no."

He eyed me. "It's not even that heavy. It's just awkward without two people maneuvering it."

"I'm sure, but I'm not your guy for it."

"You'll be fine." Dad motioned for me to follow him as he started down the hall. "You're tough. You can handle—"

"That's not really how it works. I can't just out-tough busted bones, you know?"

"The bones are healed." He stepped back into the kitchen. "You said so yourself."

"The fractures, yeah. But I did a fair amount of damage. They don't replace your hip when you're twenty-eight for nothing."

He scowled. "Those doctors were morons. That was overkill and—"

"Dad." I closed my eyes and pushed out a breath through my nose. "Just stop. Please? It's done, and—"

"And there's no reason for you to be moping around while you could be getting back on your feet and—"

"I *am* back on my feet," I growled. "But I have to be careful so I don't set myself back. Maybe it looks like it to you, but I'm *not* completely recovered from the accident."

Dad released one of those long sighs that meant he was so over it. "You've got to stop making excuses, son." Then he set his jaw and narrowed his eyes. "You know what I think?"

I glared right back at him. "That I should try playing hockey with a prosthetic hip and see what happens?"

He crossed his arms. "I think you wanted to quit hockey, and that crash just gave you an excuse."

"What?" I laughed humorlessly. "You think I *wanted* this? Do you really think—"

"I think you were a mediocre player, and instead of improving your game to hold your own in the pros, you made excuses about pain."

My lips parted. I was speechless.

Dad, however, was not. "Pain is part of hockey. The crash just gave you an excuse to be as lazy as you wanted to be during all those years I was pushing you to be the best."

"That's..." My mouth had gone dry. "That's really what you think? That I was a shitty hockey player who was looking for an excuse to slack?"

He shrugged indifferently. "You sure haven't put a lot of effort into getting off the bench, have you?"

"Besides multiple surgeries and hundreds of hours of physical therapy?"

He laughed. "And look at you. You gave up, Brent. You could have fought through this, but you gave up, and—"

"All right, you two," Mom broke in. "Enough. Ken, the dresser can wait, and Brent doesn't need your pressure while he's trying to recover. Brent, why don't you call Luna inside so I can feed the little dogs?"

I gritted my teeth. Dad and I exchanged glares, but we didn't push. Once Mom stepped in, that was it unless we wanted to catch hell from her.

I went back out to the deck and called Luna inside. As soon as she heard my voice, her ears perked up, and she gave a little yip as she came sprinting up the steps. It was impossible not to smile as she skidded to a halt beside me. "At least somebody's always happy to see me."

She licked my hand and gazed at me with those big brown eyes. I patted her gently, and we headed into the house. Dad had disappeared, probably to deal with the dresser I wouldn't help him move, and I sat down in the living room. Luna sat beside me and leaned against my knee. It smarted a little, but quite frankly, I didn't mind.

My conversation with my dad echoed in my mind. A lump rose in my throat despite my best efforts to push it back. That was what he thought of me? That I was mediocre and lazy, and had jumped on the first opportunity to be permanently benched? Christ, did that mean he'd *always* been disappointed in me as a hockey player? I knew he'd never gotten over my career ending prematurely, but I wasn't good enough? I couldn't hold my own in the pros?

I spent my entire life destroying my body to make you proud, and I was just...mediocre?

Luna licked my hand again. I cleared my throat and looked down at her. Scratching her neck, I quietly said, "We should've just gone to McDonald's tonight, shouldn't we?"

She rested her chin on my thigh, and my eyes welled up a little as I kept petting her. Luna may not have been a certified emotional support animal like my dad snarked about, but she was doing more to keep me going right now than anything else.

Yeah. We definitely should've gone to McDonald's.

Because there weren't many things I did right, but I could definitely get my dog a hamburger.

I was so eager to get the hell away from my parents' house, I didn't even look at my phone until I was back at my own place. When I did, Jon had texted me with, *I'm home. Come by whenever.*

Usually, that message would make me smile, but tonight, it just made my heart sink.

I wanted to see Jon, and I wanted to stay as far away from him as I could. I wanted to lose myself in his gentle, loving warmth, and cuddle together as much as my stupid body allowed, and watch a movie until we fell asleep.

But I also didn't want to face him right now. It was as if everything my dad had said, all his criticism and disapproval, were painted on my skin, and I wanted to hide from the world until the stain was gone. If Jon looked at me now, he'd see what my dad saw every time: failure. Disappointment. Defeat.

I didn't want him to see me like this. I could barely breathe because I was in so much fucking pain, hurting so much I was sweating just from walking into the house from my truck. Jon had seen me in pain before. It wasn't news to him. Especially after how miserable last night had been, though, I didn't want to have to admit to him that I was hurting *this* much because I'd stupidly knuckled through when I should have used a cane, sat down, taken something, iced something...

I sighed, pressing back against the couch cushions. I felt like shit tonight, and it was my own damned fault, and I deserved whatever disapproving look or "you dumbass" comment Jon gave me for doing this to myself. He'd never said anything to that effect, but who was I kidding? It was only a matter of time before he saw what my dad saw.

Not just the pain. Not just the utter defeat. How long before he realized that coddling me was more trouble than it was worth? Or before he figured out that my barrage of injuries had saved us all from witnessing how utterly mediocre I was at hockey? The one thing in my life I'd ever been good at. The one thing I'd *thought* I was good at. It was bad enough that thing was gone, but the person who'd pushed me the hardest, who I thought had believed in me...

I wiped my eyes. I had nothing without hockey. I *was* nothing without hockey. And maybe I hadn't even been anything when I'd had hockey. Where the fuck did that leave me now?

What in the holy hell made me think I was good enough for someone like Jon? Even my own parents could barely tolerate what I'd become.

My feelings for Jon were real, but they didn't change the reality of being with me. I'd always have to walk slower than he obviously wanted to. Everywhere we went would have to be strategized and thought through so I wouldn't find myself two miles from the car and unable to walk the rest of the way. Pain would be, to whatever degree, a constant companion. Sex would probably never be normal. The best I could hope for was whatever modern medicine could scrape together or I could find in an adult toy store, and it wasn't like sex with me had exactly been anything to write home about for Jon. What kind of idiot was I if I thought he wanted to sign up for the kind of sex that meant shoehorning in a medical device and pretending that counted as foreplay? He knew and I knew that was the best we could do unless a medical miracle happened.

"Goddammit," I muttered into my silent living room.

Before my pain had started cascading last night and my visit with my parents today, I'd been flying high, convinced I was on the road to normal. But normal was gone now. I didn't know who I was anymore, only that I wasn't the young, fun-loving hockey player I'd been a year ago. And I was never going to be that guy again. The sooner I accepted that, the sooner I could get the hang of whatever came next instead of living in denial.

And part of that meant accepting that I was nowhere near good enough for Jon. It was only a matter of time before he figured that out, so I needed to save us both the trouble.

The jingle of tags and click of nails on hardwood signaled that Luna was coming into the living room.

I lifted my head. "Hey, baby. You hungry?"

She studied me, tail wagging uncertainly. We'd stopped for that hamburger on the way home, but she probably did want some food.

"Okay." I put a hand on the armrest. "Let's get you some—*fuck*." Every muscle protested as I tried to get up. With some effort, I got to my feet, and I limped into the kitchen.

After I'd put some food down for Luna, I leaned against the counter and stared out at Lake Champlain. It was getting dark, but I could still make out the water. Hadn't this view relaxed me before?

Yeah. Before the hot tub right outside the window had become a place full of steamy memories with Jon. Before the shoreline had become a place for our dogs to play together, chasing each other or toys in the yard and in the water.

I'd deluded myself into believing that would go on. That the memories wouldn't turn into something that made it hurt whenever I looked out at my peaceful view.

I was falling hard for Jon. Hell, I'd already fallen hard for him.

But I had to accept reality. I was deluding myself if I kept thinking there was any future for us. His patience would run out. He'd find someone who wasn't so much effort for so little return. I could barely cope, living with chronic pain and all these newfound limitations. Who was I to ask Jon to saddle himself with all that just so he could be with a train wreck like me? Fact was, I was stupid if I thought I could—or had any right to—hold on to him any more than I'd held on to my hockey career.

And the sooner I made peace with that, the better.

30

JON

Brent didn't return my text. When I called later, he didn't answer, and he didn't return the call.

The next day, he still didn't respond.

I alternated between frustrated and worried. Had something happened? It didn't seem like him to disappear on me. Okay, he'd bolted the first night we'd been together, but then he'd come back and told me what happened and why. We knew each other now. He could talk to me.

So what the hell was going on?

By Monday evening, I was definitely worried, so I bit the bullet and drove to his place. His truck was outside and the living room lights were on. I couldn't decide if those were good signs or not.

With my heart in my throat, I walked up the path and onto his front porch, paused to steel myself, then rang the doorbell.

Instantly, Luna started barking from somewhere in the house. Thundering paws and skittering nails punctuated her barks as she rushed toward the door.

"Calm down, calm down." Brent's voice sent a rush of relief and renewed apprehension through me. He was here. He was okay.

So then the radio silence meant…?

Luna quieted down. Then the deadbolt clicked.

When the door swung open, Luna immediately rushed forward to say hello, and of course I petted her and let her lick my hand. After a moment, Brent gently told her to go back in the living room, and she trotted down the hall, tags jingling with every step.

Brent gestured for me to come inside, but we didn't get any farther than the foyer. Now that we were alone, he didn't look surprised to see me, but he didn't look thrilled either. Expression sheepish, he broke eye contact after only a split second and muttered, "Hey."

"Hey." I slid my hands into my pockets. "I, um… I didn't hear from you all day. I got worried, so I came to…" I trailed off, not sure if my explanation even mattered.

"I'm sorry." He rubbed the back of his neck. "Yesterday was… It was rough."

"Pain? Or your parents?"

"Parents. The pain is a little better, but my parents…" He deflated.

Sighing, I stepped closer, ready to offer some comfort, but he stiffened, so I did too. "What's wrong?"

"I'm sorry, Jon," he whispered. "I just… I think I need to be alone."

The words were a gut punch, but I tried not to let it show. "Oh. Okay." I swallowed, backing off a little so I didn't crowd him. "Just… call me, I guess? Text me? Whenever you're ready?"

His features tightened, and he still didn't look at me, and the gut punch intensified.

"Brent?"

He drew his tongue across his lips, then pulled in a deep breath. When he finally looked at me, fatigue radiated off him along with a dozen emotions I couldn't begin to parse. "I'm sorry," he said again. "I need… I can't do this."

"You… When you say you want to be alone, you mean…"

Flinching, he looked away again, and the subtle nod may as well have been a kick to the back of my knees for all I had to struggle to stay upright.

"Can we talk about this?" I sounded so desperate, but I didn't try to hide it because I suddenly *was* that desperate.

"I just can't do it." He looked at me again, bone-deep hurt coming through the exhaustion in his eyes. "I thought I could handle this right now. All of it. But I can't."

"Handle what? Do you want to go back to being friends with—"

"We haven't been friends with benefits from the start," he said shakily. "You know that as well as I do."

I pressed my lips together. He wasn't wrong.

Voice soft and unsteady, he went on, "I wasn't lying when I told you how I felt. I just… I overestimated how much I was ready for. With everything happening, I…" He trailed off, shaking his head.

I wanted to fight back. I wanted to tell him I loved him, that we could make this work, that neither of us had done anything wrong, so for the love of God, couldn't we at least be friends? But this was eerily similar to that moment when Ashley had told me she wanted a divorce. There was nothing to discuss. The decision had been made, even if it was the first I'd heard about it. I wanted to beg him to stay, but just like Ashley had been back then, he was already gone.

So what else could I do?

"All right." I nodded sharply and took a step toward the door. "All right, I'll… I'll get out of here, then."

He didn't look at me. I thought he murmured another apology as I was slipping out the door, but it didn't matter. It was over.

I got into my car and drove away from his lakeside house. From his exclusive neighborhood. From everything that had become a fixture in my world and had given me faith that there was life after divorce.

I didn't know why I was surprised, though. Yeah, it had fallen from the clear blue sky without any warning aside from twenty-four hours of silence, but I'd suspected from the start that this would come sooner or later. Didn't matter how much I'd tried to deny it. I'd had a feeling. I mean, did I really think I was enough for someone like him? I could barely convince myself I was enough for anyone. A young, hot former athlete with money to burn and an irresistible smile? Yeah, no shit, I wasn't enough for him. Not now that the kind of sex he was used to—or at least something close to it—was on the table again. He had the pump now, and it was working for him. He hadn't been ready to bring it out with me yet, but he'd said it was working and—

And maybe that *was* the issue. Maybe now that he was on the upswing sexually, he'd realized he didn't need to settle for me anymore.

Fuck. That *was* it, wasn't it? The minute there was a glimmer of hope that he could have a normal sex life again, I was tossed aside like cast or a brace he didn't need anymore. As a massage therapist, I was encouraged when someone no longer needed me because it meant I'd done my job and they were more functional and in less pain.

As a person, as a partner, the effect wasn't quite the same.

I should've known. After he'd told me early on how he was figuring out who he was, after he'd started coming out of his shell—what the hell did I expect? He didn't need me now that he had his feet under him and had a handle on life after hockey. Maybe he still had a lot of pain to get through, but at least when it came to sex, he'd seen the light at the end of the tunnel. So what the fuck did he need me for?

Exhaling, I thumped the wheel with my fist.

I should've seen it coming. In fact, I had. I'd warned myself not to get too close to a flight risk, and I'd gone and done it anyway.

But I damn sure wouldn't make that mistake again.

Maybe I was just depressed and lonely. I didn't know. I just knew that as I watched Ashley hugging Cody hello on our custody transfer day, it was a struggle to remember a time when I'd thought it would be the two of us till death. We were strangers now. More and more, I realized we'd been strangers for a long time. We had to be, if I'd been so out of touch that I hadn't realized she was that unhappy until the minute she'd asked for a divorce.

First you. Now Brent. Am I the problem here?

What was it about me that couldn't hold on to someone I loved? Was I doing something wrong? Not doing something right? Was I just…not someone who could be a lifelong companion for someone else?

"Good night, Dad." Cody's voice pulled me out of my thoughts.

"Good night, kiddo." I gave him a quick hug. "See you next week."

He smiled, and as he headed for his room, I started to leave, but I paused. Turning to Ashley, I said, "Listen, can we talk for a minute?" I nodded toward the door. "Outside?"

She pressed her lips together, clearly not wanting to talk to me, but she sighed and gestured at the door.

Once we were out in the breezeway, I leaned against the railing and faced her, thumbs hooked in my pockets as I tried to look more casual than I felt. "I know nothing is going to change. And I'm not asking for anything to change." I steeled myself. "But just tell me why."

Ashley's features tightened. "Why, what?"

"Come on. You know what I'm asking."

"And I told you the day I said I wanted a divorce."

"Yeah. You did." I shifted my weight. "I guess I just don't understand. I thought we were building a life together. You thought your life was passing you by." Shaking my head, I exhaled. "How were we so far from the same page?"

"I don't know." She tucked a strand of hair behind her ear. "I mean, we got married when we were young and stupid, and we thought we knew what love was. We thought we knew what life was." She laughed bitterly. "We didn't even know who *we* were."

"Didn't we kind of figure that out as we went along?"

"Maybe you did." Her tone was cold. "I didn't know who I was or what I wanted. I still don't quite know."

"You just know you don't want to be with me."

She shrugged tightly, maybe a little apologetically, but didn't deny it. "Why is this coming up now?"

"Because I haven't had the nerve to ask before now. It doesn't change anything. I just wanted to know."

Silence hung between us, thick and heavy and miserably uncomfortable. Before I could break away and head for the stairs, though, she said, "Look, we were kids. I went from being a kid to being a wife to being a woman whose life was *consumed* by not being able to have a kid of my own. And then I was a mom, and..." She sighed, shrugging tightly. "I guess I just realized that I never got a chance to be *me*."

"You couldn't be you while we were together?"

"I don't know. I really don't. I never figured myself out when everyone we knew did in their twenties. All I knew was that I didn't know who I was anymore, and I felt like my life was passing me by." She chewed her lip and seemed to think for a moment before she went on, "All the years we were trying to get pregnant, that was all I could think about. Everything I did revolved around it."

That caught me off guard. "It did?"

"Of course it did," she snapped, folding her arms. "I was in my twenties and my friends were having babies like they were going out of style, and I was failing at basic biology. So I was always either trying to figure out why I couldn't get pregnant, or I was planning my future in six-month increments."

"Six-month increments?"

"Well, yeah. Because when I did finally get pregnant, then whatever plans I made were going to have to adapt. I put off grad school because I didn't want to have a baby right in the middle of my Masters program. I never committed to traveling more than a few months out because I could be dealing with morning sickness or not fit into a swimsuit. Everything I did in the long term had to have the caveat of 'unless I get pregnant.'" Her voice wavered a little. "I did that for *eight years*."

I exhaled. "Jesus, Ash. Why didn't you tell me? I had no idea."

"Because I didn't really realize it either until later." She avoided my eyes. "I knew I was worn down and exhausted, but I didn't realize why. And then we had Cody, and the postpartum depression just wrecked me."

I winced. "I know. That was rough."

She nodded, still not looking at me. "So then when Cody was old enough to be a little more independent, especially once he started going to school, suddenly I was almost forty and had spent over fifteen years of my life fixating on getting pregnant, having Cody, and raising him. And I never went to grad school. I never took those trips we talked about." She shrugged again. "Everyone else moved on and grew up and did things, but I went nowhere. So I decided I needed to live my life."

"Ash." I shook my head. "I get all that. I promise, I do. And I'm sorry I didn't see how unhappy you were. What I don't get is why all of that meant we couldn't be together. Whatever you wanted in your life, I would've supported you, and—"

"I just needed to start over." Her tone was flat, almost cold. "I wanted more out of life."

The words hit me in the chest. I didn't think I'd ever figure out how to feel about her perception of our life and our family as "going nowhere," and I had no idea how to respond to everything she'd just said. I knew we were over and there was no going back, and I knew she wanted more than what I could provide and what I could be, but it still hurt to hear again that I wasn't enough for her. That after twenty years together, her solution for her unhappiness was to cut me loose and go searching for greener grass that, in her eyes, I could never provide.

She shifted her weight, her expression taut and her voice full of impatience. "Is there anything else?"

I shook my head. "No. No, that's… That's all I needed to know."

"Okay." She tightened her arms across her chest. "I'll see you in a week."

"Yeah. See you in a week."

We exchanged a look that didn't feel right between two people who'd ever been lovers or partners or…anything other than strangers, if I was honest. It wasn't even contempt. Indifference, maybe. Because whatever we'd been in the past was dead and gone, and if we didn't have a kid together, we'd probably never speak again.

I mumbled a goodbye and again started to go, but hesitated. As long as we were ripping off bandages, we might as well rip them all off. "Actually, there is one more thing."

Her jaw worked and her eyes narrowed. Folding her arms across her chest, she had *hurry the fuck up* written all over her face.

"I'm not asking because I want to take this back to court, or…" I gestured dismissively. "I just want to know. For me."

An eyebrow flicked up as she tightened her arms across her chest.

I gestured past her. "How long have you been with Ray?"

She jumped, eyes widening, but she quickly recovered and adopted a hostile expression again. "Why? What difference does it make? We're divorced now."

"But when did the two of you started seeing each other?"

She held my gaze. I held hers.

The longer the silence went on, the deeper my heart sank. I didn't know what I'd expected. That I'd feel *better* once I confirmed what I'd suspected all this time?

Ashley finally pushed out a resigned breath, and her shoulders dropped along with her gaze. "Fine. If you really want to know? Yes." She shrugged, but it wasn't nearly as flippant as she'd probably intended, and she couldn't look me in the eye as she said, "It started before we split up."

I had no idea what to say, or even what to feel. I'd suspected. Somewhere deep down, I'd known. But finding out for sure...fuck. There'd been a time when I probably would have lit into her for cheating on me, but I didn't have it in me today. I'd been tossed against too many emotional rocks—all I could do now was let this wave hit me and try not to let it knock me off my feet.

"He was what I was missing," Ashley said with another shrug, this one a bit more flippant. "I wasn't happy. So I moved on."

"All right. Now I know."

This time, I really did leave. Driving away in my empty car, I felt like shit and wished I'd brought Winston along. At least then I'd have some company right now. But I hadn't. Damn it.

Tomorrow, I promised myself. I didn't know where we'd go, but I was loading Winston in the car, and we were going to find a place for him to play until we ran out of daylight.

Right now, I just drove.

I'd always understood that those long years of infertility had taken their toll on Ashley and on our marriage. They'd been hell for me, and I'd known all along they'd been even worse for her. I just hadn't imagined that we'd get to the other side, have the baby we'd wanted for so long, and then I'd suddenly be part of a past she wanted to leave behind. That when she wanted something better out of life, it wouldn't matter that I'd been willing to give her anything in the world or support any endeavor she had. It wouldn't matter because she wanted more than *me*.

I'd been enough for her for a while. Then I wasn't. Not when she decided she wanted better.

I exhaled into the silence of my car. Was that all I was to people? Someone to tide them over until something better came along?

Well, whatever. I shouldn't have asked. Going into that conversation, I had stupidly hoped for some closure. Some kind of an answer so I could put a bow on this and move on.

But now I just felt worse.

And it occurred to me now that maybe it was just as well Brent walked away. Letting him go hurt like hell, but that in itself was a sign that it was time to call things off. I had feelings for him I had no business having, and they'd blown up in my face. That had come out of nowhere, but now it kind of felt inevitable. Hadn't I suspected all along that we were temporary? Hadn't I been bracing myself for that moment when he didn't need me anymore?

Guess I should've listened to myself. On the heels of a divorce from a woman who'd needed to leave me so she could find out who she was and what it meant to really live, being with a man who was trying to figure out who *he* was...didn't leave me feeling very confident about any kind of future together.

Maybe that was a good thing. I shouldn't feel confident about a future with a man like Brent. Why in the world would an up-until-recently professional athlete tie himself down with an over-the-hill single dad? I was probably just his speed for right now while his body was still on the long road of recovery from a career-ending injury, but what happened when he found his stride again? Even if he never fully regained the strength and mobility he'd had before, he'd adapt and be active again.

And hadn't he already bolted on me once? I still remembered how awful and rejected I'd felt in that hotel room the first night. When he'd come back and explained everything, we'd found our stride, but then he'd taken off again. This time it was even worse because holy fuck, it hurt. I knew him now. I had feelings for him. I'd introduced him to my son. I'd fallen hard for him, and he'd left without warning, just like he had the first night.

Clearly, Brent and I weren't in the cards.

So what *was* in the cards for me? What did I want? What could I reasonably expect someone else to want with me?

I missed the quiet stability I'd had while I was married, but I didn't want to fall in love again. Not for a while, anyway. I definitely didn't need to be with someone who was in the middle of finding himself; it was only a matter of time before he followed Ashley's example and found himself looking for someone who wasn't me. I should've known that a young, restless guy with no direction was a heartache waiting to happen.

But aside from the cold comfort of realizing it was a good thing

Brent had walked sooner than later, I didn't feel any better. If anything, I felt a whole lot worse.

I'd wondered for a long time why Ashley had suddenly wanted out of our marriage. I'd wondered if she'd started seeing Ray before she'd broken things off with me.

Now I knew.

And I wished I'd never asked.

31

BRENT

"What happened?" Ethan stared at me as we sat down in my living room. "You were practically glowing, and now…" He gestured at me before cupping his coffee mug in both hands. "I thought you two were happy together."

I deflated, absently petting Luna, who was perched on the couch beside me with her head on my leg. "We were, but I mean, let's be real." I met my best friend's eyes. "How long was he really going to saddle himself with a guy like me?"

Ethan blinked. "Are you—Brent. My God." He put his coffee cup on the end table and leaned forward, elbows on his knees as he looked right in my eyes. "You dumped him, didn't you?"

I straightened. "How did you know?"

He gave one of those long, heavy sighs he always gave when he thought I was being an idiot. "Because I know you. And look, I don't know what kind of poison your dad or your depressed brain are feeding you, but anyone who dates you would be lucky to have you." He wrinkled his nose. "Saddling himself with you, my ass."

"Easy for you to say." I sipped my coffee, wondering if it really was that bitter or if it was just me. "Have you seen how much advance planning and strategizing it takes just to figure out where to park? *I* don't even like being saddled with me."

Sighing, he rolled his eyes. "Dear God, you need to cut yourself some slack. My ex? The one who interrogated every server for ten minutes about every ingredient in every item on the menu just so he could sneer at them for not being paleo and whatever? *That* is someone who's a pain in the ass. You're dealing with an injury, not being a pretentious asshat with a superiority complex."

I laughed quietly. "Okay, Dean was a piece of work. I'll give you that."

"Ugh. Right?" Ethan groaned theatrically. "But you're not. If anything, you bend over backwards to accommodate everyone else even when you're obviously in pain."

My shoulders slumped. "Because I don't want people to get tired of accommodating me." I ran a hand through my hair and exhaled. "*Being* me is exhausting. I can't imagine what it's like being *with* me. Especially while I'm flailing my way through life, trying to figure out what the fuck I'm even doing."

Ethan furrowed his brow. "What do you mean?"

"I mean, I don't know what I'm doing now that I'm not playing hockey." I watched myself petting my dog. "I have no purpose in life right now, and I don't know what to do with that."

"Well, what kinds of things do you enjoy besides hockey?"

"That's the problem." I lifted my gaze to look at Ethan. "I lived and breathed hockey. I spent literally my entire life focusing on hockey. I don't know who I am without it."

"You have a degree, right?"

"Yeah. Don't know how many places will hire me without much experience. And it's not really a job I'm looking for. I've got money saved that'll last me a while. I just… I need some fucking *direction*. Like, a purpose, you know?"

"Honey." He smiled. "I think the answer is right here staring at you with big brown eyes."

I stared at Ethan. His eyes were bluer than mine. What the hell was he talking about?

With an exasperated sigh, he nodded downward.

I followed, and…

Luna.

Her head was still on my lap, and yes, she was staring up at me with the big brown eyes that had turned me to mush the instant I'd met her.

I petted her, which got her tail thumping on the cushion. To Ethan, I said, "So just…do stuff with my dog?"

He tsked. "Think bigger, dude. You love animals. You always have." Gesturing at Luna, he added, "Maybe that's a place to start."

I gazed down at Luna again. She rolled over, pawing at me as her tail nearly knocked Ethan's coffee off the end table. Chuckling, I patted her chest, and she tried to lick my arm.

My mind went back to the day I'd adopted her. My throat got a little tight as I remembered Jon and me laughing as we watched our new dogs playing in the tiny yard.

But then…

"It's a shame we don't have more space than this," the woman had said. *"Not just living space, but so they can get out and run around. You know—be dogs."*

"They'd probably love that," I remembered saying.

"They would. I mean, the best case scenario is they all get adopted out to forever homes. But some of them are with us for a while. The least we could do is give them more than…this."

My heart jumped, and I turned to Ethan. "What if I opened up like an animal rescue?"

"Ooh, see? Now you're thinking." He sat up straighter, smiling broadly. "Keep going."

"Well, I mean, the place I got Luna—the lady said the dogs would be happier with more space." I chewed my lip and looked around my huge, cavernous house.

"You're not thinking of adopting like forty dogs and keeping them in here, are you?"

"No, no." I shook my head. "But if I sold it and bought some land…"

"So, like, a farm?"

"Something like that, yeah." I considered it. "Except I don't know if I could keep up a place like that on my own."

"Hmm, maybe not, but you can always hire people or see if volunteers are willing to come help out."

"True. Maybe I should talk to the shelter and see if they want to work together. Even if it's just to let dogs come play outside for a few days now and then."

"Aww, doggy field trips!" He put a hand to his heart. "That would be adorable."

I laughed and looked down at Luna. "What do you think? Should we move out of this place and get a big backyard we can turn into a giant dog park?" Her tail thumped harder. Chuckling, I scratched her side. "Hmm. Maybe I should look into that."

"Good." Ethan paused. "And maybe while you're at it..."

I lifted my gaze, and he was biting his lip as he watched me cautiously. "What?"

He straightened a bit and folded his hands. "Okay, don't take this the wrong way, but I think you might want to consider talking to someone. Professionally."

"About what? Financing a farm? I still have enough money I can pay cash for—"

"No. No." Ethan shook his head. "No, I mean talk to someone about..." He hesitated. "Look, I worry about you. I know this has been a long and ugly road for you, and I'm worried it's hurting more than just your body." He tapped his temple and cautiously asked, "Like, the depression you've had for years, but magnified?"

"Wait, are you telling me you think I need a therapist?" I shook myself. "And the depression I've had for years? What are you talking about?"

His eyebrows rose. "Um, I'm talking about the depression you've had for years. Like since we were teenagers."

I stared at him. He stared back.

Then he straightened. "You thought it was normal."

"Thought *what* was normal?"

"Seriously?"

The only thing keeping me from raising my voice was my dog, and in the interest of not startling her, I quietly said, "Yes, seriously. I have no idea what you're—"

"Oh my Lord." He sighed with about as much exasperation as I felt. "This is why I was so worried about you and dragged you out to the wine bar in the first place! I know you, and I know that if left to your own devices, you'll wallow. And you'll keep wallowing."

"Not... Not forever."

"You sure about that?"

"I..." Cocking my head, I narrowed my eyes. "Why?"

"Okay, you remember that funk you got into after your rookie season?"

"Of course." I shrugged. "Who wouldn't get into a funk after a season that ended like that?"

"Sure. But how were you feeling before the season went tits up?"

"What do you mean?"

"Think about it, sweetheart. Were you in a good place that entire season?"

"I was exhausted. The regular season is no joke." I paused. "And how can I have been depressed my whole life? You and everyone else have always said I was the life of the party before..." I gestured at my leg.

"Uh-huh. And I think it was Robin Williams who said that people with depression become comedians and clowns and shit like that because they want to make others happy. That way no one else feels as miserable as they are." He paused, then waved his hand. "Or something. I'm paraphrasing. But the point is that a lot of depressed people *are* the life of the party. It keeps them going, and it keeps everyone around them going. The minute something knocks them down though, and they can't keep the façade anymore, they're flat on their back and can't function."

"Don't most people get knocked on their ass like that, though?"

"Mmhmm. But most of us can pick ourselves back up and keep moving. People with depression..." He grimaced. "Sometimes it's not that simple. Sometimes it's physical. Like you're sitting on your couch and you know you have a million things you need to do, and probably even some things you want to do, but you literally can't muster up the energy to get up, go in the kitchen, and have a glass of water."

My hand stopped moving on Luna's coat. "That's... Don't most people do that?"

"Once in a while if life is really shitty and they're grieving or they just got dumped or something? Sure." He nodded sharply. "But when it just comes out of nowhere, or it happens because of something and then it won't go away? That's not a good sign."

I swallowed, wondering why that was a struggle. "But my body is fucked up and my career is over. My dad is constantly telling me how much of a disappointment I am. And I just broke up with someone! I'm going to be depressed over all that. That's normal. Right?"

"Of course it is. But when you're depressed over that on top of being depressed because your brain is falling asleep at the serotonin switch, that's kind of a recipe for disaster." He took my hand and squeezed it. "I'm not trying to be judgy, and I'm not calling you weak or anything like that. I've been worried about you for years, and now… I mean, with your whole life getting tossed on its ass, and especially now that you just broke up with someone…" He blew out a breath. "I won't lie, sweetheart. It makes me worried to leave you alone. Because I know you can get into a low place, and I'm always terrified of how low that place can get."

I stared at him. The fear in his voice was no joke, and now I recalled more than a few times in my life when he'd dragged me kicking and screaming back out into the light after I'd been trying to hide in the dark. After a breakup. After a lost championship. After the knee surgeries that had threatened my professional prospects. After a dark cloud had consumed me for no apparent reason.

"Fuck," I whispered. "I never… I didn't realize…"

"I know. And, um, feel free to tell me if I'm overstepping or if I'm completely wrong." His brow pinched. "But do you think it's at all possible this might be why you dumped Jon?"

My heart dropped. I wanted to get defensive and say no, but… "Do you think it is?"

"Well, that's kind of been your pattern since we were kids. When it really kicks in, especially if it's after your dad's been on your ass about something, the *first* thing you do is keep people at arm's length. And whoever's closest to you gets shoved even farther away."

I blinked. "What?"

"Am I wrong?"

"You're…" Well, hell. *Was* he wrong? Of course he was. I mean, aside from the time I'd shut off my phone and abandoned social media after a nasty and public breakup, and a couple of my teammates had gotten our coaches involved because they were afraid I was losing it. And there was the time I'd caved in under the combined athletic and academic pressure my senior year in high school. And my senior year in college, for that matter. I'd drunk my way through some dark periods. Just hidden at home through others. All but canceled my cell phone and internet service a few times.

The common thread: I was alone.

Completely, utterly, and *deliberately* alone.

Oh fuck. Ethan was right.

Dad had come at me, hitting every exposed raw nerve with slapshots, and he'd left me feeling like a worthless failure.

And what was the first thing I did when it was over? Shove away everyone close to me, especially the one who'd gotten in closer than anyone else.

"Oh God." I raked a hand through my hair. "I totally fucked up with Jon, didn't I?"

"You can fix it, though!" Ethan squeezed my hand. "He knows what a piece of work your father is, doesn't he?"

I nodded.

"Okay, so tell him what happened. I mean, don't blame your dad—own your mistake—but tell him why you were in the space you were that day."

It sounded so simple. So easy. Lay it out, apologize, and then everything would be fine. It wasn't that easy and I knew it, but damn if I didn't want to cling to the possibility that it was.

"Do you mind one more somewhat bitchy piece of unsolicited advice?" Ethan asked.

I managed a halfhearted laugh. "Well, now I'm curious, so…"

He sat straighter and looked me right in the eye. "You need to cut off your dad."

"Cut off—" I stared at him. "What?"

"Think about it. How do you feel whenever you leave that place?"

I shifted uncomfortably. "Like shit."

"Uh-huh. And how many times have you told him to let the subject drop?"

I didn't answer.

"That's what I thought. Look, I know it's easier said than done. But stress isn't going to help with your pain, depression, or just, you know, being happy and functional. Even if you were totally uninjured and still playing hockey, you deserve better than the stress and pressure you get from him."

"But he's…" I swallowed. "Dude, he's my dad."

"He is. Which means he of all people shouldn't be treating you the way he does." He made a disgusted noise. "Who the hell grooms their kid to be a professional athlete, and then acts like that kid is the world's biggest disappointment when a fucking *car* wrecks his body? Like seriously, he's encouraged your entire self-worth to revolve around a *puck*. Do you really need that in your life?"

I dropped my gaze, and I watched myself petting Luna as Ethan's words banged around in my head like that proverbial puck. I couldn't argue with him. I really couldn't. As far as my dad was concerned, I started and ended with hockey, and God knew when or if he'd ever let go of *his* dream now that *my* body was permanently damaged.

So maybe Ethan was right. Maybe the best thing was for me to let go of my dad the way I'd let go of hockey. Let go of the thing that was damaging me the most.

It hurt to imagine, but I couldn't argue with him. I couldn't think of a single justification besides "he's family" to maintain contact with the man who kept shoving me back into the dark I was struggling so hard to pull myself out of.

Without my dad's constant haranguing and belittling, God knew how much better off I'd be mentally right now. One thing was for damn sure—I wouldn't have hit the bottom so hard that I'd stupidly let go of Jon.

Ethan was right. Even if I didn't cut off my dad, I needed to start putting my foot down and refusing to let him stomp me down.

And more than anything, I needed to fix where I'd fucked up with Jon.

I still had Jon's Vino and Veritas schedule committed to memory, so on a night when I knew he'd be singing, I headed into town. After parking in the garage closest to the wine bar, I carefully made the short walk, trying like hell to ignore the pain in… Oh hell, where *wasn't* there pain right now?

By the time I got to the wine bar, my eyes were watering and I had to swallow the nausea from the pain in my hip and knees. Should've brought my cane. Why did I leave it in the truck? It didn't matter. I had. And on some level, I was afraid Jon would think I was using it to squeeze some sympathy out of him. On another, I worried the sight of the cane would remind him of everything I brought to the table, and he wouldn't be interested in getting back together. Assuming he had any interest to begin with.

I hung out beside the door of Vino and Veritas, but I didn't go in—lurking in the audience would just distract him, and he didn't need that. And I kind of felt like if I walked in, everyone there would glare at me and tell me to get the fuck out after I'd hurt their friend. This was Jon's world, not mine, and I was too much of a coward to face the people who had to know by now that I'd walked.

Had I blown it with him? Fuck. I'd blown it with him. There was no point in even standing here. He was probably relieved that he didn't have to walk on eggshells to keep from jostling me. Sex with me had to be stressful as hell, so why in the world would he—

The door opened for the umpteenth time, and the guitar case appeared a heartbeat before Jon did.

"Jon," I said, and he jumped.

"Brent." He blinked. "I, uh…" He glanced behind him, then stepped aside so he was away from the door. Once we were safely out of anyone's way, he faced me again. "This is unexpected."

"Yeah, I…." I swallowed. "I didn't want to distract you while you were performing, but I wanted to talk to you. Face to face."

"Oh. Um." He glanced around. "Okay?" He didn't seem hostile. A little uneasy and uncertain, but not angry. Hopefully that was promising.

"Listen, to cut right to the chase," I said. "I fucked up. I shouldn't have called things off with you."

"You practically ghosted me." He sounded more hurt than angry, which made me feel like an even bigger asshole. "If I hadn't chased you down, how long before you would've finally said something?"

"I…" Crap. I didn't have an answer. "I don't know. I honestly don't, and I'm sorry for that. All of it. Ghosting you, making you pry the truth out of me—I shouldn't have done that."

He watched me, and his eyes were full of a single resounding question: *Why?*

I swallowed hard. "I let my dad get under my skin again, and… I mean, you were right when you said I needed to spend more time away from my parents. Going over there?" I shook my head. "It's not healthy, and it's been fucking me up a lot."

"So, this is because of your dad?" His tone was flat.

"It's..." I sighed. "No, I'm not trying to use him as an excuse. My dad was the reason I was feeling like shit, but pushing you away—that was on me. I own it. I guess I was just down and depressed about everything. I felt like a failure, and like... It doesn't really matter. What matters is that I thought the answer was to push everyone away. I've always convinced myself that everyone was going to shove me away sooner or later, so I've saved them the trouble and shoved them away first. And I was wrong, especially when I shoved *you* away."

He avoided my gaze, his features tight but still impossible to read.

"I'm sorry," I whispered. "I've done a lot of thinking, and my friend helped me get my head out of my ass, and I guess... I guess I've been spending so much time feeling sorry for myself, I stopped living my life at all. I didn't know who I was without hockey. Now I think I'm figuring that out." Despite my nerves, I smiled as I said, "I'm finally starting to see what I should be doing besides just moping around and wishing I could still play hockey."

"Yeah?" He sounded interested, but still guarded.

I shifted my weight, suppressing a wince at the pain that shot through my right knee. "Yeah. For one thing, I'm going to talk to someone about..." I gestured at my head. "My friend pointed out that I've had problems with depression my whole life, and I didn't realize it. With everything that's happened since last year, I need help."

Jon nodded slowly. "That's, um... That's probably a good idea."

"I think so, yeah. And I didn't realize that the first thing I do when I'm depressed is to shove everyone away. My family. My friends." I swallowed hard. "My boyfriend."

He flinched.

"I'm going to get help for that," I whispered. "I should have done it a long time ago, but I'm looking into it now. And I'm also working on getting off my ass and living again." I paused. "You remember how the lady at the animal shelter said they don't have a lot of space? So the dogs don't have much room to play?"

His eyebrows rose, as if he hadn't anticipated the new direction. "Uh-huh."

"Okay, well, I think that's what I want to do. Have a place where I can foster dogs while they're waiting to be adopted. And I talked to Taylor at the shelter, and she thinks we can work something out where the dogs can come and play for a little while so they get a break from the kennels and stuff."

"Oh." His expression softened a little. "That…actually sounds like a great idea."

"I think so." I paused, studying him. "And I'm not asking you to take me back because I finally figured out what I'm doing with my life. I'm asking you to take me back because it was a mistake to let you go. I love you, Jon, and I miss you."

His eyes darted away from mine, and his jaw worked subtly as he adjusted his grip on the guitar case handle. He didn't say anything, though.

"I'm sorry," I said again. "I was in a bad spot, and I messed up. I don't know what else I can say or do, but if there is something, tell me. Because I don't want to lose you."

Our eyes met, and my heart pounded.

Tell me I haven't already lost you.

After a long moment, Jon took a deep breath. "I've done a lot of thinking lately too. Being on my own, it gave me some time to…" His eyes lost focus. Finally, he continued, "The bottom line is I realized I don't need someone to be happy. I think that's why I jumped in with you in the beginning—because I was married so long, I don't know how to be alone anymore." He moistened his lips. "I still don't know, but I need to figure it out."

It took a moment for me to make sense of what he was saying, and as the meaning came through, my heart dropped. "Jon, I—"

"And come on," he continued. "Let's be real—how long before you realize a single dad in his forties isn't what you want? We both know you can do a hell of a lot better than…" He gestured at himself.

I blinked. "What? No! I want *you*."

He watched me, his expression unreadable, and I had a fleeting second to think I might have gotten through before he shook his head. "Your whole life is in flux right now, Brent." He sounded exhausted and resigned, not angry. "When you find your footing and figure out where to go from here, I don't want to be left in the dust."

I stared at him. "Left in the—Why would you be left in the dust?"

"Because that's what happens when I get tangled up with people who don't know who they are or what they want. The minute they figure it out…" He made a gesture like a plane taking off. "They're gone."

"But that's not—"

"Don't," he whispered, shaking his head again. "Listen, I was somebody's placeholder for twenty years without even realizing it." Breaking eye contact, he started to walk away, and he added over his shoulder, "I'm holding out for someone who actually wants *me*."

And he kept going. Kept walking away. Kept heading right toward the place where he'd kissed me for the first time.

I wanted to stop him, but I couldn't. I was so stunned by what he'd said, by the fact that he thought I just wanted him as a placeholder until something better came along, I had no idea how to respond. Had I really made him feel that way? That whole time I was getting in over my head with him, he'd thought I was just keeping him around to entertain me while I got my life back on track?

Why the fuck was I just standing here instead of stopping him and telling him how wrong he was about what he meant to me?

Pain warned me against running or even speed-walking after him, but I called out, "Jon! Wait!"

I had no idea if he heard me over the bustle and noise of the Marketplace. All I knew was that he kept walking. I called to him again, but…no response. He didn't even slow down.

Just before he turned the corner, I looked away, and I had to fight back tears. Goddammit. He was gone.

Except…he still had to get to his car.

I fumbled with my phone and quickly typed out, *Can we please talk about this?*

Then I waited, but no answer came. He saw the message, but he didn't respond.

Minutes passed. Long enough he could have backtracked if he'd wanted to see me. Definitely long enough he could have replied to the message, even if it was just to say no.

I guess I had my answer.

With a heavy sigh, I shoved my phone into my pocket, then started numbly heading toward my truck.

Maybe it was just as well he hadn't responded and hadn't come back. What could I even say? That I'd magically figured out who I was overnight just because I had a pipe dream of an idea about some direction my future could go? Or…hell, anything? I didn't know how to explain to Jon that he wasn't a placeholder for anyone or anything. He'd filled a gap in my world that I hadn't even known was there. Like I'd just been waiting my whole life without even knowing it for him to drop out of the sky, and now that he was gone, nothing was right.

It reminded me a little of the feeling I'd had when I'd woken up in a hospital and realized this wasn't just another dislocated hip or torn muscle. When there were a whole lot of things that were suddenly not part of my life anymore, and they'd been there for so long that I didn't even know how to process them being gone.

Except hockey—not to mention mobility and a relatively pain-free existence—had been there my whole life. As long as I could remember, anyway. Jon had only been here a few short months.

But damn if he hadn't made himself such a regular fixture that I could barely comprehend him being gone.

And if I hadn't stupidly let him go, how long before he'd have bailed anyway?

I had no idea what to make of any of this or where the future was going to take me. I still had no idea who the hell I was.

All I knew right then was that I was alone.

Again.

32

JON

The afternoon was sunny and comfortable, so I loaded Cody and Winston into the car to find a place for them to play outside. Cody wanted to go to Starr Farm Park. The name of the place had made my throat burn with acid, but I'd smiled and said of course, and that was where I took him. I just didn't let on that going to that park meant following Starr Farm Road, the street that led toward Brent's exclusive neighborhood. I'd been bringing Cody here since he was a toddler, long before I'd ever known who Brent was, and he didn't need to know that this whole area made me think of Brent now.

I pushed those thoughts away. Brent was gone, and I only got to spend every other week with Cody. I needed to focus on him, not on feeling sorry for myself and missing the man who occupied so many of my thoughts these days. It was over. Cody needed to be my priority now.

At the park, Cody unclipped Winston from his restraint in the backseat, and we all headed toward the grassy play areas. I smiled as I watched the two of them. Cody was absolutely in love with Winston, and it was mutual. Winston was always happy to see me, but one look at Cody, and it was like he turned into a puppy all over again. This was clearly a dog who had not only needed a home, but a kid, and now he had both.

Shame he doesn't have Luna to play with anymore.

Christ, don't go there.

I sat on a bench beside a picnic table and watched while Cody threw Winston's toy for him. They were adorable. Winston kicked up grass and dirt. Cody giggled. Sometimes Winston wouldn't let go of the toy and wanted to play tug-of-war instead, and Cody laughed while he indulged him. Then the dog would let go, and Cody would toss the toy again.

Cody couldn't throw as far as some of the bigger kids in his grade probably could have, but Winston didn't care. He'd tear all the way across a field if Brent—if *I* tossed a ball that far, or he'd happily chase it if it just rolled a few feet.

While they played, I watched, and I let my thoughts wander. I was still finding my footing post-Brent, and somehow that was harder after our weeks-long thing than it had been after my twenty-year marriage. Or maybe it just seemed that way because it was fresher. And because Brent had abruptly been *gone*, rather than living across the hall in a house that was *way* too small to contain all that tension.

Was that it? Because by the time Ashley and I had gotten out from under the same roof, I'd wanted to be as far away from her as I could get. Brent? That had come out of nowhere. And then he'd tried to patch things up, and I kind of hated him for that because he couldn't possibly understand how much it had hurt to tell him no. I wanted him. I wanted to be with him. I felt things for him I'd never felt before, and I didn't want to lose any of that.

But how long before he bailed again? If what his dad had said to him was enough to send him packing, then I was hard-pressed to think Brent hadn't had a foot out the door the entire time. If I took him back, I'd just be waiting for him to hightail it again.

I'd get over him. I hadn't thought it would be possible to get over Ashley, and I had. Eventually, I'd do the same with Brent. Hopefully sooner than later, too, because this sucked.

A shriek of terror snapped me out of my thoughts, and I jerked my head toward the playground. There, a little girl had been playing in the sandbox, and Winston was loping toward her, probably to retrieve his toy.

I was immediately on my feet, and so was a woman who I assumed was the girl's mother. We sprinted toward the kids and my dog.

Then we stopped a few yards short when we realized Cody had beaten us there, and he was talking to the little girl.

"It's okay," he was saying as he petted Winston, who was sitting beside him. "He's nice."

The girl didn't seem convinced.

"Winston," Cody said firmly. "Down."

Winston immediately dropped all the way onto the grass, and he put his head between his paws. His tail wagged, the long fur hissing across the grass. He reached out with one paw, trying to grab his toy, which was just out of his reach.

Cody nudged it toward him with his foot, and Winston immediately grabbed it, tail wagging even faster now. "See? He just wants to play."

The little girl glanced at him, then eyed Winston. "Does he bite?"

"No. He might lick you, though."

That got a tentative little giggle out of her. Cautiously, with Cody gently coaxing her and assuring her that Winston was friendly, she came closer. She held out her hand, but when Winston put his head up, she jumped back.

"It's okay," Cody said again. Then he turned to Winston. "Roll over."

Winston obediently rolled onto his back, and the little girl giggled with a bit more feeling as his paws flailed in the air.

After some more encouragement from Cody, she came close enough to pet Winston.

Beside me, her mom sighed. "Wow. We've been trying to get her to warm up to dogs for a while." Nodding toward Winston and the kids, she added, "This is the closest she's ever gotten to one without crying."

"Winston's pretty chill. She's got nothing to be afraid of."

The mom nodded.

In front of us, Cody tossed Winston's toy, and the dog flailed to his feet and tore after it. When he started back at a dead run, the girl cringed behind Cody, and she glanced at her mom for reassurance, but she didn't cry or run away.

Cody took Winston's toy and handed it to her. I couldn't hear what he was saying, but from the gestures, he was telling her to throw it.

She did, and it didn't go far. Winston lunged after it, snatched it up off the ground, and spun around again, dropping it at her feet. Then he got down on his forearms and yipped excitedly, tail going wild.

"He wants you to throw it again," Cody said.

The little girl reached for it, and Winston trotted a few steps before facing them again. With a giggle, she tossed the toy, and it went a few feet farther this time.

As Winston ran for the toy, Cody met my gaze, and we both smiled. Hell, I was probably beaming with pride. My son would never be a tough guy, and that was fine with me. He was a sweet kid who patiently encouraged a scared little girl to pet his dog. He didn't make fun of her. He didn't try to rile Winston up to make her more nervous. He just quietly told her that the dog was nice, then encouraged her to play with him, and now Winston was in seventh heaven, playing with two kids instead of one.

I mentally sent up a little *fuck you* to my ex-wife's boyfriend, who didn't think Cody was tough enough, and at the same time, I was once again grateful that Brent had countered some of Ray's bullshit.

Which…had me thinking about Brent again. Damn it.

Everything circled back to Brent. It was because of him that I had Winston at all. It was because of him that I knew about Ray trying to toughen up my kid. Ugh. Not even three months in my life, and he'd already left an indelible mark.

I missed him so much, but I needed to let go. I'd put my son through enough hell over the last couple of years, and he was struggling enough with letting go of Brent already.

Eventually, I'd put out feelers again, but I'd go back to what I'd set out to do with Brent—friends with benefits the way they were supposed to be. Casual sex. Nothing more. Something I could do while my son was at his mom's, and then the rest of the time, I'd focus on Cody. When he was older, I'd think about finding something with some staying power.

For the foreseeable future, I just needed to focus on being Dad.

33

BRENT

Why the fuck am I doing this to myself again?

Because I was a coward, that was why. And a doormat.

I couldn't think of any other reason why, after everything Ethan and I had talked about, I was pulling into my parents' driveway yet again. On a Saturday this time, since my parents were taking a trip out of town starting early tomorrow morning. At least that meant I was off the hook for Sunday dinners for the next month.

But I still had to get through tonight.

And tonight was going to be a challenge because after months of avoiding it, I had to give in this time—I needed my cane. I didn't know if it was stress after breaking up with Jon, or if I'd slept wrong, or… I mean, it didn't matter. Everything hurt, and I didn't feel stable when I walked. My knee kept threatening to give out. My hip felt like something wasn't right. When I tried to walk unaided, I was sure I was going to fall, and even more sure that if—when—I did fall, I'd be in a world of hurt.

Pride be damned—my dad was going to see me leaning on the cane tonight.

I turned to Luna, who was sitting in the passenger seat. "You ready to go in and play with the other dogs?"

She wagged her tail.

I chuckled and tousled her ears. At least I had her with me. My mood could never be completely sour with that sweet face looking at me.

I unclipped her from the seat and attached her leash. She waited patiently for me to get out of the truck, and then she sat in the driver's seat while I got situated with my cane in my hand. When I picked up her leash and said, "Okay," she stepped down on the floorboards, then hopped onto the ground. "Good girl."

She again waited while I locked up the truck, and then we headed for the front porch.

As he always did, my dad stepped out. Damn it—I *felt* the instant he saw the cane. His lips pulled tight, and his eyes darted toward me, silently asking, *Really?*

I shifted my attention to Luna, who had stopped to sniff one of my mom's plants. With a gentle tug, I reminded her we were still walking, and she followed. As I slowly and carefully climbed the steps, she stayed right beside me, never pulling and never trying to get ahead.

"A cane, huh?" Dad asked.

"Sometimes," I gritted out, pretending sweat wasn't beading on the back of my neck from the climb up the steps. It wasn't the exertion—it just fucking hurt. And there was still one more flight up to the kitchen and living room. Son of a bitch.

"How about I take her leash?" Dad offered in a patronizing tone. "Then you can hold the rail and your cane."

"I'm fine."

He didn't argue, and I tried not to notice his condescending expression.

"Think about it," I heard Ethan saying. *"How do you feel whenever you leave that place?"*

"Like shit," I'd replied. And didn't I feel like shit right now? Before I'd even settled in for the evening? I was already in a world of pain, and I already felt low as hell because of Jon, and now this. Awesome.

I greeted my mom, and Luna played with the papillons for a little while. Around the time Mom went in to finish cooking dinner, Luna came into the living room and sat beside me, resting her head on my knee. "Worn out already?"

She just stared up at me. The papillons came wandering in too, and before long, they'd found places to curl up and go to sleep. Yep—worn out.

Dad sipped his beer and studied me across the living room. "So this is what you're doing these days? Just…got a dog, and not doing anything else?"

I pursed my lips. "I got a dog because I can finally have a dog. Otherwise, I'm just trying to get through physical therapy and—"

"So now if you healed enough to play hockey, you've got her as an excuse not to."

I straightened, pretending not to notice the twinge in my lower back. "I didn't—Dad, there is no healing enough. We've been through this. I don't know how else I can explain to you that I am *not* a failure. I was in a car crash that I'm lucky I survived. Hockey is *not* in the cards."

"It didn't have to end your career and you know it," Dad threw back. "You've seen plenty of other players come back after all kinds of terrible injuries, so there's no reason you—"

"Dad, I can barely walk!" I threw up my hands. "How am I supposed to skate? Especially that fast and that hard?"

Sighing, he shook his head. "I just don't want to see you give up. Not after you worked so hard to get there. You've seen what other players have come back from, Brent! If Lemieux can come back, then—"

"Dad, for God's sake, *enough.*" I glared at him, chest tight with fury. "I'm not Mario Lemieux, and I'm not ashamed of that. No, I'll never be a legend like him or anyone else, but I had a damn good career. And whether I like it or not—whether *you* like it or not—I have to put that career behind me. Because it's gone, okay? And it's never coming back. *Nothing* you say will change that. *Nothing.*"

He took a breath, no doubt getting ready to speak, but I beat him to it because I didn't want to hear it.

"You had plans for me to be a pro hockey player before I could even write my own name," I said. "Yeah, I loved playing hockey, and yeah, I loved being a professional, but let's not pretend this was my idea, all right? My entire life was hockey because that's what *you* wanted it to be."

"And now you got your way and found an excuse to quit."

I rolled my eyes and huffed an impatient breath. "No, that isn't what happened. Or haven't you noticed that I didn't just lose my hockey career? You're disappointed because *your* dream got cut short, but I have to live with this every damn day. Every minute of every day. I'm always in pain, Dad. *Always*. Do you understand that?" I gestured at myself. "There is *never* a moment where something doesn't hurt, and there never will be. I have to live with that. Not you. The least you can do is back the hell off and stop trying to paint me as a failure because—"

"You can't just give up like that, Brent!"

"Yes! I can!" I threw up my hands. "I absolutely can!"

Beside me, Luna ducked, her tags jingling, and damn it, I suddenly wondered how long she'd been cowering as our voices had steadily grown louder.

"Oh no." I leaned down and petted her, speaking softly to her. "I'm so sorry, baby. I'm sorry. I didn't mean to yell."

She pressed against my leg, shaking a little.

"I'm sorry," I whispered again. When I faced my dad, I kept my voice even for my dog's sake and petted her as reassuringly as I could. "Dad, you've had me in skates since I could walk. You've had me playing hockey since I could hold a stick. Which means hockey has been wearing down my body since before I'd even finished developing." Gesturing sharply at myself, I growled, "You see a twenty-nine year-old breaking down like an old man because he's weak. My doctors? They see all the damage twenty-five years of hockey did to me even before the crash. I mean, when I was in college, they were already telling me my joints were twenty years older than I was. My hips were at least another ten years older than that."

"That's nonsense," he threw back, making Luna jump. "They're just—"

"Hey." I said it sharply, but not enough to scare my dog. "Don't yell around her."

He glared at me, then rolled his eyes, and I didn't give him a chance to start again.

"The doctors who gave me those opinions are experts in sports medicine," I ground out. "And the bottom line is that you wanted a professional hockey player for a son and never gave any thought to what kind of price I might pay for that. Because it wasn't just the car accident that messed me up. Hockey is the reason some of my injuries didn't heal properly. You're so concerned with what's happening to your dream, you've never thought about what happened to your son's body along the way." My voice tried to shake, but I refused to let it crack as I said, "I'm not a failure, Dad. I'm human. I'm mortal. Hockey broke me, a car accident finished me off, and all I can do now is move on with what's left."

He pushed out an impatient sigh. "I just don't think a twenty-nine-year-old should be this—"

"Would you rather the accident had killed me?" I snapped, glancing at Luna and petting her before looking at my dad again. "Would that be easier for you to swallow? This"—I gestured at myself again—"is the best case scenario after that crash. I don't get why you refuse to accept that I'm doing the best I can with what hockey and the accident left for me to work with."

He studied me, and I could hear the next lecture on the tip of this tongue, so I kept going.

"My entire life—my entire identity—was hockey. I have to let that go now. I have to figure out who the hell I am without hockey, because I never had the chance to be me without hockey until hockey was taken away from me. You didn't let me be anything but a hockey player, so I don't know how to be anything else. And maybe I'd make some headway in figuring that out if you could accept that I'm still your son even though I will never go back out on the ice." I gritted my teeth and swallowed against the lump in my throat, and I petted Luna as much to reassure her as myself. "So you can either drop it and accept who I am without hockey, or you can join hockey in my past. Your call."

With a sharp sigh, he slammed his hand down on the armrest.

I didn't even hear what he said, though, because Luna whined softly and ducked, tail firmly between her legs as she tried to bury her head behind my calf.

"Even if you were totally uninjured and still playing hockey," Ethan had told me, *"you deserve better than the stress and pressure you get from him."*

Goddammit. He was right. Why was I putting up with this? Especially when my dad was terrifying my dog, too?

"Dad, stop." I put up my hand as I reached down with the other to comfort Luna. "Keep your voice down."

"For God's sake," he barked. "Brent, I just don't think you're—"

"Enough." I picked up my cane and gingerly pushed myself to my feet. "We can talk about this another time, but I'm not going to let you keep scaring my dog like this."

"Brent, we—"

"No. I'm done." I picked up my cane and gestured at Luna. "Come on, baby."

She stuck close, but she ducked when my Dad stood up to try to stop me.

"Sit down, son," he said in his most condescending voice. "We're not—"

"No." I set my jaw. "We're done here. And I'm leaving."

"Brent!" My mom appeared in the kitchen doorway. She squeezed past my dad to get in between us. "Honey, don't leave."

I shook my head. "I'm not staying and listening to this anymore. It's the same thing every week, and I'm exhausted." I gestured down at Luna, who was still ducking behind me. "And now he's scaring my dog, too."

Dad rolled his eyes.

Mom huffed impatiently, shooting him a look. I could hear the appeasement coming a mile away. She'd tell my dad to back off, she'd tell me to stay, and the evening would be full of passive-aggressive barbs that I'd be expected to tolerate.

No, thanks.

"We can talk about this when you're back from your trip." Nodding toward the stairs, I said, "But I'm leaving now."

They didn't move. I didn't move.

Finally, my mom sighed and gently nudged Dad toward the kitchen. Dad tried to protest, but she just said, "Let him go, honey. You both need to cool off, and then we can talk about this."

I winced, both from the pain as I started hobbling down the stairs, and from my mom's words. In her mind, I *would* go home and cool off. Dad would calm down. We probably wouldn't even talk about it —by the time they came back from their trip, everything would be fine. It would all blow over just like it always did.

I felt bad for it, but Mom was in for a surprise, and she wasn't going to like it.

Not a moment too soon, Luna and I were in the truck, and I got us the hell out of there. A few blocks from my parents' house, though, I pulled over, put the truck in Park, and closed my eyes. I needed a minute. To pull myself together? To process? I didn't know. I just knew my stomach was somersaulting and my heart was pounding, and I couldn't decide if I felt drained, or like I was full of nervous energy. Getting that all out of my system left me feeling seriously weird. Like I was glad I'd finally gotten it off my chest, and I felt guilty and vindicated and I wanted to curl up and die and I wanted to do a triumphant fist pump.

Luna whined softly, and when I looked at her, she was watching me, her ears down and her eyes wide. Her tail wagged cautiously, and her expression said nothing if not, *You okay, Dad?*

I petted her and quietly said, "I'm sorry everyone yelled. I know you hate that." Jesus. I couldn't believe I'd subjected her to that. I was so careful not to raise my voice or make any sudden noises or movements around her, but I'd been so frustrated and angry today, and…

With a heavy sigh, I wrapped my arms around her and kissed the top of her head. "I won't take you over there anymore. I promise."

She leaned against me and tried to crane her neck to lick my face. She'd get some extra treats when we got home. Maybe we'd go play in the lake, too, if the daylight held. Anything to get this evening as far out of her mind as possible.

As I sat up and gazed at her, it occurred to me how little I'd ever done to distract myself. I usually wallowed and moped after seeing my parents. Sometimes I'd gone to Jon's, but a lot of times I'd stayed home just to avoid being a downer to everyone else.

And after one visit, I'd all but ghosted Jon, then let my depression and battered self-esteem kick on at just the right time to break things off with him. Now I was alone except for the dog my dad and I had scared tonight.

But at least we'd left, because no way in hell was he making Luna shake like that anymore.

Funny—for all my dad regularly gave me shit, it had taken this for me to finally walk out. Not berating me, not belittling me, but raising his voice around my nervous dog.

What does it say about me when I'll protect my dog more than I'll protect myself?

I cleared my throat and put the truck in gear. "What do you say we go home and play?"

Luna wagged her tail, ears perking up a little as she cocked her head.

I laughed halfheartedly and reached over to pet her as I pulled away from the curb. Maybe I'd feel like shit for the rest of the night, but there was no way in hell my dog would.

As I drove, Ethan's voice echoed in my mind: *"You need to cut off your dad."*

"Yeah," I muttered aloud. "I think you're right."

34

JON

With my evenings wide open, I was getting stir crazy, especially after I'd dropped Cody at his mom's the other night. The unfinished house was emptier and quieter without Cody or Brent. Even with Winston there, the whole place rang like a hollow shell.

It had been a long time since I'd had much in the way of nerves before going onstage at Vino and Veritas. Stage fright wasn't an issue. I knew the lyrics. I knew what I was doing.

My head wasn't in the game, though. I'd barely been able to think about anything except for Brent. Was I going to be able to concentrate enough to get through my set? Maybe I should talk to Tanner about bailing on some of my regular nights.

Not tonight, though. There wouldn't be enough time to replace me, and Tanner really didn't like having people show up for music only to be greeted by a sign apologizing for the last minute cancelation. So I was here, and I was as ready as I would ever be.

Come on. Get it together. You know these songs inside and out.

With a deep breath and a skyward prayer of, "Please don't let me fuck this up," I took my usual spot on the stage, and I started my set. Hopefully the longer I was up here, the more normal I'd feel. The more normal my whole world would feel.

Except that wasn't what happened. I'd been nervous and distracted before taking the stage, but there was definitely one circumstance I hadn't anticipated.

"The river runs; doesn't ask for more," I managed to sing despite the unexpected lump in my throat. "Doesn't ask for the rain to fall."

Goddammit. What the hell was wrong with me? I'd gotten used to singing these lyrics. As the pain of my divorce had faded and the raw heartbreak had become a distant memory, it had been easier to sing about it. Still with feeling, still with all those visceral emotions that had gone into the lyrics in the first place, but without actually *hurting* like this.

Because I didn't hurt like this over Ashley anymore. There'd probably always be a piece of my heart that ached when I thought about losing her, but it was more like an arthritic joint flaring up on a cold night to remind me of an old injury.

That wasn't what I was feeling tonight.

"A steady pace can break through stone." And every time I landed on one of those lines that dug right into the sore spots in my heart, it wasn't Ashley I was thinking of: "Gentle water's gonna bring you home." I'd written every word of these songs to cope with letting her go, and every word I sang tonight broke me all over again for Brent.

Damn it. When did all these songs start being about you?

Aw, fuck. Now how was I going to keep it together while I sang? I paused between songs for a deep swallow of water, hoping the small crowd didn't realize I was seizing the opportunity to pull myself together. I'd done this in the wake of my divorce. I could do it now. I *would* do it now.

Calling on everything that had carried me through those earliest post-divorce performances, I pushed through one song after another until, mercifully, I reached the end of my set list. While the audience applauded, I gave a polite bow, then stepped off the stage. As I always did, I went up to the bar in search of more water.

Rainn handed me an ice-cold bottle. "Wow, you were on fire tonight!" He smiled broadly. "You're so talented, Jon."

I forced a smile and thanked him as graciously as I could, but inside, I felt like shit.

That's not talent you're hearing. That's pain.

And why does it hurt more to sing these than it did when I wrote them?

I managed to extract myself from the conversation as gracefully as possible, and I left Vino and Veritas to head home for the night. Home to my empty house, since Cody wasn't there.

My heart sank deeper as I walked toward the parking garage. I'd promised myself I'd just focus on being Dad for a while, but what about the weeks when my son wasn't with me? Was I just supposed to go back to living alone in that house I would probably never finish renovating?

Though Brent had made headway on a lot of projects. I could use the time I was no longer spending with him to make more progress.

God. Why did that sound a million times more draining than it should have?

I sighed and kept walking. When my car came into view, I unlocked it and slid my guitar into the backseat. Then I dropped into the driver's seat, started the engine, and…sat there.

It felt so damn weird not to be texting Brent after I'd been at the wine bar. But I couldn't text him. Because I'd been up there singing about him. Because he was gone.

He tried to come back, you know.

I squeezed my eyes shut and exhaled. Yeah, he had. And yeah, I turned him down. I couldn't do it. I just couldn't. It was too big of a risk.

Right?

Except the more I thought about it, the harder it was to convince myself. Was it worth it to hurt like this just to keep myself from hurting in the future? What if we *did* have something with legs?

Being with someone like Brent would be a risk. Being with *anyone* was a risk. But I'd thought I had something low-risk and easy with Ashley, and look how *that* turned out.

Fuck. So what do I do?

Maybe it would be worth the risk to dive in and find out what this thing could be with Brent. For that matter, I'd been worried I wasn't worth loving. That being with me meant a partner letting their life go by.

But a young former pro athlete who could have anyone he wanted had fallen in love with me.

Brent was young. He was rich. He was hot.

And he'd fallen for me?

Maybe I was worth loving for real. Maybe there was someone who could see me as the man they wanted to be with, not the man to tide them over until something better came along. Or holding them back while something better passed them by.

I was afraid of falling for someone who saw being with me as letting their life pass them by. So what was I doing? Letting a good man slip through my fingers just because he'd hit a low spot and thought… God, he'd thought *he* wasn't good enough for *me*. He'd left because he'd wanted to cut his losses before I figured out I could do better. And when he'd realized he'd made a mistake, I'd pushed him away because I was a fucking idiot who couldn't see past my own insecurities to what the most amazing man I'd ever met was saying to me.

So why the fuck was I still sitting here?

35

BRENT

As soon as we were home, I went outside with Luna so she could play and relax. Of course it took all of ten seconds before she was in the water, splashing around like everything was perfect in her world. She brought me a stick, which I threw, though the best I could do right now was a weak underhand toss. She didn't seem to mind.

She also didn't seem to be upset anymore. I felt *terrible* for scaring her when I'd raised my voice at my dad, and I was glad I'd gotten her out of there before anyone had lost their temper. Dad and I could butt heads all we wanted. Luna didn't deserve to be terrified by people shouting.

But she'd apparently gotten over it enough to enjoy playing in the lake and the backyard. When I called her in, she dropped her stick and loped up the back steps. As she always did, she shook, spraying water all over me and everything within a ten-foot radius. I laughed—it was cold and smelled like the lake, but my dog was happy, so who cared?

As best I could, I toweled her off, which she loved even though it was excruciating for me this time. I seriously debated just letting her in while she was still wet, but I really didn't want the house to smell like lake water. At least she enjoyed it—she wagged her tail and wiggled her rump and tried to lick me in the face.

I laughed through gritted teeth. "Someone's feeling better after today."

As soon as I said it, I paused. She really had bounced back fast. She'd been nervous after we'd left my parents' house, but by the time we'd gotten home, she'd calmed down, and now that she'd played, she was back to her usual self. In fact, now that I thought about it, this was how she was more often than not. She was still nervous sometimes, and she still ducked if I startled her by accident, but she seemed to have accepted that I was safe and so was my house. Now that she was home and away from my dad, she shook off this evening like she shook off the lake water.

Man, I could learn a thing or two from this dog.

Now that Luna was relaxed and happy, chewing away on one of her bones in the living room, it was time to take care of me.

My pain was still high, so I took a couple of anti-inflammatories and sat in the hot tub for a while. To my surprise, that helped a lot, which told me today's pain must have been stress and tension more than anything. Over seeing my parents. Over everything I wasn't doing in this hot tub right now because I hurt too much and because Jon was gone. Over just existing in this frustrating body. Could've been any or all of that. Sitting here in the hot water, letting one of the jets beat on my lower back, I closed my eyes and tried not to think.

Half an hour or so in the hot water eased some of the twinges in my back and the bitchiness in my left leg. By the time I got out, I was moving a hell of a lot more comfortably than I had been earlier. I wondered how much of that was the hot tub and the ibuprofen, and how much was the relief over finally standing up to my dad. Because as much as it had hurt to be in a position to sever contact with him, it had turned out kind of like my hip replacement surgery—it sounded scary as all hell, and I'd been sure the aftermath would be awful, but as soon as it was over, I'd felt a million times better. There was still healing that needed to be done, and it still fucking hurt, but it was a gigantic improvement over how I'd felt that morning.

Just to be on the safe side, I kept using the cane as I moved around in the house. In fact, I tried not to move around too much. Where was the balance between sitting still so long that I got stiff, and moving around so much I made myself sore? Guess I'd find out.

I was hobbling toward the living room with a cup of coffee when the doorbell rang. Instantly, Luna was off and running, barking her head off as her nails skittered across the hard floor.

What the hell? Oh God, was my mom here to try to smooth things over with my dad? Or worse, was it Dad? Fuuuck.

Sighing, I put the coffee down and headed for the door. I paused —cane? Or no cane? Would it cause more tension than it was worth?

Oh, fuck it. This was my house. I'd use a cane if I damn well wanted to.

When I opened the door, I almost dropped the cane in question.

"Jon." I swallowed, watching him crouch to say hello to Luna. "This is… What are you doing here?"

He tousled Luna's ears, then rose and met my gaze. "Can we talk?"

"I, um…" I couldn't read him at all. He didn't seem hostile, so that was good, I supposed. Numbly, I nodded and stepped out of the way.

He came inside and shut the door. Glancing down at my cane, he said, "Should we, um, sit down?"

I hesitated. I wanted to ask how long he thought this conversation would be, but I also wanted to sit before anything seized up again. "Okay. Sure."

We moved into the living room. I eased myself down on the couch, and he sat down with almost a cushion between us. It didn't feel right, being this far away from him. It also didn't feel right to have him in the house at all. And why the hell was he here?

Staring down at his wringing hands, he swallowed hard. "I fucked up."

"You did?"

"Yeah." He chewed his lip, then finally met my eyes. "The thing is, I've been so afraid from the beginning that you'd realize you can do better than me. After the way things went with my ex-wife, I guess… I mean, I've had a hell of a time thinking I could be enough for anyone."

"Enough?" I breathed. "Are you kidding?"

"Look at you, Brent," he whispered, brow pinched. "You're young. You're hot. You've—"

"I'm a physical train wreck."

Jon was already shaking his head. "You were a professional athlete, and you were in an accident. Those aren't character flaws."

I blinked. Why did those words threaten to choke me up? Being physically battered… I had no illusions that it was easy for anyone around me, and I was petrified of people getting tired of accommodating, but Jesus, he was right. No, it *wasn't* a character flaw.

I cleared my throat. "But it's still rough, being with someone like me."

"No, it isn't." Jon looked right in my eyes. "It's hard to see you in pain and not be able to do anything about it. But being with you?" He smiled nervously. "That part's easy. And like I said, I guess I've just been afraid all along that you were going to figure out you could do better than a guy my age with a kid and a receding hairline."

"I, um, don't know if anyone's mentioned it," I said quietly, "but none of those are character flaws either."

He straightened a little. Then he laughed softly. "Touché."

Our eyes locked, but only for a second.

He dropped his gaze and took another deep breath. "Look, when you came back and tried to fix things, I should've listened. I was so angry and hurt because I thought..." He paused, then shook his head. "The point is that I'm sorry I pushed you away when you came back. I guess I was afraid you'd have one foot out the door."

I studied him. "One foot out the door?"

He nodded, apparently unable to hold my gaze. "Well, yeah. I'd been worrying all along I wouldn't be enough for you like I wasn't enough for my ex. So when you left, I thought..." He sighed, shaking his head. "I don't know. I guess I thought it meant you'd been looking for a reason to bail all along."

"No. No way!"

"I know. I was..." Jon rubbed the back of his neck. "I was scared, and I jumped the gun, and the bottom line is that I love you. I'm terrified of not being enough for you, and of you finding someone better, but if you'll give me a chance, I'll try my damnedest to be enough."

I was speechless for a moment. Not only because I couldn't fathom how he'd ever thought he wasn't enough for me, but because he was here. He was scared he wasn't enough, and coming here tonight, he had to have been terrified I was going to show him the door. But he'd done it anyway. He came. He was here. He'd poured his heart out. He wanted me back.

Pulse pounding, I reached across the space between us and put my hand over his. "You've been more than enough for me from the start."

Jon looked in my eyes. "Really?"

"Yes. And I'm sorry about everything," I said on a sigh. "I let my dad get under my skin on a day when I was in horrible pain, and… I mean, *every* time I leave that place, I feel like shit, but that day, I guess he just got to me more than he usually does. In fact, I'm starting to think it was him more than anything that had me living like a recluse and hiding from people for so long. Like yeah, I was trying to figure out who I was after my whole life got yanked out from under me, but then there was this weekly dose of what a disappointing failure I am."

"A failure?" Jon scoffed. "Why? Because a car crashed into yours?"

"Because apparently I was a mediocre player who jumped on the first excuse that came along to permanently bench myself."

Jon's eyes widened. "Did he actually say that?"

Nodding, I grumbled, "Almost word for word, yeah. And I let that get in my head, and I convinced myself it was only a matter of time before you realized I'm more trouble than I'm worth."

His eyes were huge now. "What? No!" He turned his hand over under mine and squeezed it. "Jesus, Brent. It's not like that at all."

"But you get what you'd be signing up for, right?" My voice was unsteady. I couldn't help it. "Some of this might get better, but it's not going away. Some of it might get worse over time, too."

"I know. And whatever happens, I'm here for it, because I want to be with you."

"Even if—"

"Yes." He squeezed my hand and slid a little closer on the couch. "I know what you're up against. And yeah, I wish it would go away, because then you could be more comfortable. But not for my benefit. I'm not in love with some fantasy of you being fully healed and functional down the line. I'm in love with *you*. Full stop. Not contingent on you magically returning to perfect health."

"Really?"

"Yes." He brought my hand up and pressed his lips to my knuckles. "I mean it, Brent. I love you. Full stop."

I had to swallow twice before I managed to whisper, "I love you too."

He smiled, and when his fingertips brushed my face, I thought I might break the fuck down right then and there.

"I'm sorry," I said. "I let my dad get into my head, and—"

"It's not your fault your dad's an idiot. I don't know what his damage is, but he used you to live out his dreams, and even after those dreams did permanent damage to your body, even after a car accident almost *killed* you, he still wants to push you to hurt yourself even more." Scowling, Jon shook his head. "Fuck him. I can tell from the way you treat my son that you're more of a man than your father will ever be."

I blinked. "Seriously?"

"Seriously. After the shit his mother's boyfriend told him, and the way he was pushing Cody to do hockey to toughen him up, I can't think of anyone better than an actual hockey player coming along and saying Cody's just fine the way he is. And it resonated, by the way."

"Good," I said. "I'm glad he's not getting hung up on what her boyfriend says."

"Me too. And since it sounds like Ray and your dad are cut from the same cloth..." He shrugged dismissively. "Fuck 'em. Both of them."

I nodded slowly. "Yeah. No kidding. And I, um... I think I'm done with my dad. At least until he gets his head out of his ass, if that ever happens."

"Oh really?"

"After tonight, you better believe it."

Jon's eyebrows rose again.

I took a breath and told him what had happened. When I'd finished, I gestured at Luna, who'd curled up on the rug in front of the fireplace. "Says a lot that I'll do more to protect my dog than I will to protect myself."

"Somehow, that doesn't surprise me." He put his hand on my knee. "But I'm glad you're protecting yourself too. You don't deserve that shit."

I wrapped an arm around him. "I feel like I don't deserve *you*."

"You do. And I'm sorry I turned you away when you came back," he whispered. "I was just so scared of being a placeholder, and..." He shook his head and sighed. "I'm sorry."

"I guess we were both afraid of something."

"We were. Probably still are. It won't go away. But…" He smiled. "Neither will I."

Returning the smile, I curved a hand behind his neck and kissed him, and suddenly everything in my world was as right as it could be. Nothing had felt right since I'd shoved him away, and now it did, and I held on and enjoyed both his kiss and the sensation of everything settling. I'd walked away from my dad. I had Jon back. Everything was the way it needed to be.

I touched my forehead to his. "I love you. I'm so sorry I bolted."

"I love you too." Jon trailed his fingertips down my cheek. "And don't be. We're both coming down from having our lives yanked out from under us. We're both scared." He smoothed my hair. "We found our way back to each other. That's the important part."

"Yeah, it is." I lifted my chin and met his lips again just because I wanted to. Just because I *could*. He was here. I was here. We were touching again.

And suddenly I didn't think we were touching enough.

I drew back to meet his gaze. "Should we take this upstairs?"

His eyes lit up. "You want to?"

Nodding, I said, "Damn right." I paused. "In fact, I want to…"

"Hmm?"

I pushed my shoulders back and tamped down my nerves. "The, um… The pump. The one the specialist gave me." I felt myself blush as I quietly asked, "You want to try it? Together, I mean?"

"Do you?"

"I want to do whatever makes this good for you. So I'm game for anything." He must have seen my skepticism, because he added, "Even if getting hard was out of the question, I'm not going anywhere."

I searched his eyes. "Really?"

"Really." Jon traced my cheekbone with the pad of his thumb. "If you hadn't noticed, sex with you has been plenty satisfying for me. As long as I'm satisfying you and not hurting you, I'm happy."

God, could this man be any more perfect?

"I'd like to try it," I said quietly. "Together. I've gotten the hang of it alone, but…"

"Then let's try it." He glanced down at the cane, which was leaning against the end table. "If you're feeling good enough to—"

"I am. I was in pretty rough shape earlier, but I'm better now." I licked my lips. "So…bedroom?"

Jon just grinned.

Upstairs, we shed our clothes and climbed into my bed. My heart was going wild now, but it was more excitement than nerves. I had a handle on using the pump, and I fully believed Jon would be onboard and not make it into something uncomfortable. Whatever doubts I'd had, whatever hang-ups had kept me from bringing this into bed with us—they were gone. Completely gone. I wanted this with him, and I wanted it now.

When I put the box between us on the mattress, he watched curiously as I opened it and pulled out the now-familiar assembly.

"So, how does it work?" he asked.

I showed him—putting on some lube, then the ring, attaching the pump. As I started pumping it carefully, he watched, but I didn't feel the least bit self-conscious or conspicuous. He wasn't eyeing it like something out of a freak show. If anything, he was studying it so he could see how it worked. Maybe one of these days, he'd be the one to use it. Why was that such a hot mental image?

I was slowly getting hard when Jon slid his hand over my chest, and then he kissed me, and—oh God, yeah, *this* was hot. Maybe the pump itself was as unsexy as it came, but slowly pumping myself hard while Jon and I made out? I could work with that. Definitely.

His kiss almost distracted me from what I was doing, but I still had the presence of mind to remember to stop pumping now and then.

When I did, Jon glanced down at the pump, and I said, "You're supposed to start and stop a few times. Keeps the… It works better that way, I guess."

"Oh. And it's, um… It's comfortable?"

I nodded. "Now that I've gotten the hang of it, yeah." I slowly started pumping it again. "The doc said it could get numb in places sometimes, but I haven't had any problems. It still takes a while to come, though." I laughed nervously. "I don't have to worry about being a minuteman, that's for sure."

Jon grinned and leaned in for another kiss. "Then I guess that means I get to spend more time blowing you, doesn't it?"

I inhaled sharply and stared up at him, arousal crackling along all my nerve endings. "Yeah?"

"Uh-huh." He brushed his lips across mine again. "I love sucking dick, so the longer it takes..." A grin finished the thought, and he kissed me.

By the time I was fully hard, I was also turned on beyond words. The way Jon kissed always curled my toes, and he had me so dizzy tonight I almost forgot how to work the pump. I remembered, though, and I deftly disconnected the cylinder from the ring. My heart was going wild. I had Jon again? In bed? And I was hard? Was this a dream?

He closed his fingers around my dick and gave it a slow, appreciative stroke, and dear God, if this was a dream, I hoped no one woke me up.

"Like that?" he asked with a grin that said he knew damn well I did.

Unable to speak, I nodded. Did I like it? Oh, fuck yeah, I liked it. I'd already known how strong and talented Jon's hands were, and having him stroke me? Twisting just a little as he used the lube to his advantage? This was unreal. It was weird to think that this was the first time he'd ever touched me when I had a hard-on, and Jesus, it was worth the wait.

And that was before he went down on me.

Holy. *Fuck.*

I hadn't had a blowjob in eons, and Jon was... Oh God, he was awesome at this. As he traced the tip of his tongue along the underside of my erection, a full-body shudder ran through me. That prompted a few twinges of protest, but not enough to distract me from how fucking amazing it was to have Jon's hot, patient, talented mouth exploring every inch of my hard cock.

I knew from experience that the lube I'd used was faintly bitter, but he didn't seem to care. And it turned out the ring around the base of my cock wasn't an issue. It was probably new and different for him, but if anything, he just seemed to be mindful of not dislodging it. Otherwise, he was licking and stroking and sucking me with all the relaxed enthusiasm of a man who really did love doing this.

I combed my fingers through his hair and squirmed as much as my body could handle comfortably, and Jon just went to town on me.

There was nothing he didn't do—deep-throating, circling his tongue around the head, licking my balls, fingering my ass.

"Holy fuck," I moaned. "That is…" I squeezed my eyes shut. "Oh God, Jon…" My fingers twitched in his hair. "I'm gonna come."

He groaned around my dick, and I squeezed my eyes shut as my back arched.

Then, with a throaty cry that seemed to echo off the high ceilings, I came in Jon's mouth for the very first time.

And before I'd even started to relax, I was already hoping like hell this wouldn't be the last time.

36

JON

I didn't think there was anything sexier in this world than Brent, flushed and trembling after a powerful orgasm. He had his arm over his eyes, and he was breathing hard, and I could have stared at him all damn night.

"Holy fuck," he slurred, letting his arm fall to the mattress. Looking up at me with blissed-out eyes, he murmured, "That was amazing."

I grinned and leaned down for a kiss. His hand curved behind my neck, and we let the kiss linger for a moment, just enjoying it like there was nothing else in the world either of us wanted. There *was* nothing else I wanted. I'd found my way back to Brent, and by some miracle, he'd taken me back. Lying here naked with him, kissing lazily all night? Hell. Yes.

When Brent broke the kiss, he glanced down. "I should, um, get rid of the ring. Give me a sec."

"Oh. Right." Lying on my side, I watched him take off the silicone ring, and he put it on the nightstand. "So that thing is comfortable for you? The ring?"

"Yeah." He settled beside me again, a hand behind his head and the other knuckles trailing lazily back and forth across my chest. "It was a little weird at first, and this one fits better than the one I tried the first few times, but...yeah. It's not bad at all." He grinned. "And it's worth it for the result."

"So I saw." I kissed him softly. "Any time you want to do that again, say the word."

"I will." He drew me down into a kiss. It started out lazy and gentle like before, but then his fingers closed around my hard-on, and I gasped, somehow managing not to break the kiss in the process. He didn't have any lube on his hand, so he didn't stroke me fast or hard. Instead, his rhythm matched the deliciously languid way we kissed, and…wow. That was… That was *hot*.

I moaned into his kiss, and I couldn't help rocking my hips, pushing myself into his fist. He tightened his grip a little, making the whole world spin around me. I was thrusting now, searching for more friction. Brent followed my lead—he kept his grip tight and he moved his hand just right to complement my movements, and Jesus, I was going to lose it. After finally getting to experience the sexiness of sucking him off, and now that I was in bed with him at all for the first time in too long, I was so turned on I could barely stand it, and making out with him while he stroked me… Oh yeah, I was going to come. I couldn't hold back, and I didn't try, and—

"Fuck, don't stop!" I gasped, and Brent growled encouragement as I neared that peak, and then I was coming, my entire body shaking with the force of my powerful orgasm. With a heavy sigh, I relaxed.

"I missed that," he said with a wicked grin. "You are so hot when you're that turned on."

I returned the grin as I tried to catch my breath. "Feel free to do it again any time."

Brent laughed. "I'll keep that in mind."

We grabbed some tissues and cleaned up. As we settled into bed again, Brent's demeanor shifted a little, and alarm prickled the back of my neck. He wasn't pulling away from me, but something in his expression had me on edge.

"What?" I asked.

He jumped, then avoided my eyes as a blush crept into his face. "Listen, um…" He chewed his lip like he couldn't quite articulate what he wanted to say.

"What?" I cupped his cheek. "Talk to me."

"Okay, well…" Brent swallowed, then looked up at me. "Look, even with the pump, I don't know if I'll ever be able to top you, but I know you enjoy bottoming."

I opened my mouth to protest, but he put up his hand.

"Let me finish."

I closed my mouth, heart thumping as I waited for him to go on.

Avoiding my gaze, he took a deep breath. "Before we, um… Before we split up, I bought something. Because I wanted to be able to do more for you than I've been able to." He gingerly pushed himself up and rolled over so he could reach into a drawer beside the bed. As he pulled it open, he said, "I don't know why I never brought it out before. I think I was…" He hesitated, then shook his head. "I don't know. It sucks to admit I need outside help, you know?"

Mute, I nodded.

He shut the drawer and rolled back, and I realized that he'd brought with him a decent-sized toy. Not one of those huge novelty dildos, but closer to the size of an average cock. Of his or mine.

Blushing brighter, he met my eyes. "It's not quite the same as topping, but it's an option."

"You…" I glanced back and forth between him and the toy. "You got it so we can…"

He nodded. "There are things you enjoy that I might not be able to do, but I don't want you missing out on them."

My lips parted and my heart ached. I could only imagine how much he'd had to swallow his pride and come to terms with some harsh realities just to get himself into that store and to make that purchase, but he'd done it anyway because he'd wanted me to be happy.

Caressing his cheek, I whispered, "For the record, we don't need it. I'm… Damn, I'm speechless that you thought of it, but I'd be perfectly happy if we didn't. I promise."

He licked his lips. "But if we *did*, would you enjoy it?"

I glanced at the toy, and I suspected my face gave me away even before I murmured, "Oh, yeah. I would."

"Then let me," he said. "I want to."

I was still utterly stunned. I'd spent twenty years with someone who wouldn't even entertain the idea of pegging or even using a finger during a blowjob—which was fine, that was her prerogative—and now Brent was willing to do this? Even if it had to bruise his pride to even admit he needed a toy to do it?

"You're amazing," I whispered, and pressed my lips to his. "One of these nights? Yes, I'm absolutely game. Anything you want to do for me, anything you want me to do for you—I'm in."

"Yeah?"

I nodded. "Of course. I love you. I want you to be happy."

"I love you too. And...same. Anything. Just say the word. If my body can't handle it..." He gestured at the toy lying mostly forgotten between us. "We'll find a way."

Our eyes locked. Oh yeah. We'd find a way. Whether it was something in bed, or everyday life, or figuring out how to navigate when he was having a bad pain day—we *would* find a way.

The lingering shyness and nervousness in his expression vanished, and he drew me down into another long kiss.

Anything he wanted, he could have it. That had been my approach whenever we were in bed, but especially now—especially after coming so close to losing this forever—I was ready and willing to give him anything he wanted in *or* out of the bedroom. If that meant spending some time with that toy he'd bought before we focused on him? I definitely wouldn't complain.

As I lost myself in Brent's sinfully perfect kiss, I was beyond relieved we'd made it back here and still blown away that, ego and pride be damned, he was ready to do whatever it took to make sure I was satisfied too. I hadn't been unsatisfied by any means, but it moved me that it was important enough for him to do what he'd done. Maybe we'd have to make some trips to the adult store together. See if there were some fun things that could help him enjoy sex without pain, and also things we could play with just for the hell of it.

We'd figure that out. Right now, all that mattered was that we'd found our way back into each other's arms. We could improvise everything else. Take it as it came. Make our own rules and do things our own way.

Tonight, I'd enjoy having the man I loved back in my arms.

And tomorrow, I had a feeling Winston would be thrilled to have his favorite playmate back.

EPILOGUE

BRENT

A few months later.

"Winston, wait!" Jon called out plaintively, but Winston galloped into the living room where Cody and I were watching TV. Luna was already up and running in circles, yelping with excitement now that her buddy was home.

Winston's long, yellow coat had snowballs clinging to the ends, and when he wagged his tail, he sent sprinkles of ice and water flying. Cody giggled. The dogs wrestled. Snow went everywhere.

Jon came into the room with a towel in hand, and he rolled his eyes. "In case it's not obvious, someone was having fun in the snow."

I laughed and gently took Luna's collar so we could separate the two of them for a minute. "Well, he had fun. That's the important part."

"Uh-huh. Something like that."

Luna sat beside me, tail wagging and ears up as she patiently waited for Jon to finish drying off his squirming, wiggling, snow-covered Retriever. When he was done, he gave Winston a pat on the rump and said, "Okay, go play!"

Instantly, both dogs were tearing through the house. The three of us laughed, and Jon and I shook our heads. One of these days, the dogs might realize they weren't puppies anymore, but apparently today wouldn't be that day. Fine by me.

"I picked up Thai." Jon gestured toward the kitchen. "Cody, why don't you go wash your hands, and we can have dinner."

Cody got up and headed for the bathroom.

I got up and, leaning on my cane, followed Jon into the kitchen.

As he pulled containers of Pad Thai out of bags, he glanced at the cane, which was in my right hand today. "Knee?"

Scowling, I nodded. "Yeah. It's not too bad today—just trying not to push it."

"Good idea."

I pulled some plates down, and we went about getting dinner on the table.

It was a challenge, moving around with the cane, but thank God I had it. Not only was it a godsend for stability now that ice and snow were a problem, but my right knee had been acting up the last few weeks. Favoring my left leg for so long had done a number on the joint, which had already been bitchy thanks to several injuries over the years. In fact, my various doctors and therapists had theorized that one of the reasons my hip had been a catastrophic injury waiting to happen because of all the time I'd spent favoring my right knee in the past. My orthopedic surgeon was keeping a close eye on my left knee and right hip for signs that they were getting jacked up. My medical record was seriously starting to look like the worst version of *Head and Shoulders, Knees and Toes* ever.

It was what it was, though, and I'd made peace with the fact that a certain amount of pain and limited mobility would be part of my life. Fortunately, I'd figured out over the last several months that pain and limited mobility didn't have to *be* my life. I'd always have to be mindful of them, and everything I did—even simple things like going to the grocery store—had to be done with my jacked-up body in mind.

It sucked, but I was learning, and I was beyond fortunate to have a boyfriend who was patient and accommodating. If we needed groceries and I was in too much pain to even think about walking in from the parking lot, never mind through the store, Jon went on his way home from work. If I'd promised to take care of a particular task around the house, and my body decided that plan could go to hell, he didn't mind.

After a lifetime of feeling like pain and injuries were things to overcome as quickly as possible in order to get back out on the ice and pull my weight for my team, it was still wild to me that the man I lived with thought of pain the same way he did ice on the road: It was there, and the best thing to do was slow down and work around it as much as we could. Have I mentioned how much I fucking love this man?

With his support and my slow, steady recovery, I was making headway on establishing some purpose in my life that didn't include chasing a black disc around on the ice. Plans for our animal rescue were coming along. My house was under contract, and the buyer wanted to close sooner than later. Jon and I were living at his place, and with Cody's help, I was finishing up the renovations so we could put it on the market in the spring.

By the time both houses were sold, the weather would be improving and we'd be ready to move to the farm I was in the process of buying a few miles outside of town.

I was still amazed that what had seemed like a pipe dream was actually coming to fruition. I'd found a farm. The animal shelter where we'd adopted Winston and Luna was onboard with the idea of bringing some of the dogs out to have some fresh air and run around while they waited to be adopted. On top of that, we were making plans to build a facility that would allow us to take some of the shelters' overflow.

It was an ambitious project, but I was excited about it. Just watching Luna come out of her shell had been amazing, and if my purpose in life was to make life better for animals who were waiting for forever homes, then I was more than happy to hang up my skates and embrace this instead.

Winston and Luna were thrilled that we were all living together. They loved the near-constant attention, and they were both a million times happier with another dog to play with any time they wanted to. The pair of them played so hard, they were usually out cold by the time Jon and I—and Cody, if he was with us—sat down to dinner. Then they'd play some more, and they'd collapse again when we went to bed.

I kind of felt bad that they weren't going to have access to Lake Champlain via my back deck anymore, but there were plenty of parks along the lake shore where they could swim. Plus the new place had a pond and a creek, and Jon and I were debating the idea of installing a swimming pool. We were already getting a hot tub—no way in hell were either of us giving that up—but we'd wait and see about a pool. Either way, the dogs would still get plenty of time in the water. Weather permitting, of course. These days, they were having too much fun playing in the snow to notice the change of scenery anyway.

Cody came into the kitchen. "Did you get crab Rangoon?"

"Hmm." Jon peeked into one of the bags and pretended he was really concerned. "I think I forgot to ask for it again."

Cody tsked and rolled his eyes. "Dad..."

Chuckling, Jon produced the crab Rangoon and put it on Cody's plate. "Don't worry, I remembered."

Cody made one of those disgusted "Dad, you're the worst" noises that I usually associated with teenagers. His dad just chuckled, and the three of us took our plates and glasses to the table.

The dogs, of course, sat beside us, ears perked up and eyes wide as they waited for some food to magically fly off the table. Or for me or Cody to toss them something, which we usually did, since we were both absolute suckers for the dogs. So was Jon, but he still wasn't so sure about feeding them from the table. He was a big softy—he'd get there.

"So." Jon looked at Cody. "We decided we're going to buy that place we went to look at last weekend. The one with the creek in the back."

"Really?" Cody asked.

"Yep," I said. "It's going to be a few weeks, but the paperwork is in."

Cody sat up a little. "And, it's a farm, right?"

"Kind of," I said. "You saw the barn, and it has—"

"Does that mean I can get a horse?" His eyes were huge, and excitement was coming off him in waves. I straightened. He'd never said anything about wanting a horse of his own, though he did love them and had quite a few toy horses in his room.

Jon pursed his lips. "Do you want a horse?"

His son nodded vigorously, that preview of irritated teenager long gone, replaced by the pure enthusiasm of a kid on Christmas. "Yeah! I do!"

"Do you know how to ride?" I asked.

"Pfft." Ah, there was that teenager preview again. "I go to horse camp every summer. Of course I can ride."

"Oh. Huh." I recalled that Jon had mentioned Cody going to horse camp, and he'd begged us to take him to tour the UVM Morgan farm in Weybridge, so I shouldn't have been surprised he could ride.

"Let's get settled in first," Jon said. "Sell this house, move into the new one, figure out where we can put a horse." He shrugged. "But yeah, I suppose we can look into getting you a horse."

I didn't think I'd ever seen Cody smile that big.

"Really?" he almost squealed.

"Yeah," Jon said, smiling the way he always did when Cody was happy. "It might not be until next spring or so, but we'll look into it, all right?" He looked at me with a semi-apologetic shrug. "We'll have room for a horse, right?"

If it makes you and your son this happy? Dude, we'll make *room.*

"Totally," I said. "We'll make it work."

Cody legitimately looked like he was going to explode with excitement.

Yeah, we'd make it happen. Definitely.

It hadn't been entirely smooth sailing with Cody. He and I got along, and I very carefully didn't intrude when it came to disciplinary things. But Cody was a kid, and kids had bad days like everybody else, and there were some days when we just did not get along. Especially after Jon and I had moved in together. Growing pains and all that.

It had been especially bad a couple of months ago. Cody had been moody and belligerent for a few days straight until his dad finally sat him down and asked what was up. Cody had been resistant about showing his cards, but Jon had gently talked him into it, and the kid had admitted he was upset because Ashley and Ray had split up. Not because he missed Ray, but because he thought it was his fault.

Fortunately, as much as Ashley and Jon struggled to get along, they were pros at putting on a united front where their son was concerned. They'd sat down together with him and explained that sometimes people broke up, and that it wasn't anybody's fault. Which wasn't entirely true—we all knew it was because Ray was a colossal asshole who'd needed to leave with Ashley's footprint on his ass—but in the interest of reassuring Cody that relationship changes were just a part of life, they'd kept that to themselves.

Ashley and Jon's relationship was improving now without Ray in the picture. Especially after they'd realized how much the recent breakup bothered their son, they'd spent some time talking in person and on the phone, trying to smooth things over enough that they could be friendlier. It helped, too, which was a huge relief for Jon, and probably for Ashley too. They had, after all, been friends long before they'd ever dated. Jon had wondered aloud a few times if part of the animosity between them had been because of her relationship with Ray, because she really had seemed miserable as hell the whole time she'd been with him. Now that she wasn't, Jon had told me, she was so much more like her usual self.

In fact, she and I got along pretty well these days. For all Ray had been a total bastard, he'd gotten her into hockey, and we'd broken the ice (so to speak) chatting about stats and scores. Maybe not the most traditional way for someone to get to know a partner's ex, but I wasn't going to argue.

I was still going to Robin multiple times a week, and she was steadily helping me regain strength and mobility. The most severe muscle atrophy was getting better now that we'd focused more on conditioning, which had helped stabilize some of my joints. The tendinosis was better, too, and there was some talk about another surgery to try to correct the worst of it.

But there was no magically curing all the havoc my injury—not to mention my entire hockey career—had wreaked on my body. I would always have some pain. My mobility would never be the same. There were things I'd done easily in the past that I couldn't do anymore, or that I struggled to do, and that was not an easy pill to swallow. Over time, though, I'd learned to focus on the things I *could* do, and on being realistic about my goals. No, I was never going to hike the Appalachian Trail or mountain bike in the Rockies like I'd fantasized about with some teammates in another lifetime, but I could walk my dog in parks and on easy trails, and I was learning to really enjoy swimming for the first time in my life. Which was great for some low-impact exercise and conditioning, and it also had the added bonus of being something I could do with Cody, since he was really interested in swimming competitively. Maybe installing that swimming pool wouldn't be such a bad idea.

So I was getting better in the ways I could expect to get better, and getting the hang of living with the things that wouldn't change. It was still tough to accept that my sex life was permanently altered, but even that was better now. The urologist had recommended a minor procedure to remove some scar tissue—probably from one of the surgeries after my injury—that was causing some minor interference with blood flow. That had helped, and the therapy, pump, and just healing over time had helped too. It wasn't perfect, but it was better. Between the ED and my chronic pain, our sex life would never be "normal," but things were improving, and Jon and I took what we had to work with and made a damn satisfying love life out of it.

There'd been adjustments beyond my physical limitations and my relationship, too. Ethan had been right about my depression, and therapy—when I'd finally managed to get in to see a therapist—had been a game changer. It was still going to be a long process, and she was still helping me grieve my career and accept the physical limitations that weren't going anywhere, but just realizing there was a process—that I didn't have to live in a semi-permanent funk—was a huge relief.

She was probably going to put me on antidepressants soon, but she and my doctor had agreed it wouldn't hurt to wait until after I'd recovered further, especially since some of them had sexual side effects. I wasn't suicidal or in danger of harming myself, and the counseling sessions were helping, so the antidepressants weren't an urgent thing.

These days, I still talked to my mom, and she'd met Jon and Cody. Cody absolutely adored the papillons, though Winston wasn't quite sure what to do with the three sentient squeak toys. He mostly followed Luna's lead and tried not to step on them.

My dad? Well, my mom wanted one or both of us to budge and break the standoff, but it wasn't going to be me. And I was pretty sure she understood that. If my dad couldn't accept me without my hockey career, then that was on him.

Meanwhile I'd be over here enjoying life with my boyfriend, his son, and our dogs while we made plans to make life better for other rescue animals.

The three of us finished dinner, and while Cody played with the dogs in the snowy backyard, Jon and I cleaned up the kitchen from dinner. After we'd finished, we went into the living room and gazed out the window at his son and our dogs. It was dark out, but the lights he'd installed on the back deck lit up the place like an airport. There were dog toys scattered all over the yard, and Cody was having a ball throwing them and watching Winston and Luna chase toys and each other.

"Should've gotten him a dog years ago," Jon mused. "He's always wanted one."

"Seems like being a sucker for animals kind of runs in the family."

"I resemble that remark."

We exchanged glances and both laughed.

"Are you sure you don't mind getting a horse?" Jon laced his fingers between mine. "That'll take up a chunk of the property."

"Nah, I don't mind. We've got fifteen acres to work with. And I don't think I can say no to him when he's that excited any more than you can."

Jon's smile was ridiculously sweet. "You're amazing, you know that?"

"I just want you and Cody happy." I wrapped an arm around his waist. "Buying him a horse really doesn't seem like a tall order."

His forehead creased. "What about buying two?"

"Two?"

"I mean, horses are social animals. So if we just had one, it might get lonely."

Oh dear Lord, I could see where Cody had inherited those puppy dog eyes.

Suppressing a smile, I said, "Jon, do you want a pony?"

He snorted. "Not a pony, but…yeah, if my kid's getting a horse, I think it would be fun for us to ride together."

"You are so cute, you know that?"

He laughed. "Uh-huh. And in all seriousness, you don't mind us getting horses?"

"Nah. But just for you two. Even if my hip wasn't a lemon, I'm terrified of them, so that's all you guys."

"You're afraid of horses?"

"Of riding them, yes. On the ground, they're fine, but I'm not getting on one."

"What?" He grinned. "You had no problem flying around the ice at a million miles an hour, but you're afraid to ride a horse."

"Uh, yeah, because my skates were inanimate objects. A horse has a brain and opinions."

Jon laughed, wrapping his arm around my waist. "I hadn't thought of it that way, but okay."

"I'll remember that the first time your horse tosses you in the mud."

"Hey! Have faith in my riding abilities."

I smirked.

He rolled his eyes. "That's not what I meant."

"Sure it wasn't." I kissed him. "Whatever you say, baby."

"Asshole," he muttered, but he was grinning, and he drew me into a longer kiss. When he pulled back this time, his expression had turned more serious. "Listen, um, what would you think about making things, I don't know…more permanent?"

"We live together and we're buying property to open up a business together. How much more permanent do—" My teeth snapped shut.

Jon smiled. "I think you know how much more permanent we can make it."

I stared at him. "Are you… Are you just floating the idea, or…"

"I don't have a ring in my pocket or anything, but that's mostly because I don't know what you'd like." He ran his fingers through my hair. "But yeah, I'm asking."

"Really?"

"Yes." He smiled. "Do I have to get down on one knee, or—"

"No, because then I'd have to let go of you." I laughed with a rush of giddiness. "And…yes. Definitely, *yes*."

Jon's eyes lit up. "Yeah?"

I nodded, drew him in, and kissed him. He held me tighter than he ever had, or maybe that was me, and… Fuck, we were doing this? We were doing this. Not just buying a place and starting an animal rescue together. Not just figuring out together what life was after our past lives. We were getting married.

This wasn't the life that had been planned for me before I'd even understood what life really was. It wasn't the future I'd worked for and expected.

But I finally felt like I had a purpose, and like I wasn't going to disappoint anybody by pursuing that purpose.

There was life after hockey, and that life meant a family I hadn't imagined. It meant doing something that made me happy instead of pleasing everyone else. Getting here had been a rough road for both of us, but we'd made it.

I wasn't a hockey player anymore. I was going to be someone who took care of animals. I was going to be a husband and a stepfather.

And the shoes I was walking in now fit better than ice skates ever had.

Guess I got lucky that night at the wine bar after all.

THE
END

ACKNOWLEDGMENTS

Thank you to Leta Blake and Jules Robin for your editing awesomeness.

Also a huge thank you to Michael Ferraiuolo for writing Jon's song lyrics.

And definitely a big thanks to Karen N. and Ilene W. for their invaluable help with my research into Brent's injuries.